凱信企管

**用對的方法充實自己，
讓人生變得更美好！**

凱信企管

用對的方法充實自己，
讓人生變得更美好！

great 大.
big 大. large 大，
差別呢？

1.65meter
要加 s 嗎？

might/may
用法有差嗎？

你的
英文
用對了嗎

基礎篇

英文翻譯專家教你
搞定易混淆文法
To Use English Correctly

User's Guide

問答的方式輕鬆點出文法盲點，
抽絲剝繭釐清從單字、片語到句子各種文法的疑難雜症！

01 | 英文翻譯專家精選，近 200 個基礎易混淆文法 Q&A

集結多年教學經驗 &
修改翻譯潤飾國人英文文章經驗之大成！

本書編排有別於一般坊間文法書，並非以英文字母排序，筆者力求對症下藥，將國人最容易誤用的英文語法依照問題的性質分為「詞彙 Q&A」、「片語 Q&A」、「句子 Q&A」和「其他 Q&A」四大主題。學習者只要靜下心仔細研讀，並予以融會貫通，就能大幅增進英文文法之功力。

易錯英文搶先看！

【詞彙 Q&A】
→ no 接可數名詞時，該名詞要用複數還是單數呢？（速翻 p.029）

【片語 Q&A】
→ can 和 able to 以及 can't 和 unable to 的用法有何不同呢？（速翻 p.166）

【句子 Q&A】
→ What does that mean? 是個正確的問句。但英美人士經常說成 What's that mean? 請問那一句才正確呢？（速翻 p.247）

【其他 Q&A】
→ C 有兩種發音，一是發 [k]，如 call, cup，另一發 [s]，如 city, cent。這是否有規則可循呢？（速翻 p.317）

02 | 最有深度的文法解析 |

透過問答方式＆大量舉例真正釐清多年誤用觀念！

多數文法書都是長篇大論，學習者只能自己囫圇吞棗，盲目學習，還不見得能抓到文法重點；本書以簡短的英文問題帶出所欲導正的文法概念，一次一題，想停隨時可以停，還可以直接從題目就看出是不是自己有疑問想學習的部份，省時間又有效率，學習無負擔。

03 隨堂測驗即時練習，絕對要學會

針對不同文法設計最適切的練習題型，發現不熟悉立即複習！

光用眼睛看完學完還不夠，沒有真正動手寫，還是很容易忘記。本書針對每一單元皆附有綜合文法隨堂測驗，學完立即測試，方能快速找出學習盲點，加深記憶，真正釐清誤解之處。學的多不如記的多，切勿貪快一口氣看完一大堆文法觀念，如若沒有真正理解吸收，只是白費力氣，反而虛耗光陰，真正弄懂才能進入下一個文法單元喔！

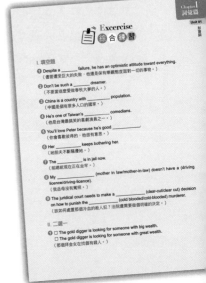

Preface

　　文法是大多數人在學習英文過程中最感頭痛的問題，許多人在學了十幾、二十年的英文之後，還是對語法一知半解或者知其然不知其所以然。在這種氛圍下，「文法很難學」的觀念深植人心，影響所及，許多莘莘學子視學文法為畏途，長此以往，文法真的再也學不會了！英文文法真的那麼難學嗎？根據筆者多年學習和研究文法的經驗，學文法需要下功夫，但並不難學，而且只要掌握重點觀念，就能駕輕就熟，駕馭文法。

　　有人可能會問，那要如何掌握英文語法的重點觀念呢？研讀文法書從中擷取重點嗎？非也！眾所周知，幾乎每本文法書都是行禮如儀、照本宣科，從名詞、形容詞……一路講下來，不但無法凸顯重點，解決文法學習所遭遇的問題，而且讀起來索然無味，只會扼殺學習的興趣與熱情。

　　文法重點觀念的建立與強化需要引導與指導。就書籍而言，如上述，大多數文法著作及相關書籍讀起來只會讓人打瞌睡，遑論引導讀者欣然地開啟文法大門，進而平順地深入文法的堂奧。鑑此，本書以學習文法重點觀念為出發點，收集文法學習過程中最多人最常碰到的問題，並以問答方式，針對這些問題所牽涉的重要文法觀念，一一做詳盡的解說，讓讀者多年不解的沈痾問題迎刃而解。

　　本書收錄近 200 個基礎易混淆文法問題與解答，由於力求對症下藥，故文法問題形式不一，在編排上無法按照英文字母排列，因此只能就問題的性質概略分為「詞

彙 Q&A」、「片語 Q&A」、「句子 Q&A」和「其他 Q&A」四個主題。不過，讀者只要用心閱讀這些 Q&A，並予以融會貫通，就能掌握英文文法中絕大多數的重點觀念，文法功力增進「一甲子」，日後的英文學習之路將會變得非常平坦，甚至成為專家。

任何書籍都無法十全十美，本書亦然，若有疏漏之處，歡迎批評指正。

作者英文學習網站：

① 網路翻譯家：http://cybertranslator.idv.tw/

② 英文資訊交流網：http://blog.cybertranslator.idv.tw/

俞亨通 2018 年 3 月

Contents

Chapter 1 詞彙篇
你的英文，用對了嗎？

Chapter 2 片語篇
你的英文，用對了嗎？

Chapter 3 | 句子篇
你的英文，用對了嗎？

Chapter 4 | 其他篇
你的英文，用對了嗎？

Chapter 1
你的英文，用對了嗎？

—— 詞彙篇 ——

001 Question

我們可以說 great wealth 但卻不能說 big wealth，是否可以多舉一些實例來說明 big, great 和 large 與一些常用名詞的固定搭配（collocations）呢？

Answer

在敘述或形容實物（physical objects）時，我們可以使用許多不同的形容詞，如 large, big, tiny, minuscule, small 等等。然而，在敘述或形容非實物的名詞（如 joy, anger, wealth）時，我們必須特別注意，慎選「加強語氣的形容詞」（intensifying adjectives）。在英文中，big, great 或 large 都是敘述非實物或非實體名詞很常用的加強語氣形容詞。茲將這三個形容詞與一些常見名詞的固定搭配分別臚列於后，供大家參考。

Big：大多用來形容不同的事件和各種類型的人，且通常不跟不可數名詞連用。

❶ 不同的事件
- ▶ a big decision（重大決定）
- ▶ a big disappointment（大失所望）
- ▶ a big improvement（重大改善）
- ▶ a big mistake（大錯）
- ▶ a big surprise（大驚喜；大吃一驚）

❷ 各種類型的人
- ▶ a big eater（食量大的人）
- ▶ a big dreamer（愛做春秋大夢的人；非常不切實際的人）
- ▶ a big drinker（酒量大的人；酗酒者 – 但不若 a heavy drinker 通用）
- ▶ a big spender（花大錢的人；揮金如土的人）
- ▶ a big talker（愛吹牛的人；說大話的人）

Great：通常用來形容表示感覺、情感、情緒或特質的名詞。

- ▶ (a) great admiration （十分欽佩）
- ▶ a great number (of) （大量；許多）
- ▶ great anger （盛怒）
- ▶ great power （大權；大國，強權）
- ▶ (a) great disappointment （大失所望）
- ▶ great pride （極為自豪；極為得意）
- ▶ great enjoyment （很大的樂趣；大樂事）
- ▶ a great quantity (of) （大量）
- ▶ great excitement （極大的興奮）
- ▶ great sensitivity （高靈敏度）
- ▶ a great failure （十分失敗的事；大為失敗的人）
- ▶ great skill （高超的技巧或技能）
- ▶ great fun （有趣的人或事物）
- ▶ great strength （很大的力氣、力量；人多勢眾，強大的兵力）
- ▶ great happiness （極大的幸福）
- ▶ great understanding （極強的理解力；很高的智力）
- ▶ great joy （很大的樂趣；大樂事）
- ▶ great wealth （巨大的財富）
- ▶ at great length （極為詳盡地）

Large：通常跟與數量和測量有關的名詞連用，且通常不跟不可數名詞連用。

- ▶ a large amount (of) （大量）
- ▶ a large proportion （很大的比例；大部分）
- ▶ a large number (of) （許多，很多）
- ▶ a large quantity (of) （大量）
- ▶ a large population （人口眾多）
- ▶ a large scale （大比例；大型；大規模）

上面所列僅為 big, great 和 large + 名詞之固定搭配的一部份而已，但應已足夠說明它們之間的主要差異。更多有關 big 和 large 的用法及意思說明請參見下一個問答。

big和large的用法及意思有何不同呢？

Answer

雖然這兩個字的中文意思都是「大的」，但它們的用法和意思其實是有出入的。Big 在書寫和口說英語中都是一個相當常用的字；事實上，它是英文前 1000 個最常用的單字之一。反之，large 是個比較不常用的字，甚至無法擠入英文前 3000 個最常用的單字之列。

如上所言，這兩個字的一般意思都是「大的」，用來表示尺寸、數量、重量或高度等大於一般的尺寸、數量...等；不過，large 是個比較正式的用字。Big 和 large 後面都要接可數名詞。所以，我們可以說 The house has a big (or large) garden.（這房子有個大花園。）— 因為 garden 是可數名詞，但卻不能說 There's a big (or large) traffic on the road next to the house.（這房子旁的道路交通流量很大。）— 因為 traffic 是不可數名詞，因此我們必須將之改為 There's a lot of traffic on the road next to the house.。雖然 big 和 large 經常可以互換，但有時卻不行。下面將舉例說明這些不同的情況。

big 可以意為「重大的」（important），如 Buying a house is a very big decision.（購屋是個很重大的決定），亦可用在口語中，表示「比較年長的」（older）意思，如 He's my big brother.（他是我哥哥。）；再者，它也有「極受歡迎的；極成功的」意思，如 Anping Castle is a big tourist destination.（安平古堡是個極受歡迎的旅遊景點。）在口語中，big 亦可意為「程度上很大的」，如 She earns a lot of money, but she's also a big spender.（她賺了很多錢，但她也是一個花錢闊綽的人。）；John is a big eater.（約翰食量很大。）

big 被用在許多固定片語中，由於這些片語是固定的，如果將其中的 big 改為 large，那就錯了。例如：It's no big deal.（那沒什麼了不起。）；She's got a big mouth.（她是個大嘴巴。）；He's too big for his boots.（他自以為了不起／他妄自尊大。）

large 亦有一些固定片語，如 Two of the escaped prisoners are still at large.（兩名逃犯仍逍遙法外）；She's larger than life.（她不同凡響）。此外，large 可與數量詞

連用來表示「大量」的意思，但 big 大多不行，如 a large amount, on a large scale, a large number of, a large quantity of, a large proportion, to a large extent, a large percentage of, a large part of, a large volume 和 a large area 等。

003 Question

You probably can't imagine that it has already taken me some quarters of an hour just to think of an appropriate subject to talk about. 這句對嗎？

Answer

這個句子的語法完全正確，但語意不合邏輯，問題出在 some 這個字上。 "Some" 的限定詞用法有重讀（stressed） 和弱讀（unstressed） 之分，而這兩種讀法的意思有相當大的出入。

some 在時間副詞中必須重讀，而在其他場合則是弱讀；在重讀的情況中，當它與可數名詞連用時，它的意思是「相當多；不少」（quite a few），而不是「一些」（a few）。所以，some days ago 的意思不是「幾天前」（a few days ago），而是「好多天前」（quite a few days ago）；for some time 的意思不是「一會兒」（for a while/a short time），而是「相當長的一段時間」（for quite a while/a fairly long time）。試比較下列兩句：

▶ I thought about your proposal for **some** weeks (i.e. for quite a few weeks). （你的提議我考慮了不少個禮拜。）

▶ I bought **some** books today (i.e. a few books). （今天我買了一些書。）

問題中的句子想要表達的意思是弱讀的 some，即「一些」，但這樣的 some 通常不出現在時間副詞中：

▶ I bought **some** books. （我買了一些書。）→（○）正確。

▶ I walked for **some** hours. （我走了好多個小時。）→（×）錯誤。

*但弱讀的some可以出現在下句中：

▶ Give me **some** time to think about it. （請給我一些時間來考慮這件事。）

因為這裡的some time是名詞片語（做動詞 give 的直接受詞），並不是時間副詞。相較之下，我們不可說：

▶ I thought about it for **some** time.（這件事我考慮了相當長一段時間。）

004 Question

ex和former的使用時機：Former president還是ex-president？Former husband還是ex-husband？

Answer

有關「前總統」、「前董事長」、「前夫」等等的「前」，英文可以使用ex-或former。根據*The New York Times Manual of Style and Usage*，ex-是口語的用法，而former則用於正式場合。例如，在報紙的文章中，您可能會看到某篇文章中從頭至尾都使用 former，但在標題（headline）或圖文（caption）中則使用ex-。據瞭解，這兩個字與所指的人是否過世或仍在世無關，不過在正式場合，最好還是使用former。

順便一提的是，當ex-意為former時，一定要使用連字號，但在ex officio（adj. & adv. 依職權的／依職權地），ex parte（adj. & adv. 單方的；片面的／單方地；片面地），ex post factor（adj. 事後的；事後追究的；追溯既往的）等拉丁片語中則不用連字號。

005 Question

複合形容詞可能：1. 以連字號（hyphen）連接在一起 2. 單獨一個字 3. 分開成兩個字。是否有規則可以知道何時該使用這三種形式中的某一種形式呢？

Answer

連字號都用在複合名詞、複合形容詞和字首（prefix）中：

複合名詞

大多數的複合名詞都被寫成兩個字 ─ 不過，這並非硬性規定：Hyphen usage（連字號用法），swimming pool（游泳池），driving licence（駕照），human being（人類），contact lens（隱形眼鏡）。

在通常以連字號連接的複合名詞中，最常見者包括 passer-by（過路人，這個字現在也寫成 passerby），dry-cleaning（乾洗），X-ray（X光），T-shirt（T恤），parent-teacher association（家長教師聯誼會，簡稱 PTA），do-it-yourself（自己動手做），mother-in-law（岳母；婆婆）和 daughter-in-law（媳婦）等。

當複合名詞被用作形容詞時，它們通常加連字號。試比較下列兩句：

▶ The afternoon was so hot that I decided to go to the **open-air** swimming pool. I love to eat in the open air in the summer.（下午太熱了，所以我決定到室外游泳池游泳。夏天時我喜歡在室外或露天用餐。）

▶ Air traffic was so dense that afternoon that **air-traffic** control could hardly cope.（那天下午的空中交通太密集了，所以空中或航空交通管制差點無法應付。）

複合形容詞

大多數的複合形容詞都是由兩個字、有時三個字所構成，而這些字之間通常會使用連字號，下面為一些常見的複合形容詞及經常與其搭配的名詞：A clear-cut decision（明確的決定），a far-fetched explanation（牽強的解釋），a low-cut dress（低胸的洋裝），a free-and-easy relationship（隨便的關係），an off-hand remark（隨

口說出的話）, cold-blooded murder（冷血、殘忍的謀殺）, an all-out effort（全力以赴）, a deep-sea diver（深海潛水伕）, full-time staff（專職職員）, a jet-black sky（烏黑的天空）, snow-white shoes（雪白的鞋子）。

注意：雖然複合形容詞在修飾名詞（放在名詞的前面）時都會加連字號，但在作主詞補語時通常不用連字號。試比較下面的句子：

▶ The products on the shelves were **out of date** and had to be withdrawn.（貨架上的產品已經過時，必須收回。）
▶ His **out-of-date** argument gathered little support.（他過時的論調難獲支持。）
▶ **Out-of-work** policemen often find employment as security guards, but it is not so easy for teachers who are out of work to find other jobs.（失業的警察經常會找到當保全人員的工作，但失業的教師要找到其他工作就沒有這麼容易了。）

字首

Co-, non- 和 ex- 這三個字首有時使用連字號與其後的名詞、形容詞或動詞連接：

▶ **Non-profit-making** organizations are non-existent in this country.（沒有獲利的公司無法在這個國家生存。）
▶ His **co-operation** in the co-production was much appreciated.（他在聯合生產方面的合作深獲感激。）

006 Question

John is a fun person.和John is a funny person.那一句正確呢？

Answer

這兩句都正確，但語意不同，因為fun和funny是截然不同的兩個字。然而，這兩個字很容易讓人搞混，致使用錯或誤用的情況不時發生，令人「啼笑皆非」！

在此，fun和funny都是形容詞；不過，fun也可當名詞用，且用得比形容詞廣泛，其

所構成的若干慣用語都頗為常用（容後再述）。當形容詞用的fun意為「有趣的；愉快的；好玩的」，而funny意為「有趣的；滑稽的；好笑的」，前者指的是令人愉快的事物或喜歡與之相處的人，後者指的是令人發笑或逗趣的人事物。例如：

▶ A comedian is **funny**.（喜劇演員很有趣 ─ 因為他們搞笑、逗趣，讓你發笑）

▶ Going to an amusement park is **fun**.（到遊樂園玩很有趣 ─ 因為你玩得很開心、很愉快）

現在來看問題中的句子：

▶ John is a **fun** person.（約翰很有趣 ─ 因為跟約翰相處讓人很愉快、很開心。）

▶ John is a **funny** person.（約翰很有趣 ─ 因為約翰很會搞笑，經常讓人覺得很好笑。）

這裡有個所謂的「做或看規則」（do/see rule）可讓您輕易判斷該用fun還是funny。如果是個人親自去做或親身經歷的，那麼就用fun，如果是看到或聽到的，則用funny。這規則的例外是看運動比賽，因為看比賽不會讓人發笑。不過，有些情況則使用fun或funny都可以，如「玩遊戲」可能很開心、很好玩，也可能很好笑、讓人笑個不停。茲舉數例供大家參考，俾讓您能確實掌握fun和funny之間的差異：

▶ Going to a dentist is not **fun**!（看牙醫不好玩！）

▶ Nobody laughed because his joke was not **funny**.（沒有人笑，因為他的笑話不好笑。）

▶ The movie was quite **funny**.（這部電影很好笑。）

▶ Playing basketball is **fun**.（打籃球很有趣。）

▶ Playing a game is **fun/funny**.（玩遊戲很有趣。）

▶ He's one of Taiwan's **funniest** comedians.（他是台灣最搞笑的喜劇演員之一。）

▶ A party with your friends is **fun**.（跟朋友的聚會很有趣。）

fun亦可當名詞用，且是不可數名詞，意為「快樂；樂趣；有趣的人事物」，其前往往用a lot of, lots of, much, great, good等詞來修飾，表示很開心、很好玩、很有意思及有趣的人事物。事實上，fun的用法很特殊，其句型有二：「事 + is/was/are/were (a lot of/lots of/much) fun（某事很好玩）」及「人 + have/has/had (a lot of/lots of/great/good) fun.（某人玩得愉快）」。由此可知，英文並無It has fun.的說法，因為這是錯誤的。例如：

- ▶ I had lots of **fun** at the party last night. （昨晚我在聚會上玩得很開心。）
- ▶ The party last night was a lot of **fun**. （昨晚的聚會很好玩。）
- ▶ We hope you have **fun** at the beach tomorrow! （我們希望明天你在海灘能玩得盡興。）
- ▶ We had great **fun** comparing the functions of our smartphones. （我們比較智慧型手機的功能比得不亦樂乎。）
- ▶ Do come tomorrow, it'll be good **fun**. （明天一定要來，那會很好玩。／那會很有意思。）
- ▶ Spending money is **fun**! （花錢真好玩！）

如上述，fun 也意為有趣的人事物（別以為人事物是可數的，在此就是不可數），在此用法中，其前往往使用 great 或 good 來修飾，構成慣用語 "great/good fun"。例如：

- ▶ Anthony is **great/good fun**. （安東尼是個很有趣的人。）
- ▶ You'll love Peter - he's **great/good fun**. （你會喜歡彼得的，他很有意思。）

請注意這裡的great/good fun（很有趣的人）與上面great/good fun（玩得很愉快）的不同；兩者構詞一樣，而且主詞都是人，但動詞一個是be動詞、一個是have/has/had。

Excercise
綜合練習

I. 填空題

❶ Despite a _____ failure, he has an optimistic attitude toward everything.
（儘管遭受巨大的失敗，他還是保有樂觀態度面對一切的事物。）

❷ Don't be such a _____ dreamer.
（不要當這麼愛做春秋大夢的人。）

❸ China is a country with _____ population.
（中國是個有眾多人口的國家。）

❹ He's one of Taiwan's _____ comedians.
（他是台灣最搞笑的喜劇演員之一。）

❺ You'll love Peter because he's good _____.
（你會喜歡彼得的，他很有意思。）

❻ Her _____ keeps bothering her.
（她前夫不斷騷擾她。）

❼ The _____ is in jail now.
（前總統現在正在坐牢。）

❽ My _____ (mother in law/mother-in-law) doesn't have a (driving licence/driving-licence).
（我岳母沒有駕照。）

❾ The juridical court needs to make a _____ (clear-cut/clear cut) decision on how to punish the _____ (cold blooded/cold-blooded) murderer.
（該如何處置那個冷血的殺人犯？法院還需要做個明確的決定。）

II. 二選一

❶ ☐ The gold digger is looking for someone with big wealth.
☐ The gold digger is looking for someone with great wealth.
（那個拜金女在找個有錢人。）

2 ☐ Let's welcome the former president.
☐ Let's welcome the ex president.
（讓我們熱烈歡迎前總統。）

3 ☐ This low-cut dress needs dry-cleaning.
☐This low cut dress needs dry cleaning.
（這件低胸的洋裝需要乾洗。）

4 ☐The party last night had a lot of fun.
☐The party last night was a lot of fun.
（昨晚的聚會很好玩。）

Answer

I. 填空題
1 great
2 big
3 large
4 funniest
5 fun
6 ex-husband
7 former president
8 mother-in-law, driving licence
9 clear-cut, cold-blooded

II. 二選一
1 第二句正確。
2 第一句正確。
3 第一句正確。
4 第二句正確。

001 Question

我拿I purchased two dozens of pencils.這個句子去問了幾個人，有人說文法或用法不對，有人說對，請問這句到底對不對呢？

Answer

不對！正確的寫法是：I purchased two dozen pencils.。dozen 這個字有兩種複數型態：dozen 和 dozens（注意：hundred, thousand, million 和 billion 也有這樣兩種複數型，而且用法也跟下面有關 dozen 的敘述完全一樣）。dozen 加 s 的複數型（即 dozens，意為「許多」）可以單獨使用，也可用 「of 介系詞片語」來修飾，即後接 of 介系詞片語，如 Complaints came the next morning by the dozens.（翌晨有很多人投訴。）；Dozens of people came to see me.（許多人來看我。）；I have been to dozens of countries.（我已經去過許多國家。）

當 dozen 前面有數字時，它是採用不加 s 的複數型（即 dozen，意為「一打」），如 Send me three dozen eggs.（給我送 3 打蛋。）；I paid eight dozen dollars for that pen.（我買那支筆花了 96 元。）不加 s 的複數型通常也不用 「of 介系詞片語」來修飾。所以，I purchased two dozens of pencils.（我買了兩打鉛筆。） 和 I purchased two dozen of pencils. 均非標準英語。

然而，當 of 後面的受詞為代名詞或特指的名詞時（所謂特指的名詞，就是名詞的前面加上 the, that, this, these, those 或所有格，如 my, John's 等等。由於 dozen 後面必須接複數名詞，所以在此不可使用 this 和 that），「數字 + dozen + of」則是一種標準的句型。請看下面的句子：

▶ Three **dozen of** them went to the U.S.（他們有 36 人去美國。）
▶ **Two dozen of** these cups were broken.（這些杯子有 24 個被打破。）
▶ **Eight dozen of** his troops were killed.（他的軍隊有 96 人喪生。）
▶ More than **one dozen of** those apples have taken away.（那些蘋果已被拿走超過一打。）

Question

一篇英文新聞報導提到 JCB 是一家同名公司所生產的工程車，但現在也被用來泛指一般的工程車。這種將專有名詞當普通名詞使用的字在英文中似乎不難見到，是否可以就此做更詳細的說明或多舉一些實例呢？

Answer

對於這些名詞，筆者通常稱之為「專有名詞通俗化」，但更精確地說應該是「商標品名普通名詞化」，因為這些專有名詞原本是各該公司的名稱，然後被用來指各該公司的產品，但現在則被用來泛指同類或同性質或同功能的商品。雖然這些專有名詞仍維持大寫型態，但已變成道道地地的普通名詞，甚至有單複數之分，如 a JCB, two JCBs。除 JCB（工程車）外，目前已知還有十幾個這樣的名詞，茲將其臚列於后供大家參考（相信一定還有漏網之魚）：

band-Aid：OK繃

chap stick：護唇膏

dumpster：大型垃圾車

hi-Liter：螢光筆

kleenex：面紙

popsicle：冰棒

post-it：便利貼

q-Tip：棉花棒

rolodex：名片整理盒

saran wrap：保鮮膜

scotch tape：膠帶

styrofoam：保麗龍

velcro：魔鬼粘

windex：玻璃清潔劑

003 **Question**

amount, number 和 quantity 的用法有何不同呢？下面三句都講得通嗎？

1. A large amount of chickens were infected with the H5N1 strain of the bird flu.
2. A large number of chickens were infected with the H5N1 strain of the bird flu.
3. A large quantity of chickens were infected with the H5N1 strain of the bird flu.

Answer

上面這三句只有第 2 句講得通，第 1 和第 3 句是錯誤的。請看下面的說明：

Amount 通常跟不可數（uncountable）、無生命（inanimate）的名詞連用：

▶ The **amount of** work I got through in September was double the amount that I did in August. （我九月份的工作量是八月份的兩倍。）

▶ She spent a very large **amount of** money yesterday. （她昨天花了好大一筆錢。）

Number 跟可數（countable）、有生命（animate）或無生命（inanimate）的名詞連用：

▶ A small **number of** chickens were infected with the H5N1 strain of the bird flu. （少數雞隻感染了禽流感 H5N1 病毒。）

▶ The president has made a large **number of** mistakes. （總統犯了許多錯誤。）

Quantity 通常跟可數或不可數、無生命的名詞連用：

▶ There are very large **quantities of** oranges on sale in the market. （目前有非常多的橘子在市場上銷售。）

▶ A vast/large **quantity of** imported beer has been sold. （已售出了大量的進口啤酒。）

再者，從上面的例句可知，amount, number和quantity的前面經常使用vast, large, small等表示數量大小的形容詞來修飾，而這些形容詞前面有時還會使用very等程度副詞來修飾。不過，要特別注意的是，在這些用法中，large不可用big來替代，亦即big不可用在amount, number和quantity的前面。

004 Question

在 He is already 29 years old but he just had (the) chicken pox. 這句中，chicken pox 前面要不要加定冠詞呢？

Answer

一般而言，疾病名稱前不加定冠詞，所以我們不能說 the cancer（癌症）、the tuberculosis（結核病 — 尤指肺結核）、the diabetes（糖尿病）或 the diphtheria（白喉），如He's dying of pneumonia.（他罹患肺炎，已不久於人世。）；Appendicitis nearly killed him.（盲腸炎差點要了他的命。）；She has cancer.（她罹患癌症。）

然而，若干疾病也可加定冠詞，如the measles（麻疹）、the mumps（腮腺炎）和the chicken pox（水痘）；換言之，有些疾病名稱，尤其是measles 和mumps等這些複數型當單數用的疾病名稱（接單數動詞），加或不加冠詞都可以。所以，在He is already 29 years old but he just had (the) chicken pox.（他已經 29 歲了，但才剛長完水痘。）這句中，chicken pox前面有無定冠詞都可以。

005 Question

guys可以用來稱呼女子(girls)嗎？

Answer

網路字典 *Merriam-Webster Online* 說，guys「複數，用來指一個群體的所有成員，而不管其性別為何」；*The New Fowler's Modern English Usage* 一書也說，guys「有時亦可指女性」。由此可知，guys 似乎是朝著可以指「所有人」（不分性別）的方向發展。不過，在正式寫作中，使用這個字來指女子並不是很恰當。

006 Question

John's and Mary's car was stolen last night.這句可否表示約翰和瑪麗各有一部車子被偷呢？

Answer

不可以。不過，在說明原因之前，我們先來複習使用所有格's來表示兩人（或多人）共同或個別擁有某項或某些東西的文法觀念。

根據文法，若要表示兩人共同擁有某項（或某些）東西，則所有格 's 只加在最靠近該項東西的人名之後，如Jack and Cindy's house（傑克和辛蒂共同擁有一棟房子）；Jack and Cindy's houses（傑克和辛蒂共同擁有至少兩棟房子）。如果是個別擁有，則每個人名的後面都要加上所有格's，如Jack's and Cindy's houses。

問題中的句子John's and Mary's car was stolen last night.有兩個謬誤之處。既然約翰和瑪麗各自有車，那麼車子的數量應該至少兩部，car應改為cars；這可能是不當使用英文省略規則，將原意為John's car and Mary's car省略為John's and Mary's car的結果，進而影響了動詞的正確性，因為無論是John's and Mary's cars 還是John's car and Mary's car，be動詞都要用were。所以，這句的正確寫法是John's and Mary's cars were stolen last night.（昨晚約翰和瑪麗的車子都被偷了。）

有人可能雞蛋裡挑骨頭，認為我們無法從John's and Mary's cars看出約翰和瑪麗各僅有一部車子，也可能各有兩部或兩部以上的車子。誠然，但對於英文這種個別擁有的表示法，有一項觀念值得我們建立或牢記，那就是：若無上下文，John's and Mary's cars都被認定等於John's car and Mary's car，即約翰和瑪麗各僅有一部車子。若要表示兩人各有兩部或兩部以上的車子或者其中一人擁有至少兩部車子，那麼寫法如下：

John's cars and Mary's cars

John's cars and Mary's car

John's car and Mary's cars

007 Question

最後一個字母為 o 的名詞，複數時加 s 或 es 是否有規則可循呢？

Answer

我們知道，字尾為 o 的名詞，它們的複數是在 o 的後面加上 s 或 es，那麼要如何判斷各該名詞是要加 s 還是 es 呢？

一般而言，若一個名詞的字尾是兩個 o，亦即母音字母 o＋o（或其他母音字母＋o），則其複數是在字尾加上 s，如 kangaroo → kangaroos、zoo → zoos、studio → studios。若字尾只有一個 o，即子音字母＋o，那麼其複數是在字尾加上 es，如 tomato → tomatoes、veto → vetoes，但 piano 和 photo 等少數名詞例外，它們的複數分別為pianos和photos。

008 **Q**uestion

no接可數名詞時，該名詞要用複數還是單數呢？

Answer

一般而言，**no**後面若接可數名詞，該名詞通常使用複數型，因為這比單數型要來得自然多了，不會顯得蹩腳。例如：

▶ **No** road accidents were reported in Pescadores throughout August.（整個八月澎湖皆未傳出道路意外事故。）

▶ **No** dogs are allowed in the restaurant.（這家餐廳不允許攜狗入內。）

不過，視個人心中所想的數量（一個或多個）而定，**no**有時可接單數或複數名詞。例如：

▶ It was 10 a.m., yet there was **no** policeman on duty outside the bank.（時間已是早上十點，但銀行外面仍無警察值勤。）

It was 10 a.m., yet there were **no** policemen on duty outside the bank.

▶ In the baseball game last Sunday, **no** players hit a home run.（在上週日的棒球比賽中，沒有任何球員擊出全壘打。）

In the baseball game last Sunday, **no** player hit a home run.

In the baseball game last Sunday, **not a single** player hit a home run.

再者，有時單複數混用會比較自然。例如：

▶ He must lead a lonely life: He has no wife and no children.（他一定過著孤寂的生活：他無妻無子。） － 男人通常只有一個太太，但往往有一個以上的小孩。

009 Question

(a) Most books (b) Most my books (c) Most of my books are in English. 這三句何者正確呢？

Answer

most 這個字可當形容詞和代名詞用，若為形容詞，其後直接接名詞，如 Most birds can fly.（大多數的鳥都會飛。），所以 (a) Most books are in English.（大部分的書都是英文書。）這句是對的。在這句中，名詞books並非指特定的書，如「我的書」、「這些書」、「那張桌子上的書」，而是泛指（generic）一般的書。

當most用作代名詞時，其後往往接介詞of再接特定或特指的（specific）名詞。所謂特指的名詞，就是名詞的前面加上the, that, this, these, those或所有格，如my, his, their, Jack's, Thomas'等等。所以 (c) Most of my books are in English.也是正確的句子；換言之，(b) Most my books are in English.這句是錯的，因為如果名詞是特指，most後面的of不能省略。然而，如果名詞是泛指，則most後面就不能有of，這就是上述most當形容詞用，後面直接接名詞的情況，所以Most of books are in English.也是錯的。

英文中這種兼具形容詞（或限定詞）和代名詞功能且用法與most完全相同的字或片語，還有all (of), both (of), some (of), any (of), many (of), much (of), a few (of), a little (of), several (of), one (of), two (of), three (of)……等等。例如：

▶ **Many students** are going to study abroad.（許多學生要出國留學。）
→（○）正確。

▶ **Many of my students** are going to study abroad.（我的學生當中有許多人要出國留學。）→（○）正確。
Many my students are going to study abroad. →（×）錯誤。
Many of students are going to study abroad. →（×）錯誤。

▶ **Some people** are Chinese tourists.（有些人是中國觀光客。）→（○）正確。

▶ **Some of those people** are Chinese tourists.（那些人當中有些是中國觀光客。）→（○）正確。

Some those people are Chinese tourists. →（✕）錯誤。
Some of people are Chinese tourists. →（✕）錯誤。

▶ **Several windows** were broken.（有幾扇窗戶被砸破了。）→（○）正確。
Several of the windows were broken. →（○）正確。
Several the windows were broken. →（✕）錯誤。
Several of windows were broken. →（✕）錯誤。

值得注意的是，當名詞為特指時，all和both這兩個字後面的of可以省略，亦即它們後面的of可有可無。不過，若名詞為泛指，則其後同樣不可有of。例如：

▶ **Almost all of my students** are female.（我的學生幾乎都是女生。）
→（○）正確。
Almost all my students are female. →（○）正確。

▶ **All children** deserve encouragement.（所有的小孩都應得到鼓勵。）
→（○）正確。
All of children deserve encouragement. →（✕）錯誤。

▶ I know **both of** his parents.（我認識他的父母親。）→（○）正確。
I know **both** his parents. →（○）正確。

▶ **Both paintings** are by the same artist.（兩幅畫都是同一畫家畫的。）
→（○）正確。
Both of paintings are by the same artist. →（✕）錯誤。

最後要提的是，half 這個亦可當形容詞（或限定詞）和代名詞用的字，若接特指的名詞，其用法與all和both相同，亦即後面的of也是可有可無。例如：

▶ **Half of** the children study Japanese.（這些孩子當中有一半學日文。）→
（○）正確。
Half the children study Japanese. →（○）正確。

▶ Nearly **half of** the employees complained of stress.（近半數的員工抱怨壓力太大。）→（○）正確。
Nearly **half** the employees complained of stress. →（○）正確。

any後面應接複數還是單數可數名詞呢？

Answer

any後面通常接複數可數名詞，但這並不表示它不能接單數可數名詞，只是兩者的用法和意思並不相同。請看下面的例句：

▶ 1. There **aren't any** books on the desk.（書桌上沒有書。）
▶ 2. There **isn't** a single book on the desk.（書桌上沒有書。）

這兩句強調的重點略有差異。在第 1 句中，我們想像的是一本以上的書，即若干書或一些書。而在第 2 句中，只有一本書。

這其中所牽涉到的文法觀念包括大家所熟悉的「不定冠詞a/an或not a/not an接單數可數名詞」以及許多人一直無法確定的「any/no接複數可數名詞或不可數名詞」。由於any大多用在疑問句、否定句或if子句中，又any通常接複數可數名詞或不可數名詞，由此可以推知，疑問句、否定句或if子句中的any都接複數可數名詞或不可數名詞，但它的意思並非「任一；任何」，而是「若干，一些」；它的相對詞就是用於肯定句、同樣接複數可數名詞或不可數名詞、意思也是「若干，一些，某些」的some。例如：

▶ Would you like **an egg** for breakfast?（早餐你想吃個蛋嗎？）--one egg 為單數可數名詞

▶ No thanks. I don't want any **eggs** today.（不，謝了。今天我不想吃蛋。）--eggs 為複數可數名詞

▶ I'm making **scrambled egg** for Jack. Won't you have any scrambled egg?（我正在為傑克做炒蛋。你不想要炒蛋嗎？）--scrambled egg 為不可數名詞

▶ Are there any **letters** for me?（有我的信件嗎？）--letters 為複數可數名詞

▶ Linda hasn't any **money** to spare.（琳達的錢都用光了。）--money 為不可數名詞

▶ The book contains no useful **information**.（這本書沒有有用的資料。）--information 為不可數名詞

- ▶ Nick has no **relatives** in Taipei. （尼克在台北沒有親戚。）--relatives 為複數可數名詞
- ▶ They have some **work** to do tonight. （今晚他們有一些事要做。）--work 為不可數名詞
- ▶ Some **cars** are very expensive. （有些車非常昂貴。）--cars 為複數可數名詞

正如上述，any亦可接單數可數名詞，但這是指any用於肯定句的情況，此時any意為「任一；任何」。在口語中，any這個字本身就是句子的重音所在。例如：

- ▶ **Any** good dictionary will give you examples of use as well as definitions of words. （任何一本好的字典都有提供用法的例句以及字詞的定義。）
- ▶ I wanted a job, **any** kind of a job. （我需要一份工作，任何工作都行。）
- ▶ Ask **any** dentist and he/she will tell you that you should go for a check-up at least once a year. （去問任何一位牙醫，他或她都會告訴你一年至少應檢查牙齒一次。）

這個 any 的相對詞也是some，但後者是指同樣用於肯定句、接單數可數名詞、意為「某一，某個」的some。例如：

- ▶ Gary is talking with **some** girl. （蓋瑞正在和一個女孩交談。）
- ▶ Alice married **some** guy she met on the train. （愛麗絲跟她在火車上邂逅的一個人結婚了。）

011 Question

最中文的「暑假」，分別有人寫成或說成summer holiday或summer holidays，它們有何不同呢？

Answer

Holiday這個單數可數名詞意為「節日，假日；假期」。例如：

- ▶ It's a **public/national/bank holiday** on Friday, so all the banks will be closed. （星期五是國定假日，所有銀行都不營業。）

▶ Sandy seems very tired. He needs a **holiday**. （桑迪似乎非常疲勞。他需要休個假。）

在表示假期、休假、度假的意思時，複數名詞holidays和holiday的用法並無二致。

例如：

▶ We have decided where we're going for our **holiday(s)** this year. （我們已決定今年要到哪裡度假了。）
▶ We are all going to Europe for our **holiday** this year. （我們今年都要去歐洲度假。）
= We are all going to Europe for our **holidays** this year.

從上述可知，summer holiday和summer holidays的意思和用法並無不同。

例如：

▶ I'd like to go to Australia for my **summer/winter holiday** this year. （今年我想去澳洲過暑假／寒假。）
= I'd like to go to Australia for my **summer/winter holidays** this year.

我們經常使用(to go/be) on holiday來表示「去／在休假／度假」。由於on holiday是固定用語，所以on不可換成at、in或其他介系詞，而holiday也不可換成 holidays。例如：

▶ I first met my wife when I was **on holiday** in Japan. （我在日本度假時初次邂逅了我太太。）→（○）正確。
I first met my wife when I was **at holiday** in Japan. →（✕）錯誤。
I first met my wife when I was **in holiday** in Japan. →（✕）錯誤。
I first met my wife when I was **on holidays** in Japan. →（✕）錯誤。

Excercise
綜 合 練 習

I. 選擇題

(   ) ❶ Two _____ their eggs were rotten.
（他們有24顆蛋已經壞掉了。）

    A. dozen   B. dozens

    C. dozen of   D. dozens of

(   ) ❷ The teacher bought two _____ erasers for the poor students.
（那老師買了兩打的橡皮擦給貧窮的學生。）

    A. dozen   B. dozens

    C. dozen of   D. dozens of

II. 填空題

❶ She spent a very large _____ of money yesterday.
（她昨天花了好大一筆錢。）

❷ There are very large _____ of oranges on sale in the market.
（目前有非常多的橘子在市場上銷售。）

❸ He has been busy like a bee since his mother got _____ (tuberculosis/ the tuberculosis).
（自從他媽媽罹患肺結核以後，他一直忙得不可開交。）

❹ _____ (Appendicitis/ The appendicitis) nearly killed the child.
（盲腸炎差點要了那個小孩的命）

❺ _____ (Brian and Julia's/Brian's and Julia's) daughter was kidnapped.
（布萊恩跟朱莉亞的女兒被綁架了。）

❻ _____ (Miss Lin and Miss Chen's/Miss Lin's and Miss Chen's) students are smart.
（林老師跟陳老師的學生都很聰明。）

7 There are many _____ in this country.
（這國家有很多的動物園。）

8 We need lots of _____ for this soup.
（我們要很多蕃茄才能做這個湯。）

9 No _____ are allowed in this area.
（乘客勿入。）

10 I have no _____ (coin), no _____ (bill).
（我沒有零錢也沒有鈔票。）

11 _____ (Many of students/Many of the students) in the class come from poor families.
（這個班有許多學生來自清寒家庭。）

12 _____ (Some animals/Some of animals) in Australia are unique.
（澳洲有些動物是獨特的。）

13 _____ (Are/Is) there any _____ (letter/letters) for me?
（有我的信件嗎？）

14 Linda hasn't any _____ (coins/coin) to spare.
（琳達的零錢都用光了。）

III. 翻譯

1 The guys are fans of the Golden State Warriors.

_____

2 Hey, guys! It's lady's room!

_____

IV. 連連看

Kleenex •　　　　　　　　• 面紙

Hi-Liter •　　　　　　　　• 大型垃圾車

Dumpster •　　　　　　　　• 螢光筆

V. 二選一

1 ☐ I purchased two dozens of pencils.
☐ I purchased two dozen of pencils.
（我買了兩打的鉛筆。）

2 ☐ A large amount of chickens were infected with the H5N1 strain of the bird flu.
☐ A large number of chickens were infected with the H5N1 strain of the bird flu.
（有許多的雞受到H5N1感染。）

3 ☐ He has cancer.
☐ He has the cancer.
（他罹患癌症。）

4 ☐ John's and Mary's car was stolen last night.
☐ John and Mary's car was stolen last night.
（約翰和瑪莉的車昨晚被偷了。）

5 ☐ I saw many kangaroos in Australia.
☐ I saw many kangarooes in Australia.
（我在澳洲看到很多的袋鼠。）

6 ☐ No children under 18 can watch this film.
☐ No child under 18 can watch this film.
（18歲以下孩童請勿觀看這部電影。）

7 ☐ Most books are interesting.
☐ Most my books are interesting.
（大部分的書都很有趣。）

8 ☐ I first met my girlfriend when I was on holiday in Paris.
☐ I first met my girlfriend when I was at holiday in Paris.
（當我在巴黎渡假時，我第一次遇見了我的女朋友。）

Answer

I. 選擇題
1 C
2 A

II. 填空題

1 amount
2 quantities
3 tuberculosis
4 Appendicitis
5 Brian and Julia's
6 Miss Lin's and Miss Chen's
7 zoos

8 tomatoes
9 passengers
10 coins, bills
11 Many of the students
12 Some animals
13 Are, letters
14 coins

III. 翻譯
1 這些人是金州勇士隊的球迷。
2 男孩們，這是女廁！

IV. 連連看

Kleenex ———————————— 面紙

Hi-Liter ⤬ 大型垃圾車

Dumpster ⤬ 螢光筆

V. 二選一
1 第二句正確
2 第二句正確
3 第一句正確
4 第二句正確
5 第一句正確
6 第一句正確
7 第一句正確
8 第一句正確

001 Question

在 There is a vacancy for a computer programmer in most every company.這句中most是否為almost之誤呢？

Answer

非也！在 There is a vacancy for a computer programmer in most every company.（幾乎每家公司都有電腦程式設計師的缺額。）這句中，most就是almost。

大多數著名的英文字典都會提到most（副詞）也有almost的意思。根據*Merriam-Webster's Dictionary of English Usage*及*The New Fowler's Modern English Usage*，這一用法自16世紀以來就已存在（最初是在蘇格蘭使用），係肇因於almost經常被寫成'most，而後來就變成了most。

儘管現今在英國僅若干方言會有使用most來代替almost的情況，但在美式英語中，這卻是一種標準或正規的用法（standard usage）－雖然是屬於非正式用法。

這個most通常僅用在anyone, anywhere, everybody, everywhere等不定代名詞以及any/every +名詞所構成的片語之前。

例如：

▶ She plays cards most **every** evening.
（她幾乎每天晚上都玩牌。）
▶ The iced tea was very sweet, as it is most **everywhere** in the South.
（冰茶非常甜，在南方幾乎每個地方都一樣。）
▶ Like most **everybody** else, I was shocked.
（就跟其他幾乎每個人一樣，我也感到震驚。）

002 Question

我們不能說I have met him five years ago.，而必須說I have met him before.。為什麼before可以跟現在完成式連用，而ago卻不行呢？

Answer

before和ago皆意為「以前」，但前者指的是「現在之前的任何時間」（亦即指過去某個不確定的時間），而後者是指「現在之前的某個確定的時間」。所以，before可以跟現在完成式連用，而ago只能用於簡單過去式。例如：

- ▶ I know that guy. I've met him somewhere **before**.（我知道那個人。我以前在某個地方見過他。）
- ▶ Have you been here **before**?（你以前有來過這裡嗎？）
- ▶ No, I've never been here **before**. This is my first time.（沒有，我以前從未來過這裡。這是第一次。）
- ▶ Your mother phoned five minutes **ago**. Can you phone her back?（你母親 5 分鐘前來電。你可以給她回電嗎？）
- ▶ I saw her for the first time at the National Palace Museum some twenty years **ago**.（我大約 20 年前在國立故宮博物院首次見到她。）

before通常跟現在完成式連用，但也可用於簡單過去式。

- ▶ I know that guy. I met him somewhere **before**.
  Were you here **before**?
  No, I was never here **before**. This is my first time.
  We were all students **before**.（我們以前都是學生。）

ago所指的時間都是從現在開始往以前推算，但before所指的時間除了上述也是從現在開始往以前推算之外，還可指從過去某個時間點往更早之前推算的時間。所以，當我們要表示比ago更早的時間時，我們只能用before (that) 或earlier或previously，而不能用ago。在這種句子中，ago用簡單過去式，而before用過去完成式。例如：

▶ My grandfather died five years ago; my grandmother had already died three years **before** (that)/previously/earlier.

（我祖父 5 年前過世，而我祖母在那之前 3 年就已經過世了。）－亦即祖母是在 8 年前過世。

▶ I met my ex-girlfriend at a hotel in Bangkok in December 2006 when she told me that she had got married four years before.

（2006 年 12 月我在曼谷一家飯店遇見我前女友，當時她告訴我，她在那之前 4 年就已結婚了。）－亦即她在 2002 年結婚。

▶ Last year I went back to my hometown that I had left ten years **before**.

（去年我回到睽違 10 年的故鄉。）－亦即我在 11 年前離開故鄉。

003 Question

He was seriously hurt by her unkind words. 這句有沒有錯呢？

Answer

錯了。這個句子犯了英文固定搭配方面的錯誤。問題的癥結就出在 hurt 上。根據字典，這個字當動詞用時有四個主要意思，都是我們經常會用到的。

hurt 的第一個意思是「弄傷，使（身體）受傷」，與其固定搭配的用語為表示受傷程度輕重的 slightly/badly/seriously（輕度／嚴重／十分嚴重）等副詞。

例如：

▶ He was only **slightly hurt** in the car accident.
（他在這場車禍中僅受輕傷。）

▶ She was **badly/seriously hurt** when she fell off the ladder.
（她從梯子上摔下來時受了重傷。）

hurt的第二個意思是「使傷心，使痛心」，與其固定搭配的用語為 very/rather/deeply（非常／相當／深感）等副詞。

例如：

- ▶ I was **deeply hurt** by the way she just ignored me.
  （她對我不理不睬的態度讓我深感痛心。）
- ▶ He was **very/rather/deeply hurt** by her unkind words.
  （她那些無情無義的話使他非常／相當／深感傷心。）
- ▶ Don't **hurt** my feelings.
  （別傷害我的感情。）

所以，在問題的句子中，seriously應改為very或rather或deeply。

hurt的第三個意思是「使感到疼痛」。值得注意的是，在這種用法中，現在進行式和簡單現在式的意思並無二致。

例如：

- ▶ "Where does it hurt/Where is it hurting, Mr. Lee?"
  （李先生，什麼地方痛？）
- ▶ "Just here, doctor."
  （醫生，就在這裡。）
- ▶ "Tell me where it hurts/where it is hurting."
  （告訴我哪裡痛。）
- ▶ "My arm hurts."
  （我的手臂痛。）
- ▶ You're hurting my arm. Ouch! Don't touch me. That hurts.
  （你弄痛了我的手臂。唉唷！別碰我，那很痛。）

hurt的第四個意思是「造成傷害（問題等）；損害」。

例如：

- ▶ This will **hurt** his reputation.
  （這將有損他的聲譽。）
- ▶ This will **hurt** his chances of being elected.
  （這將損害他當選的機會。）

▶ Have another drink — one more won't **hurt**.
（再喝一杯 － 多喝一杯不會有問題的。）

004 Question

Especially men have this problem.這句對嗎？

Answer

這句不合語法，請看下面的說明。大家都知道，副詞可以修飾動詞、形容詞和副詞，但其實副詞也可以修飾名詞，其中最常見和最典型的是especially。例如：

▶ Married men and women, **especially** men, are likely to live longer than those who are not married.
（結婚者－尤其是男性－的壽命可能比不結婚者來得長。）

在上句中，副詞especially修飾名詞men。然而，especially卻不能用在句首來修飾名詞，所以問題中的句子不對。但若改成下句就對了：

▶ Men, **especially**, have this problem.
（尤其是男性都有這種問題。）

順便一提的是，also也不能用在句首修飾名詞。例如：

▶ **Also** men have this problem.
→（╳）錯誤。
▶ Men **also** have this problem.
→（○）正確。

但這並不表示also不能放在句首，如果它的後面接個逗點就可以了。不過，此時它的意思相當於furthermore（而且；再者）。例如：

▶ **Also**, most women would agree.
= **Furthermore**, most women would agree.
（而且大多數女性都會同意。）

quite在會話中的意思很難瞭解，它到底是「完全，十分，非常」（totally, perfectly, completely）還是「有幾分，頗為，相當」（partially, somewhat, fairly, rather）呢？

Answer

答案是：quite兼具這兩種意思。如果我們說 "I am quite happy."，這可能意為「我頗為高興但不是十分高興」（I'm partially, fairly, somewhat happy but not completely happy），但也可能意為「我十分／非常高興」（I'm totally, entirely, completely, 100% happy）。

所以接下來您可能會問：我們要如何辨別它們的意思呢？當有人說 I am quite happy. 時，要怎麼知道他們是表示「我有些高興」還是「我十分高興」呢？如果光看這個句子，確實無法知道它表示那個意思。不過，別氣餒，有一些線索可以幫助我們解決這問題。

首先，英語中有些形容詞被稱為極限形容詞（limit adjectives）或不可分等級的形容詞（non-gradable adjectives），這些形容詞本身的含意已包括極度的意思，因此通常沒有比較級和最高級形式，如perfect, unique, enormous, worthless, impossible以及現在分詞和過去分詞形容詞，如disgusting, exhausted, tired, amazed, terrified, delighted等等。這些形容詞雖沒有比較級和最高級形式，但卻可以用 absolutely, completely, perfectly, quite, simply, totally, utterly和wholly等副詞來修飾以表示最高程度（亦即已達極限），或者用almost, nearly, practically, virtually來修飾以表示接近最高程度－但請注意，現在分詞和過去分詞形容詞不能用almost, nearly, practically, virtually來修飾。所以，如果我說I am quite exhausted.時，這一定意為「我極度／十分／非常疲倦」，因為它不可能表示「我有些極度／十分／非常疲倦」，這講不通。

其次，從上下文來判斷。我們往往可從說話者所說的話清楚地知道他或她所要表達的quite的意思。假設John最近生了一場病：

Mike: Are you feeling better now?
John: Yes, I'm feeling quite healthy, thank you. In fact, I feel great!

從上面的對話可知，由於John説I feel great!（我覺得身體狀況棒極了。），所以他可能表示他已完全康復，因此quite healthy應是意為「十分／非常健康」。

然而，他們的對話也有可能如下：

Mike: Are you feeling better now?
John: Well, I'm feeling quite healthy, but I still have a terrible headache.

在這裡，由於 John 説 I still have a terrible headache.（我的頭還是痛得很厲害。），所以quite healthy應是意為「有些、部分健康但不是百分之百復原、十分健康」。

再者，如果這些句子是用講的，那麼我們通常可以從説話者的語氣和語調獲得線索。如果他或她説話的語氣肯定且句末的語調下降，那麼quite通常意為「完全，十分，非常」；然而，如果他或她説話的語氣比較不確定且句末的語調上揚，那麼quite通常意為「有幾分，頗為，相當」。

事實上，用quite來表示「完全，十分，非常」的意思現在是 "quite old-fashioned"（十分／非常老式的用法）－起碼在口語是如此。在寫作，尤其是在正式寫作中quite有時還是會被用來表示「完全，十分，非常」的意思，所以在小説中您可能還會看到這樣的用法；但在現代英語口語中，quite通常意為「有幾分，頗為，相當」。

006 **Question**

在He needs must come.這句中，needs的詞類和意義為何呢？

Answer

Needs這個字本身的拼法就是N-E-E-D-S，是個副詞，但僅跟must連用，構成must needs和needs must，不過這兩者的意思並不完全相同。Must needs和needs must均有「必須，務必，不得不」的意思，但must needs還意為「偏偏，偏要；堅持」－含有譏諷、不滿的意思，而needs must則無這項意思。例如：

▶ I **must needs** go there now.（我現在非去那裡不可。）-- 可用 needs must 代替 must needs。

▶ He **must needs** come.（他不得不來。）-- 可用 needs must 代替 must needs。

▶ She **must needs** go away when I want her.（我需要她時，她偏偏離開了。）-- 不可用 needs must。

▶ The telephone must needs ring when I went to bed.（我上床睡覺時偏偏有人來電話。）-- 不可用 needs must。

英文中有句成語就是使用needs must，那就是 "Needs must when the devil drives."，意為「人在屋簷下不得不低頭；情勢所逼，不得不然」。

007 Question

hopefully到底可不可以修飾整個句子呢？

Answer

hopefully可當一般副詞用，位於句首、句中或句末，意為「滿懷希望地；抱著希望地」如 He smiled hopefully in their direction.（他朝著他們的方向滿懷希望地微笑著。）；hopefully亦可當句子副詞（sentence adverb）用，位於句首，修飾整個句子，意為「但願」，如 Hopefully we will be there by five.（希望我們能在五點之前趕到那裡。）

雖然 hopefully 當句子副詞用的情況已經很普遍，尤其是在口語中，而且有些人認為，既然其他副詞（如 apparently, fortunately 和 obviously）可以修飾整個句子，完全合乎文法，那麼 hopefully 亦可修飾整個句子，但許多作者、編輯和文體指南都認為這樣用是錯誤的。

因此，為了避免爭議，謹慎的作者和編輯往往僅在描述句子的主詞「滿懷希望；抱著希望」（with hope, in a hopeful manner）時才使用 hopefully。例如：

▶ **Hopefully**, the dog sat by the dinner table.（那隻狗滿懷希望地坐在餐桌旁。）

▶ **Hopefully**, Carlos looked at her.（卡洛斯滿懷希望地看著她。）

然而，其他作者和編輯則使用hopefully來表示「但願」、「希望」（it is hoped, It is to be hoped, we hope, I hope）的意思。例如：

▶ **Hopefully**, we'll get more news next week.（希望我們下週能得到更多消息。）

▶ **Hopefully**, this ambivalent answer won't frustrate readers.（但願這一矛盾的解答不會讓讀者感到灰心。）

008 Question

maybe和perhaps的用法有何不同呢？

Answer

無論是英式英語或美式英語，這兩個副詞迄今都仍相當常用。它們不僅意思相同（意為「也許，或許，大概，可能」），而且用法也幾無二致，兩者皆可當句子副詞（sentence adverb），修飾整個句子或子句，亦可用作一般副詞（ordinary adverb）。再者，它們皆可用來指過去、現在或未來事件。

所以，在絕大多數的情況中，maybe和perhaps都可互換。不過，maybe適合用於比較非正式的上下文，而perhaps則適合用於比較正式的場合；換言之，maybe比較口語化。在美式英語中，maybe比perhaps要常用得多。例如：

▶ I can't find the car key anywhere. **Perhaps/Maybe** I threw it away.（我到處找不到車鑰匙。也許我把它丟掉了。）

▶ There were **perhaps** as many as fifty badly wounded victims in the hospital.（醫院裡可能有多達 50 位重傷的受害者。）

▶ St Paul's Cathedral is **perhaps** one of London's most prominent landmarks.（聖保羅大教堂可能是倫敦最著名的地標之一。）

▶ **Maybe** you are right! **Perhaps** it would be best if you didn't invite David.（也許你是對的！如果你不邀請大衛，可能是最佳的作法。）

值得一提的是，maybe和perhaps皆可用於禮貌性的建議或請求。例如：

▶ **Maybe** we should meet sometime next week.（也許我們應該在下週某個時候見個面。）

▶ You could put it over here, **maybe.**
（也許你可以把它放在這裡。）

▶ **Perhaps** you would like to join us for dinner.
（也許你願意跟我們共進晚餐。）

▶ You'd better go now, **perhaps.**
（你最好還是現在就走。）

009 Question

(1) She also was carrying an umbrella. (2) She was carrying an umbrella also. (3) She was wearing a raincoat and she was also carrying an umbrella.這三句的意思有何不同呢？

Answer

從這三個句子來看，問題的關鍵在於 "also" 這個字！Also跟only和just一樣，視其在句子中的位置而有不同的意思，但它們都是修飾它們最靠近的字詞。

句 (1) 的意思是説「除了其他人帶傘外，她也帶傘」，句 (2) 的意思是「她除了帶其他東西外，也帶傘」，而句 (3) 的意思是「她穿雨衣，也帶傘」。根據上述的解釋，可以明顯看出，這三句中的also分別修飾 "She"、"umbrella" 和 "carrying"，而位置的不同，意思也不同。

在also的其他應用上，有些人使用此一副詞來代替連接詞 "and"。這種用法被許多人視為錯誤，所以應該避免，尤其是在正式寫作中，如Please send me a copy of your CV and a list of the local companies you worked for.（請將你的履歷和本地你任職過的公司名單寄一份給我。）不可寫成... a copy of your CV, also a list of ...。但 "and also" 的組合則是合乎語法的，如Please send me a copy of your CV and also a list of the local companies you worked for.。

010 Question

Answer

這兩者的意思並不相同。anymore為美式英語用字，意為「（不）再；再也（不）」(any longer)，是個副詞，用來指時間，通常用於否定句或疑問句。例如：

- ▶ Teresa doesn't live here **anymore**.（泰瑞莎不再住這裡了。）
- ▶ Don't you love me **anymore**?（你不再愛我了嗎？）
- ▶ My father doesn't work **anymore**.（我父親不再工作了。）

至於any more，這兩個字連用時，它們的意思就是字典個別對其所定義的意思，其中any意為「少許，些微，一點點」（a small amount, number, or quantity），而more意為「更，更加；更多的（數量），較多的（數量）」。any more係用來指數目或數量，通常也用於否定句或疑問句，可當副詞用，修飾形容詞、動詞及其他副詞，亦可用作形容詞，修飾名詞。例如：

- ▶ I don't want **any more**.（我不想多一些了。）
- ▶ Don't eat **any more**.（別再吃了。）
- ▶ I don't want **any more** pie.（我不想再吃派了。）

值得注意的是，除any more外，any這種本身當副詞用，後接形容詞或副詞的比較級的結構相當常用，如any better（好一點點）、any bigger（大一點點）等。茲再舉數例如下來凸顯這種結構有多麼常用：

- ▶ I don't want to eat **any more**.（我不想再吃了。）
- ▶ Are you feeling **any better**?（你覺得好些了嗎？）
- ▶ Don't go **any closer**.（別再走近。）
- ▶ If your headache gets **any worse**, you should see a doctor.（如果你的頭痛加劇，你得去看醫生。）

現在我們將anymore和any more放在同一句子中來區別它們之間的差異：

- ▶ I don't buy books **anymore** because I don't need **any more** books.（我現在不再買書了，因為我不需要更多的書了。）

Answer

also, as well和too都是副詞，也都意為「也」，而also還有「此外」的意思。

also常用於書寫中（亦即比較正式），在講話時比較不常用，它可以放在句中不同的位置。首先來看also意為「此外」的情況，此時它位在句首，其後須有逗點，是用來強調後面的句子或提供前一句的補充資料或提出新的論點或主題。例如：

▶ Rose is a beautiful girl. **Also**, she is very kind-hearted.
（蘿絲是個漂亮的女孩。此外，她有好心腸 — 人美心也美。）

▶ OK, I'll call you tomorrow and we can discuss it then. **Also**, we need to buy a new computer.
（好，我明天會打電話給你，屆時我們可以討論這件事。此外，我們需要買一部新電腦。）

當also意為「也」時，它跟一般副詞一樣，通常位在句子的中間，亦即位在主詞和主動詞之間（即普通動詞之前），或位在語氣助動詞或第一個助動詞之後，或位在當主動詞的be動詞之後。例如：

▶ I **also** like tennis.
（我也喜歡打網球。）

▶ This word can **also** be used as an adjective.
（這個字也可用作形容詞。）

▶ She was **also** a famous singer about three years ago.
（大約三年前她還是個名歌手。）

在句末，使用also並沒有錯，但通常不這麼用，而是使用as well或too來代替also，尤其是在講話時。例如：

▶ John called/contacted his wife at work/in the office but she didn't answer the phone. Her mobile phone was silent **as well**. （約翰打電話到他太太辦公室，但她沒有接電話。她的手機也沒人接。） — 注意：別把這裡的 silent 跟「靜音（模式）」的 silent (mode) 搞混了。「把手機調為靜音／振

動（模式）」的英文是 to have/put the mobile (phone) on silent/vibrate (mode)。
John called/contacted his wife at work/in the office but she didn't
answer the phone. Her mobile phone was silent **too**.

as well用於口說的頻率比用於書寫或寫作高出許多，且比 also 更常用於講話中，它
幾乎都位在句末位置。例如：

▶ I'm going to Taipei and my brother's going **as well**.
（我要去台北，我弟弟也會去。）

▶ We'll need a new computer **as well**.
（我們還需要一部新電腦。）

as well 不可放在句首。例如：

▶ I must buy a new smartphone **as well**.
（我也要買一支新的智慧型手機。）→（○）正確。

▶ **As well** I must buy a new smartphone. →（×）錯誤。

too 通常位在句末位置，其前有無逗點皆可。例如：

▶ Mrs. Lee is kind, but she's strict **too**.
（李太太人很好，但也很嚴厲。）

▶ My wife can speak Tagalog, **too**.
（我太太也會講菲語。）

too也可直接放在主詞之後來修飾主詞，它的前後有時可加上逗點，但它不可放在語
氣助動詞或助動詞之後。例如：

▶ I **too** thought she was a decent sort of woman.
（我也認為她是好女人。）

▶ They, **too**, have been to Thailand.
（他們也去過泰國。）
They have **too** been to Thailand. →（×）錯誤。

在祈使句中，as well或too通常優於also。例如：

▶ Give me a bowl of braised pork rice and a bowl of clam soup **too/as
well** then please.
（請給我一碗滷肉飯，然後也給我一碗蛤蜊湯。）

然而，意思為「也」的too只能用在肯定句；若為否定句，則須使用either。同樣地，either通常位在句末位置，其前有無逗點皆可。例如：

▶ He is a teacher, and I am (a teacher), **too**.
（他是老師，我也是（老師）。）

▶ She can dance; she can sing **too**.
（她會跳舞，也會唱歌。）

▶ Cindy: I like that metrosexual.
（辛蒂：我喜歡那位型男。）

Judy: Me **too**.
（茱蒂：我也是。）

▶ She can't dance; she can't sing **either**.
（她不會跳舞，也不會唱歌。）

▶ Jack's not here. I don't think Tom is (here), **either**.
（傑克不在這裡。我認為湯姆也不在（這裡）。）

▶ They tried another method, but that didn't work **either**. →（○）正確。
（他們試了另一種方法，但也沒有用。）

They tried another method, but that didn't work **also/as well/too**.
→（×）錯誤。

▶ A: I can't sleep.（我睡不著。）
B: Me **neither**/Me **either**. (= I can't, either)（我也睡不著。）

在上面最後一句中，**Me neither**是正規的標準英語，也是英式英語認為唯一正確的講法，考試時也應據此作答，否則肯定會被認為錯誤。然而，在美國口語中，許多人使用**Me either**來表示**Me neither**的意思。

Excercise
綜合練習

I. 填空題

1 She has visited _____ everywhere in Taiwan.
（她幾乎去過台灣所有的地方了。）

2 _____ every time I see you, I can hear my heart beat fast.
（幾乎每次看到你，我都可以感覺到我的心跳得很快。）

3 I made the dishes that my grandmother had made _____.
（我做了我祖母以前常常做的料理。）

4 She decided to support her brother though he had never treated her well
_____.
（她決定支持她哥哥，雖然他以前從來沒有對她好過。）

5 I was _____ hurt in the car accident.
（我在這場車禍中僅僅受了輕傷。）

6 She was _____ hurt in the relationship.
（她在這段感情中嚴重地受了傷。）

7 He _____ go away when I need his help.
（我需要他的幫助時，他偏偏離開了。）

8 The bell _____ ring when I took a shower.
（我洗澡時偏偏有人按門鈴。）

9 I don't love you _____.
（我不再愛你了。）

10 She doesn't need _____ love.
（她不需要更多的愛了。）

11 A:I am looking for Professor Lee.
B: Me _____.
（A: 我在找李教授。
B: 我也是。）

⑫ _____, I need some more drink.
（此外，我還需要一些飲料。）

II. 排序題

❶ agree /,/most/Also/citizens./would
（而且大多的市民都會同意。）

_____

❷ especially/many/people/children/are/risky/,/.
（很多人，特別是小孩，有極大的風險。）

_____

❸ You/coat/need/a/winter/also/in. （你冬天還需要一件大衣。）

_____

❹ I am tired. I/also/sleepy/,/ am. （我很累，而且我還想睡覺。）

_____

III. 英翻中

❶ I am quite satisfied with the result.

_____

❷ I am quite sad because my grandfather passed away last week.

_____

IV. 中翻英

❶ 希望奶奶的病情好轉。

_____

❷ 但願這本書不會很無聊。

_____

❸ 他可能是因為下雨了才沒來吧。（用perhaps中翻英）

_____

❹ 他可能錯了。（用maybe中翻英）

_____

V. 二選一

❶ ☐ There is a vacancy for a computer programmer in most every company.
☐ There is a vacancy for a computer programmer in most company.
（幾乎每家公司都有電腦程式設計師的缺額。）

❷ ☐ I have met him five years ago.
☐ I have met him before.
（我曾經見過他。）

❸ ☐ He was seriously hurt by her unkind words.
☐ He was deeply hurt by her unkind words.
（他被她說的話嚴重地傷害了。）

❹ ☐ I am quite unhappy.
☐ I am not quite happy.
（我很不開心。）

❺ ☐ Especially men have this problem.
☐ Men, especially, have this problem.
（尤其是男性都有這種問題。）

❻ ☐ We all were carrying umbrellas. She was carrying an umbrella also.
☐ We all were carrying umbrellas. She also was carrying an umbrella.
（除了我們帶傘外，她也帶傘。）

❼ ☐ I must buy a new computer also.
☐ I must buy a new computer as well.
（我還需要買一台新電腦。）

Answer

I. 填空題

① most
② Most
③ before
④ before
⑤ slightly
⑥ deeply

⑦ must needs
⑧ must needs
⑨ anymore
⑩ any more
⑪ too
⑫ Also

II. 排序題

① Also, most citizens would agree.
② Many people, especially children, are risky.
③ You also need a coat in winter.
④ I am tired. Also, I am sleepy.

III. 英翻中

① 我對成果十分滿意。
② 我很難過，因為我爺爺上週過世。

IV. 中翻英

① Hopefully, Grandma's getting better.
② Hopefully, the book is not boring.
③ Perhaps, he didn't come because of the rain.
④ He maybe was wrong.

V. 二選一

① 第一句正確
② 第二句正確
③ 第二句正確
④ 第一句正確

⑤ 第二句正確
⑥ 第二句正確
⑦ 第二句正確

001 Question

a friend of mine的所有格是a friend's of mine還是a friend of mine's呢？而 sister-in-law這種複合字的複數所有格呢？是sisters'-in-law還是sisters-in-law's或是其他呢？

Answer

A friend of mine 的所有格是在 mine （不是 friend） 的後面加 's，變成 a friend of mine's，如 a friend of mine's bad habit （我一位朋友的壞習慣） － 當然，我們也可寫成 the bad habit of a friend of mine。

Sister-in-law （嫂嫂；弟媳；妯娌；丈夫的嫂子；丈夫的弟媳；小姑；大姑；小姨子；大姨子）和daughter-in-law （媳婦） 的複數分別為sisters-in-law和 daughters-in-law。它們的所有格也是直接在後面加上's，如my sisters-in-law's assets （我嫂嫂們的資產） －當然，我們最好寫成the assets of my sisters-in-law。其他類似的複合字（如brother-in-law, son-in-law等）也是如法炮製。

002 Question

代名詞one, it和that之間有何不同呢？

Answer

one是泛指，而it和that是特指。It與所指的名詞是同一個，而that與所指的名詞是同類，但不是同一個。請看下面的例句與說明：

▶ I can't find my pen. I think I should buy one. （我找不到我的筆。我想我該去買一支。）--One 是泛指，即不特定指哪一類或哪一支筆。

▶ I can't find my pen. I don't know where I put it. （我找不到我的筆。我不知道我把它放在哪裡。） -- It 是特指，指的是同一支筆。

▶ The pen you bought is cheaper than that I bought. （你買的那支筆比我買的便宜。） --that 是特指，指的是同類的筆，但不是同一支。

003 Question

在同一句中同時使用名詞和代名詞時，其順序是否有規則可循呢？據了解，在 Tom, Mary, you and I were selected to head the committee.這類句子中，名詞都放在最前面，接下來是第二人稱代名詞，而第一人稱代名詞總是位在最後。

Answer

目前並不清楚英文是否有任何規則規定一定要將這些專有名詞放在"you"的前面，但合理的作法是先處理人名，然後再對代名詞進行排序，如問題中的例句（當然，一定要把"I"放在最後）。寫作時最好堅守這一「原則」，但如果我們圍坐在一張桌子談事情，筆者認為像"You, Tom, Mary, and I were selected to head the committee."（你、湯姆、瑪麗和我被挑選來領導這委員會。）這樣的說法也沒有什麼不對。

004 Question

我們可以使用it來指稱jeans, glasses或scissors嗎？

Answer

不可以。雖然（a pair of/some）jeans, glasses或scissors指的是單一物品，但它們被用作複數名詞，所以要說I've lost them.或They're ripped.

值得一提的是，這些複數字不具「數」的概念。我們可以說These scissors/My other trousers are old.，但究竟是一把剪刀（或一條褲子）還是多把剪刀（或多條褲子），只能從上下文中得知，除非同時使用pair或pairs，否則從這些字詞的本身是看不出「數量」的，如a pair of pants（一條褲子），two pairs of glasses（兩副眼鏡），three pairs of scissors（三把剪刀）等等。

此外，以 pair, piece和slice等量詞來量化的名詞（包括不可數名詞在內），在使用形容詞來修飾時，該形容詞是加在量詞的前面，而非直接放在名詞的前面，如 a new pair of glasses = some new glasses（一副新眼鏡），a nice bottle of wine（一瓶好酒），a thin slice of cake（一片薄蛋糕）等等。

005 Question

anybody, any body, anyone和any one有何不同呢？

Answer

※anybody和anyone都是不定代名詞，兩者皆意為「任何人」（any person），可以互換，通常用於否定句、疑問句及條件句，如Did anybody hear of such a thing?（有誰聽說過這樣的事嗎？）；Anyone can cook because it's easy.（任何人都會做飯，因為那很容易。）不過，anyone比較常用，而anybody被視為非正式用字。當主詞用時，兩者都接單數動詞，而其相對應的代名詞可以是單數he/she, him/her, his/her（正式）或複數they, them, their（非正式），如If anybody[anyone] comes, ask him/her[them] to wait.（要是有人來，叫他／她（們）等著。）

※any one是一個由any所修飾的代名詞或形容詞，意為「任何一個人」（any single person）或「任何一件事情或一樣東西」（any single thing），如（代名詞）Any one of them may speak at the meeting.（他們任何人都可以在會議中發言）；（形容詞）Linda has more work than any one person can handle.（琳達的工作量比任何人所能處理的工作量都要來得多。）

※any body是一個由any所修飾的名詞，意為「任何人的身體或形體」（any human form）或「任何團體或組織」（any group），如Can anybody communicate with any body of government?（任何人都可以跟任何政府機關溝通嗎？）

006 Question

若不知某人的性別，那麼該用那個代名詞來指涉呢？另外，everybody, anybody, somebody等的正確代名詞又是什麼呢？

Answer

以前若是不知某人的性別，我們都使用he來指涉，如If I find the person who has stolen my iPad, I'll wring his neck!（如果讓我找到那個偷我 iPad 的人，我會扭斷他的脖子！）。但這樣的用法現在往往被視為性別歧視。現今可能的作法之一是使用 "he or she"（這是主格，其受格為him or her，而所有格為his or her；但它們也可以且往往寫成 he/she, him/her, his/her）或 "(s)he"，但這看起來或聽起來都怪怪的。例如：

▶ A baby cries when **he or she** is tired.
（嬰兒累了就會哭。）

▶ If a student is absent because of illness, **(s)he** should call in sick.
（如果學生因病缺席，他或她應打電話請病假。）

▶ If in doubt, ask your teacher. **He/she** can give you more information.
（如果拿不定主意，可以問你的老師。他或她可以給你更多資訊。）

這些寫法迄今仍不時用於正式寫作或書面文件中，但目前一般比較喜歡的作法是使用 they（**them** 或 **their**），尤其是在非正式談話中，即使所指涉的是單數名詞亦然。例如：

▶ If a student is absent because of illness, **they** should call in sick.
（如果學生因病缺席，他們應打電話請病假。）

這些結構相當常用，尤其在everybody, everyone, anybody, anyone, somebody, someone, nobody以及「every, each, no + 單數的人（如person, child, boy, girl 等）」之後，它們的代名詞通常使用they（**them**或**their**）。例如：

▶ Everyone should take **their** belongings with them. Don't leave them on the shuttle bus.
（每個人都應隨身帶著他們的物品。別把它們留在交通車上。）

▶ Does everybody know what **they** want?
（每個人都瞭解他們想要什麼嗎？）

▶ Somebody's left **their** wallet here.
（有人把他們的錢包留在這裡。）

▶ If anybody/anyone comes, ask **them** to wait.
（要是有人來，叫他們等著。）

▶ Nobody plans to go on a trip to Phnom Penh, do **they**?
（沒有人打算到金邊旅遊，對吧？）

▶ Every student in the English class must have **their** own textbook.
（英語班的每個學生都要有自己的課本。）

這種結構對不知某人性別的情況以及男女性別皆有的情況都非常有用。當然了，若是單一性別，這種結構可能就不需要了。譬如說，如果交通車上的乘客都是女性，有人把傘留在車上，那麼我們可以簡單地這樣說：

▶ Somebody has left her umbrella on the shuttle bus. Could **she** please come and collect it?
（有人把她的傘留在車上。可以請她來拿回去嗎？）

然而，即使性別已知，我們也經常使用they（them 或 their），尤其是在泛稱的敘述中。例如：

▶ No boy under the age of 18 should be allowed to get married in Taiwan because **they** are not mature enough.
（未滿 18 歲的男孩不應被允許結婚，因為他們還不夠成熟。）

Excercise 綜合練習

I. 填空題

1 A _____ (friend of mine's/friend's of mine) clothes are all expensive.
（我有個朋友，她的衣服都很貴。）

2 My _____ (mother's-in-law/mother-in-law's) temper is terrible.
（我婆婆的脾氣很差。）

3 I love Maroon 5's songs. Could you play _____ for me?
（我喜歡魔力紅的歌，你可以為我演奏一首（他們的歌）嗎？）

4 Mom, I want to buy this coat. Could you buy _____ for me?
（媽媽，我想要買這件外套，你可以幫我買嗎？）

5 My pants _____ too long. （我的褲子太長了。）

6 A pair of glasses _____ needed. （你需要一副眼鏡。）

7 _____ (Anyone/Any one person) of the guests in the wedding thought they were a match made in heaven.
（婚禮上每個人都認為他們是天作之合。）

8 _____ (Is/Are) there anyone? （有人在嗎？）

9 Does everybody know what _____ want?
（每個人都瞭解他們想要什麼嗎？）

10 Every student in the English class must have _____ own textbook.
（英語班的每個學生都要有自己的課本。）

II. 排序題

1 he/I/you/are/going to school. （我跟你還有他都正要上學。）

_____

2 you/I/Laura/have to come. （我跟你還有羅拉都必需要來。）

_____

III. 二選一

1 ☐ These friends of mine's favorite basketball player is Stephen Curry.
☐ These friends' of mine favorite basketball player is Stephen Curry.
（我的這些朋友最喜歡的籃球球星是史帝芬柯瑞。）

2 ☐ Apples are good for health. Please give me one.
☐ Apples are good for health. Please give me that.
（蘋果對身體很好，請給我一顆。）

3 ☐ Mary, you and I were tired.
☐ You, Mary and I were tired.
（我跟你還有瑪莉都很累了。）

4 ☐ Have you seen my glasses? I've lost it.
☐ Have you seen my glasses? I've lost them.
（你有看到我的眼鏡嗎？我把它弄丟了。）

5 ☐ Any one of them may speak at the meeting.
☐ Anyone of them may speak at the meeting.
（他們任何人都可以在會議中發言。）

Answer

I. 填空題

1 friend of mine's
2 mother-in-law's
3 one
4 that
5 are
6 are
7 Any one person
8 Is
9 they
10 their; his or her

II. 排序題

1 He, you and I are going to school.
2 Laura, you and I have to come.

III. 二選一

1 第一句正確
2 第一句正確
3 第一句正確
4 第二句正確
5 第一句正確

001 Question

Everyone was tired except John.（除約翰外，大家都累了。）
這句為何可以寫成 Everyone except John was tired.，但卻不
能寫成 Except John everyone was tired. 呢？

Answer

※except 意為「除了...之外」（這是除去 except 後面所接的人事物，不包括在
內）。在學習英文的過程中，相信有不少人被這個字以及與其形義相似、詞類相同
（皆為介系詞）的 except for 和 excepting 搞得一個頭兩個大。因此，在此將就這
三個意思相近、但用法不盡相同的字作一詳盡的說明，讓大家從此不再為其所苦。

首先來看 except 和 except for 用法上的差異：Except 後面可以接名詞、代名詞、動
詞、副詞、介詞片語或子句，而 except for 僅能接名詞或代名詞；所以，如果它們
的後面是接名詞或代名詞，except 和 except for 在大多數情況中都是可以互換的。
例如：

▶ Everyone was tired **except** John.（除約翰外，大家都累了。）－接名詞。

▶ They all went to the public library last Sunday **except** him.
（除了他之外，上星期天他們都去了公立圖書館。）－ 接代名詞。

▶ Every day Mary does nothing **except** watch TV.
（瑪麗每天除了看電視外什麼事都不做。）－ 接動詞。

附帶說明：若句子的主動詞為 do/does/did，則 except 後面一般都是接省略 to 的原
形動詞，如上句；若主動詞不是 do/does/did，則 except 通常是接帶 to 的不定詞，
如 I had no choice except to obey his order.（我除了服從他的命令外別無選擇。）

▶ He always goes to work by bike **except** recently.
（除最近外，他都是騎腳踏車上班。）－ 接副詞。

▶ I can take my holidays at any time **except** in August.
（除八月外，我什麼時候休假都可以。）－ 接介詞片語。

▶ I know nothing about him **except** that he lives next door.
（我除了知道他住在我隔壁外，其他事情毫無所悉。）－ 接子句。

▶ My father usually goes to work by motorbike **except** when it rains.
（除下雨天外，我爸爸通常騎機車上班。）－ 接子句。

再者，

※在 all, any, every, no, none, anything, anybody, anyone, everything, everybody, everyone, nobody, nothing 等表示泛指的不定代名詞之後，一般都用 except 而不用 except for。例如：

▶ She ate everything on the plate **except** the carrots.
（除胡蘿蔔外，她把盤子裡的東西都吃了。）

▶ I've cleaned all the rooms **except** the toilet.
（除廁所外，所有房間我都清掃了。）

※except 用於表示同類事物之間的關係，而 except for 表示非同類事物的比較。例如：

▶ Everyone was tired **except** John.
（除約翰外，大家都累了。）－句中 everyone 和 John 同類。

▶ We go to school every day **except** Sunday.
（除星期天外，我們天天上學。）－句中 every day 和 Sunday 同類。

▶ **Except** for one old lady, the bus was empty.
（除一位老太太乘坐外，這部公車空無一人。）－句中 old lady 和 bus 不同類。

▶ The road was empty **except** for a few cars.
（除了幾輛汽車外，這條路空蕩蕩的。）－句中 road 和 car 不同類。

附帶說明：儘管問題中的例句也可寫成 Everyone was tired except for John.，但根據第 1 和第 2 項敘述，我們還是寫成 Everyone was tired except John. 比較好。

※except for 可置於句首，但 except 卻不行 － 這就是為何 Everyone was tired except John. 不能寫成 Except John everyone was tired. 的原因；所以，正確的寫法是 Except for John, everyone was tired.。再舉一例：

▶ **Except** for Mike, we are all under 40.
（除麥可外，我們都不到 40 歲。）

※except for 在表示對整體大部分的肯定及對小部分的否定 — 亦即包含大部分，除去小部分。例如：

▶ Mr. Lin is a good man **except for** his bad temper.
（除了脾氣不好外，林先生是個好人。）

▶ Your composition is quite excellent **except for** several spelling mistakes.
（除了幾處拼字錯誤外，你的作文棒極了。）

※僅 except for 有「若非；要不是」的意思，except 並無此義。例如：

▶ She would have left her husband years ago **except for** the children.
（要不是為了小孩，幾年前她就離開她丈夫了。）

= She would have left her husband years ago **but** for the children.

= She would have left her husband years ago **if** she had not had the children.

= **But that** she had the children, she would have left her husband years ago.

最後來談 excepting。這是個比較正式的用字，可置於句首，其後通常接名詞或代名詞，或用於 not, without, always 等詞之後。例如：

▶ **Excepting** Sundays, the library is open daily.
（除星期天外，圖書館天天開放。）

▶ Dogs are not allowed in the shop, always **excepting** blind people's guide dogs.
（除了盲人的導盲犬外，其他的狗一律不准帶進那家商店。）

▶ I think we must keep improving our English not **excepting** those who have mastered it.
（我認為我們必須不斷地增進我們的英語能力，就連那些業已精通英語的人士也不例外。）

▶ All of us, without **excepting** those who know more about the subject, should study.
（我們所有人都要研究這主題，就連那些比較瞭解這主題的人也不例外。）

002 Question

He wanted to find a companion to travel. 這句對嗎？

Answer

不對！這牽涉到不定詞放在名詞之後當後置修飾語的問題。當不定詞放在名詞之後作形容詞用時，若該不定詞為不及物動詞，則它的後面需有適當或必要的介系詞。就問題的句子而言，由於 companion 是 travel 的受詞，而 travel 是不及物動詞，當不及物動詞要接受詞時，其後須有介系詞，所以這句若改為 He wanted to find a companion to travel with.（他想找個旅行的同伴。）或改為意思稍微不同的 He wanted to travel with a companion.（他想要和同伴去旅行。）就對了。

由於有不少人在寫英文時往往會漏掉這麼一個重要的介系詞，因此有必要再多舉幾個例子來做說明：

▶ He has a big house to live.（他有一棟大房子可住。）→（✕）錯誤。
▶ He has a big house to live **in**. →（○）正確。
  = He has a big house which/that he can live **in**.
  = He has a big house **in** which he can live.

（由於 live 是不及物動詞，所以要接受詞 house 時，其後須有介系詞in－to live a big house 是錯的，必須寫成 to live in a big house）

▶ I need a friend to talk.（我需要找個朋友來談一談。）→（✕）錯誤。
  I need a friend to talk **with**. →（○）正確。

（由於 talk 是不及物動詞，所以要接受詞 friend 時，其後須有介系詞 with－to talk a friend 是錯的，必須寫成 to talk with a friend）

同樣地，下面例句的不定詞也需要介系詞，否則就錯了：

▶ They have no children to take care **of**.（他們沒有小孩要照顧。）
▶ She wanted to have a chair to sit **on**.（她想要有張椅子來坐下。）

當不定詞的動詞為及物時，它們就不需要介系詞了。例如：

▶ I have a lot of homework to do. （我有許多家庭作業要做。） --do 是及物動詞，直接接受詞，無需介系詞 — to do a lot of homework

▶ Give me something to eat. （給我食物。）

▶ Would you like something to drink? （你想要喝東西嗎？）

▶ I need a book to read. （我需要找本書來讀一讀。）

▶ Do you have anything more to say? （你還有其他事情要說嗎？）

當不定詞的動詞可為及物或不及物時，必須根據句意來判斷是否需要介系詞或需要什麼介系詞。請看下面的例句：

▶ I have nothing to write. （這句的 write 是及物動詞，直接接 nothing 當受詞，所以這裡的 nothing 是表示「沒有要書寫的內容」）

▶ I have nothing to write with. May I use your pen? （這句的 write 是不及物動詞，是說我有東西要寫，但沒有筆可寫 — with 後面接書寫工具，也就是筆，所以這裡的 nothing 是表示「沒有筆」）

▶ I have nothing to write on. Please give me a piece of paper. （這句的 write 也是不及物動詞，是說我有東西要寫，但沒有紙讓我寫在上面，所以這裡的 nothing 是表示「沒有紙」）

003 Question

Japan lies _____ the east of Asia. (1) in (2) on (3) to (4) at 這句的正確答案是那個呢？

Answer

in, on, to, at 這四個介系詞在此都是表示位置。

※in

表示在所指地點的範圍內，我們知道日本位在東亞，亦即亞洲東（北）部的範圍內（境內），所以 in 是這問題的答案。再舉一例：Unemployment rate in the east of Taiwan is very high. （台灣東部的失業率很高。）

※to

在與表示方向的字連用時，是表示在所指地點的範圍外，如 Taichung is a few hundred kilometers to the north of Kaohsiung.（台中位於高雄北方數百公里處。） － 表示台中是在高雄以外的地方，不是在高雄境內。

※on

在表示位置時，通常意為「在...的上面」，這是大家都瞭解的意思。但當 on 與 sea, river, lake, border, side（海洋、河流、湖泊、邊界、旁邊）等字連用時，亦經常表示「在...的邊緣，瀕臨；沿著」(at the edge of; along) 的意思，這也表示在所指地點的範圍外，如 a town on the border （邊界城鎮，亦即靠近邊界的城鎮）；New York is situated on the Hudson River.（紐約位於哈德遜河畔）；trees on both sides of the street（街道兩旁的樹）。當然，on the sea, on the river 也有「在海上」、「在河上」的意思，但我們應該很容易就可從上下文判斷出來。在此要強調的是，on 在表示位置時，並非總是意為「在...的上面」。

※at

表示在所指地點的某一點。然而，與 on 一樣，at 在表示位置時，並非都是這意思。當 at 與 door, table, desk 等字連用時，意為「在...的前面」，不是在某一點，如 He was standing at the door.（他站在門口 － 是站在門的前面不是門上。）；My wife is sitting at the desk reading newspaper.（我太太正坐在書桌前看報 － 不是坐在書桌上。）

004 Question

Mike: What was John talking to you in the office this morning?
David: He was like I've got a new girlfriend. 請問在 David 所說的句子中，like 是什麼意思呢？

Answer

在回答這問題之前，筆者先將問題中的對話修改如下：

Mike: What was John talking to you in the office this morning?
David: He was like "Why are you doing that?" and I was like "Actually, it's quite fun" and he was like "No way!" and I was like "Way!"

從這些對話可知，like 是個介系詞，意思大概是「好像說」，所以 Mike 和 David 兩人對話的意思大概如下：

Mike：約翰今天早上在辦公室跟你談了什麼？
David：他好像說「為什麼你在做那件事？」，我好像說「其實那滿有趣的」，他好像說「一點也不！」，我好像說「有，滿有趣的」。

在敘述某一事件或與某人的相遇時，現在說話者很常使用 like 這個字來引導每一直接引句。它被用作一種模稜兩可的話或表達大概意思的方式（因為說話者已無法十分肯定當時確切的用字）且經常帶有一些頗為複雜的輔助語言特徵（paralinguistic features）以重建原始的談話，並佐以臉部表情、手勢等等。

(Be) like 的這項用法最初是來自南加州聖費爾南多谷地 (San Fernando Valley) 一這個地區是由數個城市所構成，包括洛杉磯的大半土地 — 常用的「社會方言」（sociolect，即 social dialect）；這種方言叫做 Valspeak。英語中有不少新字新詞或舊字新義都是來自 Valspeak。

在此之前，英文還有一些類似的工具與 like 的作用一樣，其中比較常用的是 "go" 和 "be all"。例如：

Go：He went "Where are you off to?" and I went "Just down to the shop for some milk."
（他好像說「你要去哪裡？」，而我好像說「只是去商店買些牛奶」。）

Be all：I was all "Why isn't anyone working?" and Mary was all "It's lunchtime, John ... calm down!"
（我好像說「為甚麼沒有人在工作」，而瑪麗好像說「現在是午餐時間，約翰，稍安勿躁」。）

然而，這些類似的工具現在已大多被 like 所取代。現今，like 這項用法不再僅限於加州或甚至美國，就連英式英語也越來越流行。

005 **Q**uestion

為何搭乘汽車是 in a car 而搭乘巴士是on a bus呢？這類介系詞用法是否有規則可循呢？

Answer

in, on等介系詞在英文中扮演舉足輕重的角色，但每個介系詞的意思少則數個，多則數十個，對於非英語系國家的人士來說，要把這些字的用法完全弄懂或用得非常自然，可說相當困難，或至少需要一段很長的時間，所以只有仰賴平常多看、多用，讓它習慣成自然。同樣是交通工具，為何有的用 in，有的用 on，誰也說不出原因，也沒有規則可循，唯有掌握英語的正確用法後多加使用才能駕輕就熟。茲將常見的交通工具與in或on連用的習慣用語臚列如下並舉例供大家參考：

※in：A car, a taxi, a truck, a helicopter, a boat

※on：A bus, a train, a bicycle, a motorbike, a plane, a ship, horseback, elephant

▶ I traveled **in** a car from Taipei to Kaohsiung.
（我從台北坐汽車到高雄。）

▶ I traveled **on** a train from Taipei to Kaohsiung.
（我從台北坐火車到高雄。）

再者，交通工具使用 in 或 on 會影響上／下車（飛機等） 的英文說法。就in而言，上／下車是 get in/get out of，如get in/get out of a taxi；就on而言，上／下車是get on/get off，如get on/get off a bus。

由上述可知，要正確使用介系詞唯有靠長時間的練習，多看、多用，習慣成自然。如果你硬要用記憶的方式把它們記下來，筆者也不反對，只是記不勝記，因為同樣的事物在不同的場合，可能就會使用不同的介系詞，譬如說，同樣是「角落」，房間的角落跟街道的角落就使用不同的介系詞，前者是 in the corner of a room，後者是 at （或 on） the corner of a street。此外，同樣是 weekend，英國人說 at the weekend，而美國人是說 on the weekend。

假設台南有一所大學叫做 Bing Bing University，那麼英文是寫成 Bing Bing University in Tainan 還是 Bing Bing University at Tainan 呢？還是兩者都可以呢？

Answer

Bing Bing University in Tainan 和 Bing Bing University at Tainan 所表示的意義並不相同，前者是說這所大學只有一個校區，就是在台南，而後者表示這所大學有多個校區，台南只是其中一個校區，或者說它有一個校區是在台南。

以世界知名的加州大學 (University of California, UC) 為例，加州大學系統總共有十個校區，包括柏克萊 (Berkeley)、洛杉磯 (Los Angeles) 和聖地牙哥 (San Diego)；所以，加大系統這三個校區的正確寫法分別為 University of California at Berkeley 或 University of California, Berkeley (柏克萊加州大學)、University of California at Los Angeles 或 University of California, Los Angeles（洛杉磯加州大學）及 University of California at San Diego 或 University of California, San Diego（聖地牙哥加州大學）。

007 Question

在 Autonomy aims to increase students' awareness, participation, and evaluation of the learning process and products. 這句中，介詞 of 搭配 awareness 和 evaluation，但與 participation 並不搭配，這是不是違反文法的平行對稱原則，如果是，問題要如何解決呢？

Answer

這個句子確實違反了英文文法所要求的平行對稱與對仗工整的原則。解決之道就是給予每個字適當的介系詞（或其他慣用的搭配字），不可為了「簡潔」而使句子不合語法。所以，這句應改為 Autonomy aims to increase students' awareness of, participation in, and evaluation of the learning process and products.（自治旨在增進學生對學習過程與學習成果的認識、參與和評估。）

這是許多人在寫作時常犯的錯誤，必須謹慎因應，以免再犯，如 I have computers both in the office and at home.（我在辦公室和家裡都有電腦。）就不能寫成 I have computers both in the office and home.。由於每個字所慣用或所搭配的介詞不盡相同，因此若遇到有兩個或兩個以上詞類相同的字連用且需搭配介詞使用的情況，我們必須分別考慮各字慣用的介詞，不可僅以這些連用字的最後一字做為判斷該使用哪個介詞的依據，除非這些字慣用同一個介詞；換言之，若這些字使用不同的介詞，那麼所有介詞都必須寫出。例如：

▶ He was **accused** and **convicted of** murder.（他被控殺人並被判有罪。）

▶ He was **charged with** and **convicted of** murder.（他被控殺人並被判有罪。）

在上面 a 句中，accused 和 convicted 使用相同的介系詞 of，所以 accused 後面的 of 可以省略；但在 b 句中，charged 慣用的介系詞是 with，與 of 不同，所以必須寫出，不可省略。

008 Question

文法書告訴我們，between 後面要接複數名詞，但像 There is twenty meters between each telegraph pole. 這樣的句子卻經常看到。請問 between 後面可接單數名詞嗎？

雖然有些人及一些文法書認為 between 後面不應接單數名詞，但實際的情況是，
between 可以跟 each 和 every 連用，後面接單數名詞。The New Fowler's Modern
English Usage 一書更指出，「這種結構必須被尊重和容忍」(This construction
must be respected and tolerated)。The Columbia Guide to Standard American
English 也指出，「between + each/every + 單數名詞」在語法上並無不妥之處，只
是它僅適用於口語和非正式場合、並不適合正式場合。老實說，這種結構的例句所
在多有。例如：

- ▶ He changed his shirt **between** every inning. （每局之間他都會更換球
  衣。）
- ▶ He had a cup of coffee **between** each class. （每節課之間他都會喝杯
  咖啡。）

不過，在正式場合（如正式寫作）中，最好將上面的例句改為：

He changed his shirt between innings. 或 He changed his shirt after each inning.

He had a cup of coffee between classes. 或 He had a cup of coffee between each
class and the next.

問題中的句子則改為：There is twenty meters between each telegraph pole and the
next. （每根電線桿之間的距離為 20 公尺。）

Excercise
綜合練習

I. 填空題

❶ Every day Mary does nothing _____ watch TV.
（瑪麗每天除了看電視外什麼事都不做。）

❷ I think we must keep improving our English not _____ those who have mastered it.
（我認為我們必須不斷地增進我們的英語能力，就連那些業已精通英語的人士也不例外。）

❸ We ate _____ the new table.（我們在桌前吃飯。）

❹ Germany is _____ the middle of Europe.（德國位於歐洲的中間。）

❺ We need a road between _____ (village/villages).
（在村子跟村子之間，我們需要一條道路連接。）

❻ Let's add some transitional sentences between _____ (paragraph/paragraphs).
（在每個段落之間要加一些句子連結。）

❼ I received the message when I was _____ a taxi.
（當我在計程車上的時候，我接到電話。）

❽ Don't call him now. He is still _____ a motorcycle.
（現在不要打給他。他還在騎車。）

❾ University of British Columbia _____ (in/at) Vancouver
（英屬哥倫比亞大學溫哥華校區）

❿ National Taiwan University _____ (in/at) Taipei
（台灣大學台北校區）

II. 選擇題

（　）❶ 選錯。
    (A). It is the school you are going to.
    (B). It is the school you are going.
    (C). It is the school to which you are going.

(　) ❷ 選錯。

       (A). I need a spoon to eat.

       (B). I need a spoon to eat with.

       (C). I need a spoon with which I can eat.

III. 英翻中

❶ When my aunt asked me the date of my wedding ceremony, I was like, what the hell! I don't even have a boyfriend.

❷ When I bumped into my professor this morning, I was like, oh, no! Don't recognize me. I haven't turned in my assignment yet.

IV. 中翻英

❶ 我將要去（go to）北京並且待（stay in）在那裡。

❷ 經理相信也堅持這計畫是有利可圖的。

V. 二選一

❶ ☐ Except John everyone was tired.
  ☐ Everyone was tired except John.
（除約翰外，大家都累了。）

❷ ☐ He has a big house to live.
  ☐ He has a big house to live in.
（他有一棟大房子可住。）

❸ ☐ Taipei lies in the north of Taiwan.
  ☐ Taipei lies to the north of Taiwan.
（台北在台灣的北方。）

④ □ There are 100 meters between every building.

　□ There are 100 meters between buildings.

（每棟建築間需要有100公尺。）

⑤ □ Are you on the MRT now?

　□ Are you in the MRT now?

（你在捷運上嗎？）

Answer

I. 填空題

❶ except
❷ excepting
❸ at
❹ in
❺ villages

❻ paragraphs
❼ in
❽ on
❾ at
❿ at

II. 選擇題

❶ B
❷ A

III. 英翻中

❶ 當我阿姨問我結婚日期的時候，我好像說：「什麼鬼啊！我連男朋友都沒有啊！」

❷ 當我今天早上遇到教授，我心裡偷偷說：「噢不，不要認我，我還沒交作業耶！」

IV. 中翻英

❶ I am going to and staying in Beijing

❷ The manager believes in and insists on the profits of the project.

V. 二選一

❶ 第二句正確
❷ 第二句正確
❸ 第一句正確

❹ 第二句正確
❺ 第一句正確

001 Question

在 We'll go by bus or train. Whatever! 這句中，whatever 後面有驚嘆號，那麼它是個感嘆詞，這種感嘆句用法在字典裡好像找不到，能不能請您說明一下呢？

Answer

在對類似的句子進行分析後，筆者認為這應該是 whatever 的新用法，因為英文字典裡似乎還找不到 whatever 有這種感嘆句用法，而且新舊用法之間還有一項很顯著的差異，那就是，我們所熟知的 whatever，重音是在第二音節，而新用法的 whatever，重音是在第一音節。所以，日後在使用這個字時，必須注意它的發音。

眾所周知，whatever 主要當代名詞和限定詞或形容詞用。當代名詞用時，在正式用法中，意為「任何，什麼……都；不管什麼，無論什麼」，而在非正式或口語用法中，意為「任何其他類似的東西；（表示驚訝）什麼，究竟」。例如：

▶ You can choose **whatever** you like.
（你可以選擇任何你喜歡的東西。）

▶ We must stay together **whatever** happens.
（不管發生什麼事，我們都必須待在一起。）

▶ **Whatever** do you mean?
（你究竟是什麼意思？）

▶ **Whatever** happened?
（究竟發生什麼事呢？）

▶ **Whatever** next? = **Whatever** will happen next?
（接下來究竟會發生什麼事呢？）

▶ You're going to keep snakes! **Whatever** next?
（你要養蛇！下一步還想幹什麼？）

▶ John's getting married? **Whatever** next!
（約翰要結婚嗎？下一件不知又是什麼事！）

whatever 當限定詞或形容詞用時,意為「任何,什麼……的;不管什麼的,無論什麼的」。例如:

▶ We shall be grateful for **whatever** help you can give us.
（我們會感謝你給我們的任何幫助。）

▶ She refuses, for **whatever** reason.
（不論是什麼理由,反正她拒絕了。）

whatever 還有一種限定詞或形容詞用法,是用來加強語氣的。這種 whatever 都用在否定句中,意為「一點……都不,任何……都不;毫不 (= at all)」;此時,whatever 是放在名詞或代名詞之後。例如:

▶ I know nothing **whatever** about him.
（我對他一無所知。）

▶ He hasn't got any brains **whatever**.
（他一點腦筋都沒有。）

現在回到問題的核心。問題中的 "Whatever!" 顯然是個代名詞,意為「任何其他類似的東西;諸如此類」,主要用於口語中。這個句子原來應該是 We'll go by bus or train or whatever else might be available.（我們將搭乘巴士或火車或任何其他可以搭乘的交通工具去）,然後簡化為 We'll go by bus or train or whatever!,然後再進一步簡化為 We'll go by bus or train. Whatever!。尤有甚者,它不但可應用於無生命的事物上,而且亦可應用於有生命的人物上。在下面的例句中,第 1 句是存在多時的用法,而第 2 句是新用法:

▶ 1. I don't really want to be a poet, dramatist, or whatever.
（我並非真的想當詩人、劇作家或其他諸如此類的人。）

▶ 2. I don't really want to be a poet or dramatist. Whatever!
（我並非真的想當詩人或是劇作家,管他的。）

注意:第 1 句的 whatever,重音在第二音節,而第 2 句的 whatever,重音在第一音節。

OK 這個字被廣泛地用在談話中，但它也可用在寫作嗎？它好像還有其他拼法！

Answer

OK 可能是唯一全世界都認識的英文字。但儘管如此，它卻有 5 種不同的拼法：OK, O.K., ok, o.k., okay，其中 OK 似乎是最被廣泛接受、最受歡迎的拼法。雖然 OK 被廣泛地用在口說英語中，但在正式和學術文章中卻非常罕見，所以在這些場合中最好別用這個字；吾人可使用 all right, acceptable, satisfactory 或 appropriate 等類義字來代替。

OK 當動詞用時（意為「同意，批准，認可」），OK's, OK'd 和 OK'ing 是最常見的第三人稱單數、過去式 （與過去分詞） 和現在分詞的書寫形式，但 okays, okayed 和 okaying 的使用頻率亦相去不遠。

Excercise 綜合練習

I. 中翻英

1 告訴我關於她的任何事情。

_____

2 他一點想法也沒有。

_____

II. 填空題

1 I haven't recovered, but I am _____.
（我還沒恢復，但我越來越好了。）

2 He was dumped last month, but he has _____ since he met this pretty girl.
（他上個月被甩了，但是自從他遇到這個正妹後就沒事了。）

III. 二選一

1 ☐ I am okaying now.
☐ I am OKing now.
（我正在康復。）

2 ☐ Whatever! I don't care about him anymore.
☐ Whatever I don't care about him anymore.
（管他的！我已經不在乎他了。）

Answer

I. 中翻英
1 Tell me whatever about her.
2 He's got no idea whatever.

II. 填空題
1 OK'ing
2 OK'd

III. 二選一
1 第一句正確
2 第一句正確

001 Question

The book is sold well.這句對嗎？

Answer

乍看之下，這是一個正確的句子，但其實它並不合乎英文語法及習慣用法，因為英文中有些動詞是以主動態來表示被動的意思，如 sell, read, cut, wash, cook 等等。請看下面的例句：

▶ The book **sells** well.（這本書賣得很好。）

▶ Her letter **reads** as follows....（她的信件內容如下……）

▶ The book doesn't **read** very well.（這本書不好讀。）

▶ This knife **cuts** easily.（這刀子很鋒利／很好用。）

▶ This shirt doesn't **wash** well.（這襯衫不耐洗。）

▶ Make sure the meat **cooks** for at least an hour.（要讓肉至少煮上一個小時。）

事實上，英文中以主動態來表示被動意思的片語動詞（phrasal verbs）亦所在多有，以 go down 為例，它常用的意思中就有三個是以主動態來表示被動。例如：

1. go down 意為「被記下來；被銘記」

▶ Everything you say will **go down** in our records.（你說的每一句話都將記入我們的檔案。）

▶ Smith will **go down** as one of the best teachers this school has ever had.（曾是這所學校最好的老師之一，史密斯將被銘記在心。）

2. go down 意為「（食物等）被吞下，被嚥下」

▶ The medicine **went down** easily.（這藥容易吞下。）

▶ You need smaller pills that **go down** more easily.（你需要小一點的藥片，那會比較容易吞下。）

3. go down 意為「被接受；被認可；被喜愛」

▶ Jim **went down** well with Mary's parents on his first visit.（吉姆初次拜訪瑪麗的父母親就給他們留下良好的印象。）

▶ The new director's appointment did not **go down** very well.（大家對新董事任命的反應並不是很好。）

002 Question

I would appreciate it if you would pay in cash. 和 I would appreciate if you would pay in cash. 這兩個經常會看到的句型為何都可以存在呢？

Answer

在進入主題之前，先來看看 appreciate （名詞：Appreciation） 的意思和用法。這個動詞的主要意思有四：1.「鑑賞，欣賞，賞識」，如 appreciate good wine（欣賞好酒。），wine appreciation （葡萄酒賞析）；2.「瞭解，明白」（= understand, realize）；3.「感激，感謝」（= be grateful or thankful for）；4.「（財產、貨幣等）增值，升值」，如 His house has appreciated considerably during the past six months.（他的房子在過去 6 個月期間已大幅增值。）然而，有些人並不喜歡 appreciate 經常被用來代替 understand 或 realize 的用法，如 Do you appreciate our problem?（你瞭解我們的問題嗎？） 一 句中的 appreciate 還是改為 understand 比較好。一些文法學者更建議，寫作時應避免使用 appreciate 後面接 how 或 that 子句的結構，如 I appreciate that you are disappointed by our failure to promote you.（我瞭解你對我們未能把你晉升感到失望。） 一句中的 appreciate 還是改為 realize 比較好。

再者，若干寫作權威對於使用 appreciate 來表示「感激」的意思，也期期以為不可，但顯然他們是不食人間煙火的「少數民族」。另外，當 appreciate 意為「感激」時，亦有人反對其後直接接 how 或 that （但筆者認為應該還要再加上 if）所引導的子句，如 *Garner's Modern American Usage* 一書的作者 Bryan Garner 就是其中之一。他認為像 We appreciate how you've worked for the community.（我們對您為社區所做的事表示感激。） 應改為 We are grateful for ...。所以，在問題的例

句中，若省略了 "it"，那就會發生 appreciate 後面直接接子句的問題。是故，這個句子有 "it" 會比較好。事實上，這也是習慣用法，我們最好不要省略 appreciate（做「感激」用時）後面的 "it"。

「主詞 + would be grateful if 主詞 + would/could...」和「主詞 + would appreciate it if 主詞 + would/could...」（這兩句可以劃上等號。）都是日常生活中相當常用的口語和書寫英文；grateful 這個形容詞前面可以加上副詞 most 或 very 來修飾，而 appreciate 前面則可加上副詞 much 或 greatly 來表示「非常」的意思。例如，在應徵函的結尾，現在流行寫上「如蒙面試，我將感激不盡」、「若蒙面試，不勝感激／深表感謝」之類的話，英文寫法如下：

> ▶ I'd be most grateful if you could/would give me an interview.
> = I'd much appreciate it if you could/would give me an interview.
> = I'd be much obliged if you could/would give me an interview.

上句中的「主詞 + would be obliged if...」亦可表達完全相同的意思，有必要一併熟知。若把主句中的 would 換成 will 也沒有錯，但 will 暗示事情發生的機會比較大，好像對方一定要如你所願，這樣一來，I will appreciate it if ... 便顯得對別人（僱主）不太禮貌了。

003 Question

To be out is in. 這句是什麼意思呢？

Answer

在這句中，out 和 in 都是形容詞。in 做為形容詞由來已久，意為「流行的，時髦的」（fashionable, trendy），至於 out 當形容詞用，則是最近才發生的事。

在 1990 年代初期，out 開始被用做動詞，如 to out someone 意為告訴全世界某人－通常是公眾人物－是同性戀者，這裡的 out 就是 coming out of the closet, out of your cupboard 或 out of your house 的簡寫，也就是大家常聽到的「出櫃」的意思。之後，昭告天下某人是同性戀者的人被稱為 outer，而這種行為則被叫做 outing。因此，如果有某位公司老闆被人家公開他或她是同性戀者的秘密，我們就說 The boss has been outed.。同性戀人權團體如獲至寶地接受這個字，目前就有好幾個網站在

站名中使用 out 這個字。

"Coming out"（出櫃）現在是個正面的用語，可以用來指任何鼓起勇氣公開他們或她們之性傾向的人，而不會有任何冒犯之意。所以，當您閱讀英文報紙看到 Quite a few British MPs have come out in parliament. 這樣的頭條新聞時也就不足為奇了，不過要注意的是，這裡是説相當多的英國國會議員在國會中公開他們是同性戀者，而不是説相當多的英國國會議員走出國會。

有一則新聞報導提到某國選出「首位出櫃的同性戀總統」（first "out" gay president）— 這裡的 out 就是當形容詞用，意為「出櫃的」。可見 out 的用法仍在擴大當中。走筆至此，讀者應該知道 "To be out is in." 這句話的意思了吧：「現在正流行出櫃」。

004 Question

在 I have (got) an appointment with my dentist tomorrow. 這句中，"have" 意為「有」（possess），是個狀態動詞。但在 The team members are having a meeting tomorrow. 這句中，have 卻用進行式，請問 have 到底是狀態還是動態動詞呢？同樣的問題也發生在 "own" 身上。Own 一般是狀態動詞，不能用進行式，但在一本英文字典中卻出現這樣的句子：More and more people are owning bicycles.。

Answer

在 to have a meeting 中，have 到底是狀態動詞（stative verb），還是動態動詞（dynamic verb）呢？先不談這問題的答案，從這問題可以看出動詞的本質在英文文法中是個非常複雜且一直在改變的領域。

所有的文法書都會談到有些動詞是動態動詞，亦即它們是在敘述動作，而這些動詞經常使用進行式，如 do, eat, watch 等動詞都是。所以我們可以這樣説 I'm doing my homework, eating a sandwich and watching television all at the same time!。有些動詞則是狀態動詞，它們是在敘述狀態而不是動作，如 possess（擁有）就沒有牽涉到動作。狀態動詞通常不使用進行式，所以不能説 I'm possessing a bike.。

然而，有很多動詞是兩者兼而有之，既是狀態動詞，亦是動態動詞。因此，如果問某位女性 Are you and your husband going to have any more children?（妳跟妳先生還要有更多的小孩嗎？），她可能回答說 No, we already have three.（不要，我們已經有三個了。）。在這兩句中，動詞 have 都是狀態動詞，可用 have got 來替換且不應使用進行式。所以，如果她說 I am having three children already.，那就錯了。但如果有位太太打電話給她先生問說 What are you doing?（現在你在幹什麼？），他可能回答 I'm having a cup of coffee with my friend.（我正在和朋友喝咖啡。）此時這個 have 是動態動詞，其意思已經改變，它是在敘述進行社交活動的動作，意思可能是「吃，喝」等等。

這種情況與問題中 have 與 meeting 連用的情況非常相似。I have/I've got a meeting. 是狀態的，意為「有」（possess），而 We are having a meeting. 則是動態的，其意思相當於 We are meeting. 或 We are holding a meeting.（我們正在開會。）。所以，to have a meeting 可以是狀態動詞，也可以是動態動詞，兩者兼而有之。由於問題中的句子 The team members are having a meeting tomorrow.（隊員明天將開會。）中有 tomorrow 這個表示未來的字眼，顯然這是個未來式句型；其實，這是英文中一種頗為常見的用法，亦即用現在進行式來表示不久的將來會發生的動作。

至於 own 被用作動態動詞，筆者不敢苟同。own 肯定只能當狀態動詞用，所以將它用於進行式是一種差勁的英文。當有人說 More and more people are owning bikes. 時，owning 真正的意思應是 getting 或 buying，否則應該說 More and more people own bikes.（越來越多人有腳踏車。）

遺憾地，這種將狀態動詞用作動態動詞的情況與日俱增。譬如說，在廣告中，為了增加「動」的效果，狀態動詞往往被用作動態動詞。大家一定曾看過一家著名速食連鎖店的廣告，其中有句廣告詞是這樣的：“I'm loving it.”。大家對於這樣的廣告詞看看或聽聽就好，別真的去學它，否則就糟糕了，因為 love 是個不折不扣的狀態動詞，不能有進行式。這樣拙劣的英語，避之都唯恐不及了，還要去學它嗎？

005 **Question**

在動詞 hope + (that) 子句的結構中，有沒有 will 的意義有何差別呢？

Answer

hope 實際上是個很有彈性的動詞，我們通常將 hope 與簡單現在式連用來表示未來的意思。例如：

▶ I **hope** that you pass your exam. （我希望你通過考試。）

這好像第一條件句（first conditional － 參見文末的附註），如 If you need anything, I will get it for you. （如果你需要任何東西，我可以幫你拿)。但在某些上下文中，也有可能使用 will。例如：

▶ I **hope** that you will be able to be a student of National Taiwan University. （我希望你能成為台大的學生。）

▶ I **hope** that you'll visit us again in the near future. （我希望不久的將來你能再度來訪。）

在幾乎所有 hope + (that) 子句的結構中，will 都可用簡單現在式來取代，兩者的意義幾乎或完全一樣，但反之則不然。例如：

▶ 1. I hope that he has his passport with him. （我希望他有帶護照。）

▶ 2. I hope that he will have his passport with him.

第 1 句不可改成第 2 句，因為前者有現在和未來的意思，但後者只有未來的意思。

所以，「hope + 簡單現在式」比「hope + will」要來得有彈性，但有時它們的意思是一樣的。再看一些例句：

▶ They **hope** that you'll remember your promise. （他們希望你記得你的承諾。）

▶ They **hope** that you remember your promise.

上面這兩句的意思幾乎相同。

▶ I **hope** that you agree to the proposal. （我希望你接受這項提案。）

這句的意思可能是你已經看過或聽過該提案，但如果有人說：

▶ I **hope** that you will agree to the proposal.（我希望你會接受這項提案。）

這句的意思比較不可能表示你已經看過提案，或許該提案都還未提出。

hope 亦可跟現在進行式連用，此時現在式與未來式之間的意思就有比較明顯的差異。例如：

▶ I **hope** that you're thinking of me.（我希望你正在想我。）

這句顯然是指我希望你現在正在想我，但

▶ I **hope** that you'll be thinking of me.

這句顯然是指在未來的某個時間想我。

所以，在此可做個結論：我們最好使用「hope + 簡單現在式」，因為這比較有彈性，可以表示現在和未來；但只有在你非常肯定你要表達的就是未來的意思時才使用「hope + will」。

附註：英文第一條件句的句型是「If + S + 簡單現在式, S + will + 原形動詞」，係表示未來極有可能發生的情況；第二條件句（second conditional）就是與現在事實相反的條件句，而第三條件句（third conditional）則是與過去事實相反的條件句。

006 Question

the period ending July 1 和 the period ended July 1 有何不同呢？

Answer

這兩者都意為 7 月 1 日結束前的某段時間，亦即這段時間是到 7 月 1 日終止，但它們的含意卻截然不同。The period ending July 1 是指未來的時間，它是片語，其中 ending July 1 是修飾 the period 的形容詞子句 that ends (on) July 1 的減化，而 the period ended (on) July 1 則是指過去的時間，它是句子，其理解方式與 The war ended in 1975.（戰爭於 1975 年結束。）或 The concert ended at 10 o'clock.（音樂會於 10 點結束。）一樣。這兩者都是標準英語的習慣用法。

007 **Question**

I forgot to bring the cases. 和 I forgot bringing the cases. 這兩句有何不同呢?

Answer

forget 這個字後面可接不定詞和動名詞,但兩者的意思卻有極大的差異。「forget + 不定詞」意為「忘記去做某事」,而「forget + 動名詞」意為「忘記曾經做過某事」。以問題中的句子為例,I forgot to bring the cases. 意為「我忘了把箱子帶來」,而 I forgot bringing the cases. 意為「我忘了已經把箱子帶來了」。再舉一例:

▶ 1. He **forgot to study** for an economics test. (他忘了唸書準備經濟學考試。)

▶ 2. He **forgot studying** for an economics test. (他忘了曾為準備經濟學考試唸過書。)

上面第 1 句的意思是說他忘了唸書,亦即他根本沒有唸書。第 2 句則是說他有唸書,但可能是因為時間過了太久或者貴人多忘事,壓根兒把曾經唸過書,準備參加經濟學考試這件事忘得一乾二淨了。

remember 這個字的用法也跟 forget 一樣,若其後接不定詞,則表示「記得去做不定詞所指的某事」,若接動名詞,則表示「記得過去所發生的某事」。例如:

▶ I **remember locking** the door as I left the house. (我記得離開家時鎖了門。)—現在我還能想起這件事。

▶ I **remembered to lock** the door as I left the house. (我離開家時記得鎖門。)—我把門鎖上了。

008 Question

He will teach his son to deceive others. 這句的意思是「他要教導他兒子去欺騙別人」嗎？

Answer

「teach + 受詞 + to do something」有兩個意思：1. 教某人做某事 2. 教訓某人不要再做某事。例如：

▶ 1. Who taught you to play the piano?（是誰教你彈鋼琴的？）
▶ 2. I'll teach you to be rude to me.（我要教訓你對我粗暴無禮，亦即我要給你個教訓，看你還敢不敢再對我粗暴無禮。）

由此可知，問題中的句子應屬於第 2 項的意思，亦即他要教訓他兒子，看他還敢不敢再欺騙別人。再舉一例：She got wet through. That'll teach her to go out without an umbrella.，這句的意思是「她全身都淋濕了。那是對她出門不帶傘的教訓」，亦即給她個教訓，看她還敢不敢再出門不帶傘（不是教她出門不帶傘。）Teach 這兩個截然不同的意思很容易讓人混淆，所以在使用上必須特別注意。

除上述外，teach 後面也常接雙受詞，即 teach + 間接受詞 + 直接受詞 （= teach + 直接受詞 + to + 間接受詞）。例如：

▶ My mother **taught** me this song.
  = My mother **taught** this song **to** me.
  （我媽媽教我這首歌。）
▶ She **teaches** foreign students Chinese.
  = She **teaches** Chinese **to** foreign students.
  （他教外國學生學中文。）

090

009 Question

He spoke to his girlfriend that he had missed her very much.
這句為何不對呢？

Answer

這牽涉到動詞後面接 that 所引導的名詞子句當受詞的問題。在英文中，有些動詞後面可接 that 子句，但有些動詞則不行。下面所列的動詞都可以接 that 子句當受詞（當然，它們只是這類動詞中的一小部份而已，但都相當常用）：

Accept, admit, announce, answer, ask, assume. authorize, believe, claim, command, complain, consent, consider, contest, declare, decide, decree, demand, demonstrate, determine, deny, desire, dictate, direct, discover, discuss, doubt, examine, expect, feel, find (out), forget, grant, guarantee, hope, ignore, imply, indicate, insist, know, move, notice, observe, order, overlook, permit, propose, prove, recommend, regret, remark, report, request, require, say, see, show, specify, suggest, suppose, think, understand, urge, wonder 等等。例如：

▶ We have to **admit that** he's a highly competent man. （我們必須承認他是個非常能幹的人。）

▶ They **decided that** John must stay there. （他們決定約翰必須留在那裡。）

▶ I **regret that** you see it like that. （我很遺憾你那樣看待這件事。）

然而，有些動詞卻不可以接 that 子句當受詞，如 contribute, describe, make, prevent, speak, summarize 等等。所以問題中的句子是錯誤的：

▶ He **spoke** to his girlfriend **that** he had missed her very much. （他對他的女友說，他非常想念她。）→（✗）錯誤。

不過，describe 後面雖不能接 that 子句，但卻可以接 what/who/how 等 wh- 子句。例如：

▶ You must try to **describe** exactly **how** it happened. （你必須盡量準確地描述這件事是怎樣發生的。）

I worry about you. 和 I am worried about you. 這兩句的意思一樣嗎，含意有沒有不同呢？

Answer

雖然這兩句的結構不同，I worry about you. 中的 worry 為不及物動詞，而 I am worried about you. 中的 worried 為分詞形容詞，但它們的意思幾無不同，皆為「我擔心你」或「我為你擔憂」；此外，它們的文法都正確。

然而，它們的含意並不相同。I worry about you. 是一般性或普遍性的陳述，是指說話者一直以來或大多數時間都為此人擔憂，是一種長期或持久性的擔憂，而 I am worried about you. 則有一項「現在」的元素存在，表示說話者對說話當時所見所聞或最近所發生的某一特殊情況的憂慮、擔心。為了讓讀者瞭解它們之間的語意差異，茲將這兩句加以延伸如下：

▶ 1. I **worry about** you because I'm your mother. （我擔心你，因為我是你母親。）

▶ 2. I'm **worried about** you; you're looking very thin. （我為你擔憂；你看起來好瘦哦。）

父母向來都為子女操心，所以在第 1 句中，母親為子女擔心是一種普遍性的情況，而非特殊情況。第 2 句則為特殊情況，因為你平常可能體重很正常，但此時此景你看起來瘦巴巴的，所以我為你擔心。

011 Question

make, have 和 get 這三個使役動詞的含意一樣嗎 還是有所不同呢？

Answer

make, have 和 get 這三個使役動詞（causative verb）在英文中相當常用，其句型分

別為 have + sb + 原形動詞、make + sb + 原形動詞及 get + sb + to + 原形動詞，它們均可用來表示「使或叫某人做某事」的意思。然而，它們的含意並不完全相同。所以，它們並非總是可以互換，也不全然都可以用在同一個句子中。

※make 含有「強迫、迫使」（force）之意。

例如：

▶ 1. Mr. Huang made his son water the flowers.
（黃先生叫他兒子澆花。）－黃先生的兒子別無選擇，因為他父親要他澆花。

▶ 2. His jokes made us all laugh.
（他的笑話把我們都逗笑了）－他的笑話使我們不得不笑。

※have含有「要求」(ask）之意。

例如：

▶ 3. I'll have the porter bring your baggage up right away.
（我會叫搬運工馬上把你的行李拿上來。）－ 搬運工會馬上把你的行李拿上來，因為我要求他這麼做。

▶ 4. I had John find me a house.
（我叫約翰幫我找房子。）－ 約翰幫我找了房子，因為我要求他這麼做。

※get 含有「說服」（persuade）之意。

例如：

▶ 5. Wendy got me to lend her some money.
（溫蒂叫我借她一些錢。）－ 溫蒂（成功地）說服我借她一些錢。

▶ 6. The students got the teacher to dismiss class early.
（學生叫老師提早下課。）－ 學生（成功地）說服老師讓他們提早下課。

綜上所述，在句 1 中，若將 made 換成 had 或 got（記住：Get 後面要接帶 to 的不定詞）也說得通，只是含意不同，但若將句子改為 Mr. Huang made his father water the flowers.（黃先生叫他父親澆花。）則不通，因為儘管兒子比老子大的情況並非罕見，但也不多見，哪有兒子強迫父親澆花的道理。句 2 不能使用 had 或 got，因為笑話不會要求或說服我們笑。在句 3 和 句 4 中，若將 have 和 had 換成另外兩個使役動詞，都還說得通。句 5 亦然，但句 6 的 got 若換成 made，則有違常

理，因為儘管現今師道式微，師生關係緊張，學生會強迫老師提早下課或老師會在學生強迫下提早下課，還是令人匪夷所思。

最後，我們就用同一個句子來說明這三個使役動詞不盡相同的含意，以彰顯其用法之真諦。

例如：

a. The doctor made the patient stay in bed.
b. The doctor had the patient stay in bed.
c. The doctor got the patient to stay in bed.

這三句的意思都是「醫生叫病人留在床上」，但含意不同：

句 a 表示病人別無選擇、不得不留在床上，因為醫生堅持他要留在床上 （醫生有權威迫使病人這麼做。）；

句 b 表示病人之所以留在床上，是因為醫生要求他這麼做；

句 c 表示醫生成功地說服病人留在床上。

Excercise
綜合練習

I. 填空題

1 The ticket _____ like hot cakes.
（票賣得很好。）

2 After the event, the society doesn't _____ well with the celebrity.
（在事件之後，整個社會對這名人的觀感不太好。）

3 I _____ that you are disappointed by our failure to promote you.
（我瞭解你對我們未能把你晉升感到失望。）

4 His house has _____ considerably during the past six months.
（他的房子在過去 6 個月期間已大幅增值。）

5 Tim Cook, the chief executive officer of Apple, is an _____ who is proud to be a gay.
（蘋果公司執行長庫克是名公開的出櫃者，並且深以同志身份為傲。）

6 The well-educated students were glad to hear one of their classmates finally had the courage to _____.
（那些受過良好教育的學生，聽到他們有位同學終於有勇氣公開出櫃了，都感到很開心。）

7 I am _____ dinner with my old friends
（我正在跟老朋友共進晚餐。）

8 She's _____ a baby.
（她有小寶寶了。）

9 It's 9 o'clock now. The meeting _____ at 12 o'clock.
（現在九點了，會議在十二點就會結束。）

10 The war _____ in August.
（戰爭在八月結束了。）

11 Sorry, I didn't do my homework. I forgot _____ (do) my homework last night.
（抱歉我沒有寫作業。我昨晚忘了要寫作業了。）

⑫ I remembered _____ (turn off) the light before I left. Why is it on now?

（我記得我出門前有關燈，怎麼現在燈是開著的？）

⑬ I _____ (am worried/worry) about you because your voice didn't sound good last night.

（我很擔心你，因為你昨晚的聲音聽起來不太好。）

⑭ Your girlfriend _____ about you because she loves you.

（你女朋友會擔心你是因為她愛你。）

⑮ The policeman _____ (made/had/got) the thief raise his hands.

（警察強迫小偷舉起雙手。）

⑯ My mother _____ (made/had/got) my grandmother to see a doctor.

（我媽媽說服我祖母去看醫生。）

II. 以現在／未來式改寫句子

❶ I hope you will be there for me.

（我希望你能支持我。）

_____

❷ I hope she is happy.

（我希望她快樂。）

_____

III. 英翻中

❶ She teaches the little girl the beauty of nature.

_____

❷ I taught the students to be impolite to me.

_____

IV. 中翻英

❶ 他們決定約翰必須留在那裡。

_____

② 他在防範自己不要被你的話傷到。

_____

V. 二選一

❶ ☐ The book is sold well.
☐ The book sells well.
（這本書賣得很好。）

❷ ☐ I would appreciate it if you would pay in cash.
☐ I would appreciate that you would pay in cash.
（如果你能付現，我會十分感激的。）

❸ ☐ The boss has been outed.
☐ The boss has been out.
（這老闆被公開出櫃了。）

❹ ☐ The team members are having a meeting tomorrow.
☐ The team members have a meeting tomorrow.
（隊員明天將開會。）

❺ ☐ I hope that he has his passport with him.
☐ I hope that he will have his passport with him.
（我希望他有帶護照。）

❻ ☐ Don't forget to take it home.
☐ Don't forget taking it home.
（不要忘記帶它回家了。）

❼ ☐ The professor summarizes that she said a lot about algebra this morning.
☐ The professor summarizes what she said about algebra this morning.
（教授總結她早上所說的諸多代數相關的問題。）

❽ ☐ I had my hair cut.
☐ I cut my hair.
（我去剪頭髮了。）

Answer

I. 填空題

1. sells
2. go down
3. realize
4. appreciated
5. outer
6. come out
7. having
8. having
9. ends
10. ended
11. to do
12. turning off
13. am worried
14. worries
15. made
16. got

II. 改寫句子

1. I hope you are there for me.
2. I hope she will be happy.

III. 英翻中

1. 她教導那小女孩大自然的美。
2. 我教訓那些學生不得對我沒有禮貌。

IV. 中翻英

1. They decided that John must stay there.
2. He is preventing not to be hurt by your words.

V. 二選一

1. 第二句正確
2. 第一句正確
3. 第一句正確
4. 第一句正確
5. 第一句正確
6. 第一句正確
7. 第二句正確
8. 第一句正確

001 Question

when 和 while 在引導時間副詞子句時，它們的用法有何不同呢？

Answer

在 when 和 while 所引導的時間副詞子句中，when 子句的動詞可以為延續性動詞或非延續性動詞，但 while 子句的動詞必須是延續性動詞。因此，當 when 子句的動詞為延續性動詞時，when 可與 while 互換，這時主要子句的動作和時間副詞子句的動作是同時發生的。以 I often missed my home a lot when I was abroad.（我在國外時常常很想家）為例，在這句中，when 可用 while 來代替，意思不變。但在 When they came home, I was cooking dinner.（他們回家時，我正在煮晚餐）這句中，由於 came 是瞬間動詞，所以不能用 while 來代替 when。這是 when 和 while 用法的主要差異之一。

when 和 while 用法的另一差異是：When 子句的動詞通常為過去簡單式，而 while 子句的動詞往往是過去進行式。這牽涉到 when 或 while 子句的動詞與主要子句的動詞之動作發生的時間先後關係。一般而言，當 when 子句的動詞與主要子句的動詞都是過去簡單式時，when 子句的動作較早發生，此時 when 相當於 after。舉例來說，Mary stood under a tree when it began to rain. 這句是說瑪麗站在樹下這個動作是發生在下雨之後（她一定淋到雨）；如果句子改成 When Mary stood under a tree, it began to rain.，那麼這是說瑪麗站在樹下之後，雨才開始下（她沒有淋到雨 — 如果樹葉可以遮雨的話）。弄懂這種動作發生的時間先後關係，可讓我們正確而清楚地瞭解或判斷兩個動作發生的先後順序。再舉一例：When the film ended, people walked out of the theater.（電影結束後，觀眾走出戲院）。

如果 when 子句的動詞為過去簡單式，而主要子句的動詞為過去進行式，那麼儘管一般文法書大都稱這兩個動作是同時發生，但其實不然。例如：

▶ I was enjoying my dinner **when** my wife came home.
= **While** I was enjoying my dinner, my wife came home.
（我太太回家時，我正在吃晚餐。）

從這句可知，吃晚餐的動作發生的時間比回家的時間還早，因為在我太太回家之前我就開始吃晚餐了，她回家之後，我還繼續在吃，所以充其量我們僅能說這兩個動作只有在她回家的那個瞬間（即 when 子句之動作發生的瞬間）同時發生。因此，過去進行式的動作一定比過去簡單式還要早發生；而在這種句型中，when 子句的動詞都是用瞬間動詞。

最後來討論如何表達同時在進行的兩個動作：主要子句和時間副詞子句都用過去進行式；當然，根據上述，我們要用 while 來引導時間副詞子句，而兩個子句的動詞必須皆為延續性動詞。例如：

▶ **While** I was studying in one room of our dormitory, my roommate was having a party in the other room.
= I was studying in one room of our dormitory **while** my roommate was having a party in the other room.
（當我在宿舍的一個房間唸書時，我的室友正在另一房間開趴。）

002 Question

because, since, as, for, in that 和 now that 的用法有何不同呢？

Answer

這幾個字和片語均意為「因為；由於」，而 since, in that 和 now (that) 還有「既然」的意思。它們都是用來引導表原因的子句，其中除 for 為對等連接詞外，其餘皆為附屬連接詞。

在這幾個字當中，because 的語氣最強，其所引導的子句係表示直接的原因，必然的因果關係，通常位在主要子句之後，但有時亦位在主句之前，如 We couldn't go out because it was too cold.（因為天氣太冷，我們不能外出）。Because 亦是回答用 why 所提出的問題時唯一可用的字，其餘皆不行。例如：

▶ Susan: Why can't I go?（蘇珊：我為什麼不能去？）
Amy: **Because** you are too young.（艾美：因為妳年紀太小了。）

此外，because 子句可用於強調句，其餘皆不行。例如：

▶ It's **because** he is honest that we like him.（就是因為他做人老實，我們
才喜歡他。）

再者，because 子句可作補語，其餘皆不行。例如：

▶ This is **because** I love her too much.（這是因為我太愛她了。）

since 和 as 的語氣都比 because 弱，而 since 比 as 略微正式。它們所引導的子句
係表示不言而喻、顯而易見或已為大家所知的原因或既成事實的原因，通常位在主
句之前，但有時亦位在主句之後，其中 since 往往被譯為「既然」。例如：

▶ **Since** you can't answer the question, I'll ask someone else.（既然你
回答不出這個問題，我就問別人了。）
▶ **Since** you feel tired, you should rest.（既然你感到疲倦，你應該休息。）
▶ **As** he was not well, I decided to go without him.（因為他身體不好，我
決定一個人去。）
▶ **As** she has no car, she can't get there easily.（她因為沒有車，要去那裡
並不容易。）

此外，since 可用於省略句，其餘皆不行。例如：

▶ **Since** so, there is no more to be said.（既然如此，就再也沒有什麼好說
的了。）

如上述，for 為對等連接詞，而它所引導的子句只能放在主句之後且其前必須有逗
點。例如：

▶ **For** he is ill, he is absent today. →（✗）錯誤。
▶ He is absent today, **for** he is ill. →（○）正確。
（因為生病，他今天缺席。）

for 所引導的原因子句可表示直接的因果關係（可用 because 來替換），換言之，若
because子句放在句末，且其前有逗點，那麼 because 可用 for 來代替。不過，for
子句有時並不表示直接的原因，而是對主句的內容加以說明、解釋或推斷，此時 for
不能用 because 來替換。例如：

▶ The ground is wet, **for/because** it rained last night.（地面是濕的，因為昨晚下過雨。）

▶ It rained last night, **for** the ground is wet this morning.（昨晚下過雨，因為今天早上地面是濕的。）-- 不能用 because

▶ It must have rained last night, **for** the ground is wet.（昨晚一定下過雨，因為地面是濕的。）

▶ He is absent today, **for/because** he is ill.（他今天缺席，因為他生病了。）

▶ He must be ill, **for** he is absent today.（他一定生病了，因為他今天缺席。）

▶ Day breaks, **for** the cock crows.（公雞啼，天亮了。）

▶ We must start early, **for/because** it will take two hours to drive to the airport.（我們得早點動身，因為開車去機場得花兩個小時。）

in that 和 now (that) 與 since 相似，語氣較弱，它們所引導的子句同樣係表示已為大家所知的原因或既成事實的原因。now (that)，與 since 一樣亦大多被譯為「既然」。例如：

▶ **Now (that)** you have come, you may as well stay.（你既然來了，不妨就住下。）

▶ **Now (that)** John's arrived, we can begin.（既然約翰來了，我們可以開始了。）

▶ **Now (that)** you are busy, let me do it for you.（既然你忙，就讓我來為你做吧。）

最後，必須特別注意的一點是，中文習慣上說「因為……所以」，但在英文中，because, since, as, for 等絕對不能與 so（所以）連用。

003 Question

在表示「是否」時，whether 和 if 有何不同呢 另外，whether 的後面是否一定要接 or not 呢？

Answer

Whether 是個連接詞，可引導名詞子句和副詞子句。若引導名詞子句，whether 意

為「是否」，可用 if 來代替；若引導副詞子句，whether（通常與 or 連用）意為「不管……（還是……）」。

雖然在引導名詞子句時，whether 經常可用 if 來代替，但在下列用法中，只能使用 whether，不可使用 if：

(1).當 or not 緊接在 whether 之後時，whether 不可用 if 來代替，亦即英文沒有 if or not 的寫法。例如：

▶ Ask him **whether** he can come **or not**. →（○）正確。
▶ Ask him **if** he can come **or not**. →（○）正確。
（問問他是否能來。）

▶ I wonder **whether or not** we should tell her. →（○）正確。
▶ I wonder **if or not** we should tell her. →（✕）錯誤。
（我不知道我們該不該告訴他。）

(2).以 whether 引導的名詞子句當主詞時，whether 不可用 if 來代替。例如：

▶ **Whether** this ended the matter remained unclear. →（○）正確。
▶ **If** this ended the matter remained unclear. →（✕）錯誤。
（這是否能使此一事件劃下休止符仍不清楚。）

(3).以 whether 引導的名詞子句當主詞補語時，whether 不可用 if 來代替。例如：

▶ The question is **whether** the man can be trusted. →（○）正確。
▶ The question is **if** the man can be trusted. →（✕）錯誤。
（問題在於這個人是否值得信賴。）

(4).在不定詞之前只能用 whether，不能用 if。例如：

▶ The question is **whether** to go or stay. →（○）正確。
▶ The question is **if** to go or stay. →（✕）錯誤。
（問題是：去還是留。）

▶ He wondered **whether or not** to go (**whether** to go **or not**). →（○）正確。
（他不知道去還是不去。）

(5).在介系詞之後只能用 whether，不能用 if。例如：

▶ There was a big argument **about whether** we should move to a new house. →（○）正確。

▶ There was a big argument **about if** we should move to a new house. →（×）錯誤。
（我們曾為是否應搬到新家而發生嚴重爭吵。）

(6).Whether 引導的名詞子句位在名詞之後當同位語時，whether 不可用 if 來代替。例如：

▶ It's your **decision whether** you go or stay. →（○）正確。

▶ It's your **decision if** you go or stay. →（×）錯誤。
（你去還是留要由你自己決定。）

▶ You have to answer my question **whether** you love him. →（○）正確。

▶ You have to answer my question **if** you love him. →（×）錯誤。
（你必須回答我所問的你是否愛他這個問題。）

在上面第 (6) 項中，You have to answer my question whether you love him. 亦可寫成 You have to answer my question of whether you love him.。根據 *The New Fowler's Modern English Usage*，在「the question (of) whether + 子句」中，有 of 或沒有 of 都是標準英語。

必須一提的是，whether or not 有時亦寫成 whether or no。儘管一般而言 no 並非副詞，但 whether or no 這一型態自 17 世紀以來一直使用至今，《牛津英語大辭典》(Oxford English Dictionary, OED) 甚至在 1923 年指出 whether or no 比 whether or not 常用，不過現在 whether or not 要比 whether or no 常用許多。例如：

▶ I don't know whether it's true or no(t) (whether or no(t) it's true).（我不知道是真是假。）

▶ Whether or no(t) he comes (Whether he comes or no(t)), the result will be the same.（不管他來不來，結果都將一樣。）

至於 whether 的後面是否一定要接 or no(t) 的問題，使用 whether 而未表示還有另一種選擇，亦即後面沒有接 or no(t)，在少數情況中是適當、合理的，如上述第 (2) 項中的例句 Whether this ended the matter remained unclear.。然而，表示還有另一種選擇的寫法，亦即後面有接 or no(t)，則較之常見許多。這裡所謂的少數情況，是指另一種選擇非常明確，所以不必說出或寫出亦能瞭解的情況，也就是不言而喻的情況。

004 Question

but 和 yet 用作連接詞表示「然而，可是，但是」之意時，兩者有何不同呢？

Answer

用作對等連接詞 （coordinating conjunction）時，but 與 yet 的意思並無二致，但 yet 的語氣較強且可能比較驚訝。例如：

▶ Tony studied hard, **but** he failed in the exam.
▶ Tony studied hard, **yet** he failed in the exam.
（東尼很用功，但考試仍不及格。）

然而，"yet" 的前面可以放 and 或 but，但 "but" 的前面卻不行。例如：

▶ Jenny's very beautiful, **yet** she's rather lazy. →（○）正確。
= Jenny's very beautiful, **and yet** she's rather lazy. →（○）正確。
= Jenny's very beautiful, **but yet** she's rather lazy. →（○）正確。
Jenny's very beautiful, **and but** she's rather lazy. →（✕）錯誤。
（珍妮非常漂亮，但她挺懶的。）

儘管 and yet 或 but yet 的寫法不時可見，但是一些文法學者卻不表苟同，認為這是累贅，因為 and 和 but 是贅詞。他們指出，雖然莎士比亞也使用 but yet，但莎翁是著名的詩人和劇作家，並非著名的文法學家。

最後值得注意的是，如果有人看到像下面這樣的句子，千萬別以為 but 前面可以放 yet：

▶ The sun has not risen **yet** but I should go to work. （太陽還沒有升起，但我該去上班了。）

上句中的 yet 並非連接詞，而是副詞，意為「還（沒）、尚（未）」，用於現在式或現在完成式的否定句或疑問句，而 yet 通常置於該子句的句末。若在 yet 和 but 之間用逗點隔開，就不會造成這樣的誤解或混淆了，如 The sun has not risen yet, but I should go to work. 。

有人將 so 與動詞連用，即 so 後面接動詞，如 I so want to go there.。這樣對嗎？

Answer

so 作副詞用時，其後通常接形容詞或副詞，用來強調感覺、品質或數量等。例如：

▶ The chocolate is wonderful, but it's **so** expensive.
（這巧克力很好吃，只是太貴了。）

▶ Why is your brother always eating **so** quickly?
（你弟弟為何老是吃得這麼快呢？）

若要與動詞連用，則須使用 really；換言之，若要強調動詞，須用 really，而 so 則用來強調形容詞和副詞。例如：

▶ I **really** want to go there.
（我很想去那裡。）

▶ I'm **so** keen to go there.
（我很想去那裡。）

really 和 so 在英文中叫做副詞加強語 （intensifiers），意思都是「非常，很」(very, very much) － 它們用來強調其後所接的字。在上面第一句中，really 加強了動詞 want 的程度。但在第二句中，so 加強了形容詞 keen 的程度。

然而，在問題的句子 I so want to go there. 中，這一「really 接動詞而 so 接形容詞」的規則被打破了 － so 竟然跟動詞連用或用在動詞之前。這種用法通常被視為「青少年俚語」(teen speak)。

這種用法是最近幾年才出現的現象，但或許是它的應用頻率越來越高或應用範圍越來越廣，最近幾年改版的英語辭典幾乎都有收錄。此種結構似乎最常被用來表達個人意見，所以它們的主詞以第一人稱 I 居多，而且大多使用「想要」、「渴望」、「期待」、「喜歡」、「喜愛」等意思的動詞，如 want, look forward to, like, love, enjoy, appreciate。此外，在口語中說這些句子時，so 的發音要加重，亦即 so 是整句的重音所在。例如：

▶ I was **so** looking forward to meeting your family.
（我非常盼望見到你的家人。）

▶ I **so** don't like his new girlfriend.
（我很不喜歡他的新女友。）

▶ I **so** didn't want to go to that concert.
（我非常不想去聽那場音樂會。）

▶ I **so** love your dress!
（我很喜愛妳的洋裝！）

▶ I am **so** going to be there!
（我一定會到那裡！）

▶ We're **so** looking forward to this movie.
（我們非常期待這部電影。）

▶ You are **so** gonna (= going to) be in trouble when you get home.
（當你回家時，你一定會遇上麻煩。）

▶ She **so** loved watching birds flying in the sky.
（她非常喜歡看小鳥在空中飛翔。）

嚴格來說，這些句子全部都文法錯誤，所以它們不大可能出現在英文寫作中。但可以肯定地說，英語系國家時下的年輕人會三不五時說出這樣的句子。

Excercise
綜合練習

I. 填空題

1 I was enjoying my dinner _____ my wife came home.
（我太太回家時，我正在吃晚餐。）

2 _____ the film ended, people walked out of the theater.
（電影結束後，觀眾走出戲院。）

3 Day breaks, _____ the cock crows.
（公雞啼，天亮了。）

4 _____ you are busy, let me do it for you.
（既然你忙，就讓我來為你做吧。）

5 _____ to be or not is a question.
（生存還是死亡仍是個問題。）

6 Do you know _____ or not it will rain tomorrow?
（你知道明天會不會下雨呢？）

7 I haven't seen her _____ (but yet/yet, but) I feel so close to her.
（我還沒見到她但是已經覺得跟她很親近了。）

8 She didn't love you _____ (but yet/and yet) you bought her such an expensive gift.
（她根本不愛你，可是你竟然還買這麼昂貴的禮物給她。）

II. 二選一

1 ☐ While I was taking a shower, the bell rang.
☐ When I was taking a shower, the bell rang.
（當我在洗澡的時候，門鈴響了。）

2 ☐ Many people got sick, for the weather changed greatly last week.
☐ Many people got sick for the weather changed greatly last week.
（由於上週天氣變化巨大，很多人都生病了。）

3 □ She loves you so much and but you cheated on her!

□ She loves you so much and yet you cheated on her!

（她這麼愛你，你竟然還是背叛她了！）

4 □ What you need to know is if you want to do it or not.

□ What you need to know is whether you want to do it or not.

（你需要知道的只有你是否想要做這件事情。）

Answer

I. 填空題

1 when

2 When

3 for

4 Now (that)

5 Whether

6 whether

7 yet, but

8 but yet

II. 二選一

1 第一句正確

2 第一句正確

3 第二句正確

4 第二句正確

001 Question

It might rain. 和 It may rain. 有何不同呢？

Answer

might 是 may 的過去式，如 We thought we might win the tournament. （我們認為我們可能贏得這項錦標賽），但兩者都可以用來表示「可能性」(possibility)，只是 might 所表示的可能性比 may 來得低；所以，It might rain. 和 It may rain. 都意為「可能下雨」，但前者下雨的可能性比後者低。同樣地，We might go to the movies. （我們可能去看電影）跟 We may go to the movies. 的主要差別在於前者去看電影的可能性略低於後者。

此外，might 和 may 這兩個語氣助動詞也都可用來表示「許可」（permission），但 might 的禮貌性或客氣的程度高於 may；所以，Might I express my opinion?（我可以表達我的意見嗎？）比 May I express my opinion? 更客氣、更有禮貌，換言之，是否一定要表達意見，前者比較不堅持。

002 Question

cannot, can't 和 can not 有何不同呢？

Answer

"cannot" 和 "can not" 是截然不同的兩個字，兩者不可互換。Cannot（不能）是 can（= be able to）（能）的否定形式。Can't 是 cannot 的縮寫形式，而且是比較後來才出現的寫法，在莎士比亞的作品中並沒有這樣的形式，《牛津英語大辭典》(Oxford English Dictionary, OED) 所提供的最早的例句是在 1706 年。由於是縮寫形

式，can't 並不適合用在正式寫作和論文中。此外，值得一提的是，cannot 通常發成 can't 的音。

can not 目前只出現在兩種情況中，第一種情況是 not 為某固定片語的一部份，如 You can not only borrow the car but you can also borrow my camping equipment. （你不僅可以借車，還可借用我的露營用品）－ 由於在這句中，not 是 not only ... but (also) 此一固定片語的一部份，因此不能使用 cannot；第二種情況是句子要特別強調 "not"，如 No, you can NOT wash the dog in the washing machine.（不！你不可以將狗放進洗衣機去洗）；You can NOT go to the movies!（你不能去看電影）。

can not 分開寫的方式現今不僅極為少用，甚至被視為錯誤。不過，can 的過去式 could 的否定和縮寫形式分別為 "could not"（不可寫成 couldnot）和 "couldn't"。

既然 can 的否定形式是 cannot 而不是 can not，那麼在否定問句中，我們可以直接將 cannot（單一個字）移到主詞的前面嗎？如 Why cannot you go to the dentist？（你為何不能去看牙醫呢？），答案是：不行。當然，若將 cannot 改為縮寫形式，使句子變成 Why can't you go to the dentist? 就合乎語法了。然而，在不適合使用縮寫形式的正式書面英語中，問題還是存在。說來可能會讓人出乎意料之外，因為這問題的解決之道就是用 can not（兩個字），使句子變成 Why can you not go to the dentist? 就可以了。

或許把 can 換成助動詞 do 來做說明，會讓我們更快速地解開這問題的迷團；此時句子就變成了 "Why DO you not go to the dentist?"，但不可以寫成 "Why DO NOT you go to the dentist?"。雖然 do not 是兩個字，而 cannot 是單一個字，但同樣不可寫成 "Why CANNOT you go to the dentist?"。原因是 not 為副詞，是修飾主動詞，不是修飾助動詞，所以它要緊鄰主動詞。若用縮寫形式，它最靠近主動詞的位置是在主詞的前面，即 "Why DON'T you GO to the dentist?"；換成 cannot 就是 "Why CAN'T you GO to the dentist?"。綜上所述，在問問題時，cannot 要打散，就像將 do 和 not 分開一樣，以使 not 可以修飾主動詞。所以，cannot 正確的問句寫法是：Why can you not go to the dentist?

Question

How CAN I help you 和 How MAY I help you 這兩個問句都有人用，那麼該使用 MAY 還是 CAN 呢？

Answer

老實說，吾人實在很難區分 may 和 can 之間的不同。不過，在正式寫作中，最好還是使用 may。當有人問你 "How can I help you?" （我該怎樣幫助你?）時，比較合理的回答應該是 "How should I know?" （我怎麼知道?）。

相較於 can，may 這個語氣助動詞所表示的可能性比較有禮貌、帶一點試探性而且比較肯定。現今，肯定句已鮮少使用 can 來表示可能性，而是以 may, might 和 could（could 也很少用了）來代之；但在問句中，則可用 can 來詢問可能性，如 Can this be true?（這可能是真的?）。

然而，這幾個表示可能性的語氣助動詞的肯定程度都低於 50%，換言之，它們的語氣充滿不確定性。這也就是為什麼當有人問 "How can I help you?" 時是以 "How should I know?" 來回答的原因，因為 should 肯定的程度幾近 90%。這一問一答含有「連你要怎樣幫助我都不確定，我又怎麼知道呢」的意思。

 **Excercise**
綜 合 練 習

I. 填空題

❶ The village _____ (may/might) be destroyed by the typhoon.
（這村子可能會被颱風摧毀。）

❷ Your boyfriend said "I love you" to that girl. He _____ (might/may) betray you!
（你男朋友跟那女生說「我愛你」！他可能背叛了你。）

❸ You _____ (can't/can not) merely visit Paris but also stay in Paris!
（你不只可以造訪巴黎，還能待在那裡！）

❹ You _____ (can't/can not) go into the room.
（你不可以進去那間房間。）

II. 選擇題

( ) A: How can I help you? B: _____.
(A). How should I know?
(B). How can I know?
(C). I don't know.
(D). Could you help me take the baggage?
（我該怎樣幫助你？）

III. 二選一

❶ ☐ Everyone brings an umbrella. It might rain.
☐ Everyone brings an umbrella. It may rain.
（大家都帶著雨傘。可能是下雨了。）

❷ ☐ You can't say that to your mother!
☐ You can not say that to your mother!
（你不可以這樣跟你媽說！）

Answer

I. 填空題
1 might

2 may

3 can not

4 can't

II. 選擇題
（A）

III. 二選一
1 第二句正確

2 第一句正確

001 Question

It's a wise man that never makes mistakes. 這個強調句中的 a 是否應改為 the，而整句的意思是「就是這位聰明的人從不犯錯」嗎？

Answer

這句的意思並非這樣。它也不是所謂「分裂句」（cleft sentence）的強調句型（It is/was + 強調的部分 + that 子句）。它是一種極為特殊的「It is ... that 子句」句型。英語中有為數不少的諺語都是使用這種句型。大家知道，許多英語諺語都是從莎士比亞時代流傳下來的，有些甚至是直接來自莎士比亞的戲劇；他那個時代和以前時代的英語跟現代英語的用法有很大不同，這就是問題的根源，也是問題中的句子的意思被誤解的原因。所以，我們不能按照現代英語的語法規範去理解那個時代的諺語。

「It is ... that 子句」這種英諺句型，意思被誤解的情況屢見不鮮。舉例來說，莎士比亞的劇本「威尼斯商人」（The Merchant of Venice）中有一句諺語 "It is a wise father that knows his own son."，如果按現行語法來理解的話，也就是如果按字面的意思來理解的話，那就是只有聰明的父親才會瞭解自己的兒子，有些人也是這樣翻譯的；但實際上並不是這意思，而是「再怎麼聰明的父親也不見得瞭解自己的兒子」或「其父未必知其子」。所以，問題中的句子的意思應是「再怎麼聰明的人，也難免犯錯」。換言之，這種句子的真正意思與字面意思恰好相反，它具有含蓄的讓步意味，吾人切勿望文生義、譯成強調句型。

「It is ... that 子句」這種諺語結構有幾個共同特點：1. 被強調的部分不是特指的某人某物，而是一般的泛指，因此它的前面是用不定冠詞，而不是表示特指的定冠詞；2. 被強調的中心詞至少有一個形容詞作修飾語；3. 從結構上來看，主句（It is ...）不同於一般的強調句，它只有現在式，沒有其他時態，也沒有否定形式 － 這道理很簡單，因為它表達的是一種普遍真理；4. 這類諺語的哲理性比較強。

總結上面的敘述，我們可以將這種句型更詳細地寫成：「It is a + 形容詞 + 名詞 + that 子句」，意為「無論多麼的……也（不）……」或「再怎麼的……也（不）……」（但往往引申為諺語）。這種句型中的 that 子句有否定和肯定兩種情況，當它為否定形式時，要譯成肯定的意思；當它為肯定形式時，則要譯成否定的意思。請看下面的例句：

that 子句為否定形式的情況

▶ It is a good workman **that** never blunders.（智者千慮必有一失。）－ 不可譯為：一個好的工人決不犯錯

▶ It is a long lane **that** has no turning.（路必有彎；凡事必有變化；耐心等待終會時來運轉。）－不可譯為：那是一條永不轉彎的長巷

▶ It is a good horse **that** never stumbles.（凡馬皆有失蹄時；凡人皆會犯錯；金無足赤，人無完人）

▶ It is a good husband **that** never stumbles and a good wife that never grumbles.（世間沒有從不犯錯的賢夫，也沒有從不嘮叨的賢妻。）

▶ It is a small flock **that** has not a black sheep.（再小的羊群也有雜色羊。）－樹多出雜木，人多出怪物

that 子句為肯定形式的情況

▶ It is a good divine **that** follows his own instructions.（能説者未必能行。）

▶ It is an ill bird **that** fouls its own nest.（再壞的鳥也不會弄髒自己的巢－家醜不外揚。）

▶ It is a good doctor **that** follows his own advice.（名醫不自醫。）

▶ It is a silly fish **that** is caught twice with the same bait.（智者不上兩回當。）

▶ It is a good dog **that** can catch anything.（世上沒有什麼東西都能抓的狗。）

002 Question

是否可以詳述冠詞的用法呢？

Answer

冠詞本身不能單獨使用，它們必須放在名詞或名詞片語的前面才有意義，係用來幫助指明名詞的含義。英語中的冠詞有三個，即 a, an, the，其中 a, an 為不定冠詞（indefinite article），the 為定冠詞（definite article）；不過，由於有些名詞不加冠詞，有人稱之為零冠詞（zero article）。

不定冠詞 a 係放在第一個字母為子音的單數可數名詞前面（如 a cow, a book, a desk），而 an 則放在第一個字母為母音或發音等同母音的單數可數名詞前面（如 an apple, an engineer, an open door）。第一個字母為 h 而且發[h]音的字通常使用 a（如 a horse, a history book, a hotel），但若該 h 字母是發真正的母音或不發音，則須使用 an（如 an hour, an honor）。相對地，一個字的開頭字母若為母音，但實際的發音卻是子音，那麼該字的前面須使用 a，如 a useful device, a union matter 等，因為 useful 和 union 的第一個 u 實際上都是發[ju]的音（相較於 an ugly old man 的 u）。同樣地，once-in-a-lifetime experience 或 one-time hero 前面的不定冠詞皆須使用 a，而非 an，因為 once 和 one 開頭的 o 都是發[w]的音。

至於頭字語（acronyms）或縮寫（abbreviations）前面的不定冠詞，也必須力求正確。例如，FBI agent 的前面該使用 an 還是 a 呢？雖然 F 是個子音，照理講，任何以 F 做開頭的字，前面的冠詞應該用 "a"，但實際的情況是，FBI 前面應使用 "an"，因為在唸 FBI 時，第一個音並非[f]的音，而是[ɛf]的音。同樣地，在 we saw a UFO. 這句中，儘管 UFO 這個縮寫是以母音 "U" 做開頭，但實際在發 "U" 的音時，第一個音並非母音。至於 URL 到底要用 a 或 an 做冠詞，端賴它是唸成[ɝl] 還是字母的 "U-R-L" 而定。

不定冠詞 a 和 an 在意義上相當於數詞 one，可以指人亦可指物。定冠詞 the 在意義上相當於指示代名詞 this/that（這個／那個 － 後接單數可數名詞）或 these/those（這些／那些 － 後接複數可數名詞），如 Do you know the woman talking to the boss?（你認識那個正在跟老板說話的女子嗎？）；Have you got the books I sent you?（我寄給你的那些書收到了嗎？）。

在文章中，首次提到某個單數可數名詞時，其前通常使用不定冠詞，但後續再提到這個名詞時則要使用定冠詞。例如：

- ▶ "I'd like **a** glass of orange juice, please," John said. （約翰說：「請給我一杯柳橙汁。」）
- ▶ "I put **the** glass of juice on the counter already," Cindy replied. （辛蒂回答說：「我已經把那杯柳橙汁放在櫃臺上。」）

名詞的泛指或通稱（generic reference）在英文中是個非常重要的文法觀念。可數名詞可用 (1) a/an + 單數名詞，(2) the + 單數名詞或 (3) 零冠詞 + 複數名詞來表示泛指。例如：

- ▶ **A dog** is a man's best friend. （狗是人類最忠實的朋友。）
- ▶ **The dog** is a smart animal. （狗是聰明的動物。）
- ▶ **Dogs** are smart animals. （狗是聰明的動物。）

在上面的例句中，a dog, the dog 和 dogs 都是泛指所有的狗，而非特指某一隻狗。一般而言，單數可數名詞大多在前面加上不定冠詞來表示泛指，樂器名稱和科技產品或最新發明則使用定冠詞來表示泛指，而動物名稱則可使用不定冠詞或定冠詞表示泛指。複數名詞是以零冠詞來表示泛指。不過，必須注意的是，在表示泛指時，單複數不可混合使用，主詞與補語的「數」必須對稱，即單數對單數，複數對複數。例如：

- ▶ **Dogs** are smart animals. →（○）正確。
- ▶ **A dog** is a smart animal. →（○）正確。
- ▶ **A dog** is smart animal**s**. →（✕）錯誤。
- ▶ **Dogs** are **a** smart animal. →（✕）錯誤。

至於不可數名詞則以零冠詞來表示泛指。例如：

- ▶ **Beauty** is in the eye of the beholder. （情人眼裡出西施。）
- ▶ **Beauty** is only skin deep. （美貌只是外表；不可以貌取人。）
- ▶ **Discretion** is the better part of valor. （謹慎即大勇；大勇貴謹慎 — 意指不該冒不必要的危險。）
- ▶ I adore **chocolate**. （我非常喜歡巧克力。）
- ▶ We adore **Baroque music**. （我們非常喜歡巴洛克音樂。）

值得注意的是，有些名詞，尤其是專有名詞，必須加定冠詞：

1. 世上獨一物二的事物：

the sun（太陽）、the sky（天空）、the moon（月亮）、the earth（地球）、the universe（宇宙）、the world（世界）、the Arctic（北極）等。

2. 複數化以及有 republic 和 kingdom 等字的國名：

The United States（美國）、the Netherlands（荷蘭）、the Bahamas（巴哈馬）、the Philippines（菲律賓）、the United Kingdom（聯合王國，即英國）等。

3. 海洋、河流、港灣（但湖泊不加）：

The Pacific Ocean（太平洋）、the Gulf of Mexico（墨西哥灣）、the Red Sea（紅海）、the Sea of Japan（日本海）、the Amazon River（亞馬遜河）、the Yangtze River（長江），但 Dongting Lake（洞庭湖）。

4. 山脈、群島、半島、沙漠（但單數的 island, mount, mountain 不加）：

The Scandinavian Peninsula（斯堪地那維亞半島）、the Mergui archipelago（緬甸丹老群島）、the Falkland Islands（福克蘭群島）、the Himalayas（喜馬拉雅山脈）、the Andes（安地斯山脈）、the Sahara（撒哈拉沙漠）、the Gobi（戈壁沙漠）、the Arabian Desert（阿拉伯沙漠），但 Wake Island（威克島）、Mt. Ali（阿里山）。

5. 報章、雜誌、經典、書籍：

The New York Times（紐約時報）、the Times（倫敦泰晤士報）、The Miami Herald（邁阿密先鋒報）、the Holy Bible（聖經）、the Koran（可蘭經）等。

6. 方向，方位：

The east（東，東方）、the south（南，南方）、the west（西，西方）、the West（美國西部；西方國家）、the past（過去）、the future（將來）、the right（右，右邊）、the left（左，左邊）等。

7. 複數化的姓氏（家族）和球隊名稱：

The Obamas（歐巴馬夫婦；歐巴馬一家人）、the Johnsons（強森夫婦；強森一家人）、the Los Angeles Lakers（洛杉磯湖人隊）、the Milwaukee Brewers（密爾瓦基釀酒人隊）等。

8. 公共建築、機關、團體組織、劇院、公路、鐵路、航線等名稱：

The Ministry of Education（教育部）、the Empire State Building（帝國大廈）、the Grand Hotel（圓山飯店）、the Taipei Theater（台北戲院）、the Central Highway（中央公路）、the House of Representatives（眾議院）、the Presbyterian Church（長老教會）等。

9. 樂器：

My daughter can play the piano/the cello/the flute.（我女兒會彈鋼琴/拉大提琴/吹長笛。）

10. 表示單位的名詞：

He has hired the assistant by the hour.（他按小時雇用助理。）；Beef is sold by the pound.（牛肉的銷售是以磅為單位。）

11. 語言名詞之後若有 "language" 時要加 the：

語言名詞單獨使用時不加 the，但若其後有 "language" 這個字，則要加 the，如 He can speak English.（他會說英文。）；His knowledge of the English language is poor.（他的英文知識很貧乏。）

有些名詞不加定冠詞，即零冠詞：

1. 地名和人名：

China has become the world's second largest economy.（中國已成為世界第二大經濟體）；He is Mary's brother.（他是瑪麗的兄弟。）

2. 季節、月份、節日、假日、日期、星期和時間：

I go on holiday in summer.（我每年夏天都會去度假。）；The company was established in October 2010.（這家公司於 2010 年 10 月創立。）；It happened on September 3.（這事發生在 9 月 3 日。）；to go skiing at Christmas（聖誕節期間去滑雪）；We go to school from Monday to Friday.（我們星期一到星期五上學。）；We'll be there around midnight.（我們將在午夜時分到那裡。）

3. 官銜和職稱：

President Barack Obama and Secretary of State Hillary Rodham Clinton urged the new Lebanese government to fight terrorism.（美國總統歐巴馬和國務卿希拉蕊敦促黎巴嫩新政府打擊恐怖主義。）；Major General Lo is Vietnam's spy.（羅少將是越南的間諜）。

4. 三餐：

Breakfast was delicious.（早餐好吃。）；He's preparing dinner by himself.（他正獨自一人準備晚餐。）

5. 學術科目：

Her major is theology.（她主修神學。）；I'm taking economics and math.（我修經濟學和數學。）

6. 疾病：

He died of pneumonia.（他死於肺炎。）；Appendicitis nearly killed his father.（盲腸炎差點要了他父親的命。）；Amy has cancer.（艾美罹患癌症。）－ 我們有時會聽到或看到 "the measles"（麻疹）和 "the mumps"（腮腺炎），但這些複數型當單數用的疾病名稱也可以不加冠詞。

7. 球類等體育運動名稱：

David likes to play badminton and basketball.（大衛喜歡打羽毛球和籃球。）；She usually plays chess with her husband.（她經常和她先生下西洋棋。）

8. 社會或教育事業機構等名稱：

Go to hospital（去醫院看病）－ 相較於 go to the hospital（去醫院，指去醫院做其他事情，不是去看病）。除 hospital 外，school, church, market, college, court, prison 等字也有類似的用法。當這些名詞前有 "the" 時，指的是地點、地方、實際的建築物，但用作抽象名詞時，指的則是建築物的功用，說明人在那裡從事相應的活動。

9. by 與火車等交通工具連用時，各該交通工具前不加冠詞：

We'll go by train.（我們將搭火車去。）－ 相較於 We'll take the train.。

Excercise
綜合練習

I. 選擇題

1 (　) It is a silly fish that is caught twice with the same bait.

(A). 智者不二過。　　　　　　(B). 愚者老犯同樣的錯。

2 (　) It is a good workman that never blunders.

(A). 一個好的工人決不犯錯。　　(B). 智者千慮必有一失

II. 填空題

1 I love to _____ (play piano/play the piano).

（我喜歡彈鋼琴。）

2 (Dogs are/ Dog is) _____ our best friends.

（狗是我們最忠實的朋友）

III. 二選一

1 ☐ We are hired by the hour.

☐ We are hired by hour.

（我們是按小時被僱用的。）

2 ☐ It is a good doctor that does not follow his own advice.

☐ It is a good doctor that follows his own advice.

（名醫不自醫。）

Answer

I. 選擇題
1 A　　　　　　**2** B

II. 填空題
1 play the piano　　**2** Dogs are

III. 二選一
1 第一句正確　　**2** 第二句正確

001 Question

在 He spends all his salary within four or five days of receiving it. 這句中是否可以將 all his salary 改為 his all salary 呢？

Answer

不可以。在 He spends all his salary within four or five days of receiving it.（他在領到薪水後的四、五天內就把它全部花光。）這句中，all 和 his 都可以叫做「限定詞」（determiners），而限定詞是位在名詞之前，用來「限定」名詞。大體而言，當有一個以上的限定詞出現在名詞之前時，它們須按照一定順序排列才合乎語法。視限定詞的相對位置而定，我們將限定詞分為三類：「前置限定詞」（pre-determiners），「中間限定詞」（central determiners）及「後置限定詞」（post-determiners）。顧名思義，在限定詞的順序中，前置限定詞位在最前面，中間限定詞在中間，後置限定詞位在最後面。例如：

在 I met all my many friends. 中，all 是前置限定詞，my 是中間限定詞，many 是後置限定詞。

事實上，上面這個句子有些不尋常，因為在同一句子中同時使用三個限定詞的情況比較少見，一般只有使用到一個或兩個限定詞。

現在就將常用的限定詞依其類別臚列如下，供大家參考：

1. 前置限定詞：all (of), both (of), half (of)；double, twice, three times 等；a third (of), three quarters (of) 等；what, such 等；only。

2. 中間限定詞：the, a(n)；this, that, these, those；my, your, Bill's 等；some, any, no, every, each, either, enough, much；what(ever), which(ever), whose。

3. 後置限定詞：one, two, three 等；first, second, third 等；next, last, other, several 等；much, many, few(er), little/less, more。

由上面可知，前置限定詞主要包括 all, both, half 以及倍數和分數。必須注意的是，前置限定詞不可同時出現，如 all his salary 是正確的，但 all half his salary 則錯誤。

中間限定詞主要包括冠詞 the, a(n)、所有格 my, your, Bill's... 以及 some, any... 等等。同樣地，中間限定詞亦不可同時出現。

後置限定詞則包括基數、序數以及 last, next, much, many 等等。但與前置和中間限定詞不同的是，後置限定詞可同時出現。

綜合以上的敘述，限定詞的順序可以寫成：all these problems, four times this amount, twice that size, one-third my salary, his fourth birthday, Mary's third husband, these three boys, our several achievements, the few friends that I have, my first three days off, our next two projects, several/many other people, all my other books, such a waste, She has become only the third woman to be nominated for the best director at the Oscars.（她已成為僅有的第三位被提名角逐奧斯卡最佳導演的女性。）等等。

但此一順序也有若干例外，如 many a child (= many children)、his every move、an only child（獨生子）等。

002 Question

多次在外國一些小報的網站及其他網站上看到類似 They are generous, not! 和 She is a good girl, not! 這樣的寫法，請問這個 not 的意義和用法為何呢？

Answer

這可謂 not 的新用法，原本只有在會話中才聽得到，但根據您的說法，這項用法也已開始出現在書面中。這是一項異於尋常的用法，它是將 not 放在句末而非句中，有點像附加問句（tag question），是一種將肯定敘述予以否定的附加問句。

然而，這個 not 不只是個否定詞而已，它其實是在強調說話者否定的觀點，相當於在表示「剛剛所說的都是廢話、垃圾」的意思。它就像 "No way!" 或 "I don't think so!"，中文的意思大概是「才不！」、「才怪！」。所以，它通常放在相反的觀點

或意見之後。譬如說，從電影院走出來的人可能會說 "'O, yeah, it was a great film, not!" （哦，那是一部很棒的影片，才怪！）。你也可能會聽人家這麼說 "This is a cool website, not!" （這是個很棒的網站，才不呢！）或 "Sure we're ready, not!" （當然我們已準備好了，才怪！）。

顯然地，這種用法的 not 是個流行用語，但可能會、也可能不會持久。如果它真的在一段時間之後就不再被使用了，那麼我們就可以說 "That's a cool bit of slang, not!" （它是個有點酷的俚語，才怪！）。事實上，英文還有一個意為「才怪；個頭」的用語：My foot （不是「我的腳」）。例如：

▶ "She says she's too busy to speak to you." （她說她忙得沒時間跟你講話。）

▶ "Busy, **my foot**! She just doesn't want to." （忙？忙個頭！她只是不想跟我講話！）

003 Question

age 這個字的用法是否有一定的規則，如 children age 6-10, children aged 6-10, children 6-10 或 children 6-10 years of age，何者正確呢？

Answer

在指某人的特定年齡時，aged 是個常用的字，它是形容詞，意為「（某人）……歲的」，如 A woman aged 50 has given birth to twins. （一名 50 歲婦女產下了一對雙胞胎。）；They've got two children, aged 3 and 7. （他們有兩個孩子，一個 3 歲，一個 7 歲。）從上面的例句可知，視年齡資料對該人物是否必要而定，aged 前面的逗點可有可無。

然而，除 aged 外，在表示「（某人）……歲的」意思時，也可使用當名詞用的 age（單數）或 ages（複數），亦即 aged 可用 age 或 ages 來替換，如 A woman age 50 has given birth to twins.；They've got two children, ages 3 and 7.；Men ages between 18 and 35 are most at risk from violent crime. （18 至 35 歲之間的男性最容易遭遇暴力犯罪的危險。）同樣地，age 或 ages 前面的逗點可有可無。此

外，我們亦可使用片語 "years of age"（注意：這裡的 age 不可用複數且其前沒有冠詞）來表達相同的意思，如 Men between 18 and 35 years of age are most at risk from violent crime. 或 Men from 18 to 35 years of age are most at risk from violent crime.。

至於「在（某人）……歲時」的意思則用 "at age/ages" 或 "at the age/ages of" 來表達，如 He died at age 80.（他 80 歲逝世。）；She entered Parliament at the age of 26.（她 26 歲時成為國會議員。）；The aim of this study was to explore how prenatal drug exposure (PDE) and caregiving environment relate to cognitive, academic, and behavioral performance at ages 6 and 7.（本研究的目的在探討產前藥物使用情況及照護環境與 6 歲和 7 歲時認知、學術和行為表現的關係。）*The New Fowler's Modern English Usage* 一書指出，at age/ages 是美式英語的用法，而 at the age/ages of 是英式英語的用法，但從實際的應用情況來看，這項區分似乎矯枉過正了，不必當真。再者，在 at age/ages 或 at the age/ages of 中，視所要表達的意思而定，at 可換成其他介系詞，如 By age 6, a child is able to cut softer foods with a knife and is able to tie his or her own shoes.（小孩子到了 6 歲就能用刀子切比較柔軟的食物且能自己繫鞋帶。）；Men between the ages of 18 and 35 are most at risk from violent crime.。

最後，值得一提的是，aged 當形容詞用時，除了「（某人）……歲的」意思外，還意為「年老的」，如 an aged man（老翁）；He helped take care of his aged grandfather.（他幫助照料年邁的祖父。）必須注意的是，意為「（某人）……歲的」aged 為單音節 [edʒd]，而意為「年老的」aged 為兩個音節 [ˈedʒɪd]。此外，aged 亦是當動詞用的 age 的過去式和過去分詞，這個字也是單音節，意為「（使）變老」，如 After his illness he aged quickly.（他病後老得很快。）；Since her husband's death, she has aged considerably.（自從她丈夫去世後，她老了很多。）

004 Question

在 I want to invite all of them. 這句中，all 後面的 of 可以省略嗎？

Answer

不可以！大多數人可能都認為，由於 all of + 名詞時，of 可以省略 (both of 和 half of 的情況亦然)，因此在所有 all of 的句型或用法中，都可以將 of 省略，非也！ 這僅適用於 all of 後接 the, our, your, this, those, his, her 等限定詞、再接名詞的情況，若是接 us, you, them, it, him 和 her 等（受格）代名詞，那麼 of 就不能省略，否則就大錯特錯了。例如：

▶ **All of you** must go there. （你們所有人都要去那裡。）→（○）正確。
▶ I want to invite **all of them**. →（○）正確。（我想邀請他們全部。）
▶ A: Where is my cake? （我的蛋糕哪裡去了？）
   B: I've eaten **all it**. →（×）錯誤。
   （我把它全部吃光了。）－ all it 須改為 all of it 才對。

有人可能會質疑，在 All you need is a good night's sleep.（你所需要的不過是晚上好好睡一覺。）這句中，all 跟 you 之間不是沒有 of 嗎？ 這也是不明就裡的說法。在此句中，all 為代名詞，而 you need 為省略關代 that 的關係子句，修飾 all，不可混為一談。

現在我們就來詳細說明 all 的用法，以免掛一漏萬、瞎子摸象，似是而非。All 可用作限定詞 （determiner，或者說形容詞）、前置限定詞 （pre-determiner）、代名詞或副詞。

All 用作限定詞時後接不可數名詞或複數名詞。例如：

▶ The mother had given up **all** hope. （這位母親已放棄所有希望。）
▶ **All** students hate exams. （學生都討厭考試。）－這是泛指所有學生。

all 用作前置限定詞時後接 the, our, your, this, those, his, her 等中間限定詞 （central determiners）。在此用法中，all 亦可用 all of 來代替，反過來說，只有這種句型才適用上述可以省略 of 的情況。再者，在「all (of) + 中間限定詞 + 名詞」的句型中，若名詞為不可數名詞，則動詞用單數，若名詞為複數名詞，則動詞用複數。例如：

- ▶ **All (of) the students** are coming to the party.（這些學生全部都會來參加聚會。）－特指大家正在談論的那些學生。
- ▶ They lost **all (of) their money**.（他們把所有的錢都輸掉了。）
- ▶ **All (of) the money** is lost.（所有的錢都弄丟了。）－動詞用單數。
- ▶ **All (of) the students** have gone.（所有的學生都走了。）－動詞用複數。

職是之故，下列兩句可明顯看出文法錯誤：

- ▶ I want to buy **all of books**.（我想購買全部的書。）－ books 前面少了中間限定詞 the, these 或 those。→（×）錯誤。
- ▶ **All of divers** returned safely.（所有潛水員都安全回來了。）－ divers 前面少了中間限定詞 the。→（×）錯誤。

all 用作代名詞時不接 of，如 I hope all goes well.（我希望一切順利。），但若與 us, you, them, it, him 和 her 等代名詞連用，則須有 of，如上述。再者，用作代名詞的 all 亦可置於句子的主詞之後、接在受格代名詞之後以及置於助動詞、語氣（或情態）助動詞或 be 動詞之後。例如：

- ▶ These houses **all** belong to that billionaire.（這些房子全部都屬於那位億萬富翁所有。）
- ▶ I want to invite them **all**.（我想邀請他們全部。）
- ▶ The author's books had **all** been sold.（那位作家的書全部賣完了。）
- ▶ You can **all** relax.（你們都可以放鬆了。）
- ▶ The students are **all** late.（這些學生全部遲到。）

此外，用作代名詞的 all 也可置於關係子句之前。由於 all 是不定代名詞（indefinite pronoun），因此關代只能用 that，但 that 通常省略。例如：

- ▶ **All** Teresa's asking for is a little respect.（泰瑞莎要的不過是一點點尊重而已。）
- ▶ That's **all** I know about it.（那是我所知道的全部。）

all 用作副詞時置於形容詞、副詞或介詞之前。例如：

- ▶ The classroom suddenly went **all** dark.（教室裡突然一片漆黑。）
- ▶ This is an **all** new hi-tech microwave oven.（這是一種全新的高科技微波爐。）
- ▶ It doesn't sound **all** that good.（事情聽起來不太好。）
- ▶ Professor Liao is **all** for my suggestion.（廖教授完全贊成我的建議。）

Excercise
綜 合 練 習

I. 填空題

❶ _____ (my/parents/of/both) like my girlfriend.
（我父母兩人都很喜歡我女朋友。）

❷ He is _____ (only/child/an).
（他是獨生子。）

❸ Boys and girls _____ are called teenagers.
（13到18歲的男孩和女孩被稱作青少年／女。）

❹ He _____ a lot in these years.
（這幾年他老了很多。）

❺ _____ (All of divers/ All of the divers) returned safely.
（所有潛水員都安全回來了。）

❻ Saying you love me is _____ (all/all of) I ask of you.
（我所要的一切只不過是說你愛我。）

II. 中翻英

❶ 我很喜歡你煮的菜，才怪呢！

_____

❷ 他愛她，才不呢！

_____

III. 二選一

❶ ☐ He spends all his salary within four or five days of receiving it.
  ☐ He spends his all salary within four or five days of receiving it.
  （他在領到薪水後的四、五天內就把它全部花光。）

❷ ☐ I want to buy all of books.

☐ I want to buy all of these books.

（我想購買全部的書。）

❸ ☐ I have known him since the age of 12.

☐ I have known him since age of 12.

（我從十二歲起就認識他了。）

Answer

I. 填空題

❶ Both of my parents

❷ an only child

❸ between 13 and 18 years of age

❹ aged

❺ All of the divers

❻ all

II. 中翻英

❶ I love the dishes you made, not!

❷ He loves her, not!

III. 二選一

❶ 第一句正確

❷ 第二句正確

❸ 第一句正確

NOTE

Chapter2
你的英文，用對了嗎？

—— 片語篇 ——

001 Question

the creation of man是「創造人」還是「人的創造」呢？

Answer

許多人對「NP1 + of + NP2」這種俯拾即是的結構（NP為 noun phrase「名詞片語」的縮寫，但事實上，英文的NP包括了名詞片語、名詞和代名詞）都想當然耳地把它們翻譯為「NP2的NP1」，如the legs of the table譯為「桌子的腳」（桌腳）。然而，這種結構並沒有這麼簡單，如the love of God表面上的意思是「上帝的愛」，但其實它有兩個不同的意思：一為 Our love for God－We love God.（我們對上帝的愛），另一為God's love for us－God loves us.（上帝對我們的愛。）

由上述可知，「NP of NP」結構可能只有殆無疑義的單一意思（如the legs of the table），也可能有模稜兩可的雙重意思（如 the love of God）。因此，當我們碰到這種結構時必須判斷它是屬於何者，以免「會錯意」了。一般而言，若of左右的兩個NP同時兼備順序（由左至右）的動詞受詞關係與逆序（由右至左）的主詞動詞關係，就會產生雙義。of右邊的NP必須是人或動物才具有做動作（當主詞）或接受動作（當受詞）的能力，而左邊的NP則必須是兼有動詞內涵的名詞型態，才能施動作於他人。當同一結構同時出現這兩種情況時，「NP of NP」就會產生兩個不同的意思。所以，在寫作時必須注意這一點，以免意思被誤解。

若右NP沒有做動作的能力，亦即該NP為非人或非動物，那麼這結構就只有順序的動詞受詞關係，沒有逆序的主詞動詞關係，這就只有一個意思，如love of nature（對大自然的愛；愛大自然）。又若左NP只是名詞，無動作的含意，就不可有受詞，因此只有逆序的主詞動詞關係，沒有順序的動詞受詞關係，同樣地也只有單義，如the works of Shakespeare（莎士比亞的作品）。再者，若右NP不能接受左 NP 的內含動作，但卻可對左 NP 施以動作，那麼亦只能產生主詞動詞關係（單義），如 the creations of Shakespeare（莎士比亞的創作／作品 ）。

至於問題中所提到的 "the creation of man"，若按「NP2 的 NP1」的翻譯方式，

則意為「人的創造」。由於名詞creation是動詞create的衍生詞，man具有做create這個動作的能力；又按宗教的信仰，man又有接受create的說法（上帝創造人），因而這一短語兼具兩種語意結構，若無上下文的判斷，無法確定真正的意思：

to create man －（上帝）創造人
Man creates something － 人類創造某物

不過，若右NP為非人或非動物，則不產生主詞動詞關係，只有動詞受詞關係，如the creation of the world（創造世界，即to create the world）、the loss of energy（精力的消耗，即to lose energy消耗精力）。或者如上述，若右NP不能接受左NP的內含動作，但卻可對左NP施以動作，那麼只能產生主詞動詞關係，也是只有一個意思，如the creations of Shakespeare（莎士比亞的創作／作品）。

「NP1 + of + NP2」結構在英文中應用得非常廣泛和普遍，但由於這種結構具有多種語意功能及語法意義，因此也是一種很難精準掌握的結構。除上述外，其他比較常見的語意及語法功能還有：

同位格關係（NP1＝NP2）：the City of New York（紐約市）－New York is the city；the art of painting（繪畫藝術）－painting is the art：the problem of unemployment（失業問題）－unemployment is the problem。

主屬關係（NP1 屬於 NP2）：the publishing industry of Taipei（台北的出版業）；the children of the family（那家的孩子）。

主屬關係（NP1屬於NP2－某人屬於某地）：the intelligentsia of Paris（巴黎的知識份子）；the Chen of Kaohsiung（高雄陳）。

修飾關係（NP1修飾NP2）：a glass of beer（一杯啤酒）；two pounds of sugar（兩磅糖）；three kilometers of bad road（三公里難以行駛的路）；ten years of age（十歲）。

修飾關係（NP2修飾NP1）：a box of wood（木箱）；a house of stone（石屋）；a girl of ten（十歲的女孩）；a matter of importance（重要事件－an important matter）；a man of ability（有能力的人－an able man）。

Question

「留學生」的英文怎麼說呢？

Answer

這必須從兩方面來考慮。如果是本國到外國求學的留學生，叫做students overseas；如果是外國到本國求學的留學生，則叫做overseas/foreign students或students from overseas。

從上述可知，雖然本國和外國留學生都使用overseas和students這兩個字，但它們前後位置的不同，意思卻有天壤之別，千萬別搞錯。

003 **Question**

無生命名詞的所有格須使用of結構，而有生命名詞的所有格則可使用of結構或's，但在無生命的時間名詞後面使用's的情況屢見不鮮且合乎文法，請問還有哪些無生命名詞也可以這樣用呢？

Answer

根據英文文法規則，無生命名詞的所有格大多使用of結構，如The collar of the shirt is dirty.（這件襯衫的領子髒了。）所以The shirt's collar is dirty.是錯的；而有生命名詞（包括人和動物）的所有格則可使用of結構或's，如John's collar is dirty./The collar of John is dirty.（約翰的衣領髒了。）或The dog's collar is dirty./The collar of the dog is dirty.（狗的頸圈髒了。）不過，就有生命名詞而言，我們通常使用's而比較少用of結構。

雖然無生命名詞的所有格大多使用of結構，但許多無生命名詞就跟有生命名詞一樣可使用of結構或's。它們可分成下列四類，前三類的界定明確，第四類的界定則比較鬆散難以掌握：

① 地名（亦即專有名詞）

Africa's modernization（非洲的現代化），England's industrialization（英格蘭的工業化），Taiwan's history（台灣的歷史；台灣史），Taipei's problems（台北的問題）。

② 地方場所（亦即表示地方場所的普通名詞）

the earth's center（地球中心），the nation's debts（國債），the city's recreation areas（這城市的娛樂區），the world's problems（世界的問題），the moon's surface（月球表面）。

③ 時間／距離／價值／重量名詞

a year's wait（一年的等待），the week's proceeds（本週的收入），today's young people（今日的年輕人），a day's work（一天的工作），this evening's storm（今晚的暴風雨），5 days' leave（五天的休假），3 years' salary（三年的薪水）。a cable's length（電纜的長度），two hours' walk/flight/drive（兩小時的步行或路程/飛行/車程），a dollar's worth（of apples）（價值一元的蘋果），two tons' weight（兩噸重）。

④ 其他

包含許多不同的名詞，它們似乎只有一項共通點，那就是它們都是表示與人類事物有密切關係的概念：at arm's length（保持一定的距離），the story's main theme（故事的主題），the car's engine（汽車引擎），the car's history（汽車史），the ship's captain（船長），the wine's quality（這葡萄酒的品質），the book's importance（這本書的重要性），the machine's function（這部機器的功能），the brain's function（腦部的功能），a word's structure（字的結構），science's influence（科學的影響），the treaty's signing（條約的簽署）。由於這一類包含許多各式各樣的名詞，因此有關無生命名詞何時可以使用's所有格形式的問題相當棘手，只能仰賴平時多看多讀來累積經驗，以免用時方恨少或使用錯誤。

最後值得一提的是，許多本身不允許使用's的無生命名詞，若以it來代替就可以了，亦即使用it的所有格its。例如：

▶ The assumption is unjustified, but its basis is very clear.（這項假設不合理，但它的基礎很清楚。）

不過，如果把上例中的basis改為 reason，那麼我們只能乖乖地使用the reason of the assumption，而不能使用its reason，因為its reason是等於the reason for it而不

是the reason of it－上例中的 its basis = the basis of it。

004 Question

英文中，一群魚、一群蜜蜂或甚至一群牛的「群」都有不同的用字，是否可以提供這方面的資料作參考呢？

Answer

在列出這些「群」的用字之前，我們要先說明若干與這些集合名詞有關的用法和文法觀念。有些集合名詞的使用場合或對象有非常嚴格的限制，如pride只能用來指獅子的一群，school只能指魚及其他水生動物的一群；其他集合名詞（如herd）的應用則比較普遍。

此外，集合名詞的主要問題（單複數問題）也是大家必須注意的重點。

❶「物」的集合名詞

「物」的集合名詞，如：silverware/cutlery（餐具）、software（軟體）、hardware（硬體）、baggage/luggage（行李）、furniture（家具）、underwear（內衣褲）等等－都是接單數動詞，如My luggage is missing.（我的行李遺失了。）

❷「人」的集合名詞

至於「人」的集合名詞，clergy（神職人員）、folk（人們）、police（警察）等都是接複數動詞，如The clergy are up in arms about it.（神職人員對此很不滿。）；但audience（觀眾）、committee（委員會）、orchestra（管弦樂團）、jury（陪審團）等則可接單數或複數動詞，一般而言，它們作總稱時使用單數動詞，指所有成員時使用複數動詞，如The orchestra was playing.（管弦樂團正在演奏。）；The orchestra have all gone home.（管弦樂團的團員都回家了。）英式英語傾向於視audience等集合名詞為複數，而美式英語則視其為單數，如The government are/is discussing the proposal.（政府正在討論這項提議。）

在英文中，不同動物的「一群」往往有不同的講法或寫法；不過，有些動物的「群」可能不只一個用字。茲將手邊的資料臚列如下（依動物字母排列），供大家參考：

an army of ants	一群螞蟻
a herd of antelopes	一群羚羊
a shrewdness of apes	一群猿
a pace of asses	一群驢子
a cete of badgers	一群獾
a battery of barracudas	一群梭魚
a sloth of bears	一群熊
a colony of beavers	一群海狸
a swarm of bees	一群蜜蜂
a singular of boars	一群野豬
a herd of buffaloes	一群水牛
a caravan of camels	一群駱駝
a clowder of cats	一群貓
a drove of cattle	一群牛
a brood of chickens	一窩雞
a chattering of choughs	一群紅嘴山鴉
a covert of coots	一群白冠雞
a bask of crocodiles	一群鱷魚
a murder of crows	一群烏鴉
a herd of deer	一群鹿
a pack of dogs	一群狗
a school of dolphins	一群海豚
a dole of doves	一群鴿子
a team of ducks	一群鴨子
a convocation of eagles	一群老鷹
a parade of elephants	一群象
a gang of elks	一群麋鹿
a business of ferrets	一群雪貂
a shoal of fish	一群魚
a skulk of foxes	一群狐狸
an army of frogs	一群青蛙
a gaggle of geese	一群鵝

a tribe of goats	一群山羊
a cloud of grasshoppers	一群蚱蜢
a bazaar of guillemots	一群海鳩
a husk of hares	一群野兔
a cast of hawks	一群老鷹
an array of hedgehogs	一群刺蝟
a brood of hens	一窩母雞
a siege of herons	一群鷺
a bloat of hippopotamuses	一群河馬
a string of horses	一群馬
a pack of hounds	一群獵犬
a troop of kangaroos	一群袋鼠
a kindle of kittens	一窩小貓
an exaltation of larks	一群雲雀
a leap of leopards	一群美洲豹
a pride of lions	一群獅子
a plague of locusts	一群蝗蟲
a tittering of magpies	一群喜鵲
a sord of mallards	一群綠頭鴨
a labor of moles	一群鼴鼠
a troop of monkeys	一群猴子
a barren of mules	一群騾子
a watch of nightingales	一群夜鶯
a family of otters	一群水獺
a parliament of owls	一群貓頭鷹
a pandemonium of parrots	一群鸚鵡
a covey of partridges	一群鷓鴣
a muster of peacocks	一群孔雀
a rookery of penguins	一群企鵝
a nye of pheasants	一群松雞
a litter of pigs	一窩豬
a congregation of plovers	一群千鳥

a school of porpoises	一群海豚
a bevy of quails	一群鵪鶉
a bury of rabbits	一群兔子
a colony of rats	一群老鼠
an unkindness of ravens	一群渡鴉
a crash of rhinoceros	一群犀牛
a building of rooks	一群白嘴鴉
a pod of seals	一群海豹
a flock of sheep	一群綿羊
a walk of snipe	一群鷸
a host of sparrows	一群麻雀
a dray of squirrels	一群松鼠
a flight of swallows	一群燕子
a mutation of thrushes	一群畫眉鳥
an ambush of tigers	一群老虎
a knot of toads	一群蟾蜍
a rafter of turkeys	一群火雞
a turn of turtles	一群海龜
a gam of whales	一群鯨魚
a rout of wolves	一群狼
a fall of woodcocks	一群山鷸
a descent of woodpeckers	一群啄木鳥
a zeal of zebras	一群斑馬

005 Question

this kind of dog和this kind of dogs何者正確呢？

Answer

根據正規文法，前者才正確，後者是不對的。但問題其實並沒有這麼簡單，因為除

kind外，manner, sort, style, type和way等名詞在「this/that，these/those或 any/many/all + kind, manner, sort, style, type或way + of +名詞」的用法中一直存在著許多問題。

書面的美式英語以及大多數保守的美國評論都堅持單數名詞 kind, manner, sort, style, type 和 way 必須用單數指示形容詞或限定詞來修飾(this/that/any kind, manner, sort, style, type 或 way)，而且其後必須接of +單數名詞，如this kind of dog, that manner of chatter, any sort of dilemma, this type of book, this way of writing。再者，當kind, manner, sort, style, type和way為複數時，其前的指示形容詞或限定詞必須為複數，而且其後必須接of +複數可數名詞，如these kinds of studies, those sorts of poems, all types of airplanes。但當of後面的名詞為不可數名詞（物質名詞和抽象名詞）時，這些名詞可以是單數，如all sorts of gravel（所有碎石種類，即各種碎石－gravel為不可數名詞），these ways of thinking（這些思考方式）。

然而，雖然書面美式英語的標準有上述要求，但英式英語以及美國口語和非正式用法仍出現許多不同的單複數組合，如these kind of men。儘管這些組合都不合文法，但在口語中卻相當常見。因此，我們建議，在書面和正式用法中，最好遵守上述合乎語法的要求。此外，儘管 "any kind of books" 不合語法，但 "books of any kind" 卻是標準英語，寫作時可以多加利用。

最後，值得注意的是，在「this/that，these/those或any/many/all + kind, manner, sort, style, type或way +of +名詞」的結構中，名詞前不可加冠詞。

006 Question

the Great Wall of China和the Tower of Pisa等世界著名奇景、古蹟或地標中為何使用of，而不使用所有格呢？它們可不可以寫成China's Great Wall和Pisa's Tower呢？

Answer

不行。of結構可用來表示所有關係，尤其是表示無生命的東西的「所有」關係，如the edge of the desk（書桌的邊緣）。然而，當of所構成的介系詞片語被用作名詞之後的修飾語時，它也是在表示地點和起源，與法文的介系詞 "de"（有時縮寫

為 d'）表示地點和起源的情形非常相似，如 Jeanne d'Arc 或 Joan of Arc（聖女貞德），不可說成或寫成 Arc's Joan。

雖然我們可以談論China's Great Wall（中國的萬里長城），但這個結構體的英文名稱卻是 "the Great Wall of China"。英文名稱採用這種of結構的其他奇景、古蹟或地標還包括the Great Pyramid of Giza（埃及吉薩金字塔）、the Rock of Gibraltar（直布羅陀岩山）、the Statue of Liberty（自由女神像）和the Tower of Pisa（比薩斜塔）等等。

007 Question

studies program也是 study program的複數嗎？

Answer

不是。大多數人可能都會將study program和studies program視為同樣的東西，也就是「研究計畫」。其實不然，僅study program才是中文的「研究計畫」，而它的複數是study programs。

studies program中的studies是一個複數形的字，意思是「學業；課程；學科」，並非「研究」，所以studies program意為「課程」，如David wants to continue his studies.（大衛想繼續他的學業。）；business/environmental studies（商業／環境課程）；The college has no queer studies department nor any official queer studies program.（這所大學沒有酷兒學系，也沒有任何正式的酷兒研究課程。）

一般而言，在「名詞＋名詞」的複合名詞中，第一個名詞通常用單數，但也有一些例外的情況，而這些特例大多是第一個名詞原本就是複數形。除studies program外，常見的第一個名詞為複數形的複合名詞還有：

the foreign languages department（外語系）
sports meeting（運動會）
talks table（談判桌）
goods train（貨車）
customs papers（海關文件）
clothes brush（衣刷）

a total of...和the total of...有甚麼不同（所接的be動詞和語意）呢？能否説明得詳細一點呢？

Answer

❶ a/the total of

a total of後接複數名詞，而該複數名詞是句子的主詞，換言之，a total of接複數動詞（be動詞就是are或 were），而the total of也是接複數名詞，但句子的主詞卻是the total，而不是該複數名詞，所以the total of 接單數動詞（be動詞就是is 或was）。兩者的語意並無差異且皆可用in total, in all, all told等同義的片語來替換。

例如：

> ▶ **A total of** thirty days were spent on the trip.
>   = **The total of** thirty days was spent on the trip.
>   = **In total**, thirty days were spent on the trip.
>   = **In all**, thirty days were spent on the trip.
>   = **All told**, thirty days were spent on the trip.
>   （這趟旅行總共花了三十天。）

顯然地，a total of和the total of的文法概念與a number of和the number of如出一轍。儘管一些文法學者認為a total of是贅字，但它卻可用來避免句子的開頭使用數字。

例如：

> ▶ **A total of** 432 people applied for the three jobs.（總共有 432 人申請這三份工作。）

❷ total 當動詞

total這個字本身可當動詞、形容詞和名詞用。當動詞用時，total意為「總計為；總共為；共達」。

例如：

> ▶ His earnings from car racing now **total** over three million dollars.（他的賽車收入現在總計超過三百萬元。）

但它還有一個俚語意思也相當常用，那就是「（車輛）撞毀，撞爛，完全毀壞」。例如：

▶ They weren't hurt in the accident, but the car was **totaled**. （他們在車禍中沒有受傷，但車子全毀了。）

▶ Her new car was **totalled** in the accident. （她的新車在車禍中撞毀了。）

total的過去式和過去分詞都是totalled或totaled，而現在分詞為totalling或 totaling－前者為英式英語拼法，後者為美式英語拼法。在英文中，對於一個音節以上的字，若其最後一個字母為子音字母，尤其是-l，英式英語通常（並非總是）重複此字母，但美式英語通常不重複，如cancel, total, travel等。

❸ total 當形容詞
當形容詞用時，total僅能用在名詞之前，意為「總共的；全部的」及用於強調的「完全的；絕對的」。
例如：

▶ The **total** cost of the project came to over three million dollars. （工程總費用超過三百萬元。）

▶ The event was a **total** failure. （活動徹底失敗。）

▶ Why on earth would you let a **total** stranger into the house? （你到底為什麼會讓一個完全陌生的人進入屋內呢？）

然而，某些英美人士反對將 total 當作absolute, complete或utter的同義詞，用來表示強調的「完全的；絕對的」之意。

❹ total 當名詞
當名詞用的total可與combined, cumulative, estimated, final, grand, overall, sum以及high, huge, large, low, small等形容詞連用。

例如：

▶ His three goals give him a grand **total** of 30 for the season. （他的三次進球使他本賽季的進球總數達到 30 個。）

▶ The **sum total** of my knowledge of astrology is not impressive. （我對占星學的知識乏善可陳。）

然而，sum total的用法也有爭議，大多數文法學者都認為total在這個片語中是贅字，違反英文簡潔的原則。

Excercise 綜合練習

I. 填空題

❶ I am going to Paris to study fashion design. I will be a _____.
（我要到巴黎唸時裝設計，我將成為一名海外留學生。）

❷ I will guide the _____ in our school to visit Taipei.
（我將要帶領本校的留學生參觀台北。）

❸ What's the meaning of _____ (the art's work/the work of art) in the age of mechanical reproduction?
（在機器複製的年代，藝術作品的意義是什麼呢？）

❹ Please tell me _____ (the main theme of the story/the story's main theme).
（請告訴我這故事的主旨。）

❺ The silverware _____ (is/are) expensive.
（這套餐具很貴。）

❻ I saw _____ (a school/a family) of fish.
（我看到一群魚。）

❼ _____ (These ways of thinking/This way of thinking) can be wrong.
（這些思考方式可能是錯的。）

❽ _____ (These types of books/This type of book) sells like a hot cake.
（這種書很暢銷。）

❾ I would like to visit _____ (the Great Wall of China/China's Great Wall) someday.
（有朝一日我要去看看中國萬里長城。）

❿ Have you ever seen _____ (Giza's Pyramid/the Great Pyramid of Giza)?
（你看過埃及吉薩金字塔嗎？）

⓫ Here comes the _____ (good train/goods train).
（貨車來了。）

⑫ Have you prepared the _____ (custom papers/customs papers)?
（你已經準備好海關文件了嗎？）

⑬ _____ (The total/A total of) 100,000 people joined the parade.
（總共有10萬人參加這場遊行。）

⑭ The car was _____ (totaled/broken)! Is the driver still alive?

（整部車都被撞毀了，駕駛還活著呢？）

II. 排序題

❶ The/men/of/women/of/the/invention/greatest/virtue/is.
（女人的道德是男人最偉大的發明。）

_____

❷ Love/time/the/fool/is/of/not.
（愛情不是時間的玩物。）

_____

III.二選一

❶ ☐ The legs of the table are rotten.
☐ The table's legs are rotten.
（桌子的腳已經爛掉了。）

❷ ☐ There are many troops of wolves around here.
☐ There are many herds of wolves around here.
（這邊有很多群狼。）

❸ ☐ This kind of dog is large.
☐ This kind of dogs is large.
（這種狗很大。）

❹ ☐ My dream is seeing the Statue of Liberty.
☐ My dream is seeing the Liberty Statue.
（我的夢想是看到自由女神像。）

5 ☐ When's the sport meeting?

☐ When's the sports meeting?

（運動會何時舉行呢？）

Answer

I. 填空題

1 student overseas

2 overseas/foreign students

3 the work of art

4 the main theme of the story; the story's main theme （兩者皆可）

5 is

6 a school

7 These ways of thinking

8 This type of book

9 the Great Wall of China

10 the Great Pyramid of Giza

11 goods train

12 customs papers

13 A total

14 totaled

II. 排序題

1 The virtue of women is the greatest invention of men.

2 Love is not the fool of time.

III. 二選一

1 第一句正確

2 第二句正確

3 第一句正確

4 第一句正確

5 第二句正確

Chapter 2 你的英文，用對了嗎？ | **片語篇**　　**Unit 02** 介系詞片語

001 Question

as such和such as有何不同呢？

Answer

這兩個片語看起來很像，但意思卻截然不同。**as such**有兩個意思，第一個意思比較難解釋，大概是「以此身份」、「就其身份而言」的意思，係用來代替其前所提過的名詞，以避免重複。請看下面三句：

▶ I'm an English teacher, and **because** I'm an English teacher I hate to see grammar mistakes.

= I'm an English teacher, and **as** an English teacher I hate to see grammar mistakes.

= I'm an English teacher, and **as such** I hate to see grammar mistakes.

（我是英文老師，因為我是英文老師，所以我不喜歡見到文法錯誤。）

這三個句子的意思一樣，但以第3句最簡潔，因為它用such來代替句中的第二個an English teacher，避免了第1和第2句出現兩次an English teacher的重複情況，合乎英文高度講究的「當省則省」要求。下面再來看兩個類似的例句：

▶ She's a famous singer, and **as such** she has made a lot of money.（她是名歌星，以此身份她已賺了很多錢。）

▶ The film was a romance, and **as such** it had the usual happy ending.（這部影片是愛情片，這種片子通常有圓滿的結局。）

as such的第二個意思是「就其真正的意義來說」。例如：

▶ The shop doesn't sell books **as such**, but it does sell magazines and newspapers.（就書的真正意義來說，這家店沒有賣書，但有賣雜誌和報紙。）－雜誌和報紙跟書相似，但它們不是真正的書。

▶ He isn't Taiwanese **as such**, but he's spent most of his life here. （就台灣人的真正意義而言，他不是台灣人，但他的大半生都在台灣度過。）

such as就簡單多了，它意為「像……之類；例如」（like; for example），但such as和like或for example的用法並不相同，需特別注意。現僅舉一例來說明such as的用法：

▶ Many countries in Europe, **such as** France and Germany, use Euros. （歐洲有許多國家，如法國和德國，都採用歐元。）

002 Question

英文中有不少像as poor as the church mouse這種由as ... as ...所構成的片語，是否可以多舉一些例子作為參考資料呢？

Answer

這種由 "as ... as ..." 所構成的片語（第一個as之後接形容詞，第二個as之後接名詞）是英文修辭手段或比喻說法（rhetorical devices or figures of speech）之一的「明喻或直喻」（simile－注意simile這個字的發音是[ˋsɪməˌlɪ]，與smile之發音和拼字都不相同）的應用。simile這種比喻方式在日常生活的談話中經常可以聽到，它是用一件事物去比喻另一事物，通常以like或as來引導。然而，在此我們僅列出使用as做開頭的片語，而不涉及使用like的simile（如a voice like thunder, teeth like pearls, to run like the wind等）；另外，simile與其他修辭工具或比喻說法－尤其是metaphor（隱喻或暗喻）－之差異，由於非三言兩語所能述盡，在此亦略過不談。

下表所列幾可算是集 "as ... as ..." 片語之大成，將是日後極具價值的參考資料。這些片語雖皆可譯為「像……一樣……」，但若有相對應的中文成語，還是以後者為佳。

英文	中文	關鍵字釋義
as bald as a coot	童山濯濯	coot：白冠雞
as black as coal/soot	漆黑，極黑	soot：煤灰；煤煙

as blind as a bat	有眼無珠	
as bold as brass	厚顏無恥；膽大包天，膽大妄為	
as bright as a button	聰明伶俐	
as brown as a berry	褐如漿果	
as busy as a bee	非常忙碌	
as clean as a new pin/a whistle	乾乾淨淨，非常整潔，光滑潔淨	
as clear as a bell/crystal	非常清楚，清晰明瞭	
as close as an oyster	守口如瓶	
as cold as ice	冷若冰霜	
as common as muck	粗俗不堪	muck：糞，堆肥；品質低劣的東西
as cool as a cucumber	泰然自若；老神在在；冷靜鎮定	
as dead as a doornail/the dodo	死定了的，完全死了的，被徹底廢棄或遺忘的；不存在的；早已過時的	doornail：（門上用作裝飾的）大頭釘子；dodo：過時之物
as deaf as a post	全聾	
as drunk as a lord	爛醉如泥，酩酊大醉	lord：統治者；君主；貴族
as dry as a bone/dust	十分乾燥的，乾透的；口渴極了，口渴得要死；枯燥乏味	
as dull as ditchwater	枯燥乏味	
as easy as A.B.C.	非常容易，輕而易舉，非常簡單	
as fat as a pig	肥胖如豬，肥得像頭豬	
as fit as a fiddle/a flea	身體健康，精神飽滿，神采奕奕	
as flat as a pancake	非常平坦	
as free as a bird/air	自由自在	
as fresh as a daisy	精力充沛；精神煥發；充滿青春活力	daisy：雛菊

as gentle as a lamb	溫順的，溫和的	
as good as gold	很乖，循規蹈矩	
as good as new	完好如新	
as green as grass	幼稚的，初出茅廬，沒有經驗的	
as guilty as sin	罪惡深重	
as happy as a sandboy/Larry	興高采烈，非常高興	as happy as Larry 為澳洲俚語
as hard as nails/iron	鐵石心腸，冷酷無情；堅硬如鐵	
as heavy as lead	十分沉重，非常重	
as helpless as a newborn babe	無助的；依賴他人的；完全不能照顧自己的	
as honest as the day is long	非常誠實	
as hungry as a horse	非常餓	
as keen as mustard	很熱心的，相當感興趣的	mustard：芥末；（俚語）熱情
as large as life	跟原物一樣大；體態容貌完整無缺；千真萬確，不容置疑	
as light as a feather	輕如鴻毛，非常輕	
as like as two peas (in a pod)	一模一樣	
as mad as a hatter/a March hare	瘋狂的，精神錯亂的，瘋瘋癲癲的（像三月交配期的兔子一樣瘋野）	hatter是「愛麗絲夢遊仙境」（Alice in Wonderland）故事中那位說話沒頭沒腦的瘋狂製帽匠，因此放在片語中引申為瘋狂的意思。
as mute as a fish	噤若寒蟬；默不作聲	
as nutty as a fruitcake	腦袋有毛病；精神不正常；傻呼呼	fruitcake：水果蛋糕

as obstinate as a mule	十分頑固的，非常固執的	
as old as the hills	十分古老的，非常老舊的	
as patient as Job	很有耐心的	聖經裡有個人叫Job，他就是約伯，是希伯來族的族長，在英語中又可引申為「極有耐心的人」。
as plain as a pikestaff	非常清楚；一清二楚；顯而易見；極為明顯	pikestaff：長矛柄
as playful as a kitten	愛玩耍的，愛嬉戲的	
as pleased as Punch	非常高興；興高采烈；樂不可支	Punch 指的是英國家喻戶曉的滑稽木偶劇《潘趣與茱迪》(Punch-and-Judy) 中的男主角Punch。
as poor as the church mouse	一貧如洗	
as proud as a peacock	非常驕傲	
as pure as the driven snow	純真無邪，玉潔冰清	
as quick as lightning	轉瞬間，快如閃電，非常快	
as quiet as a mouse	非常安靜	
as regular as clockwork	非常有規律	clockwork：鐘錶的機械；發條裝置
as right as rain	非常健康	
as round as a barrel	很圓的	
as safe as houses	十分安全	
as sharp as a needle	很有鑑別力的，異常精明的；非常機敏的	
as sharp as a razor	厲害的；非常鋒利的；機警的	
as sick as a dog	病得很嚴重	
as sick as a parrot	非常失望	
as silent as the grave	寂靜無聲	

as slippery as an eel	滑頭滑腦；奸詐狡猾	
as slow as a snail	慢如蝸牛，慢吞吞	
as sly as a fox	像狐狸般狡猾	
as snug as a bug in a rug	非常舒適，極其安逸	
as sober as a judge	非常嚴肅	
as soft as butter	很柔軟	
as sound as a bell	非常健康；十分健全；狀況極佳	
as steady as a rock	堅若磐石；堅定不移	
as stiff as a poker	（風度、舉止）拘謹；生硬；刻板	
as straight as a die	絕對真實的，非常老實的	
as straight as an arrow	筆直，非常直	
as strong as an ox/a horse	非常強壯	
as sure as eggs is eggs	的的確確，千真萬確，無疑地，肯定地	
as sweet as honey	甜如蜜	
as thick as thieves	親密無間	
as thick as two short planks	非常遲鈍，愚笨的，愚鈍的	plank：木板，厚板
as thin as a rake	瘦骨嶙峋，骨瘦如柴	
as tough as old boots	非常硬的，非常堅強的；（尤指肉）很硬的，很老的，咬不動的	
as ugly as sin	奇醜無比	
as weak as water	身體虛弱；意志薄弱	
as white as a sheet/a ghost	蒼白如紙；（尤指因病或恐懼而）臉色慘白；面無血色	
as white as snow	潔白如雪	
as wise as an owl/Solomon	聰明絕頂/像所羅門一樣智慧過人	所羅門王（聖經人物）被西方認為是世界上最有智慧的人。

003 **Question**

more than和over的用法有何不同呢？

Answer

根據 *The New Fowler's Modern English Usage* 一書，美國的報紙和一些英文用法指南自19世紀中期以來一直有一項根深柢固的慣例，那就是反對在數字前面使用 "over" 來表示「多於……」或「……以上」(more than, in excess of)的意思。反之，除年齡外，在所有數字前面，他們都是使用more than 來表示這項意思。

然而，在英國，在數字前面使用 "over" 並無任何限制且未遭遇任何反對聲浪；換言之，在數字前面使用over或more than來表示「多於……」或「……以上」的意思，都被英國人所接受。不過，無論在英國或北美，在年齡的前面使用over皆無異議。

例如：

▶ You don't look a day **over** forty.
（你看起來最多四十歲。）

▶ She was a little **over** twenty.
（她二十出頭。）

儘管美國新聞界迄今仍沿襲上述慣例，但在平常的談話中，

例如：

▶ There were **over** four thousand runners in last year's marathon.
（去年的馬拉松賽有四千多位跑者參加。）

▶ He's well **over** six feet tall.
（他的身高遠遠超過六呎。）

上述這樣的句子，經常耳聞；然而，在寫作中，最好還是使用 "more than"，至少在美國或針對美國人士時應採用這樣的寫法。

Question

between ... and 和 from ... to 的用法有何不同呢？

Answer

這兩個片語的用法並無不同，但都是固定搭配，不可混合使用。所以，我們可以寫成 "between \$118 and \$176" 或 "from \$118 to \$176"（118至176美元）以及 "from 1993 to 1996" 或 "between 1993 and 1996"（1993至1996），但不可寫成 "between \$118 to \$176" 或 "from 1993 and 1996"。

此外，在 from ... to 中不可使用連字號或破折號來取代 to，所以 He was chair from 1994-98. 是錯的，必須寫成 He was chair from 1994 to 1998.（他在1994至1998年擔任主席。）但在形容詞用法中，使用連字號或破折號來取代 to 是可以的，如 his 1994-98 stint as chair（他在1994至98年的主席任期），her Jan. 10-15 trip to Europe（她 1 月 10 至 15 日的歐洲行。）

Excercise
綜合練習

I. 填空題

1 Children like junk food, _____ (such as/as such) soda, potato chips and hamburgers.

（孩子們喜歡吃垃圾食物，像是汽水、洋芋片還有漢堡。）

2 She is just a kid, _____ (such as/as such) she can't watch this film.

（她只是個孩子，所以她不可以看這個影片。）

3 A: Mom, Tom said I don't need bras because I am as flat as a _____ (plate/pancake).

（媽媽，湯姆說我不需要胸罩，因為我是飛機場。）

B: Honey, there is always someone who likes you and someone who dislikes you. You have to learn the value of yourself in spite of their cruel judgments.

（親愛的，世界上總是會有人喜歡你，也總是會有人不喜歡你，重要的是不論他們如何毒舌評論你，你都要找到自己的價值。）

4 Can love be as steady as a _____ (lead/rock)?

（愛情有可能堅若磐石嗎？）

5 You don't look a day _____ (over/ more than) forty.

（你看起來最多四十歲。）

6 There were _____ (over/more than) forty people in the room.

（這房間裡面有超過四十個人。）

7 The price is between $100 _____ $120.

（這價錢是介於100跟120元之間。）

8 It happened from 1900 _____ 1915.

（那事件發生在 1900 至 1915年期間。）

II. 二選一

1 ☐ The shop doesn't sell books as such, but it does sell magazines and newspapers.

☐ The shop doesn't sell such as books, but it does sell magazines and newspapers.

（就書的真正意義來說，這家店沒有賣書，但有賣雜誌和報紙。）

② ☐ When she opened the gift, she was as sick as a parrot.

☐ When she opened the gift, she was as sick as a dog.

（當她打開禮物的時候，她簡直失望透頂了。）

③ ☐ He is more than 100 kg.

☐ He is over 100 kg.

（他超過100公斤。）

④ ☐ He was the chair from 2008 to 2016.

☐ He was the chair from 2008-2016.

（他在2008至2016年擔任主席。）

Answer

I. 填空題

① such as

② as such

③ pancake

④ rock

⑤ over

⑥ more than

⑦ and

⑧ to

II. 二選一

① 第一句正確

② 第二句正確

③ 第一句正確

④ 第一句正確

001 Question

two and one-half inches和two-and-one-half inches這兩種寫法那一種才正確呢？還是兩者都可以呢？

Answer

根據*Chicago Manual of Style*這本著名修辭書籍裡所寫的 "four and one-eight inches"，我們應該寫成 "two and one-half inches"。CMOS説，在表示「幾又幾分之幾（整數＋分數）」的帶分數時，整數不必用連字號(hyphen)來跟分數結合在一起。

注意：分數無論是單獨存在或是當複合形容詞用，其中間一定要有連字號，如 two-thirds, three-eighths, one-third apple, two-tenths point。這與21到99一定要有連字號的寫法一樣，如twenty-one, ninety-nine。

另外，在此提供幾個與「分數」有關的英文供大家參考：

分數：fraction
假分數：improper fraction
真分數：proper fraction
帶分數：mixed fraction
整數：integer 或 whole number。

002 Question

Nice to meet you和Nice meeting you有何不同呢？

Answer

1 Nice to meet you

(It is) Nice to meet/see you.（很高興認識／見到你。）是剛見面時的寒暄語。你也可以用I'm glad/happy to meet/see you.來表達相同的意思。

2 Nice meeting you

而(It was) Nice meeting/seeing you.則是雙方見了面、交談過後要道別時所説的話，所以其後往往接著説「再見」（Goodbye, Bye-bye, Bye, See ya, cheerio等等－cheerio大多是英國人的説法）或「保重」（Take care）之類的話。

Nice meeting/seeing you.
= My pleasure meeting/seeing you.
= Nice to have met/seen you.

003 Question

in front of和in the front of的意思有很大的不同，前者是指一物在另一物的前面，而後者則指一物在另一物內部的前部，如 There is a desk in front of the chair.（椅子的前面有張書桌。）；There is a desk in the front of the classroom.（教室的前部有張書桌。）英文中像這種同一名詞前面有無定冠詞，意思相差極大的例子一定不少吧？

Answer

針對這問題，筆者去找了一些資料，發現有幾個類似的例子（也許還有更多），兹

160

説明如下：

❶ future

in future：日後，往後，今後

in the future：未來，將來

▶ Try to do better **in future**.（今後要努力做得更好。）

▶ **In future**, make sure you go to school on time.（今後要確定準時上學。）

▶ What will you do **in the future**?（你將來要做什麼？）

▶ We're hoping to move to the United States **in the not too distant future**.（我們希望在不太久的將來搬到美國去住。）

❷ charge

in charge of：主管，負責，看管（含有主動的意味）

in the charge of：在……主管，負責，看管之下（含有被動的意味）

▶ The nurse is **in charge of** the old men.（這位護士負責照料這些老人。）

▶ The old men are **in the charge of** the nurse.（這些老人由這位護士負責照料。）

▶ Who's **in charge of** the department?（誰負責這一部門？）

❸ case

in case of：萬一……發生，如果發生……，要是……，遇到……的時候

in the case of：就……而論，就……來説，至於（這裡 case 意為「情況」、「實例」）

▶ **In case of** fire, ring the bell.（如果發生火災，請速按鈴。）

▶ **In case of** any difficulties, you must consult with your aunt.（萬一碰到困難，你必須跟你阿姨商量。）

▶ Many people want to be famous singers and make a lot of money, but **in the case of** me, it's otherwise.（許多人都想成為名歌手，賺很多錢，但就我而言，情況則不然。）

❹ hospital/school/church/prison

in hospital：住院，在醫院裡接受醫療

in the hospital：在醫院裡，指在醫院這個建築物裡面

注意：美式英語也用in the hospital來表示in hospital的意思（in university和in the university也有同樣的情況）。除hospital外，school, church, market, college, court, prison等字也有類似的用法。當這些名詞前有"the"時，指的是地點、地方、實際的建築物，但用作抽象名詞時，指的則是建築物的功用，說明人在那裡從事相應的活動。

▶ His father is **in hospital**. （他父親在住院。）

▶ "Where is John?" 「約翰去哪裡？」

▶ "He is **in the hospital**. He goes there to see his sick friend." 「他在醫院，他去看他生病的朋友」

▶ I'm a high school student, and I **go to school** every day. （我是個中學生，每天上學。）

▶ My father sometimes **goes to the school** to speak to the headmaster. （我父親有時會去學校跟校長談話。）

▶ Are they **in church**? （他們在做禮拜嗎？）

▶ Are they **in the church**? （他們在教堂裡面嗎？）

▶ He is **in prison**. （他在坐牢。）

▶ He is **in the prison**. He is there to see his brother. （他在監獄裡面，他去那裡探視他的弟弟。）

004 Question

lots of, a lot of 和 a lot 這三者有何不同呢？

Answer

a lot of或a whole lot of和lots of的意思完全一樣（意為「大量；許多」= a great quantity, number, or amount of），而用法也幾乎如出一轍，唯一的小差異是，lots of 大多用於口語；換言之，lots of 比 a lot of要來得非正式。所以，我們可以說成或寫成：

▶ There are **a (whole) lot of** people over there.
  = There are **lots of** people over there.
  （那裡有很多人。）

就文法而言，a lot of和lots of是用在名詞或名詞片語之前，而名詞可以是可數(countable)或不可數(uncountable)。

例如：

- ▶ There are **a lot of** people working for the company.（有很多人為這家公司工作。）--句中的people為可數名詞，而people working for the company就是名詞片語。
- ▶ What **a lot of** food there is!（好多的食物啊！）-- 句中的 food 為不可數名詞。

至於a lot或lots，則可當名詞或副詞用。從lot前面可以加冠詞，本身可以加s就知道它是個名詞，所以a lot和lots是名詞。

例如：

- ▶ I've got **a lot** (of work) to do.（我有很多工作要做。）
- ▶ They gave us **lots** to eat.（他們給了我們好多吃的東西。）

然而，a lot 或 lots 亦可當副詞，經常用來修飾副詞或形容詞的比較級，在此它們意為「在很大程度上，非常」。

例如：

- ▶ This is **a lot** better.（這個好多了。）
- ▶ Thanks **a lot**. = Thank you very much.（非常感謝。）

a lot或lots也經常用來回答問句。

例如：

- ▶ Are there **a lot of** people working for the company?（有很多人為這家公司工作嗎？）
- ▶ Yes, a lot. = Yes, lots.（是的，很多。）

最後要提的是一個與a lot of和lots of有關的非常重要的文法觀念，那就是：在否定句和問句中，若名詞為可數，往往使用many來代替a lot of或lots of；若名詞為不可數，往往使用much來代替a lot of或lots of。

例如：

- ▶ There aren't **many** Spanish tourists in Taiwan.（台灣的西班牙觀光客不多。）
- ▶ Are there **many** Spanish tourists in Taiwan?（台灣有很多西班牙觀光客嗎？）

▶ I haven't got **much** money.（我沒有很多錢。）

005 Question

too much和much too要怎麼用呢？He is too much intelligent. 是什麼意思呢？

Answer

❶ too much

too much是一個修飾用的片語，意為「太多；非常，很」，可當形容詞或副詞用。例如：

▶ He drank **too much** beer last night.（他昨晚喝太多的啤酒。）
▶ She doesn't like traveling **too much**.（她不太喜歡旅行。）

然而，儘管too much/too little/too many/too few（其中too為副詞，修飾much, little, many和few）當形容詞用時，後面可直接接名詞，但這並不表示「too＋形容詞＋名詞」這種結構可一體適用，因為too不能用於一般形容詞之前，例如我們可以說The coffee is too sweet.（這咖啡太甜。），但卻不能說the too sweet coffee。因此，在「too＋形容詞＋名詞」這種結構中，若形容詞為一般形容詞，則此結構的詞序必須做調整方能合乎文法。例如：

▶ It was a too good opportunity to miss. →（✕）錯誤。
▶ It was too good an opportunity to miss. →（○）正確。
　（那是一個不能錯失的極好機會。）
▶ It's a too cold day. →（✕）錯誤。
▶ It's too cold a day. →（○）正確。
　（天氣太冷了。）

❷ much too

再者，儘管too much亦可當副詞用，但卻不能修飾形容詞，亦即too much不能直接放在形容詞的前面，所以問題中的He is too much intelligent.是個錯誤的句子，原因可能出在too much和much too被搞混了。

too本身是個加強語氣用的副詞，意為「太，過分」，但其前經常還會使用much, far, a bit/a little等副詞來修飾，例如：

> ▶ You're going **much too** fast, slow down!（你開得太快了，慢一點！）
> ▶ There's been far **too** little rain lately and the crops are suffering.（近來雨水太少，農作物都受害了。）

因此，在much too中，much是做為已是加強語氣用的副詞too的語氣加強語。

大家應該知道，too有個句型相當常用，那就是「too＋形容詞＋不定詞（to＋原形動詞）」，意為「太……而不能……」，如He is too young to go to school.（他年紀太小，還不能上學。）值得注意的是，在「too＋形容詞＋名詞」結構中，too不能用於一般形容詞之前，但在「too＋形容詞＋不定詞」句型中，too一定用於一般形容詞之前。所以，He is too much intelligent.應是He is much too intelligent. 之誤。綜上所述，much too可以說是具有「雙重加強語氣」的作用，以上句為例，它是從He is intelligent.（他聰明。）加強語氣為He is too intelligent.（他太聰明了。）再加強語氣為He is much too intelligent.（他真的太聰明了。）

006 **Question**

在Winning the championship is his no mean achievement.這句中，no mean是什麼意思，no在此做什麼詞類用呢？一般而言，no的前面不是不可以加上人稱代名詞嗎？

Answer

no mean意為「了不起的；不凡的；很好的」，其中no為形容詞，mean也是形容詞，意為「低劣的，平庸的」。據瞭解，no前面可以加上人稱代名詞（如his, her等等）和定冠詞the的用法，目前僅剩下no small和no little等片語而已，如 her no small achievement（她不小的成就）。再舉一例：

> ▶ It was **no small** achievement getting her to agree to the deal.（能讓她同意那筆交易可是個不小的成就。）

至於no mean的前面也加上人稱代名詞的情況，似乎很少見。"no mean"可以修飾人事物。例如：

▶ She was **no mean** performer on a variety of instruments.（她是位不凡的演奏家，擅長多種樂器。）

▶ Winning the championship is his **no mean** achievement.（贏得錦標賽是他一項不凡的成就。）

▶ To destroy 121 enemy aircraft is **no mean** record.（摧毀 121 架敵機是個非凡的紀錄。）

007 Question

can和able to以及can't和unable to的用法有何不同呢？

Answer

can和be able to都是表示能力，意為「能，會」，它們有時是同義詞，可以互換，但有時卻不行。同樣地，它們的否定詞can't和am not/aren't/isn't able to或am/are/is unable to也是有時可以互換，有時則不行。例如：

▶ I can drive. = I **am able to** drive.（我會開車。）

▶ I can't drive. = I **am not able to** drive. = I am **unable to** drive.（我不會開車。）

can的過去式could係表示過去能做某事或會做某事，而could的否定詞couldn't 則表示過去不會做某事，即缺乏做某事的能力。同樣地，could和was/were able to 以及couldn't和wasn't/weren't able to或was/were unable to亦是有時可以互換，有時則不行。例如：

▶ I **could** swim. = I **was able to** swim.（以前我會游泳。）

▶ I **couldn't** swim. = I **wasn't able to** swim.
= I was **unable to** swim.（以前我不會游泳。）

既然can和be able to的意思相同，那麼該使用那一個比較適當呢？在非正式場合，尤其在口說英語中，一般都使用can（亦適用於can't, could和couldn't；以下的敘述亦同），而be able to（亦適用於am/are/is/was/were able to, am not/aren't/isn't/wasn't/weren't able to或am/are/is/was/were unable to；以下的敘述亦同）則用在比較正式的場合，不是很適合用於日常生活的情況中。

從上述可知，can和be able to可以互換的情況是發生在現在式和過去式的句子中。若是未來式、現在完成式和過去完成式，那麼它們就不能互換了，因為can 在這些時式中並非表示能力；所以，在未來式、現在完成式和過去完成式中僅能使用be able to。例如：

▶ My six-year-old son has **been able to** read for two years. （我六歲兒子已經會看書兩年了。）

▶ I thought he had **been able to** swim. （我認為他一定會游泳。）

最後值得一提的是，unable to比not able to來得正式一些。

008 Question

Fewer-Less than two hundred people went to the concert.這句該用Fewer than或 Less than還是兩者都可以呢？

Answer

fewer和Less分別為few和little的比較級，few後接複數可數名詞，little後接不可數名詞。但few跟a few的用法並不相同，few意為「（少之又少）幾乎沒有」，表否定，而a few意為「一些」，表肯定。Little和a little的用法亦有如此的差異，little 意為「（少之又少）幾乎沒有」，表否定，而a little意為「一些」，表肯定。例如：

▶ Allen has **few** friends in Tokyo, does he? （艾倫在東京幾乎沒有朋友，對吧？）

▶ Allen has **a few** friends in Tokyo, doesn't he? （艾倫在東京有一些朋友，不是嗎？）

▶ Mary got **little** help from John, did she? （瑪麗沒有從約翰那兒得到什麼幫助，對吧？）

▶ Mary got **a little** help from John, didn't she? （瑪麗從約翰那兒得到一些幫助，不是嗎？）

few可當代名詞和形容詞用，fewer（及最高級 fewest）亦然。但little和less（及最高級 least）除了用作代名詞和形容詞外，還可當副詞用。例如：

▶ Sam ate **little**, so I urged him to eat a little more.（山姆幾乎沒吃，所以我勸他多吃一些。）一句中的 little 和 a little 都是副詞用法。

▶ I had **fewer** books than he did.（我擁有的書比他少。）

▶ Eat **less** or you're getting fatter and fatter.（吃少點，否則你會越來越胖。）一句中的 less 為副詞用法。

fewer欠缺的副詞用法，正是它經常被用錯的癥結所在，尤其是在fewer than的比較句型中。在「形容詞／副詞比較級＋than」的句型中，若主動詞為be動詞，須使用形容詞比較級 + than，若主動詞為普通動詞，則須使用副詞比較級＋than。由於fewer僅能用作形容詞，不能當副詞用，因此它不是位在be動詞或連綴動詞之後，就是位在名詞之前。例如：

▶ Cars made in Korea are **fewer** than those made in Japan.（韓國車比日本車少。）

▶ He worked **fewer** hours than I did.（他的工作時數比我少。）

所以，問題中的句子只能使用less than，不可使用fewer than，因為less是副詞，而fewer是形容詞：

▶ **Less** than 200 people went to the party.
= **Fewer** people than 200 went to the party.
（參加派對的人數不到兩百人。）

如果你曾經像這樣用錯fewer than而被老師或指導教授責備，現在應該可以釋懷了，因為連英國人都會用錯，何況我們大多數人只是第二語言學習者。英國《太陽報》（The Sun）2012 年 4 月初有一篇關於雙子宮婦女兩個子宮同時受孕懷雙胞胎的報導；該報在報導中使用了下面這個令筆者無言以對的句子：

▶ Research shows fewer than 100 women worldwide have fallen pregnant with twins in separate wombs.（研究顯示，全世界兩個子宮同時受孕而懷雙胞胎的雙子宮婦女不到百人。）

然而，no fewer than （不少於，至少，用於數字前，表示強調）是固定用法，似乎不受上述語法的規範，因為在若干英文辭典和正式文件中不時可見類似下面的句子：

▶ There shall be **no fewer than** three guards on duty.（值班警衛不得少於三人。）

▶ **No fewer than** 50 celebrities went to the concert.（至少有 50 位名流出席音樂會。）

009 Question

be full of和be filled with可以互換嗎？

Answer

這兩個動詞片語雖都意為「充滿，裝滿」，但含意並不相同，所以不能互換。

full of中的full為形容詞，意為「滿的」，但full of的含意是having or containing a lot of things or people or a lot of something，而filled with的含意是making something full或becoming full of something，其中filled為動詞fill的過去分詞形容詞。由此可知，在這兩個片語中，只有be filled with能表達真正裝得滿滿沒有剩下任何空間的意思，而be full of是表示含有或裝有很多東西、許多人或大量的某種東西，相當於「都是；滿是」的意思。例如：

▶ The room **was full of** books. →（○）正確。
▶ The room **was filled with** books. →（╳）錯誤。
  （這個房間都是書。）除非這個房間沒有其他任何東西，而且書籍從地板疊到天花板，整個房間都堆滿書，第二句才講得通。

▶ The restaurant **is** always **full of** customers. →（○）正確。
▶ The restaurant **is** always **filled with** customers. →（╳）錯誤。
  （這家餐廳總是門庭若市。）除非這家餐廳的客人摩肩接踵，大家擠成一堆，沒有任何移動或用餐空間，第二句才講得通。

▶ His trousers **are full of** holes.（他的褲子都是洞。）
▶ Her essay **was full of** grammatical errors.（她的論文滿是文法錯誤。）
▶ Her eyes **were full of** tears. →（○）正確。（她眼中滿是淚水）
▶ Her eyes **were filled with** tears. →（○）正確。（她眼淚盈眶。）
▶ The room **is filled with** smoke.（這個房間煙霧瀰漫。）

再者，在這兩個片語中，只有filled with可與grief（悲痛）、horror（恐懼）、shock（震驚）、terror（驚恐）等表示強烈情緒的字眼連用，不可使用full of。例如：

▶ Mary **was filled with** shock and grief when she found that her husband had an affair with a colleague at work.（當瑪麗發現她老公跟他同事有染時，她震驚不已、悲痛欲絕。）

I. 填空題

1 _____ inches.
（四又八分之一英吋。）

2 _____ meters.
（六又四分之一公尺。）

3 _____ (In the case of/In case of) any difficulties, you must consult
with your aunt.
（萬一碰到困難，你必須跟你阿姨商量。）

4 What will you do _____ (in the future/in future)?
（你將來要做什麼？）

5 Is there _____ (a lot of/much) food in the refrigerator?
（冰箱裡有很多食物嗎？）

6 That is _____ (lots/much) interesting.
（那有趣多了。）

7 He is _____ sick _____ work.
（他病得太重了，沒辦法工作了。）

8 The ticket is _____ (too much/much too) expensive for the students.
（對學生來説，這張票太貴了。）

9 Joanne Kathleen Rowlin is _____ writer.
（JK羅琳是位了不起的作家。）

10 It was her _____ achievement.
（這是她不小的成就）

11 He'll _____ speak really good English by the end of the year.
（到了年底，他將會説一口真的很好的英文。）

12 He _____ speak Japanese.
（他以前不會説日文。）

⑬ I drank _____ coffee than she did.
（我喝的咖啡比她少。）

⑭ The stadium holds _____ 100,000 people.
（這個體育場能容納至少 10 萬人。）

⑮ Her eyes _____ tears.
（她眼中滿是淚水。）

⑯ John looked at the teacher, _____ horror.
（約翰充滿恐懼地看著老師。）

II. 圈圈看

❶

A: John, say hi to Danny.
（約翰，跟丹尼打聲招呼。）

B: Nice to meet you./Nice meeting you.
（很高興看到你。）

❷

A: Thanks for having me here. I had a great time.
（謝謝你邀請我來。我今天很開心。）

B: Nice to see you./Nice seeing you.
（今天看到你來我很開心！）

III. 選擇題

（   ）選對。

(A). I haven't got a lot of money but I've got much love.

(B). I've got much money but I haven't got a lot of love.

(C). I haven't got much money but I've got a lot of love.

IV. 二選一

1 ☐ It's two and one-half inches.

☐ It's two-and-one-half inches.

（這是兩吋半。）

2 ☐ Hello. Nice to meet you.

☐ Hello. Nice meeting you.

（哈囉，很高興認識你。）

3 ☐ Are they in church?

☐ Are they in the church?

（他們在做禮拜嗎？）

4 ☐ I haven't got a lot of money but I've got much love.

☐ I haven't got much money but I've got a lot of love.

（我沒有很多錢但是我有很多的愛。）

5 ☐ It was a too good opportunity to miss.

☐ It was too good an opportunity to miss.

（那是一個不能錯失的極好機會。）

6 ☐ The shirt is much too small for me.

☐ The shirt is a bit too small for me.

（這件襯衫對我來說有點太小了。）

7 ☐ Little sum is involved

☐ No little sum is involved.

（相關的金額不小。）

8 ☐ Fewer than two hundred people went to the concert.

☐ Less than two hundred people went to the concert.

（參加這場音樂會的人數不到兩百人。）

9 ☐ The room was full of books.

☐ The room was filled with books.

（這個房間都是書。）

Answer

I. 填空題

1 four and one-eighth
2 six and one-fourth
3 In case of
4 in the future
5 much
6 lots
7 too; to
8 much too
9 no mean
10 no small
11 be able to
12 wasn't able to/was unable to
13 less
14 no fewer than
15 were full of
16 filled with

II. 圈圈看

1 Nice to meet you.
2 Nice seeing you.

III. 選擇題

（C）

IV. 二選一

1 第一句正確
2 第一句正確
3 第一句正確
4 第二句正確
5 第二句正確
6 第二句正確
7 第二句正確
8 第二句正確
9 第一句正確

001 Question

「兩起事件相距不到多少時間發生」及「兩棟建築物相距不到多少距離」中的相距不到多少時間及相距不到多少距離，如何用英文表達呢？

Answer

英文中似乎有個「慣用語」可以表達這樣的意思，那就是 "within (…) of each other"，括弧中放的是「多少時間」以及「多少距離」的數量和單位。舉例來說會比較容易瞭解。

例如：

▶ Seventy-year-old twin brothers have been run over by Lorries and killed while cycling in separate accidents **within three hours of each other**.

（兩名 70 歲的孿生兄弟先後在騎單車時遭到卡車輾斃，兩起意外事故相距不到 3 小時。）

▶ Two young Palestinians fall victim to landmines **within one hour of each other**.

（兩名巴勒斯坦青年相距不到一小時先後成為地雷的受害者。）

▶ There are two bird's nest specialty shops here. They are **within 2.5 kilometers of each other**.

（這裡有兩家燕窩專賣店，兩者相距不到 2.5 公里）。

當然，括弧內也可以用其他計量單位，視你要表達的意思而定。

002 **Q**uestion

> 由於in與時間長短的字詞連用時有「在（一段時間）之內」和「在（一段時間）之後」這兩個不同的意思。那麼在I'll be back in an hour.這句中，in an hour是 within an hour還是after an hour呢？

Answer

❶ 過去

如果是過去發生的情況，那麼 in an hour 的意思是「一小時內（within an hour）」（這亦適用於in與其他表示時間長短的字詞連用的情況）。例如：

▶ My boss thought it would take longer, but I completed the report **in half an hour** yesterday afternoon.（我老闆認為要花更長的時間，但我昨天下午不到半小時就完成了這份報告。）

▶ He wrote the novel **in six weeks** last summer when he was on holiday in Japan.（去年夏天他在日本度假時花了不到六週的時間就完成了這本小說。）

❷ 未來

如果是未來的情況，那麼in an hour的意思通常是「一小時後 (after an hour)」。此外，我們常見的一種類似的時間表示法或寫法，如in an hour's time, in three days' time等等，它們的意思就相當於用在未來情況的in an hour, in three days等等，不過後者的寫法比較簡單。例如：

▶ It'll be ready in about half an hour. － 約半小時後；過了大約半小時之後（大約半小時後就會準備好了。）

▶ It'll be ready in half an hour's time.（半小時後就會準備好了。）

▶ It won't be ready for half an hour.（這無法在半小時準備好。）

▶ I'll see you again in six months. － 六個月後；過了六個月之後（六個月後我會再和你見面。）

▶ I'll see you again in six months' time.（六個月後我會再和你見面。）

▶ I shan't see you again for six months. （未來六個月我不會再和你見面。）

上面的例句中有兩句的介系詞是用for而不是in，是因為在first、only、否定詞和最高級之後，美國用in而英國用for。

在肯定句中，for 通常表示動作或事件持續的時間，所以in an hour跟for an hour 的意思是不同的。試比較下面的句子：

▶ He learnt English **in three weeks**. （他在三個禮拜內學會了英語。）
▶ He learnt English **for three weeks**. （他學了三個禮拜的英語。）
▶ It's two o'clock; I'll come **in an hour**. （現在是兩點鐘；我將在一個鐘頭之後來。） － 也就是三點過後來。
▶ It's two o'clock; I'll come **for an hour**. （現在是兩點鐘；我將會待一個小時。） －也就是從兩點待到三點。

003 Question

He didn't come home all the night.和He didn't come home all night.這兩句是否一樣呢？

Answer

這兩句的意思是一樣的，都意為「他整晚都沒有回家」，但語法則有對錯之分。一般而言，在否定句中，all與其後所接的時間名詞之間是不可以有定冠詞the的。雖然不少英國人在談話時可能會在否定句中使用the，如all the day, all the week等等，但這是很奇怪的事。美國人無論在肯定句或否定句中，似乎都不用定冠詞。

例如：

▶ He sings all day. （他整天都在唱歌。）
▶ He didn't sing all day. （他整天都沒有唱歌。）

這規則並不適用於副詞片語 all the time （一直，始終），此片語無論在肯定句或否定句中都需要the。但形容詞 all-time （空前的，創紀錄的）也沒有定冠詞，如 Our company's sales have reached an all-time high this year.（本公司今年的銷售額達到歷來最高。）

004 Question

at the bank和in the bank以及on the street和in the street之間
有何不同呢？

Answer

這些表示地點的介系詞片語都正確無誤且很常用，但它們之間的含意並不完全相同。首先來看at the bank和in the bank，後者指的一定是在銀行裡面（inside the bank），但前者可能是在銀行裡面或外面的任何地方，亦即沒有指出確切的地點。例如：

▶ I will meet him **at the supermarket**.
（我將和他在超市見面。）
-- 沒有指出確切的地點，可能在超市裡面，也可能在超市外面。

▶ I will meet him **at the checkout in the supermarket**.
（我將在超市裡面的結帳櫃台跟他見面。）
-- 指出了確切的地點。

至於on the street和in the street之間的區別，一般而言，這要看你從什麼角度來看。如果有一條街聚集了很多人，而當時你人是在距離不遠的另一條街上，你要說There were a lot of people on the street.。如果當時你人就在那條有很多人的街上，你要說 There were a lot of people in the street.。

簡言之，當你使用in the street 時，你是以「那條街的一份子」或「人在那條街上」的角度來看事情，如There are speed bumps every fifty meters in the street where I live.（在我住的那條街上，每 50 公尺就有減速丘。）。一 speed bump 亦叫做 speed hump 或 sleeping policeman。

有個外國英文教學網站説，「8點15分」(8:15)不能説成fifteen past eight，而要説成 quarter past eight。以前學的英文不是説8點15分可以説成eight fifteen或fifteen past eight嗎？難道這是新的講法嗎？

Answer

如果讀者上Google網站，以兩岸三地的中文網站為範圍，搜尋英文的時間表示法，有人可能會被嚇了一大跳，因為原來大家竟錯得這麼離譜，就連一些所謂的著名教學網站也是一樣，絕大部分的網站均稱8:15可以説成eight fifteen或 fifteen past eight，真是自誤誤人！

一般而言，時間都有兩種表示法

❶ 順讀法

這是比較正式的説法，即不管時間是在半小時以內或半小時以上都由左至右讀，如10:25讀作 ten twenty-five、11:15讀作eleven fifteen、2:30讀作two thirty、4:45讀作four forty-five。

❷ 逆讀法

逆讀法就是使用「分鐘 + past（英）/after（美）+ 小時」（這是半小時以內的表示法）或「分鐘 + to（英）/of/before/till（美）+ 小時」（這是半小時以上的表示法，就是差幾分幾點的意思）的結構。就逆讀法而言，英語教學大多使用 past和to這兩個英國用法的介系詞，但事實上美國人也使用after和of/before/till 來表達相同的意思。例如：

八點二十分 (8:20)：(It's) twenty past/after eight.
九點二十一分 (9:21)：Twenty-one minutes（註）past/after nine
九點四十六分 (9:46)：Fourteen minutes（註）to/of/before/till ten（差14分10點）
十點五十分 (10:50)：Ten to/of/before/till eleven（差10分11點）

現在進入主題：當時間為半小時或一刻鐘（15分鐘）時，順讀法如上述由左至右讀，如22:15讀作twenty-two fifteen或ten fifteen、10:30讀作ten thirty；然而，如果是使用有past和to等介系詞的逆讀法，則「半小時」不用thirty而要用half 來表達，「一刻鐘或15分鐘」不用fifteen而要用(a) quarter來表達，其中"a"可以省略（註），如9:15讀作quarter past nine、11:45 讀作quarter to twelve，而 9:30 讀作half past nine。另外，根據 The new Fowler's Modern English Usage 一書，在英格蘭和威爾斯，許多年輕人現在使用像 half seven（省略 past）這樣的寫法或讀法來表示「七點半」（7:30 a.m. 或 7:30 p.m.）。

註：事實上，英文的時間說法滿複雜的。在一般會話中，大多數英美人士對於5分鐘、10分鐘、15分鐘及其他5之倍數的分鐘，都直接說成five past two、ten past four、twenty to six、a quarter to ten 等等，但對於非5之倍數的分鐘，通常要加上minutes，如「七點四分」要說成four minutes past seven（不是four past seven），而「九點四十八分」要說成twelve minutes to ten（不是twelve to ten），其餘依此類推。另外，在「半小時」和「一刻鐘」的說法中，half的前面不可有"a"，所以我們可以說half past six或甚至half six，但不能說a half past six；而quarter的前面則可以有"a"，但"a"可以省略，所以說quarter past six或a quarter past six都可以，會話中通常省略"a"。然而，在其他非表示時間的情況中，quarter前面的"a"不能省略，譬如我們要說I ate a quarter of an orange.（我吃了四分之一個橘子。）而不能說 I ate quarter of an orange.。

至於整點時間，常用的有下列幾種表示法：

The train arrived at three o'clock on the dot.
= The train arrived on the dot of three o'clock.
= The train arrived at three o'clock on the hour.
= The train arrived at three o'clock sharp.
= The train arrived at three o'clock exactly (或 at exactly three o'clock).
（火車三點整準時抵達。）

006 Question

on a team和in a team那個是英式英語，那個是美式英語呢？

on a team為美式英語，而in a team為英式英語。英式英語和美式英語除了在某些拼字（如colour, color）、字彙（如lorry, truck）和文法上有所不同外，在介系詞的用法上亦有一些差異，如「在週末」，英式英語是at the weekend，美式英語為on the weekend。(be) on a team/in a team意為「在……隊裡；入選……隊」。例如：

▶ I am **on the football team**. （我是足球隊的一員。）
▶ Are you **in the baseball team** this year? （今年你入選棒球隊了嗎？）

此外，我們經常使用的Please write me soon.＝Please write to me soon.（請快點寫信給我。）其實也有英式英語和美式英語之分，其中Please write me soon.是美式英語，而Please write to me soon.為英式英語。

007 Question

for example和such as的用法有何不同呢？

Answer

事實上，for example、for instance、such as 和like都可用來舉例，列舉同類的人事物，意思均為「例如；比如像……；像……之類；諸如……」，但它們的用法並不相同。

for example或for instance可置於句首、句中或句末；當置於句中時，for example 前後都要用逗點隔開，置於句首時，後面須有逗點，而置於句末時，前面須有逗點。

例如：

▶ I can play quite a few musical instruments, **for example**, the flute, the guitar, and the piano.

= I can play quite a few musical instruments, **for instance**, the flute, the guitar, and the piano.

= I can play quite a few musical instruments, **e.g.**, the flute, the guitar, and the piano.（我能彈奏很多樂器，如長笛、吉他和鋼琴。）

▶ My father loves going to restaurants which serve exotic foods. **For example**, last week he went to a restaurant which serves deep-fried rattlesnake.

= My father loves going to restaurants which serve exotic foods. **For instance**, last week he went to a restaurant which serves deep-fried rattlesnake.（我父親喜歡到供應奇特食物的餐廳用餐。譬如說，他上週到一家供應油炸響尾蛇的餐廳用餐。）

▶ You can buy fruit here – oranges and bananas, **for example/for instance**.（你可以在這裡買水果，如買橘子和香蕉。）

從上面的例句可以看出，當 for example 置於句中或句末時，它所列舉的人事物是名詞或名詞片語；若置於句首，則 for example 後接句子。然而，在「for example＋子句」的結構中，for example 其實並非都位在句首，因為在實際的應用上，句中表示時間和地點的介系詞片語往往被挪到句首，而使 for example 位於句中，因此我們必須區別 for example 置於句中、後接子句與後接名詞或名詞片語之間的不同。

例如：

▶ In New Zealand, **for example**, it was very difficult to introduce disciplinary measures for public servants.（譬如說，在紐西蘭，很難對公務員採取懲戒措施或紀律處分。）

▶ In the 1950s and 1960s, **for instance**, it was very difficult to introduce disciplinary measures for public servants.（譬如說，在 1950 和 60 年代，很難對公務員採取懲戒措施。）

▶ In New Zealand between the 1950s and 1960s, **for example**, it was very difficult to introduce disciplinary measures for public servants.（譬如說，在 1950 至 60 年代的紐西蘭，很難對公務員採取懲戒措施。）

such as 也可用來舉例，列舉同類的人事物。

例如：

▶ I can play quite a few musical instruments, **such as** (= **like**) the flute, the guitar, and the piano. （我會演奏許多種樂器，像是長笛，吉他還有鋼琴。）

從上面的例句可以看出，such as 的前面雖有逗點，但其後卻沒有逗點。這是such as與for example或for instance的主要差異之一。另一差異是，such as用於列舉時不可接子句。在此，such as亦可用like來替代。

然而，such as用於句中時也可以完全不用逗點。

例如：

▶ Boys **such as** (= **like**) John and Tom are very friendly. （像約翰和湯姆這樣的男孩都很友善。）

▶ Car companies **such as** (= **like**) Toyota and Ford manufacture their automobiles in many different countries around the world. （豐田和福特等汽車公司在全球許多不同國家製造汽車。）

在上面兩句中，such as或like前面為何沒有逗點呢？這是因為such as或like及其後所列舉的項目是使句意完整或正確不可或缺的資料。如果你把這些字拿掉，意思就會發生變化。

例如：

Car companies manufacture their automobiles in many different countries around the world.

上句可以意為，所有汽車公司都在全球許多不同的國家生產汽車，但這並非事實，因為有些汽車公司僅在一個或兩個國家製造汽車。所以，such as (= like) Toyota and Ford這片語是必要的。如果這些字是必要的，那麼such as或like前面就不能有逗點。這種情況與關係子句的「限定」(restricted) 與「非限定」(non-restricted) 用法一樣。

再者，雖然上述我們都將such as和like劃上等號，但事實並非都是如此，因為 such as在實際應用上亦經常被分開，此時such as就不能用like來替換。

例如：

▶ He has several **such** reference books **as** dictionaries and handbooks. （他有幾本像字典、手冊之類的參考書。）

▶ **Such** countries **as Thailand, Malaysia, and Brunei** are called Southeast Asian nations. （像泰國、馬來西亞和汶萊這些國家都被叫做東南亞國家。）

008 Question

在Most important(ly), you must work hard to catch up.這句中，我們應使用most important還是most importantly，或是兩者都可以呢？

Answer

Most important和most importantly以及more important和more importantly都是用來強調事物的片語。嚴格來說，在這兩組片語中，正確的寫法是most important（最重要的是）和more important（更重要的是），因為它們通常是what's most important和more important than that的簡寫。

most importantly和more importantly分別意為「最重要地」和「更重要地」。因此，即使我們將整個片語都寫出來也會有文法上的瑕疵，如What's most importantly is that we try our best.（最重要地，我們盡自己最大的努力。）這就好像把What's most clear to us is that she's trying her best.（我們最清楚不過的是，她正在盡自己最大的努力。）寫成What's most clearly to us is that she's trying her best.一樣；眾所周知，後面這一句的文法是不對的（be動詞後面要用形容詞，不是副詞）。因此，筆者會建議問題中的句子寫成Most important, you must work hard to catch up.（最重要的是，你必須努力學習，迎頭趕上。）

然而，現今在許多文章和新聞報導，甚至著名作家的作品中經常可見使用most importantly和more importantly的情況。鑑此，儘管有人說這些名作家未必是文法學家，但現在大多數英語人士都認為most important和most importantly以及 more important和more importantly是可以互換的。他們包括 The New Fowler's Modern English Usage 一書的作者 Henry Watson Fowler 和 R. W. Burchfield；這兩位現代

英語專家在該書中指出，most important 和 more important 以及 most importantly 和 more importantly 的用法（尤其是 most importantly 和 more importantly 的用法）在 1970 年代和 1980 年代曾遭到強烈反對，但現在必須將其皆視為標準用法。

009 Question

for ages和in ages的用法一樣嗎？

Answer

for ages (= for a long time)和in ages (= in a long time)的意思完全一樣，都是「很長時間；很久」，只是前者為英式英語，後者為美式英語，如I haven't seen him for/in ages.（我很久沒有見到他了。）

雖然這兩個片語的意思完全一樣，但用法卻不盡相同。for ages和in ages皆可用於肯定句和否定句，但for ages僅能用於表示動作已持續一段很長時間（且該動作可能還在持續當中）的肯定句以及動作已經結束一段很長時間或動作已經很久沒有進行的否定句，而in ages僅能用在表示動作已經結束一段很長時間或動作已經很久沒有進行的肯定句和否定句。請看下面的例句和說明：

- ▶ I haven't read a good book **in ages**. → （○）正確。
  （我很久沒有閱讀好書了。）--in ages 用於動作已經很久沒有進行的否定句。
- ▶ I haven't read a good book **for ages**. → （○）正確。
  （我很久沒有閱讀好書了。）--for ages 用於動作已經很久沒有進行的否定句。
- ▶ I've been reading that book **for ages**. → （○）正確。
  （我讀那本書已有好長一段時間。）－讀書的動作仍在持續當中。for ages 用於動作已持續一段很長時間的肯定句。
- ▶ I haven't been reading that book **for ages**. → （○）正確。
  （我已經好長一段時間沒有讀那本書了。）－讀書的動作早已停止。for ages 用於動作已結束一段很長時間的否定句。
- ▶ That's the worst book I've read **in ages**. → （○）正確。
  （那是很久以來我所讀過最爛的書。）－這句含有讀那本爛書的動作，既然是爛書，那麼閱讀的動作顯然已經結束。in ages 用於動作已經結束一段很長時

間的肯定句。

▶ That's the worst book I've read **for ages**.（那是很久以來我所讀過最爛的書。）— 這句含有讀那本爛書的動作，既然是爛書，那麼閱讀的動作顯然已經結束。for ages 不能用於動作已經結束一段很長時間的肯定句。（這句有問題）

▶ I haven't read a book **in ages**.
　→（○）正確。
　（我很久沒有讀書了。）--in ages 用於動作已經很久沒有進行的否定句。

▶ I have read a book **in ages**.
　→（×）錯誤。
　（我讀書已經很久了。）--in ages 不能用於動作已持續一段很長時間且該動作可能還在持續當中的肯定句。

010 Question

What time do you go to school和At what time do you go to school那一句正確呢？

Answer

這兩句都正確且都是一般使用的句型。它們的主要差異在於At what time do you go to school?（你幾點上學？）是用在非常正式的場合，亦即這一問句是屬於正式的文法，因為它的回答應該諸如It is at seven o'clock. (7 點)，句中含有介系詞 at。

然而，在日常生活中，也就是在比較不那麼正式的場合，大多數人都是使用What time do you go to school?--亦即省略at；這種寫法或說法相當常見且廣泛被接受。

再者，你可能也會看到或聽到What time do you go to school at?這樣的寫法或說法，亦即將at放在句末。這也是一種比較不那麼正式的用法，但同樣是一般使用的句型。

總的而言，在詢問上述時間時，視at之有無及其在句中的位置而定，我們可以用三種句型來表達同一意思。同樣的情況亦適用於表示日期的介系詞on及表示月份和年份的介系詞in，不過，在許多情況中，我們往往使用when來取代what。

例如：

▶ **What day** is your birthday?
  = **On what day** is your birthday?
  = **What day** is your birthday **on**?
  = **When** is your birthday?
  （你的生日是哪一天？）

▶ **What year** did Ma Ying-Jeou re-elect President?
  = **In what year** did Ma Ying-Jeou re-elect President?
  = **What year** did Barack Obama re-elect President in?
  = **When** did Barack Obama re-elect President?
  （歐巴馬哪一年當選連任？）

最後值得一提的是，雖然 "At what time ..." 和 "What time ..." 的意思相同，但它們之間其實還有一項細微的差異，那就是 "At what time ..." 可能是在詢問確切或特定的時間。譬如說，有位刑事調查員問說 "At what time did the bomb go off?" （炸彈何時爆炸？），對方可能回答 "4:23 p.m." （下午4點23分－時間非常明確）。不過，這位調查員也可能這樣問 "What time did the bomb go off?"。事實上，在大多數情況中，"What time ..." 都要比 "At what time ..." 來得自然，因為一般時間片語前面的介系詞通常省略。例如：

▶ I am very busy. Can you come another time? （我現在很忙。你可以找另外時間來？）－這比 Can you come at another time? 來得自然。

Excercise
綜 合 練 習

I. 填空題

1 There are two bird's nest specialty shops here. They are _____ 2.5 km _____.

（這裡有兩家燕窩專賣店，兩者相距不到 2.5 公里。）

2 The twin sisters gave birth to their babies _____ 2 hours _____.

（這對雙胞胎姊妹在兩小時間相繼產下嬰兒。）

3 I shan't see you again _____.

（未來六個月我不會再和你見面。）

4 It'll be ready _____.

（半小時後就會準備好了。）

5 I didn't practice playing the piano _____.

（我並非總是在練鋼琴。）

6 He didn't come home _____.

（他整晚沒有回家。）

7 I couldn't move! There were a lot of people _____ the street.

（我動彈不得了！街上有好多的人喔！）

8 I will meet you _____ the bank.

（我將會在銀行跟你見面。）

9 Some of the European languages come from Latin, _____ French, Italian, and Spanish.

（歐洲有些語言源自拉丁語，如法語、義大利語和西班牙語。）

10 Such countries _____ Thailand, Malaysia, and Brunei are called Southeast Asian nations.

（像泰國、馬來西亞和汶萊這些國家都被叫做東南亞國家。）

11 _____ (Most important/What's most importantly), you have learned a lot from the experience.

（最重要的是，你從這次經驗中學到很多東西。）

187

⑫ _____ (More important/What's more importantly), you have done your best.
（比較重要的是，你已經盡你最大的努力了。）

⑬ I haven't seen a movie _____ ages.
（我很久沒有看電影了。）

⑭ It seems that he has lived in Taiwan _____ ages.
（她彷彿已經住在台灣很久了。）

II. 圈圈看

❶ It's (quarter to twelve/fifteen to twelve).
（現在十一點四十五分。）

❷ I ate (quarter of/a quarter of) a cake.
（我吃了四分之一塊蛋糕。）

❸ I will see you (on/in) the weekend.
（我週末會去見你。）

❹ I was (on/of) the basketball team in high school.
（我中學時期是籃球隊的。）

❺ (At what time/What time) did you go to bed last night?
（昨晚你什麼時候睡覺？）

❻ (On what day/In what day) is the Dragon Boat Festival this year?
（今年的端午節是在哪一天？）

III. 二選一

❶ ☐ I'll be back in an hour.
   ☐ I'd be back in an hour.
   （我會在一小時後回來。）

❷ ☐ He didn't sing all day.
   ☐ He didn't sing all the day.
   （他整天都沒有唱歌。）

3 □ I saw this product on the shelf in the convenient store.
　　□ I saw this product on the shelf at the convenient store.
（我在便利商店的架上看過這產品。）

4 □ It's fifteen past nine.
　　□ It's a quarter past nine.
（現在九點十五分。）

5 □ I can play quite a few musical instruments, such as the flute, the guitar, and the piano.
　　□ I can play quite a few musical instruments, for example the flute, the guitar, and the piano.
（我會演奏許多種樂器，像是長笛，吉他還有鋼琴。）

6 □ Most importantly, you must work hard to catch up.
　　□ Most important, you must work hard to catch up.
（重要的是，你必需要努力追上進度。）

7 □ I haven't liked cartoons in ages.
　　□ I have disliked cartoons in ages.
（我很久以前就已經不喜歡卡通了。）

Answer

I. 填空題

❶ within; of each other
❷ within; of each other
❸ for six months
❹ in half an hour's time
❺ all the time
❻ all night
❼ in

❽ at
❾ such as
❿ as
⓫ Most important
⓬ More important
⓭ in/for
⓮ for

II. 圈圈看

❶ quarter to twelve
❷ a quarter of
❸ on
❹ on
❺ What time
❻ On what day

III. 二選一

❶ 第一句正確
❷ 第一句正確
❸ 第一句正確
❹ 第二句正確
❺ 第一句正確
❻ 第二句正確
❼ 第一句正確

Chapter 2
你的英文，用對了嗎？ | 片語篇　　　**Unit 05 動詞片語**

001 Question

Class is supposed to begin at 10.和Class was supposed to begin at 10.這兩句的意思有何不同呢？

Answer

be supposed to表示的是一種預期的情況：現在式的be supposed to意為「應該」，因此語意上相當於should或ought to（ought to的語氣比should來得強）；過去式的be supposed to意為「本該發生的事，但實際上卻沒發生」，因此相當於should have + P.P.或ought to have + P.P.。

Class is supposed to begin at 10.的意思是説，課應該在 10 點開始上（預期）；而Class was supposed to begin at 10.的意思是説，課原本應該在10點開始上，但事實卻沒有（即預期沒有實現），所以這相當於，譬如説，Class was supposed to begin at 10: 00, but it didn't begin until 10: 15.（課原本應該在10點開始上，但直到10點15分才上)。我們亦可用下面的句子來表達相同的意思：

Class should have begun at 10: 00, but it didn't begin until 10: 15.
Class ought to have begun at 10: 00, but it didn't begin until 10: 15.

be supposed to 除了上述的意思外，還有一個頗為常見的意思，那就是「一般認為」(to be generally believed/considered)。請看下句：

▶ It **is generally believed that** mice are afraid of cats. （一般認為老鼠怕貓。）

這種以it做假主詞或形式主詞來代表其後 that 所引導的名詞子句的句型，在英文中用得很多，應該加以熟悉。現在我們使用 be supposed to 來改寫如下：

▶ Mice **are supposed to** be afraid of cats. （老鼠應該怕貓。）

若不用 be supposed to，這句也可以改成：

▶ Mice **are generally believed to be** afraid of cats. （一般認為老鼠怕貓。）

大多數的 "It ... that" 句型都可以如上述地加以改寫，其方式就是將名詞子句的主詞拿來當句子的主詞，並將名詞子句的動詞變成to-不定詞。最後要提的是，supposed to中的d不發音，它的發音就跟suppose to一樣，但在拼寫時切記不可漏掉 "d"。

002 Question

You can try and love her.和You can try to love her.這兩句有何不同呢？

Answer

這兩句的意思（你可以試著愛她）完全一樣，因為try and和try to幾乎可以互換。Try and是口語用法，而且相當常用，如We are going to try and (= try to) find a solution to the problem. （我們將設法找到這問題的解決辦法。）但它不能用在正式書面文件和正式寫作中。

然而，必須注意的是，在否定句中，用try to會比用try and來得好，如She didn't even try to be polite. （她甚至不想試著客氣一點。）此外，當try有數、時態等的變化時，亦即try變成tries, tried, trying時，一般都用try to而不用try and，如We're trying to improve our teaching methods. （我們正設法改進教學方法。）。

003 Question

「做決定」的英文是take a decision還是make a decision呢？

Answer

兩者都正確。take a decision是英式英語，而make a decision是美式英語。雖然take a decision於20世紀末開始「入侵」美國，但現今美國人仍大多使用make a decision。

不過，要注意的是，「決策者」幾乎都是拼成decision-maker，不是拼成 decision-taker；同樣地，「（做）決策的」是寫成decision-making，而不是decision-taking。

004 Question

He had to call in sick to work....這句真令人困惑，為什麼他請病假去工作呢？這不是矛盾嗎？

Answer

我們平常所說的「請病假」，英文最常用的講法是call in sick或take a sick leave。call in sick通常是指上班族請病假不上班，因此有些人亦說成call in sick to work，來明確指出這是上班族的「請病假」，俾與學生的「請病假」有所區別。

然而，由於 call in sick後面可以接一個不定詞片語來表示「請病假去做某事」（假病假之名，行做其他事情之實）的意思，如He called in sick (for one day) to go on a date with his new girlfriend.（他請一天病假去跟他的新女友約會。）有些人往往把call in sick to work中的to work誤解為不定詞。這裡的to是介系詞，而work是名詞－這可從學生請病假可以說成call in sick to school中得到證明。它們的意思是說「向工作場所請病假」、「向學校請病假」。所以上面的例句亦可寫成He called in sick to work (for one day) to go on a date with his new girlfriend.。

既然談到請假，如果不提一些與請假有關的用語，似乎有點說不過去。一般而言，「請（一天）假沒去上班」就是take a day off，「請兩天假沒去上班」就是take two days off，依此類推。同樣地，為了區別上班族與學生的請假，我們可以更明確地說take a day off from work/school。若是只請半天假的話就說成take the morning/afternoon off。「早退」是leave early、「遲到」是come in late。不過，美語中並無細分「事假」和「喪假」，只要是私人因素請假都可以說成He took a day (or the whole day) off to take care of some personal business/affairs.（他請了一天假去處理私事。）

值得一提的是，美語中有個俚語，意思與call in sick完全一樣，那就是bang in或bang in sick (to work)，如I banged in sick to work for two days to finish my book.（我請了兩天病假來完成我的書。）。

在 You may well say so.這句中，may well的意思為何？另外，may or might (just) as well和may or might as well ... as的意思又是為何呢？

Answer

❶ may/might well

may/might well意為「很可能；儘可，有足夠理由」。例如：

▶ She **may/might well** refuse to speak to you. （她很可能拒絕跟你說話。）

▶ You **may/might well** say so. = You have good/enough reason to say so. （你有足夠的理由這麼說。）

這種句型也可變成倒裝句，如She may well refuse to speak to you.可以變成Well may she refuse to speak to you.－請注意詞序。再舉一例：Well may you ask why! （你儘可以問原因啊！）。

❷ might well have + p.p.

這種句型僅意為「很可能」，它的用途主要有二：

(a). 在與過去事實相反的假設語氣中用於結果子句。例如：

▶ We lost the baseball match, but we **might well** have won if one of our players hadn't been hurt. （我們輸了這場棒球賽，但如果我們有個球員不受傷的話，我們很可能會贏。）

(b). 對過去所發生事情的推測。例如：

▶ Your mother **might well** have been looking for you. （你媽媽很可能一直在找你。）

注意：在否定句中，not是位在 "well" 之後（意為「很可能不」）。例如：

▶ You **may well not** recognize him. （你很可能認不出他了。）

3 may/might (just) as well

may/might (just) as well (= had better/best)意為「最好（還是）；還是……的好」。例如：

▶ You **may/might as well** not fool around all day long.
= You had better/best not fool around all day long.
（你最好別整天遊手好閒。）－ not 同樣位在 "well" 之後（意為「最好不」）

may as well A as B意為「與其 B 不如 A」。
might as well A as B意為「做 B 等於做 A」。例如：

▶ One may as well not know a thing at all as know it imperfectly.（與其一知半解不如完全不知。）
▶ We might as well negotiate with a tiger for its hide as try to make peace with Kim Jong-un.（與金正恩謀和無異於與虎謀皮。）

006 Question

I wouldn't go so far as to say that.這句是什麼意思呢？

Answer

這句話意為「我還不至於說那樣」，是一種表示不完全同意某人的看法或意見的禮貌性說法，相當於說I don't wholly/entirely/completely agree with you.或I am not in complete agreement with you.

一般人比較不容易瞭解 "go so far as to + V" 這個片語的意思；它的主要意思為「竟然」、「到了……的程度」。例如：

▶ They **go so far as to** call him a genius.（他們竟然稱他是天才。）
▶ He went **so far as to** call her names.（他竟然說她的壞話。）

注意： "call someone names" 是個口語，意為「罵人；說某人壞話」（不是「叫某人的名字」），call後面是接受格（不是所有格），而names要用複數。舉例說明：

▶ More often than not his wife goes so far as to **call him names**.（他太太經常數落他的不是。）

▶ Those children were **calling each other names** in the street.（那些小孩在街上你罵我，我罵你的。）

007 Question

為何不能說I want to go to shop or go to swim or go to hike呢？這是因為go shopping or go swimming or go hiking是慣用語嗎？

Answer

go shopping/go swimming/go hiking等本來就是慣用語，但這並不表示有了慣用語就不能有其他表示相同意思的說法，只是英文確實沒有go to shop/go to swim/go to hike這樣的說法，因為這樣是錯誤的。 "go to" 意為「前往」、「前去」，所以to的後面應該接表示目的地、場所或地方等的名詞或名詞類用語，如go to the beach（去海灘）、go to the concert（去聽音樂會）、go to the movies（去看電影）、go to where his daughter works（去他女兒工作的地方）等等。問題中所提到的shop, swim, hike都是動詞，並非名詞。

這位讀者之所以認為go to後面可以接動詞，可能是將它與going to混為一談。在英文中，be going to是個很常見的片語，但它有兩個用法：一是當作表示未來的助動詞，意為「將要」，相當於will，這時to後面接原形動詞，如I am going to swim tonight.（今晚我要去游泳。）；另一個be going to是上述go to的進行式時態，所以to的後面也是接名詞或名詞類用語，而這個進行式時態可以表示正在進行的動作，也可以表示事先已計畫好的未來要做的動作，亦即用現在進行式表示未來，如 I am going to the beach.就有兩個意思，一是「我正在去海灘」，另一是「我將要去海灘」（在講這句話之前就已決定要去了。）

還有一點要注意的是，在口語和英文歌曲中，going to往往被唸成 gonna，但並非所有going to都可以唸成 gonna，只有 "be going to + V" 中的going to才能讀做gonna，如I'm gonna getcha.「妳是我的」/「我將會得到妳」，而 "be going to + N" 中的going to則不行。

008 Question

影片中有人説Get a move on!，字幕上打的中文是「快點」。事後查字典確實有這個片語。口語不是要越簡潔越好嗎？為什麼他不説Hurry up!呢？

Answer

一個片語中字數的多寡與它是不是口語無關；換言之，口語所用的片語並非總是由一、兩個字所構成，有時是「又臭又長」。譬如説， "to put one's foot in one's mouth" （意為「説錯話，説話不得體」）這個成語有好幾個字，但它卻是一句很常講的話，一句很常用的口語；又如「事實上；實際上」在英文口語中大多説成 "as a matter of fact" ，而 "in fact" 反而少用。因此，該片的人物説「快點」時用get a move on而不用hurry up，應該是個人習慣的問題。

除 "get a move on" 外，英文中意思與 "hurry up" 相當的口語還有 "Step on it." 、 "Step on the gas." 和 "Make it snappy." 。這些口語都是經常耳聞的，它們通常用於祈使句。

009 Question

是否可以詳述had better的用法呢？

Answer

had better意為「最好」、「應該」，後接原形動詞，與語氣助動詞should的用法相似，其中的had在口語和非正式寫作中經常縮略為'd或完全省略。例如：

▶ You **had better** go before it rains.
  = You**'d better** go before it rains.
  = You **better** go before it rains.
  （你最好在下雨前就去。）

▶ I'**d better** be making tracks.
　= I'**d better** get going.
　= I'**d better** be off in a (little) bit.
　（我該走了 / 我要走了。）

然而，在正式或學術文章中，一般並不建議使用had better或better，而應使用should或ought to。例如：

▶ You **should** go to school today. = You **ought to** go to school today.
　（你今天應該上學。）

在上面的例句中，should和ought to的意思相同，都是表示建議、勸告的「應該」。另外，順便一提的是，ought to在口語中經常寫成 "oughta" 或發 "otta" 的音，就像 have to經常變成 "hafta" （has to發 "hasta" ）的音一樣。

雖然had better與should（或ought to）都是表示勸告或建議，但had better只能對特定的情況而不能對普遍的情況提出勸告或建議，若要對普遍的情況提出勸告或建議，則須使用should。例如：

▶ You **should** brush your teeth before you go to bed. （睡覺前你應該刷牙。）
▶ He **should** dress more appropriately for the office. （上班時他的穿著應該要更得體。）

不過，should亦可針對特定的情況提出勸告或建議。例如：

▶ You **shouldn't** say anything. （你什麼都不該說。）
▶ He **should** get back to work. （他應該回去工作。）
▶ We **should** meet early. （我們應該早點見面。）

然而，had better針對特定情況所提出的勸告或建議，帶有警告或威脅會有不良後果的意味。例如：

▶ You'**d better** do what I say or else you will get into trouble. （你最好按照我的話去做，否則你就會有麻煩。）
▶ I'**d better** get back to work or else my boss will be angry with me. （我最好回去工作，否則我老闆就要生氣了。）
▶ We'**d better** get to the airport by five or else we may miss the flight. （我們最好在五點之前到達機場，否則我們可能會搭不上飛機。）

值得注意的是，had better中的had不能用have或has來替換；再者，"had"雖是過去式，但從上面的例句可知，had better是表示一種現在或未來的情況。不過，had better可用had best來代替，但had best的使用頻率比had better來得低。例如：

- ▶ You **had best** get home before midnight. （你最好在午夜之前回到家裡。）
- ▶ We**'d best** get going. （我們最好現在就走 / 我們該走了。）

had better的否定形式是將否定副詞not放在had better的後面，不是放在had的後面。例如：

- ▶ You**'d better** not disturb him. （你最好別去打擾他。）
- ▶ You **had better** not miss the last bus. →（○）正確。
  （你最好別錯過末班公車。）
- ▶ You had not better miss the last bus. →（✕）錯誤。

had better通常不以一般疑問句的形式出現，若要使用這種疑問形式，則將had（不是 had better）置於主詞之前，如What had we better do?（我們該怎麼辦呢？）had better用於否定疑問句的情況比較多，常用「Hadn't＋主詞＋better ...?」結構，這是一種勸告形式，比肯定句的語氣來得委婉。例如：

- ▶ **Hadn't you better** take an umbrella? （你是不是該帶一把傘呢？）
- ▶ **Hadn't you better** ask him first? （你是不是該先問問他呢？）
- ▶ **Hadn't we better** go now? （我們是不是現在就去呢？）

至於had better的附加問句如下列所示：

- ▶ You'd better not go out today, **had you**? （你今天最好不要外出，好嗎？）
- ▶ You had better go for a doctor, **hadn't you**? （你最好去看醫生，不是嗎？）

had better後接動詞進行式（had better + be + V-ing），係表示最好馬上做某事；若接完成式動詞（had better + have + P.P.），則表示本該做某事但並未去做。例如：

- ▶ I think I**'d better** be/get going. （我想我該走了。）
- ▶ We**'d better** be getting our clothes ready. （我們最好馬上把衣服準備好。）
- ▶ We **had better** be watching TV. （我們最好馬上就看電視。）
- ▶ We **had better** be starting back now. （我們最好現在就動身回去。）

▶ You **had better** have done it.（你本來應該把那件事做好的。）— 但實際上卻沒做。

▶ You **had better** have stayed with us.（你本來應該跟我們待在一起的。）— 但實際上卻沒有。

had better亦可用於祈使句，此時had往往省略。例如：

▶ **Better** not wait for him.（最好不要等他了。）

▶ **Better** say yes, if your wife asks you.（如果你太太問你，你最好說「是」。）

010 Question

「go + 形容詞」結構的意義為何呢？

Answer

「go + 形容詞」結構在英文中頗為常見，go在此結構中是當連綴動詞用。一般而言，「go + 形容詞」結構大多能從字面上看出或猜出大概的意思，如go hungry（挨餓）、go mad（發狂）、go wrong（犯錯，出錯）、go green（變綠了；邁向環保）、go bad（「食物」變質了）；然而，有些「go＋形容詞」結構則無法或很難從字面看出它們的意思，如go postal（勃然大怒；怒火中燒）、go Dutch（各付各的帳）、go straight（改過自新；正正當當地做人）以及現今非常盛行的go viral（在網路上爆紅）。就go viral而言，這個片語通常用來指影片、音樂或笑話。例如：

▶ A video of four youngsters dancing on a rainy street corner has **gone viral**.（一支顯示 4 個青少年雨中街頭跳舞的影片在網路上爆紅。）

▶ After the video went viral, visitors to our blog doubled overnight.（那段影片被 PO 上網後，我們部落格的點閱人數一夜間暴增一倍。）

現就「go＋形容詞」結構的使用規律及其意義歸納整理如下：

❶ go ＋顏色形容詞

go常與顏色形容詞連用，通常表示情況變化的結果或程度。例如：

▶ The grass was **going green**.（草變綠了。）

▶ Her hair's **going grey**. （她的頭髮變白了。）

必須注意的是，這類句子中的go均可用turn來代替，這在正式文體中尤然。

❷ go ＋形容詞

「go＋形容詞」結構亦可表示某人或某物的情況變壞，而這種變化通常是不可逆的或永久性的。例如：

▶ Eggs are apt to **go bad** in summer. （雞蛋在夏天容易變壞。）
▶ He has **gone mad/crazy**. （他瘋了。）
▶ Tom has **gone bald/blind**. （湯姆禿頂了／失明了。）
▶ Mr. Smith has **gone quite deaf**. （史密斯先生的耳朵聾得很厲害。）
▶ The heat has caused the milk to **go sour**. （高溫使牛奶酸掉了。）

❸ go ＋形容詞

go還可與一些一般性形容詞或帶有字首un-的過去分詞連用，來表達各種不同的意思。例如：

▶ The telecommunications workers decided to **go slow**. （電信工人決定怠工。）
▶ The telephone has **gone dead**. （電話不通了。）
▶ You'll never **go wrong** if you follow my advice. （你只要遵從我的忠告就決不會出錯。）
▶ All my letters **went unanswered**. （我寫的信都沒有回音。）
▶ The robbers must not **go unpunished**. （絕不能讓這些搶匪逍遙法外。）

值得一提的是，go的相反詞come也有後接形容詞的結構；同樣地，come在此結構中亦當連綴動詞用。一般而言，「come＋形容詞」結構中的形容詞往往是意義比較正面的形容詞。例如：

▶ Wrong never **comes right**. （[諺] 錯誤終究是錯誤，絕不會變成正確。）
▶ My dream has **come true**. （我的願望實現了。）
▶ Everything will **come clear** if you make an investigation. （如果你調查一下，一切都會一清二楚。）
▶ It **comes easy** with practice. （只要練習就容易了。）

I. 填空題

1 I _____ have a crush on someone like you!
（我不該愛上像你這樣的人的。）

2 She _____ be here now!
（她現在應該要在這裡的！）

3 They _____ break into the house last night.
（他們昨晚試圖闖入那房子。）

4 He is _____ wake her up.
（他試著叫醒她。）

5 He had to c_____.
（他今天必須要向公司請病假。）

6 Many of our company's employees b_____ today.
（本公司許多員工今天請病假。）

7 _____ you ask why!
（你儘可以問原因啊！）

8 No one will eat the food; it _____ be thrown away.
（沒有人要吃這些食物，最好還是扔掉算了。）

9 He _____ call her names.
（他竟然說她的壞話。）

10 More often than not the teacher _____ call him names in the class.
（那老師經常在班上數落他的不是。）

11 I _____ to the movies.
（我去看電影了。）

12 I _____ hiking.
（我要去健行。）

⑬ After the video _____, visitors to our blog doubled overnight.
（那段影片被PO上網後，我們部落格的點閱人數一夜間暴增一倍。）

⑭ The heat has caused the milk to _____.
（高溫使牛奶酸掉了。）

II. 圈圈看

❶ She is the _____ (decision-maker/decision-taker) of the family.
（她是家裡的決策者。）

❷ Every _____ (decision-making/decision-taking) process produces
a final choice.
（所有的決策過程後都會產生一個結果。）

III. 改寫句子

❶ I'd better be making tracks.
= _____
（我該走了。）

❷ We should meet early.
（我們應該早點見面。）
= _____

IV. 英翻中

❶ Make it snappy.
_____

❷ Step on the gas.
_____

V. 二選一

1 □ Class is supposed to begin at 10.
□ Class was supposed to begin at 10.
（十點就會開始上課了。）

2 □ I try to love her.
□ I try loving her.
（我很努力要試著愛她。）

3 □ We might well negotiate with a tiger for its hide as try to make peace with Kim Jong-un.
□ We might as well negotiate with a tiger for its hide as try to make peace with Kim Jong-un.
（與金正恩謀和無異於與虎謀皮。）

4 □ I wouldn't go so far as to say that.
□ I can't agree with you more.
（我不完全認同你。）

5 □ I am gonna the beach.
□ I am going to the beach.
（我正要去海邊。）

6 □ He should dress more appropriately for the office.
□ He had better dress more appropriately for the office.
（上班時他的穿著應該要更得體。）

7 □ My dream has gone true.
□ My dream has come true.
（我的願望實現了。）

Answer

I. 填空題

1. am not supposed to
2. is supposed to
3. tried to
4. trying to
5. call in sick to work
6. banged in
7. Well may
8. may/might just as well
9. went so far as to
10. goes so far as to
11. went
12. am going to go
13. went viral
14. go sour

II. 圈圈看

1. decision-maker
2. decision-making

III. 改寫句子

1. I'd better get going.
2. We ought to meet early.

IV. 英翻中

1. 快一點！
2. 快踩油門！（快點！）

V. 二選一

1. 第一句正確
2. 第一句正確
3. 第二句正確
4. 第一句正確
5. 第二句正確
6. 第一句正確
7. 第二句正確

Chapter3
你的英文，用對了嗎？

——句子篇——

001 Question

I don't want there to be any misunderstanding.的意思及句子結構為何呢？

Answer

這是 "there is/are"（有）句型的不定詞表示法，句子的意思是「我不希望有任何誤解」。再舉一例：

▶ I don't want **there to be any** doubt about this.（我不希望對此有任何懷疑。）

這種句型還有動名詞表示法，如：

▶ I have dreamed **of there being** such a beautiful girlfriend.（我一直夢想有這樣漂亮的女友。）

句中there is/are的be動詞由於是介系詞of的受詞，所以須用動名詞 "being"。

002 Question

有人說I am glad to see you tomorrow.這句不對，這到底是怎麼回事呢？因為我認為這句的文法並沒有錯。

Answer

這個句子確實不合邏輯，因為I am glad to see you指的是現在的時間，而 tomorrow 是未來時間，把兩者放在一起顯然矛盾。在英文中，形容詞後面的不定詞稱為「不定詞後修飾語」，係用來修飾它前面的形容詞。如果不定詞後修飾語指的是主動詞所表示的時間之後所發生的事件或狀態，那麼此不定詞必須使用進行式(to + be +

V-ing)，而非簡單現在式（to + 原形動詞）。所以，問題中的句子若要合乎邏輯或語法，我們必須將它改為I am glad to be seeing you tomorrow.（我很高興明天會見到你。）茲再舉一例說明之：

She is very happy to be soon married to him.

這句也犯了相同的錯誤。**She is very happy to be married to him.**只能表示她已嫁給他的意思，亦即她已嫁作人婦，現在兩人是夫妻。然而，從句中的soon可以看出，她是要說，她對於即將和他結婚感到樂不可支（她還沒結婚）。所以這句應改為：

▶ She is very happy **to be marrying** to him soon.
= She is very happy **to be getting married** to him soon.
= She is very happy **that she is going to marry** him soon.

003 Question

在省略if的條件句，若為否定形式，好像不能將had not縮寫後移到句首（如不能將Had it not been ......寫成Hadn't it been...），這是否屬實呢？

Answer

沒錯！英文的條件句有三種情況可以省略if：當條件句的動詞部分含有were（與現在事實相反）、had（與過去事實相反）或should（與未來事實相反－即假設的情況不太可能發生）時，我們可將它們移到句首並省略if，使句子變成倒裝句。例如：

▶ If I were you, I wouldn't do that.
= **Were** I you, I wouldn't do that.
（如果我是你，就不會那麼做了。）

▶ If he had taken my advice, he might not have made such a bad mistake.
= **Had** he taken my advice, he might not have made such a bad mistake.
（要是他聽我的勸告，就不會犯這樣嚴重的錯誤了。）

▶ If I should have a chance to try it, I would do it in another way.

= **Should** I have a chance to try it, I would do it in another way.

（要是我有機會試一試，我會用另一種方法去做。）－ Should 係表示有機會一試的可能性微乎其微。

▶ If we were to have children, we'd need to move to a bigger house.

= **Were** we to have children, we'd need to move to a bigger house.

（如果 / 要是將來有小孩，我們必須換一間較大的房子。） －「were to + 原形動詞」是另一種與未來事實相反的條件句型。

如果條件句為否定形式，那麼在寫成倒裝句時，not必須置於主詞的後面，不能將它與were、had或should縮寫後移到句首。但如果將倒裝句改回正常的詞序，那麼were、had或should就可與not縮寫在一起。例如：

▶ **Were** she **not** my daughter, I'd have no hesitation in phoning the police.

（如果她不是我女兒，我會毫不猶豫地打電話報警。）→（○）正確。

Weren't she my daughter, I'd have no hesitation in phoning the police. →（╳）錯誤。

▶ **Had** it **not** rained last Saturday, we would've celebrated Tom's birthday with a barbecue in the garden.

（上週六要是沒下雨，我們會在花園烤肉慶祝湯姆的生日。）→（○）正確。

Hadn't it rained last Saturday, we would've celebrated Tom's birthday with a barbecue in the garden. →（╳）錯誤。

▶ **Should** you **not** wish to sign the contract, you must let them know before the end of June.

（要是你不想簽約，你必須在六月底之前讓他們知道。）→（○）正確。

Shouldn't you wish to sign the contract, you must let them know before the end of June. →（╳）錯誤。

但如果將倒裝句改回正常的詞序，那麼 were、had 或 should 就可與 not 縮寫在一起。請看下面的例句（其它條件句亦同）：

▶ If she **weren't** my daughter, I'd have no hesitation in phoning the police and telling them about the crime that has been committed. （如果她不是我女兒，我會毫不猶豫地打電話報警，告訴警方她所犯的罪。）

004 Question

(1) Please let me know when you arrive. 和 (2) Please let me know when you will arrive.這兩句有何區別呢？

Answer

這兩句雖只有一個will之差，但詞性與語意卻有天壤之別。第(1)句的when you arrive 是副詞子句（時間子句），用現在簡單式表示未來式，因為時間子句中不能有表示 未來的will或be going to等字眼（注意：這一文法規則幾乎是TOEFL, TOEIC及其他 英檢必考的問題）。而第(2)句的when you will arrive為名詞子句，當know的受詞。

再者，句 (1) 的意思是說「請你在抵達時告訴我」，至於告訴什麼事情則不明確， 可能是到達的時間，也可能是此行的目的或其他事情。然而，句(2)則明確表示了是 要告訴抵達的時間，所以這句的意思是「請你告訴我抵達的時間」，亦即 Please let me know your arrival time.。句(2)指的是未來的時間，如果我們要請對方告訴過去 抵達的時間，那麼名詞子句的時態要改成過去式，如Please let me know when you arrived yesterday.。

005 Question

在 It's high time we send（不是 sent）him a registered letter. 和 It's about time you spent（不是 spend）a little less money. 這兩句中，附屬子句的動詞為何一用現在式另一用過去式呢？

Answer

一般字典都只將 "It is high time...." 和 "It is about time ...." 解釋為「正是…… 的時候」、「該是……的時候」，英文的意思就是 "right time" 或 "appropriate time"。事實上，它們還有「早該……」的意思，尤其是 "It's about time ...."。

這兩個句子在time的後面大多接子句，而且使用簡單過去式，尤其是 "It's about time ...."，這可由問題中的例句得到證明。它表達的意思就是上述的「早

該……」，如It's about time you spent a little less money.（你早該少花一點錢了。－現在花錢的習慣還沒改。）；It's about time you had your hair cut.（你早該理髮了。－現在還沒理髮。）

至於 "It's high time ...."，附屬子句的動詞可以是現在式或過去式。如果是現在式，它指的是一種未來動作的「真實情況」，表示說話者有計畫去做那件事。如果是過去式，它指的是對過去應做卻未做的事情感到遺憾，且希望未來能夠去做，但會不會去做則不確定，所以是一種未來動作的「非真實情況」。例如：

▶ **It's high time** we send him a registered letter.（該是我們寄掛號信給他的時候了。）－打算要寄了。

▶ **It's high time** I have my hair cut.（該是我理髮的時候了。）－計畫要理髮了。

▶ **It's high time** I had my hair cut.（我早該理髮了。）－現在還沒理髮，想要理，但會不會理則還是未知數。

由上述可知，「It's high time/It's about time ＋ 子句（簡單過去式）」的句型，可視為一種與現在事實相反的條件句，這就是子句的動詞使用簡單過去式的原因。不過，雖然使用過去式時，"It's high time...." 和 "It's about time...." 都有「早該」的意思，但 "It's about time...." 的時間比 "It's high time...." 更早，亦即前者比後者「更早該」。

006 Question

在I'll face the fact that my girlfriend will move to Taipei tomorrow.中，the fact that 的語法功能為何呢？

Answer

這句的意思為「我將要面對我女友明天搬到台北的事實」。儘管中文翻譯有「事實」二字，但它並非 "the fact" 的翻譯，而是筆者為了讓中文翻譯變得通順而加入的，因為the fact that中的the fact雖具有舉足輕重的語法功能，但本身並無意義。

the fact that的語法功能有下列三項，其對英文寫作的幫助尤其宏大：

❶ 用來引導名詞子句

在許多情況中，當that所引導的名詞子句比較複雜時，若直接將其置於句首當主詞，可能會顯得「頭重腳輕」。這時我們通常使用形式主詞或虛主詞it來代替that子句，而將that子句置於句末。注意：that子句當主詞時，動詞須用單數。例如：

▶ **That** my son has passed all the exams makes me feel very happy.
  = It makes me feel very happy that my son has passed all the exams.
    （我兒子已通過所有考試，令我很高興。）
▶ **That** he lost his job suddenly worried his parents very much.
  = It worried his parents very much that he lost his job suddenly.
    （他突然失業，使他的父母非常憂慮。）
▶ **That** she did not go to Cindy's birthday party surprised everybody.
  =It surprised everybody that she did not go to Cindy's birthday party.
    （她未參加辛蒂的生日派對，讓大家很驚訝。）

有時候，尤其是在比較正式的場合，在不使用形式主詞it的情況下，我們可使用the fact這一輔助工具，以使句意不致造成誤解：

▶ **The fact that** my son has passed all the exams makes me feel very happy.
▶ **The fact that** he lost his job suddenly worried his parents very much.
▶ **The fact that** she did not go to Cindy's birthday party surprised everybody.

the fact與that所引導的名詞子句為同位語。原本引導名詞子句的that是連接詞，在加上the fact當同位語後，that變成關係代名詞。

❷ 用於介詞之後引導當受詞用的名詞子句

根據英文文法，介系詞後面不能直接接that子句當受詞，但我們可以在that子句的前面加上the fact，使the fact作為介詞的受詞，這樣其後的that子句就成了the fact的同位語，百分之百合乎語法要求。例如：

▶ Rachel was absent due to **the fact that** she was sick.
  （瑞秋因生病沒來。）
▶ The father was worried over **the fact that** his son was suddenly taken ill.
  （那父親為他兒子突然病倒憂心忡忡。）

▶ But for **the fact that** you helped me, I would not have succeeded.
（要不是你幫忙，我就不會成功。）

▶ Carl had to face up to **the fact that** his family disapproved of his plan.
（卡爾必須正視家人不贊同他的計畫的事實。）

▶ The bad weather is responsible for **the fact that** the attendance at the party is small.
（參加聚會的人稀稀落落，是由於天氣不佳。）

事實上，英文中至少還是有個我們常用的介詞可直接接that子句，那就是 except。例如：

▶ I know nothing about him except **that** he lives next door.
（我除了知道他住在我隔壁外，其他事情毫無所悉。）

▶ Gary has no special fault except **that** he drinks too much.
（蓋瑞除了喝酒喝太多外，沒有什麼特別的毛病。）

❸ 用於原本不可接 that 子句的及物動詞之後引導當受詞用的名詞子句

英文中有些動詞雖為及物動詞，可接名詞或代名詞當受詞，但卻不能接 that 子句當受詞。因此，這些動詞 (如 contribute, describe, dislike, escape, face, make, prevent, speak, summarize, want) 若要接 that 子句，則可借助 the fact 結構以使其合乎語法要求。例如：

▶ Linda dislikes **the fact that** her husband smokes.
（琳達不喜歡她先生抽菸。）
→（○）正確。
Linda dislikes that her husband smokes.
→（×）錯誤。

▶ We were lucky to escape **the fact that** we were punished.
（我們很幸運，沒有受罰。）
→（○）正確。
We were lucky to escape that we were punished.
→（×）錯誤。

▶ We must face **the fact that** our son might fail the General Scholastic Ability Test.
（我們必須正視兒子的學測可能不過的事實。）

→（○）正確。

We must face that our son might fail the General Scholastic Ability Test.
→（✕）錯誤。

最後，順便一提的是，下面所列的動詞都可以接 that 子句當受詞，當然，它們只是這類動詞中的一小部份而已，但它們都是很常用的動詞：

accept, admit, announce, answer, ask, assume. authorize, believe, claim, command, complain, consent, consider, contest, declare, decide, decree, demand, demonstrate, determine, deny, desire, dictate, direct, discover, discuss, doubt, examine, expect, feel, find (out), forget, grant, guarantee, hope, ignore, imply, indicate, insist, know, move, notice, observe, order, overlook, permit, propose, prove, recommend, regret, remark, report, request, require, say, see, show, specify, suggest, suppose, think, understand, urge, wonder 等等。例如：

▶ We have to **admit** that Benson's a highly competent man.
（我們必須承認班森是個非常能幹的人。）

▶ We **decided** that Anna must stay here.
（我們決定安娜必須留在這裡。）

▶ I **regret** that you see it like that.
（我很遺憾你這樣看待這件事。）

007 Question

Andy was very tired because he had been jogging. 這句顯然是在表示因果關係，這種句型的使用時機為何呢？

Answer

在這句中，had been jogging是過去完成進行式(had been + V-ing)，而was是過去簡單式。根據文法，在過去兩個先後發生的動作中，發生在前的動作要用過去完成式(had + P.P.)，而發生在後的動作用過去簡單式。換言之，過去完成式係用來表示發生在過去某個動作或某一特定時間之前的動作。例如：

▶ Mr. Chen **had studied** English before he moved to San Francisco.
（陳先生搬到舊金山之前已學了英文。）

▶ I **had never seen** such a beautiful beach before I went to Pescadores.
（在我去澎湖之前，我從未看過這麼美麗的海灘。）

▶ A: **Had you ever visited** the U.K. before your trip in 2011?
（在 2011 年的英國行之前，你有去過英國嗎？）

B: Yes, I had been to the U.K. once before.
（有，我之前去過一次。）

然而，若過去完成式的動作一直持續至過去某個動作或某一特定時間，那麼我們須使用過去完成進行式來表示。例如：

▶ James **had been waiting** there for more than two hours when Mary finally arrived.
（當瑪麗終於抵達時，詹姆斯已在那裡等了超過兩小時。）

▶ Carla **had been** working at that company for three years when it went out of business.
（在那家公司歇業時，卡拉已在該公司工作了三年。）

▶ How long **had** you **been** waiting to get on the bus?
（你等多久才坐上公車呢？）

由於過去完成式或過去完成進行式的動作都發生在過去簡單式的動作之前，兩者自然很容易就形成因果關係；是故，過去完成式＋過去簡單式或過去完成進行式＋過去簡單式，乃成為表示過去發生的兩個有因果關係的動作或事件的完美組合，而問題中的句子Andy was very tired because he had been jogging.（安迪很疲憊，因為他一直在慢跑。）是屬於過去完成進行式＋過去簡單式的組合。例如：

▶ I did not have any money because I **had lost** my wallet.
（我身無分文，因為我遺失了錢包。）

▶ Sam knew Bangkok so well because he **had visited** the city several times.
（山姆對曼谷瞭若指掌，因為他已去過曼谷好幾趟。）

▶ We were not able to get a hotel room because we **had not booked** in advance.
（我們沒有飯店房間可住，因為我們事先沒有預訂。）

▶ Barry failed the final test because he **had not been** attending class.
（貝瑞期末考不及格，因為他一直沒來上課。）

▶ Kevin was very tired because he **had been** washing cars.
（凱文非常疲憊，因為他一直在洗車。）

▶ Amy gained weight because she **had been** overeating.
（艾美體重增加了，因為她一直暴飲暴食。）

值得一提的是，在過去完成進行式 + 過去簡單式的情況中，過去完成進行式的動作在過去簡單式的動作或狀態生時可能還在持續中，但也可能已告結束。

事實上，現在完成進行式(has/have been + V-ing)＋現在簡單式亦是一種表示因果關係的完美句型，它是用來表示最近的動作產生現在的結果或對現在造成的影響。但必須注意是，現在完成式(has/have + P.P.)並沒有這樣的用法。例如：

▶ My hands are so dirty because I **have been** working in the garden.
（我的雙手很髒，因為我一直在花園工作。）

▶ The ground is soaking wet because it **has been** raining all night.
（地面濕透了，因為整晚都在下雨。）

▶ Kevin is very tired because he **has been** jogging/washing cars.
（凱文非常疲憊，因為他一直在慢跑 / 洗車。）

同樣地，在現在完成進行式＋現在簡單式的情況中，現在完成進行式的動作在現在簡單式的動作或狀態發生時可能還在持續中，但也可能已告結束。以The ground is soaking wet because it has been raining all night.這句為例，在講這句話的時候，雨可能已經停了，但整晚下雨對現在所產生的結果或造成的影響（地面濕透了。）是顯而易見的。

Excercise
綜合練習

I. 填空題

1 I don't want _____ any problems.
（我不希望這有任何的問題。）

2 I have dreamed _____ such a lovely baby.
（我一直夢想要有這麼可愛的一個小貝比。）

3 I am glad to _____ you tomorrow.
（我很開心明天要跟你碰面。）

4 We are happy _____ travel next month.
（我們很開心下個月要去旅行了。）

5 I don't know when you _____.
（我不知道你將會在幾點睡覺。）

6 I will use your computer when you _____.
（當你睡覺時，我要用你的電腦。）

7 It's high time we _____ this song.
（我們早該演奏這首歌了。）

8 It's high time you _____ hard.
（是時候你該好好唸書了。）

9 _____ he lost his job suddenly worried his parents very much.
（他突然失業，使他的父母非常憂慮。）

10 Rachel was absent due to _____ she was sick.
（瑞秋因生病沒來。）

11 I _____ such a beautiful beach before I went to Pescadores.
（在我去澎湖之前，我從未看過這麼美麗的海灘。）

12 How long _____ to get on the bus?
（你等多久才坐上公車呢？）

II. 改寫句子

1 If he had taken my advice, he might not have made such a bad mistake.

= _____

（要是他聽我的勸告，就不會犯這樣嚴重的錯誤了。）

2 If we were to have children, we'd need to move to a bigger house.

（要是將來有小孩，我們必須換一間較大的房子。）

= _____

III. 二選一

1 ☐ I don't want there to be anything wrong.

☐ I don't want there is anything wrong.

（我不要有任何差錯。）

2 ☐ She is very happy to graduate soon.

☐ She is very happy to be graduating soon.

（她很開心要畢業了。）

3 ☐ Had it not rained last Saturday, we would've celebrated Tom's birthday with a barbecue in the garden.

☐ Hadn't it rained last Saturday, we would've celebrated Tom's birthday with a barbecue in the garden.

（上週六要是沒下雨，我們會在花園烤肉慶祝湯姆的生日。）

4 ☐ Please let me know when you are ready.

☐ Please let me know when you will be ready.

（請告訴我你何時準備好。）

5 ☐ It's high time we sent him a registered letter.

☐ It's high time we send him a registered letter.

（該是我們寄掛號信給他的時候了。）

6 ☐ Linda dislikes the fact that her husband smokes.

☐ Linda dislikes that her husband smokes.

（琳達不喜歡她先生抽菸。）

7 ☐ The ground is soaking wet because it had been raining all night.

☐ The ground is soaking wet because it has been raining all night.

（地面濕透了，因為整晚都在下雨。）

Answer

I. 填空題

1 there to be

2 of there being

3 be meeting

4 that we will

5 will sleep

6 sleep

7 played

8 study

9 That; The fact that

10 the fact that

11 had never seen

12 had you been waiting

II. 改寫句子

1 Had he taken my advice, he might not have made such a bad mistake.

2 Were we to have children, we'd need to move to a bigger house.

III. 二選一

1 第一句正確

2 第二句正確

3 第一句正確

4 第二句正確

5 第二句正確

6 第一句正確

7 第二句正確

001 Question

在She would have liked to go to Hong Kong for the weekend. 這句中，would have liked的意義為何呢？

Answer

would have liked是would like的過去式，兩者後面都是接現在式不定詞（to＋原形動詞），但前者是表示過去想要做但卻沒有做的情況。這種情況也可以用「would like＋完成式不定詞（to + have + P.P.）」或「wanted＋完成式不定詞」來表示。例如：

▶ My sister would have liked to study abroad.
= My sister would like to have studied abroad.
= My sister wanted to have studied abroad.
（我妹妹本來想出國留學。）－但事實上並沒有去。

所以，問題中的句子是說她本來想去香港度週末，但事實上並沒有去。

002 Question

I cannot wait to see my family.這句是什麼意思呢？

Answer

這句意為「我渴望見到我的家人」或「我迫不及待想要見到我的家人」。從這個句子可以看出，雖然句中使用了否定詞cannot，但它卻無否定之意，反而是表示肯定的意思。英文中，有些形式上看似否定的句型，實際上卻是表示肯定的意思。雖然這類句型有些是大家所熟知的，但都是零零碎碎，所以在此將它們作個有系統的整理，供大家參考。

❶ nothing/none（或 no ＋名詞）but ... －「只有；僅僅」。

nothing/none（no＋名詞）but ...等於only，表示肯定的意思，後接名詞、代名詞、不定詞等。例如：

No one but him in our class can swim across the river.（我們班上只有他能游過這條河。）

▶ She could do **nothing but** wait here.（她別無他法，只好在這裡等待。）
▶ He chose **none but** the best.（他只選最好的。）

❷ never (not) ...but (that) －「每當……，總是……；沒有哪次不是……」。

▶ I **never** see you **but** I think of my mother.（每當看見你，我就會想起我的母親。）
▶ It **never** rains **but** it pours.（不下則已，一下傾盆；禍不單行；屋漏偏逢連夜雨。）

❸ not...until －「直到……才」。

在這個句型中，until可作介詞，也可作連接詞。作介詞時，後接名詞、代名詞或片語；作連接詞時，後接子句。not後面接非延續性動詞或瞬間動詞。例如：

▶ He did **not** go to bed **until** his mother came back.（他直到他媽媽回來才睡覺。）

not...until ...也可用於強調句和倒裝句中。例如：

▶ It was **not until** this morning **that** he finished the work.（他直到今天上午才完成那項工作。）

❹ not long before －「不久……就……」。

▶ It was **not long before** he appeared.（他不久就出現了。）

❺ not/no...without... －「沒有……就沒有……」。

在這個句型中，使用兩個否定來加強語氣，表示肯定的意思（雙重否定等於肯定）。

▶ One **cannot** live even a few minutes **without** air.（沒有空氣，人們甚至連幾分鐘也不能生存。）
▶ There is **no** smoke **without** fire.（無風不起浪；事出必有因。）

❻ too...not to... 和 never (not) too...to... 這類雙重否定的句型，也表示肯定意思。

－too...not to...是too...to...的否定，意為「非常……必定能；太……不會不」。例如：

▶ The boy is **too** clever **not to** work out this math problem. （這個男孩很聰明，不會解不出這道數學題。）

－not too... to...，意為「不太……所以能」。例如：

▶ He is **not too** old **to** do it. （他做這件事，年齡並不老。）

－never too...to ...，意為「決不；永不」。例如：

▶ It is **never too** late **to** give up prejudices. （放棄偏見永遠不晚。）

❼ cannot/couldnt + too －「愈……愈好；再……也不為過；無論怎樣……也不過分」。

在這個句型中，cannot也可改用can hardly, scarcely, never, impossible；too也可改用over, enough等。例如：

▶ We **cannot** be **too** careful in choosing friends. （我們在擇友時愈謹慎愈好 / 無論多謹慎也不為過。）

▶ A man can **never** have **too** many friends. （朋友越多越好。）

❽ hardly/ scarcely...when/before... －「一（剛）……就……」。

在這個句型中，when/before前面的主句要用過去完成式，而其後的子句則用簡單過去式。例如：

▶ He had **hardly/scarcely** arrived **when** it began to rain. （他一到達，天就開始下雨了。）

❾ no sooner ... than ... (= hardly/ scarcely ... when/before ...) －「一（剛）……就……」。

在這個句型中，no sooner位在主句中，主句要用過去完成式，而than引導的子句則用簡單過去式。例如：

▶ **No sooner** had they got to the theater **than** the concert began. （他們一進入劇院，音樂會就開始了。）

❿ can't/couldn't + 比較級－相當於最高級。

▶ It **couldn't** have happened to a **nicer** man!（再也沒有人比你更好或更棒了；你最棒了！）

▶ I **can't/couldn't** agree (with you) **more**.（我完全同意。）

⓫ none other than －「正是」。

▶ She is **none other than** my teacher.（她正是我的老師。）

▶ The letter was written by **none other than** Mary.（寫這封信的正是瑪麗。）

more often than not－「經常，往往」。

▶ The street is crowded **more often than not**.（這條街經常擁擠不堪。）

⓬ not a little －「非常，十分，相當；很多」（注意：not a bit = not at all －「一點也不」）。例如：

▶ He is **not a little** tired.（他非常累。）

▶ He has **not a little** experience.（他有豐富的經驗。）

▶ His business is **not a little** promising.（他的事業很有前途。）

003 Question

I do love you.（我確實愛你）這個敘述句使用do＋原形動詞來加強語氣。是否可以談談英文中其他加強語氣或表示強調的字、片語或句子呢？

Answer

英文中加強語氣的方法不一而足。除了用助動詞do＋原形動詞來加強語氣外，另外至少還有七種加強語氣或表示強調的方法。茲將這八種方法臚列於後，供大家參考：

❶ 用反身代名詞來加強語氣

▶ We **ourselves** will hold a press conference.（我們將親自召開記者會。）

▶ He can do it well **himself**.（他自己能做好這件事。）

❷ 用助動詞 do 來加強語氣

▶ **Do** be quiet. The baby is sleeping.（務必安靜。嬰兒正在睡覺。）

▶ The baby is generally healthy, but every now and then she **does** catch a cold.（嬰兒的健康狀況尚好，但就是偶爾會感冒。）

❸ 用副詞 very, only, even, too 等來加強語氣

very 用於形容詞最高級或first, last, opposite, own等字的前面，意為「真正地，極其」；too意為「真的」

▶ She ate it to the **very** last mouthful.（她把它吃得一乾二淨。）

▶ **Only** in Paris can you buy shoes like that.（只有在巴黎你才能買到那樣的鞋子。）

▶ He didn't answer **even** my letter.（他甚至連我的信都不回。）

▶ I will **too** go!（我真的要去！）

❹ 用形容詞 very, single 來加強語氣

very 意為「正是；恰好是」

▶ She died in the **very** room.（她就是在這個房間裡過世的。）

▶ Not a **single** person has gone to her wedding ceremony.（竟然沒有一個人參加她的婚禮。）

❺ 使用下列片語來加強語氣

by all means（當然；一定；不論如何）、by no means（絕不；一點也不）、in no way（絕不；一點也不）、all too（極，甚，太）、only too（極，甚，太）、in heaven's name, in the world, on earth, the dickens, the devil, the hell, under the sun（後面這幾個片語的意思都是「到底；究竟」，而under the sun還有「全世界；全天下」的意思）

▶ **By all means** wash your dirty shirt.（一定要洗你的髒襯衫。）

▶ These scenes of violence are **all too** familiar.（這些暴力場面簡直是太熟悉了。）

▶ What **in the world** are you doing?（你到底在幹什麼？）

▶ He was the last person **under the sun** I expected to see there.（他是我在那裡最最沒有料到會見到的人。）

❻ 用倒裝句來加強語氣

▶ **Not** a word **did** she say the whole two hours. （整整兩個鐘頭，她一句話也沒說。）

▶ **In wine** is the truth. （酒後吐真言。）

▶ **Never will they** give up the struggle for freedom and peace. （他們絕對不會放棄為自由與和平而奮鬥。）

▶ **More serious was** the problem of environmental pollution. （更嚴重的是環境污染問題。）

❼ 用強調句型（It is/was ＋被強調部分＋ that 子句）來加強語氣

在此句型中，that子句前的先行詞若是人，則that可用who或whom來代替，其餘情況只能用that。

▶ **It was** your mother-in-law that (whom) I met in the park the day before yesterday. （前天我在公園裡碰到的正是你的岳母。）

▶ **It is** only when one is ill that one realizes the importance of health. （只有在人們生病時才知道健康的重要。）

▶ **It was** Professor Wu that (who) sent me the letter. （寄信給我的正是吳教授。）

❽ 用「主句（主詞＋動詞……）, and that ...」句型來加強語氣（that 代替前面主句的全部或部份句子）

▶ You must apologize to me, **and that** in public. （你必須向我道歉，而且是公開道歉。）

▶ You must do it, **and that** at once. （你必須做這件事，而且要馬上做。）

▶ She speaks English, **and that** very well. （她講英文，而且講得很好。）

`004` Question

I didn't go home.和I wouldn't go home.有何不同呢？

Answer

這兩個句子的意思截然不同。I didn't go home.是過去簡單式，這句非常簡單，它

是在敘述過去一項簡單的事實，僅在提供資訊，讓人家知道「我沒有回家」。至於I wouldn't go home.則比較複雜，因為它使用了語氣助動詞would的否定型態。這句可以有兩個完全不同的意思。當然了，若沒有上下文，我們將無從判斷它指的是那個意思。

would除了做為will的過去式來表示「過去的未來式」（表示在過去某個時間點你認為某事未來會發生。至於你的想法或看法是否正確則不重要）外，還有兩個主要意思，一是表示意願，另一是表示過去習慣性和經常性的動作，但現在已經不做或不再發生：

① 表示意願

就第一義而言，wouldn't就是不願意，所以I wouldn't go home.這句是說「我不想回家」或「我不願意回家」。雖然大家都要我回家，想方設法要我回家，但我堅持不回家，我不想回家，我不願意回家。

② 過去習慣性和經常性的動作，但現在已經不做或不再發生

第二個意思wouldn't是指在大部分的時間或在大多數的情況中，我都不回家。或許由於在我的求學時代，我的父母親都在工廠上大夜班，每天日落黃昏時，家裡都空無一人，所以我放學後都不回家，而是直接去外婆的家或是去一些朋友的家，但我就是不回家或沒有回家（因為家裡沒有人）--這是我過去一種經常性的習慣，即「過去我經常不回家」。

005 Question

Could I borrow your pen?和May I borrow your pen?哪一句比較有禮貌呢？

Answer

在英文中，有幾種句型可以表示禮貌性請求。在此我們將討論最常見的以 "I" 和以 "you" 作主詞的禮貌性請求。

❶ 以 I 當主詞

首先來看以 I 當主詞的禮貌性請求，如 Could I borrow your pen (please)?；May I (please) borrow your pen?（注意：please 可以放在句末或主詞後面）。這兩句都意為「我可以借你的筆嗎？」，而且禮貌程度等量齊觀、不相上下。不過，要注意的是，在禮貌性請求中，could係表示現在或未來的意義，並非過去的意義。此外，我們亦可使用Can I borrow your pen?，但Can I係用於非正式場合，尤其是用在說話者對他或她相當熟識的人提出請求的場合。一般通常認為Can I的禮貌程度略低於Could I或May I。事實上，Might I也可以表示禮貌性請求，如Might I borrow your pen?，但Might I係用於非常正式且講究禮貌的場合，所以它的使用頻率比Could I或May I低很多。

對於以I當主詞的禮貌性請求，一般典型的回應是 "Certainly"、"Yes, certainly"、"Of course"、"Yes, of course" 或 "Sure"（非正式）。吾人亦經常使用動作來回應禮貌性請求，如點頭、搖頭或只是「嗯」(uh-huh) 一聲。

❷ 以 you 當主詞

接著來看以 you 當主詞的禮貌性請求，如Would you (please) pass me the salt?；Will you pass me the salt (please)?。這兩句都意為「請你把鹽遞給我好嗎？」，亦即在禮貌性請求中，Would you和Will you的意思是一樣的。但Would you比較常用，且通常被認為比較有禮貌。然而，禮貌的程度往往取決於說話者的口氣。此外，我們亦可使用Could you (please) pass me the salt?，基本上，Could you和Would you的意思僅有微乎其微的差異，而且禮貌程度也不分伯仲。事實上，Can you也可以表示禮貌性請求，如Can you pass me the salt (please)?，但Can you通常用於非正式場合，且其禮貌程度通常低於Could you或Would you。必須注意的是，以you當主詞的禮貌性請求，不能使用May，否則就錯了。在禮貌性請求中，May僅能跟I或we連用。

對於以 "you" 當主詞的禮貌性請求，一般典型的回應是 "Yes, I'd (I would) be happy to/be glad to"（好，我很樂意。）、"Certainly" 或 "Sure"（非正式）。吾人對於禮貌性請求通常會給予肯定的回答，但若必須做出否定回應，那麼可以用 "I'd like to, but …" 做開頭，來表示禮貌性拒絕，如 "I'd like to pass (you) the salt, but I can't reach it."（我想把鹽遞給你，但我拿不到。）

Excercise
綜合練習

I.填空題

1 His wife would _____ commit suicide.
（他太太本來想要自殺的。）

2 She _____ get married at 18.
（她本來要在18歲就結婚的。）

3 He chose _____ the best.
（他只選最好的。）

4 It _____ rains _____ it pours.
（不下則已，一下傾盆。）

5 The baby is generally healthy, but every now and then she _____ catch a cold.
（那嬰兒的健康狀況尚好，但就是偶爾會感冒。）

6 I will _____ go!
（我真的要去！）

7 She _____ admit her affair with her boss.
（她不願承認她和她老闆有染。）

8 I _____ go home last night.
（我昨晚沒有回家。）

II. 回答句子

1 A: Would you please pass me the salt?
（你可以把鹽遞給我嗎？）
B: _____.
（好，我很樂意。）

2 A: Would you help me?
（你可以幫幫我嗎？）

B: _____

（我很想幫你，但是我沒辦法。）

III. 二選一

❶ ☐ I can't agree with you more.
　☐ I can agree with you more.
（我完全同意。）

❷ ☐ More serious the problem of environmental pollution was.
　☐ More serious was the problem of environmental pollution.
（更嚴重的是環境污染問題。）

❸ ☐ I wouldn't go home. My mom would beat me.
　☐ I didn't go home. My mom would beat me.
（我不想回家，回家我媽會揍我。）

❹ ☐ May you come here?
　☐ Could you come here?
（可以請你過來一下嗎？）

Answer

I. 填空題

❶ have liked to
❷ would have liked to
❸ none but
❹ never; but
❺ does
❻ too
❼ wouldn't
❽ didn't

II. 回答句子

❶ Yes, I'd (I would) be happy to/be glad to
❷ I'd like to, but I can't.

III. 二選一

❶ 第一句正確
❷ 第二句正確
❸ 第一句正確
❹ 第二句正確

001 Question

It couldn't have happened to a nicer man這句是什麼意思呢？

Answer

這句的意思是「再也沒有人比你更棒了！」這是一句很常用的會話。當某人告訴你壞消息時，如I've failed my exam.（我考試沒過。）你可以回答：What a pity!（真遺憾！）或What a shame!（真可惜！）或I'm sorry to hear that.（聽到這樣我很難過。）如果某人告訴你好消息，如I've passed my exam.（我通過考試了。）你就可以說It couldn't have happened to a nicer guy!

此外，英文還有一句也很常用的會話，它的構造和理解方式亦頗為神似，那就是 I can't/couldn't agree (with you) more.。It couldn't have happened to a nicer guy!字面上的意思是「某事不可能發生在更好的人身上了」，換言之就是「再也沒有人比你更好了」；而I can't/couldn't agree (with you) more.字面上的意思是「我同意你的程度已達極限，無法再同意更多了」，換言之就是「我完全同意（你的看法或意見等）」，即I completely agree (with you).。

002 Question

在「the＋比較級……，the＋比較級……」這句型中，the應該不是定冠詞吧！若不是，它們是什麼詞類呢？

Answer

「the＋比較級＋（子句），the＋比較級＋（子句）」這種常見句型意為「越……，越……；愈……，愈……」。與 "both... and ..."、"either ... or ..."、"neither ... nor ..."、"not only...but also..." 等一樣，它也是一種相關字組，亦即與其兩個元

素連用的詞類和結構必須平行對稱、對仗工整。倘若這句型中沒有括弧所示的子句 (S + V)，那麼其中的逗點可以省略，如The sooner the better.（越快越好。）；The more the merrier.（多多益善；人越多越熱鬧。）

誠然，句中的兩個the都不是定冠詞。由於在這個句型中，前面部分是附屬子句，而後面部分為主要子句，因此國內有些文法書認為前面的the為連接詞，而後面的the為副詞，但筆者認為，由於「比較級」不是形容詞就是副詞，因此第一個 the應該也是副詞才對，因為只有副詞才能修飾形容詞和副詞。著名的 *The New Fowler's Modern English Usage* 一書在其 "Supplement"（補遺）中也針對這句型及其兩個 the 的詞類做了說明，該書也認為它們都是副詞。

003 Question

He is as wrong as wrong can be.這句是什麼意思呢？

Answer

這句的意思是「他大錯特錯；他錯得很離譜」。這是一種比較特殊的句型，乍看之下，有人可能會認為句子寫錯了。此種句型的結構為：「主詞＋be動詞＋as＋形容詞＋as＋形容詞＋can be」，它係藉著重複同一個形容詞來強調該形容詞，意為「極為……」、「不亞於……」、「再……不過了」。

例如：

▶ She is **as wise as wise can be**.（她極為聰明；她再聰明不過了。）
▶ He is **as handsome as handsome can be**.（他英俊極了。）
▶ He may not be so clever as Peter, but he is **as industrious as industrious can be**.（他也許不如彼得聰明，但卻用功極了。）

can be亦可用 "may be" 來代替，而過去式則用 "might be"。

例如：

▶ I was **as hungry as hungry might be**.（我餓極了。）

Question

過去分詞形容詞要用very還是much來修飾呢？例如，I am very disappointed at you.和I am much disappointed at you.（我對你很失望。）哪句才對呢？

Answer

截至目前，這問題還沒有一定的規則可尋，充其量只能說「部分規則」。現在先來看一些例句，如His father was much respected in that pretty town.（他父親在那個美麗的城鎮非常受敬重。）；I am very annoyed.（我很生氣。）

上述的「部分規則」是這樣的：如果過去分詞的形容詞成分比較多，那就用very 或 very much來修飾，如disappointed；如果是被動態成分比較多，或明顯就是被動態，則使用much來修飾。所以，在I am much tired.中，顯然much須換成 very，因為tired是個不折不扣的形容詞；而在I am very inconvenienced.中，very無疑地須換成much，因為這句是被動態結構。然而，這中間還有灰色地帶，讓我們很難做出正確的判斷，所以只能從習慣用法上著手，這當然需要多看多讀。另外，有不少過去分詞既不能用very也不能用much來修飾，如unsolved, undetected, located, finished, defeated等等。

005 **Question**

在More than one of my students are (or is) going to study abroad this semester.這句中，More than one是單數還是複數呢？

Answer

根據 *The New Fowler's Modern English Usage*，"more than one" 一定是單數，必須接單數動詞及使用單數代名詞，所以問題中的句子應寫成More than one of my students is going to study abroad this semester.（我的學生中有一人以上這學期將出國唸書。）如果 "more than" 後面的數目大於1，那麼就要使用複數動詞，如

More than two of my students are going to study abroad this semester.。

同樣地，在Not one of the houses was left standing after the 9-21 earthquake.（921大地震後未倒塌的房子一幢也沒有。）和I have three children and at least one of them is a boy. He usually rides his bicycle to school.（我有三個小孩，其中至少有一位是男孩。他經常騎腳踏車上學。）這兩句中，not one和at least one也是單數主詞，必須接單數動詞及使用單數代名詞。簡言之，在「one of＋複數名詞」句型中，主詞是one，恆為單數，必須接單數動詞及使用單數代名詞，即使one的前面使用了more than, not , at least等修飾語，亦不影響其單數性。

有人可能提出質疑，認為 Not one 的 Not 等於將主詞的單數「否定」了，這樣主詞就變成了複數，所以動詞應使用複數。Come off it!（別胡說了；別瞎扯了；別開玩笑了！）Not並未否定主詞的單數性。Not one相當於Not a single one，意為「一個也沒有」(not even one)，所以動詞不可能使用複數。

然而，在「one of＋複數名詞」句型中，若複數名詞後面接關係代名詞，那麼關代的先行詞是one還是複數名詞呢？這牽涉到關代後面接單數或複數動詞的問題。正確的答案是，關代的先行詞是複數名詞，亦即關代後面接複數動詞。相信不少被這問題所困擾的人將從此豁然開朗。是故，上述的句型可以寫成「one of＋複數名詞＋關係代名詞＋複數動詞」，如David is one of the students who are absent.（大衛是缺席的學生之一。）但這句型也有例外，若one的前面加上the only，那麼關代的先行詞就變成了one，亦即關代後面用單數動詞，如David is the only one of the students that is absent.（大衛是唯一缺席的學生。）

006 Question

有些副詞既可以位在語氣助動詞的前面，也可以在後面，如We most likely will be late.或We will most likely be late.。這兩句何者才是正確的寫法，還是兩者都可以呢？

Answer

副詞是出了名的「滑溜」，可能在句子任何奇怪的地方突然冒出來。所以，問題中的We will most likely be late.（我們很可能會遲到。）當然是對的，但We most likely will be late.也沒有錯。若干文法書將部分副詞稱為「句中副詞」，其中大多是一般所謂的頻率副詞，如ever, always, usually, often, frequently, generally, sometimes, occasionally, seldom, rarely, hardly ever, never, already, just, probably 等。這些副詞通常位在助動詞的後面、主動詞的前面，但位在be動詞的後面，如You should always tell the truth.（你應該都要說實話。）

如果有兩個助動詞，則句中副詞可以放在第一或第二個助動詞的後面，如It must already have been done.（那件事必定已經做好了。）或It must have already been done.。然而，在報章雜誌中，常常會見到將句中副詞置於助動詞前面的情況，如I never would tell you the truth.（我絕不會告訴你真相。）

007 Question

We are the best of friends. 和We are best friends. 的意思一樣嗎？

Answer

這兩句的意思並不完全相同。We are best friends.意為「我們是最好的朋友」，表示我們之中任何一人與其他朋友的關係或感情都沒有我們來得麻吉。至於We are the best of friends.，這是「the＋形容詞最高級＋of＋(the)複數名詞」的句型，在這種結構中，複數名詞前面定冠詞之有無會影響句子的意思。

在「the＋形容詞最高級＋of＋複數名詞」的句型中，若複數名詞前面沒有定冠詞，如問題中的句子，那麼它是表示泛指，沒有比較的範圍，其意思相當於 very/ extremely＋形容詞原級，所以這句相當於We are very/extremely good friends.（我們是非常/極為要好的朋友。）－這表示雖然我們極為要好，但我們之中任何一人與其他朋友的關係或感情，有可能也同樣極為要好、非常麻吉。

例如：

▶ Mary is **the wisest of** women.
= Mary is **a very/an extremely wise** woman.
（瑪麗是個非常聰明的婦女。）

▶ My grandma lives in **the quietest of** places.

= My grandma lives in **a very/an extremely quiet** place.

（我祖母住在一處極為安靜的地方。）

▶ He has **the most beautiful** of gardens.

= He has **a very/an extremely** beautiful garden.

（他有一個非常漂亮的花園。）

在上述句型中，若複數名詞前面有定冠詞，那麼它是表示特指，其意思相當於形容詞比較級＋than，後接any other＋單數名詞或all other＋複數名詞或the others。這是指特定範圍內的比較，表示主詞比該範圍內其他人事物都來得如何如何，也就是說，主詞在該範圍內具有形容詞最高級的性質。例如：

▶ Mary is **the wisest of the** women (in that group).

= Mary **is wiser than** any other woman/all other women/the others (in that group).

（瑪麗比 [該團體中] 其他任何 / 其他所有婦女都要聰明。） — 瑪麗是該團體所有婦女中最聰明的。

▶ My grandma lives in **the quietest of** the places (in Taipei).

= My grandma lives in a place which **is quieter than** any other place/all other places/the others (in Taipei).

（我祖母在台北所住的地方比台北其他任何 / 其他所有地方都來得安靜。） — 我祖母所住的地方是台北最安靜的。

▶ He has **the most beautiful of** the gardens (in this community).

= His garden is **more beautiful than** any other garden/all other gardens/the others (in this community).

（他的花園比本社區其他任何 / 其他所有花園都要漂亮。）—他的花園是本社區最漂亮的。

但這種句型並不常用，一般都用比較級來表達，如上述。不過，倘若「the＋形容詞最高級＋of＋複數名詞」結構中，複數名詞是以「the＋形容詞＝集合名詞」的型態出現，而前面的形容詞最高級就是此型態中形容詞的最高級，那麼這種結構就相當常見，因為它具有強調作用。

例如：

▶ We must care about **the poorest of** the poor.（我們必須關懷那些最窮的人。）

▶ Bill Gates is **the richest of** the rich.（比爾・蓋茲是有錢人當中最有錢的。）

▶ He is **the strongest/weakest of** the strong/weak.（他是強者/弱者當中最強/最弱的。）

世界知名的《富比士》(Forbes) 雜誌每年都會公布全球富豪排行榜，它的英文標題就是 The Richest of the Rich。

Excercise 綜合練習

I. 填空題

1 _____ the merrier.
（多多益善；人越多越熱鬧。）

2 The cheaper the _____.
（越便宜越好。）

3 I am _____ annoyed.
（我很生氣。）

4 I am _____ tired.
（我很累。）

5 Mary is _____ of women.
（瑪麗是個非常聰明的婦女。）

6 Bill Gates is _____ the rich.
（比爾・蓋茲是有錢人當中最有錢的。）

7 I have three children and at least one of them _____ a boy. He usually rides his bicycle to school.
（我有三個小孩，其中至少有一位是男孩。他經常騎腳踏車上學。）

8 David is one of the students who _____ absent.
（大衛是缺席的學生之一。）

II. 回答句子

1 A: I've passed my exam.
（我通過考試了。）
B: _____
（再也沒有人比你更棒了！）

2 A: I was dumped.
（我被甩了。）

B: _____

（聽到這樣我很難過。）

III. 中翻英

❶ 他英俊極了。

_____

❷ 我開心極了。

_____

IV. 重組句子

❶ never/Mary/seen/has/snow.
（瑪麗從未看過雪。）

_____

❷ Taipei/It/cold/been/never/so/in/has.
（台北從來沒有那麼冷過。）

_____

V. 二選一

❶ ☐ It couldn't have happened to a nicer guy!
☐ It could have happened to a nicer guy!
（再也沒有人比你更棒了！）

❷ ☐ I am very disappointed at you.
☐ I am much disappointed at you.
（我對你非常失望。）

❸ ☐ More than one of my students is going to study abroad this semester.
☐ More than one of my students are going to study abroad this semester.
（我的學生當中，至少有一個會在這學期出國。）

Answer

I. 填空題

1. The more
2. better
3. very (much)
4. very (much)
5. the wisest
6. the richest of
7. is
8. are

II. 回答句子

1. It couldn't have happened to a nicer man!
2. I'm sorry to hear that.

III. 中翻英

1. He is as handsome as handsome can be.
2. I am as happy as happy can be.

IV. 重組句子

1. Mary has never seen snow.
2. It has never been so cold in Taipei.

V. 二選一

1. 第一句正確
2. 第一句正確
3. 第一句正確

001 Question

(1) I run every day to lose weight. 和 (2) I'm running every day to lose weight.的意思有所不同嗎？有何不同呢？

Answer

這兩句的意思的確有所不同。句 (2) 的現在進行式是在表達「暫時的動作」，可與 He is running for President.的用法等量齊觀，此句是說「競選總統」這個動作現在正在進行中，但不會永遠持續著，一定會有結束的時候。我們無法用He runs for President.來表達相同的意思，除非我們要表達的意思是：每當有總統選舉，他一定出馬競選，也就是說他一直不斷地參加總統競選。必須注意的是，這裡的「暫時動作」是指「比較長的暫時動作」，與一般「比較短的暫時動作」在含意上也有些不同。

例如：

▶ (a). He **is studying for** the college entrance exam next year.
（他正在準備明年大學聯考。）

▶ (b). More people than ever before **are running** for the city council.
（比以前都要來得多的人正在競選市議員。）

▶ (c). I am **sitting**.
（我正坐著。）

▶ (d). They **are watching** television.
（他們正在看電視。）

句(a)和(b)是屬於「比較長的暫時動作」，而句(c)和(d)則是屬於「比較短的暫時動作」。前兩句的動作雖然都是在進行中，但在說話者說話的當時可能沒有在進行。以句(a)為例，說話者說話的當時可能沒有在唸書，因為他不可能不吃不睡地一直在唸書。至於後兩句的sit和watch，一定是說話者說話當時正在發生的動作。但無論如何，這些動作都有「結束的時間點」，這也就是為何稱之為「暫時」的原因。

問題中句(1) I run every day to lose weight.（我每天跑步來減重。）的簡單現在式是在表達「跑步」這個動作是習慣性的，它已經進行或發生好一段時間，而且不預期這動作會結束，亦即不預期會有結束的時間點。

002 Question

I never knew it.和I've never known it.這兩句的意思有何不同呢？

Answer

首先來看I never knew it.，這句有兩個意思。由於過去式是在表示動作或狀態發生在過去、結束在過去，所以I never knew it.可能被認為主詞所指的那個人已不在人世，因此他或她再也不知道或永遠都不知道那件事了。譬如說，She never married.這句十之八九會被認為她已過世，所以我們才說「她從未結過婚」，否則即使七老八十都不能被排除結婚的可能性。不過，"I never knew"也是一句現在常用的口語，意為「我以前一直不知道」，如I never knew that John was married.（我以前一直不知道約翰結婚了。）－這是說，我在說話當時才知道約翰已經結婚了，以前並不知道。再舉一例：

▶ A: Vivian's got a 20-year son.
（薇薇安有個 20 歲大的兒子。）
▶ B: Oh, **I never knew**!
（哦，我以前一直不知道！）

同樣地，這是我第一次知道薇薇安有個這麼大的兒子，以前並不知道，到現在才知道。

至於I've never known it.，這是現在完成式與never連用的句型。現在完成式是在表示動作或狀態發生在過去，一直持續到現在或到現在依然存在。所以這句的意思是說，我一生中或有生以來直到現在都不知道、不瞭解或不懂得某件事。例如：

▶ I**'ve never had** any problems with my teeth.
（我的牙齒從未發生任何毛病。）
▶ I**'ve never known** how to do algebra.
（我一直以來都不會代數。）

▶ I**'ve never understood** why you moved to Vietnam.
（我一直不瞭解你搬到越南的原因。）

這三句都是說，從出生開始或過去某個時間點開始一直到現在，我都沒有過某種經驗、不知道或不瞭解某件事，即使在說話的當時亦然。

值得注意的是，由於have, know和understand都是狀態動詞，而一般通常使用簡單現在式來敘述目前存在的狀態。所以，下面三句比上面三句更為常見：

例如：

▶ I don't have any problems with my teeth.
（我的牙齒沒有發生任何毛病。）

▶ I don't know how to do algebra.
（我不會代數。）

▶ I don't understand why you moved to Vietnam.
（我不瞭解你搬到越南的原因。）

Excercise
綜合練習

I. 填空題

1 More people than ever before _____ the city council.
（比以前都要來得多的人正在競選市議員。）

2 Many people _____ Thai nowadays.
（現在有很多人在學泰文。）

II. 圈圈看

1 I _____ (have never eaten/didn't eat) apples.
（我一直以來都不吃蘋果。）

2 She _____ (has never been to/doesn't go to) Japan.
（她從來沒有去過日本。）

III. 二選一

1 ☐ I run to lose weight.
☐ I run every day to lose weight.
（我每天跑步來減重。）

2 ☐ I have never seen her.
☐ I didn't see her.
（我從來沒有看過她。）

Answer

I. 填空題
1 are running for
2 are studying

III. 二選一
1 第二句正確
2 第一句正確

II. 圈圈看
1 have never eaten
2 has never been to

244

001 Question

Let's go.和Let us go.有何不同呢？

Answer

雖然 Let's是Let us的縮寫，但兩者的含意並不完全相同。Let's是表示將說話對象包括在內，如Come on, Mary, let's dance!（瑪麗，我們來跳舞吧！）—這裡的 "us" 是指你跟你說話的對象Mary。但Let us則不包括說話對象，如Father, let us marry!（父親，讓我們結婚吧！）—這裡的 "us" 是指你跟你的男友或女友；換言之，這是說你建議你父親讓你跟你的男友或女友結婚，不是你要跟你父親結婚。

值得一提的是，Let's的否定形式有三：最常見、也是被大多數人視為正規英語的是Let's not，如Let's not go.（我們別走。）但在英式英語中，有時亦用Don't let's，如Don't let's go.，而在美式英語中，有時亦用Let's don't，如Let's don't go.。其實，這三種寫法都是正規或標準英語（Standard English）。

Excercise
綜合練習

❶ _____ sing a song.
（大家來唱歌吧！）

❷ Mom, _____ go on the seesaw.
（媽媽，讓我們玩翹翹板吧！）

Answer

❶ Let's
❷ Let us

001 Question

What does that mean?是個正確的問句。但英美人士經常說成
What's that mean?請問那一句才正確呢？

Answer

在極為輕鬆的非正式場合或在隨意的書寫中，疑問助動詞does常被縮寫為's。

儘管這樣的說法或寫法不合文法（因為what's = what is），但這是習慣用法，我們也不能說它不對。同樣的情況也發生在What does she do for a living?= What is her job?（她靠什麼生活？／她從事什麼工作？）這個相當常用的問句上－這問句經常被寫成或說成"What's she do for a living?"。

002 Question

It's not that big of a deal.是什麼意思呢？

Answer

這句話的意思是「沒什麼大不了的」，這是一句常用的口語。儘管許多人認為這是屬於非正規或粗鄙的英文，其中的of更是累贅到無以復加的程度，但這種「形容詞＋of a＋名詞」的結構卻越來越常見，相信不久就可取得慣用語的地位。

一般認為，這種結構其實是個名詞片語（冠詞＋形容詞＋名詞，如a big deal），但由於形容詞前面還使用too, that（如問題中的that，意為「那麼，那樣」，通常用於疑問句和否定句）或how等副詞來修飾，因而發生了詞序上的變化。舉例來說，「天氣太熱」可以說成The day is too hot.或It's too hot a day.，但不能說成It's a too hot day.；同樣地，「咖啡太甜」可以說成The coffee is too sweet.，但不能說成too sweet coffee（例外：只有too much/little才可以使用「too＋形容詞＋名詞」的結構，如too much/little money）。

因此，對於「形容詞＋of a＋名詞」結構，我們可以「a＋形容詞＋名詞」這樣的名詞片語形式來理解，其意自明，只是因為形容詞前面還有副詞，而使詞序改變，以符合語法（如問題中的句子若寫成 "... a that big deal" 就不通了）。例如：How hard of a job do you think it'll be?（你認為那件工作會有多困難呢？）可以(It'll be) a hard job.來理解，而She didn't give too long of a talk.（她的演講不太長。）可以(She didn't give) a long talk.來理解－to give a talk (on/about) 意為「發表演講；作報告」。

「形容詞＋of a＋名詞」的結構屢見不鮮，經常從名流口中説出。*Webster's Dictionary of English Usage*就舉了一個例子説，前美國職棒游擊手Reewee Reese在他就其入選名人堂發表感言的前夕被媒體問到該項感言時，他回答説：It won't be that long of a speech.。而美國兩度入選高球名人堂的世界知名高球名將Lee Trevino有次在電視上説：A particular stroke wouldn't be that difficult of a shot.。前紐約市長Edward Koch曾對紐約時報説：I don't want to be considered too good of a loser.。

如上所言，It's not that big of a deal.可以It's not a big deal.來理解，其實這兩者的意思並無二致，都是説「沒什麼大不了」、「沒什麼了不起」、「那有什麼了不起」－big deal原意為「大交易」，在此為「了不起」。這又相當於另一句常用的口語 What's the big deal?，這同樣在表示「那有什麼了不起」或「那又怎麼樣」(So what?) 的意思。

003 Question

英文老師説，「我要回家了」這句話的禮貌説法是I must get going.，而非I'm going home now.。除這句外，在表示「我要回家了」，「我要走了」等意思時，是否還有其他比較有禮貌的説法呢？

Answer

對英美人士來説，I'm going home now.顯得太直接了，有些人聽了會覺得説話者不

太懂禮貌。在英文中，要表示上述意思時，常用的比較有禮貌的說法有下列幾句：

I'd better be making tracks.
I'd better get going.
I'd better be off in a (little) bit.
I've (got) to go (now).
I must get/be going.
I guess I should get/be going.

004 Question

It is cold today.是否可以改成Today is cold.呢？

Answer

一些人習以為常地說 "Today is cold."，其實這並非正規的英語。在It is cold today.中，today是當副詞用，意為「在今天」；當today被拿來用作主詞時，其句子必須如Today is Sunday.這樣表示日期的結構。

但在這裡，it是指天氣、氣候，如It must have rained last night.（昨晚必定下過雨。）或It snowed a lot yesterday.（昨天下了很大的雪。）此外，it也可表示時間或日期、距離或環境等：

▶ It is ten o'clock now.（現在是 10 點鐘。）-- 時間
▶ It is a long way to Taipei.（去台北的路很長。）-- 距離
▶ It is very noisy.（這裡很吵。）-- 環境

關於用it來表示日期，有兩個問句是我們日常生活中經常會用到的，其一就是問人家「今天星期幾」，另一是問「今天幾月幾號」。在此，我們分別列出這兩個問句常用的三種說法，供大家參考：

What day is today?（最多人使用）
What day is it today?
What is the day today?（最少人使用）
（今天星期幾？）

What date is today?
What date is it today?（最少人使用）
What is the date today?（最多人使用）
（今天幾月幾號？）

005 Question

一位外國朋友每次寫email給我，第一句話都是寫I hope this email finds you well.。這句話是什麼意思？是否可以說明find在此的用法？

Answer

"I hope this email finds you well." 這句話是書信的問候語或祝福語，它的字面意思是「我希望您收到此email時身體健康」，相當於我們常見或常用的「收信好」、「收信安好」、「收信快樂」、「收信愉快」等的意思。類似的例句還有I hope this card finds you in better health.（我希望您收到這張卡片時身體更健康。）

這是「find＋受詞＋副詞或介系詞片語」的句型應用，其中find意為「發現，發覺，感覺到」，而整個句型的意思為「發現處於某種狀態」。例如：

▶ When we arrived this morning, we **found** Cindy (= she was) **in a good/bad mood**.（今天早上我們到達時，發現辛蒂心情不錯／心情不好。）

▶ Sam woke up to **find** himself (= that he was) **in the hospital**.（山姆醒過來時，發現他已在醫院裡。）

▶ Saturday midnight **found** Robert (= he was) **lying** drunk on the floor.（星期六午夜羅伯特醉臥在地板上。）

▶ Mary: I thought his act was despicable.（瑪麗：我認為他的行為卑劣。）
Amy: I didn't **find** it so.（艾美：我不覺得他的行為是這樣。）

Excercise 綜合練習

I. 填空題

1 A: I'd better be making _____. (我該走了喔！)
   B: See you!（再見了！）

2 A: I guess I should _____.（我想我該走了。）
   B: Bye.（掰掰。）

3 I found him _____ (in trouble).
   （我發現他陷入困難中）

4 I found her _____ (sleep on the sofa).
   （我發現她在沙發上睡著了。）

II. 改寫句子

1 It's not a big deal.（沒什麼大不了的。）
   = _____.

2 It's a big problem.（這是個大問題。）
   = _____.

III. 圈圈看

1 (It/Today) is Friday.
   （今天星期五。）

2 (It/Here) is dirty.
   （這裡很髒。）

VI. 二選一

1 ☐ What's that mean?
   ☐ What's you mean?
   （那是什麼意思？）

② ☐ The coffee is too sweet coffee.

☐ The coffee is too sweet.

（咖啡太甜了。）

③ ☐ I must get going

☐ I'm going home now.

（我要回家了。）

④ ☐ It is cold today.

☐ Today is cold.

（今天很冷。）

⑤ ☐ I fell asleep on the train and woke up to find myself in Kaohsiung.

☐ I fell asleep on the train and woke up to find myself arrive in Kaohsiung.

（我在火車上睡著了，醒來時發現已經到了高雄。）

Answer

I. 填空題

❶ tracks

❷ get/be going

❸ in trouble

❹ sleeping on the sofa

II. 改寫句子

❶ It's not that big of a deal.

❷ It's so big a problem.

III. 圈圈看

❶ It; Today

❷ It

VI. 二選一

❶ 第一句正確

❷ 第二句正確

❸ 第一句正確

❹ 第一句正確

❺ 第一句正確

001 Question

在I would like to thank my wife, Teresa, for her wise decision in selecting a school for our child.這句中，Teresa前後是否一定要有逗點呢？有沒有逗點的意義是否有所差別呢？

Answer

在 I would like to thank my wife, Teresa, for her wise decision in selecting a school for our child. （我想要感謝我太太泰瑞莎在挑選小孩就讀的學校時所做的明智決定。）這句中，Teresa的前後都要加上逗點。若沒有這兩個逗點，即I would like to thank my wife Teresa for her...，那就表示我有一個以上的老婆，而我想要感謝的是其中一位叫做Teresa的老婆；因此，Teresa是必要的資料、不可或缺，否則有人可能會認為我指的是我另一位老婆春嬌。然而，這顯然有悖普遍的事實，因為除了中東國家的回教徒可能有一個以上的太太外，絕大多數人都只有一個太太。因此，在Teresa前後各加一個逗點，使 Teresa 成為插入語，目的只是在補充資料，可有可無，並不影響句意。現在再舉一例來說明：

▶ 1. My sister Margaret plans to attend Wellesley this fall.
▶ 2. My sister, Margaret, plans to attend Wellesley this fall.
（我妹妹瑪格麗特計畫今秋就讀衛斯理女子學院。）

第1句表示我有一個以上的妹妹，而計畫今秋就讀衛斯理學院的是其中一位叫做Margaret的妹妹，其他妹妹並沒有這樣的計畫；第2句是說我只有一個妹妹，即使沒有把她的名字講出來，別人也知道My sister是誰，所以Margaret這個名字只是補充資料，可有可無，並不影響句子的意思，故用逗點隔開。

在It is books that are a key to the wide world.這句中，關係代名詞that所指的先行詞books是複數，為何可以「等於」單數的a key呢？

Answer

It is books that are a key to the wide world.是個強調句，意為「書正是通往廣闊世界之鑰」。這句若改為一般的句子，則變成Books are a key to the wide world.（書乃通往廣闊世界之鑰。）句中books是主詞，a key是主詞補語。在英文中，主詞和主詞補語之間通常都會有數的一致。例如：

> ▶ My child is an angel.（我的小孩是天使。）-- 句中 child 和 angel 都是單數。
> ▶ My children are all students.（我的小孩都是學生。）-- 句中 children 和 students 都是複數。

然而，主詞和（主詞）補語的一致經常出現例外的情況，而這種例外的句子俯拾即是。根據 *The New Fowler's Modern English Usage* 一書，當單數主詞和複數補語或複數主詞和單數補語是由be動詞分開時，be動詞要跟主詞的數一致。

❶ 單數的情況：

> ▶ My only hope for the future **is** my children.（我未來唯一的希望是我的孩子。）
> ▶ Their principal crop **is** potatoes.（他們的主要作物是馬鈴薯。）

❷ 複數的情況：

> ▶ These boys **are** a real problem.（這些男孩真是麻煩人物。）
> ▶ Good manners **are** a rarity these days.（彬彬有禮現今非常罕見。）

尤有甚者，be動詞有時是跟補語的數一致，但比較少見，如More nurses is the next item on the agenda.（「更多護士」是議程下一個要討論的事項）；不過，這一句可視為The subject/question of more nurses is the next item on the agenda.的減化，這就變成了主詞和補語一致的一般情況，即subject/question是單數，item也是單數。

此外，由what所引導的名詞子句當主詞時也會發生主詞和補語一致的例外情況。一般而言，子句當主詞時，動詞應該用單數，但由於what既可意為 "the thing that" 亦可意為 "the things that" ，因此在What we need most is/are books.（我們最需要的是書。）這句中，be動詞可以是is或are。不過，當what指的顯然就是單數時，be動詞就只能用單數，如What is needed most is books.（目前最需要的是書。）因為從what之後的is可看出，句中的what= The thing that，因此主詞和補語之間的be動詞只能用is，不能用are。

最後值得一提的是，be all ears（聚精會神地聽；洗耳恭聽）、be all eyes（聚精會神地看）和be all fingers and thumbs（笨手笨腳的）等這類成語是當形容詞用的主詞補語，與上述名詞類的主詞補語不同，因此若主詞是單數，主詞和補語之間並不存在數的一致問題，如Tell me what happened; I'm all ears!（快告訴我發生什麼事，我正洗耳恭聽呢！）I'm sorry I dropped your cup – I'm all fingers and thumbs today.（很抱歉，我摔壞了你的杯子－我今天真是笨手笨腳。）

003 Question

在 It is you who play (or plays) an important role in that matter. 這句中，who要接單數還是複數動詞呢？

Answer

在It is you who play (or plays) an important role in that matter.（該事件中扮演重要角色的人就是你。）這句中，who 是主詞，也可以說是它所引導的形容詞子句（即關係子句）的主詞，指的是先行詞you，所以動詞要用"play"。

值得一提的是，關係子句幾乎從不用來修飾人稱代名詞，如 I who am a student at this school come from a country in Asia.（我是這所學校的學生，來自亞洲國家。）是個錯誤的句子。然而，問題中的句子是一種所謂「分裂句」的強調句型（It is/was...that），不受此限，如It was they that cleaned the classroom yesterday.（就是他們昨天打掃教室。）－在此that也可用who來代替，但僅限被強調的元素是人，如上述的例句，其他情況只能用that，不能用其他關係代名詞。

不過，在非正式或新聞英語中，分裂句中的主格人稱代名詞經常被寫成受格型態，

如It is us who will come up with the solutions.（日後提出解決方案的人就是我們。）
另外，著名的成語 "He who laughs last laughs best." 也使用同樣的句型，意思是說，不要在乎眼前的輸贏，要到最後才見分曉，也就是說「最後笑的人才是真正的笑」；不過這裡的he係用做不定代名詞，意為anybody, any person。

004 Question

在 I don't know what to do.這句中，what to do是當know的受詞，那麼它是不是某個句子的減化呢？若是，它的原句為何呢？

Answer

what, which, when, where, who, whom, whose, how等wh-字和whether的後面都可以接不定詞來用作名詞片語。既然是名詞片語，那麼它們一定是從名詞子句減化而來，換言之，它們的原句都是名詞子句。

在進入主題之前，我們先來談關係子句（形容詞子句）的一個減化規則，那就是若子句中含有should, would, must, can, may等情態助動詞（或稱「語氣助動詞」，modals or modal auxiliaries），那麼句子減化時須將情態助動詞變成不定詞。

例如：

▶ The man **to remember** (= whom you/we/everyone should remember) is Bill.
（吾人應該記得的人是比爾。）

這規則亦適用於名詞子句。所以，「wh-字 + 不定詞」的原句一定含有情態助動詞。然而，「wh-字 + 不定詞」中的不定詞只有「應該」或「能」的含義，亦即它們只對應 should 或 can/could（現在式用 can，過去式用 could），並無其他情態助動詞的意思。

例如：

▶ I don't know **what to do**.
（我不知道做什麼。）

= I don't know **what I should do**.
（我不知道我該做什麼。）

▶ Wendy found two smartphones she liked, but she had difficulty deciding **which one to buy**.
（溫蒂發現兩支她都喜歡的智慧型手機，但她難以決定買哪一支。）

= Wendy found two smartphones she liked, but she had difficulty deciding **which one she should buy**.
（溫蒂發現兩支她都喜歡的智慧型手機，但她難以決定她該買哪一支。）

▶ Tony can't decide **whether to** hang out with his friends or (to) stay home tonight.
（東尼不能決定今晚是要和朋友廝混在一起還是留在家裡。）

= Tony can't decide **whether he should** hang out with his friends or stay home tonight.
（東尼不能決定今晚他該和朋友廝混在一起還是留在家裡。）

▶ Please tell me **how to find** these reference books?
（請告訴我怎樣找到這些參考書。）

= Please tell me **how I can find** these reference books?
（請告訴我怎樣我才能找到這些參考書。）

▶ Professor Lee told me **how to teach** English.
（李教授告訴我怎樣教英文。）

= Professor Lee told me **how I could teach** English.
（李教授告訴我怎樣我才能教英文。）

在上面這五組例句中，各組兩句的意思並無不同。

Excercise
綜合練習

I. 填空題

1 Their principal crop _____ potatoes.
（他們的主要作物是馬鈴薯。）

2 Good manners _____ a rarity these days.
（彬彬有禮現今非常罕見。）

3 It is I _____ should be responsible for the fault.
（該為這項過錯負責的人就是我。）

4 It is the salary _____ makes him work hard.
（是薪水讓他努力工作。）

II. 圈圈看

1 (Her father Allen/Her father, Allen,) mistreated her.
（她的父親，艾倫，虐待她。）

2 (My hometown Taipei/My hometown, Taipei,) has a lot of rain.
（我的家鄉，台北，雨量豐沛。）

III. 改寫句子

1 Please tell me how I could get to the train station.
（請告訴我該如何走到火車站。）

= _____.

2 I want to know how I can avoid the mistakes.
（我想要知道如何能避免錯誤。）

= _____.

IV. 二選一

❶ ☐ One of my friends, Lori, is getting married.
☐ One of my friends Lori is getting married.
（我有一個朋友，勞賴，要結婚了。）

❷ ☐ It is books that are a key to the wide world.
☐ It is books that is a key to the wide world.
（書正是通往廣闊世界之鑰。）

❸ ☐ It is you who plays an important role in that matter.
☐ It is you who play an important role in that matter.
（是你在這件事情中扮演很重要的角色。）

Answer

I. 填空題
❶ is
❷ are
❸ who/that
❹ that

II. 圈圈看
❶ Her father, Allen,
❷ My hometown, Taipei,

III. 改寫句子
❶ Please tell me how to get to the train station.
❷ I want to know how to avoid the mistakes.

IV. 二選一
❶ 第一句正確
❷ 第二句正確
❸ 第一句正確

001 Question

there is or are及something or somebody等不定代名詞的附加問句為何呢？

Answer

附加問句（tag questions）是英文一項重要的特色。附加問句構成的基本原則是：

1. 附加問句的主詞與陳述句的主詞一致。

2. 附加問句的助動詞與陳述句的助動詞（be動詞和語氣助動詞）一致，若陳述句的動詞為普通動詞，則附加問句就使用 do, does 或 did。

3. 若陳述句為肯定，則附加問句通常為否定，反之亦然。

請看下面的例句：

▶ You won't forget to check my emails, **will you**?（你不會忘記查收我的電子郵件，對吧？）

▶ You play tennis on Thursdays usually, **don't you**?（你經常在週四打網球，不是嗎？）

▶ You didn't play baseball last Friday, **did you**?（上週五你沒有打棒球，是嗎？）

關於 there is/are 句型的陳述句，其附加問句的主詞仍使用 there 這個「假主詞」(preparatory subject)。例如：

▶ There's nothing wrong, **is there**?（沒有什麼不對，是吧？）

▶ There weren't any problems when you talked to Jack, **were there**?（你和傑克談話時沒有發生任何問題，對吧？）

至於以something, somebody, anything, anybody, nothing, no one等不定代名詞做主詞的陳述句，如果是something, anything, nothing等，那麼附加問句是使用 "it" 做

主詞；若是somebody, anybody, no one等，則使用 "they" 做為附加問句的主詞。
例如：

Something happened at John's house, **didn't it**?（約翰家裡發生了事情，不是嗎？）

No one phoned, **did they**?（沒有人打電話，對吧？）

Somebody wanted to borrow John's bike, **didn't they**? Who was it?（有人想要借約翰的單車，不是嗎？是誰呢？）

肯定附加問句是在表示說話者預期的回答是否定的，而否定附加問句是在表示說話者預期的回答是肯定的。例如：

▶ You haven't fed the goldfish, **have you**?（你沒有餵金魚，對吧？）
No, I haven't. You do it.（對啊，我沒有餵。你現在去餵。）
▶ Excessive speed was the cause of the accident, **don't you agree**?（超速是這起事故的致因，你同不同意？）
Yes, I do.（是的，我同意。）

Let's 的附加問句是 shall we?（表示建議）：

▶ Let's go to the movies tonight, **shall we**?（我們今晚去看電影，好嗎？）

英文還有所謂的「肯定的陳述句--肯定的附加問句」；在此情況中，我們是先用肯定的敘述來做猜測，然後用附加問句來詢問我們的猜測或假設是否正確。例如：

▶ This is the final match of the season, **is it**?（這是本季最後一場比賽，是嗎？）
Yes, that's right.（是的，沒錯。）
▶ She's going to marry him, **is she**?（她將嫁給他，是嗎？）
▶ You think she'll sue for divorce, **do you**?（你認為她會訴請離婚，對吧？）

最後，祈使句也有附加問句：

▶ Open the door, **will you**?（把門打開，好嗎？）
Open the door, **won't you**?

這裡使用will you?或won't you?的意思並沒有什麼不同，只是won't you?是指說話者預期的回答是否定的。這種附加問句具有將祈使句的命令意味轉換為禮貌性請求的效果，它的作用與please一樣。所以，上面的句子也可改成下面的講法，意思並無

二致：

> ▶ Open the door, **please**.
> Open the door, **will you please**?
> Open the door, **would you**?
> Open the door, **could you please**?
> **Could you** open the door?

不過，要注意的是，在祈使句中不可使用couldn't you?或wouldn't you?。

002 Question

What does she look like?、How does she look?和What is she like?的用法和意思有何不同呢？

Answer

這三個句子是日常生活中經常聽到的問句，茲將它們的用法以及意思上的差異敘述如下：

How + do (does, did)＋主詞（人）＋look?／What＋do (does, did)＋主詞（人）＋look like?－用來詢問長相（長得怎麼樣）、外表（外表、穿著打扮看起來怎麼樣）。注意：How ...?通常指比較正面的外表，而What ...?則是指不好不壞或比較負面的外表。

例如：

> ▶ **What did you look like** when you were young?（你年輕時長得怎麼樣？）
> Short, fat, and spotty.（矮矮胖胖的，還有雀斑。）
> ▶ **What does she look like**?（她的穿著打扮看起來怎麼樣？）
> As if she hasn't bought any new clothes in the last twenty years.（她好像 20 年沒買新衣服一樣。）
> ▶ **How do I look**?（我看起來怎麼樣？）

Fantastic! That outfit really suits you. （棒極了！那套衣服很適合你－很適合你的外表。）

What + be + 主詞（人）＋like?－用來詢問性格、個性（某人是個怎麼樣的人）。

▶ **What's** Bob **like**?
（鮑柏是個怎麼樣的人？）

Always losing his temper.
（動不動就發脾氣。）

▶ **What's** John **like**?
（約翰是個怎麼樣的人？）

Very sociable. He's the life and soul of any party.
（很善於交際。他是社交聚會的靈魂人物。）

▶ What's his wife like?
（他的太太是個怎麼樣的人？）

She's serious and shy. I've never seen her smile.
（她既嚴肅又害羞。我從未見到她笑過。）

另一類似的問句 － 即把 "What + be + 主詞（人）＋like?" 問句中的What改為Who－也很常見：

▶ **Who** are you **like** in your family?
（你在家中像誰？）

My mother I suppose, we're both quite moody.
（我想是像我媽媽，我們兩人都很情緒化。）

How＋be＋主詞（事物）?／What＋be＋主詞（事物）＋like?－用來詢問經驗。在詢問人家的經驗時，這兩種問句的用法和意思並無太大的差別。此外，這兩種問句也可用來詢問做好的食物或吃了的食物好不好，但一般大多使用 "How ...?" 的問句形式。至於也可用來詢問心情和身體健康的How + be + 主詞（人）?（如 "How are you today?"，"How is your wife?"），由於是大家所熟知的，在此就不再贅述了。

▶ **How** was your exam? （你的試考得怎麼樣？）
Fine. I think I did OK. （很好。我想我考得不錯。）

▶ **What** was your exam **like**? （你的試考得怎麼樣？）
Fine. I think I did OK. （很好。我想我考得不錯。）

▶ **What** was your holiday **like**? （你度假度得怎麼樣？）

Not wonderful. The hotel was awful.（不是很好。旅館糟透了。）
▶ **How** was your steak?（你的牛排怎麼樣？）
Delicious. Beautifully tender and very juicy.（美味可口。鮮嫩多汁。）

003 Question

must, used to和ought to的附加問句呢？

Answer

I、由於must有兩種意思，所以它的附加問句必須分別考慮。

1. 當must意為表示義務、責任、要求的「必須」時，它的附加問句使用「needn't＋主詞」。

例如：

▶ He **must** get up early tomorrow, **needn't he**?（他明天必須早起，不是嗎？）

2. 當must意為表示推測的「一定，肯定，想必，諒必」時，它的附加問句須視時態及其他情況而定。就現在式（must＋be）的情況而言，其附加問句為「be＋not＋主詞」。

例如：

▶ He must be a doctor, **isn't he**?（他必定是個醫生，不是嗎？）
▶ They must be staying there, **aren't they**?（他們現在肯定留在那裡，不是嗎？）

3. 就過去式（must＋have＋P.P.）的情況而言，其附加問句可以為「haven't/hasn't＋主詞」或「didn't＋主詞」。但這兩者的含意並不相同，「haven't/hasn't＋主詞」表示過去的動作對現在產生了影響，而「didn't＋主詞」則只單純表示過去的動作。

例如：

▶ Your English is very good. You must have studied English for several years, **haven't you**?（你的英文很好，想必你已唸了好幾年的英文，不是嗎？－ 過去的動作產生現在的結果。）

▶ The road is wet. It must have rained last night, **hasn't it**?（地上是濕的，昨晚一定下過雨，不是嗎？）－過去的動作對現在的影響。

▶ He must have finished it yesterday, **didn't he**?（他一定是在昨天完成工作，不是嗎？）－僅單純表示 finished 這個動作。

雖然第 1 義的must可等於have/has to（現在式）或 had to（過去式），但當陳述句使用have/has to或had to時，附加問句須使用「don't/doesn't＋主詞」或「didn't＋主詞」。

例如：

▶ We have to get there at eight tomorrow, **don't** we?（我們必須在明天八點到那裡，不是嗎？）

▶ He has to get up early tomorrow, **doesn't** he?（他明天必須早起，不是嗎？）

▶ They had to take the early train, **didn't** they?（他們必須搭早班火車，不是嗎？）

II、接著來看used to的附加問句。由於used to的否定可為didn't use to或usedn't to，所以它的附加問句可為「didn't＋主詞」或「usedn't＋主詞」。

例如：

▶ He used to take pictures there, **didn't he? / usedn't he?**（他過去常常在那裡拍照，不是嗎？）

不過，在 There used to be ... 的句型中，其附加問句為「wasn't/weren't there」。例如：

▶ **There used to be** a banana tree in the garden, wasn't there?（這花園以前有棵香蕉樹，不是嗎？）－ there 為虛主詞，真正的主詞為單數的 a banana tree。

▶ There used to be many children playing there, **weren't there**?（以前那裡有許多小孩在玩耍，不是嗎？）－ there 為虛主詞，真正的主詞為複數的 many children。

III、至於ought to的附加問句，陳述句若為肯定，則附加問句使用「shouldn't/oughtn't＋主詞」。

例如：

▶ He ought to know what to do, **oughtn't he? / shouldn't he?** （他應該知道要做什麼，不是嗎？）

004 Question

What do you say to going to a movie with me tonight?這句是什麼意思呢？

Answer

這句話的意思是「今晚跟我去看電影好不好？」。我想這位讀者想要問的問題應該是 "What do you say to..." 在句中的意思。它的意思與 "How about ..." （如何呢？／怎麼樣呢？／好不好呢？）完全一樣，其中to是介系詞（並非不定詞），所以其後接動名詞－這與about後接動名詞正好相符。例如：

▶ **What do you say to** going out for lunch? （到外面吃午餐好嗎？）
= **How about** going out for lunch?

005 Question

電影中有這樣的對話I will always love you.，另一人回答説And I you.。以前從未聽過這樣的回答。這是什麼意思，文法正確嗎？

Answer

英語是一種非常講究省略（ellipsis）的語言，只要是前面提過的，後面「當省則省」，尤其日常生活會話更是力求精簡。問題中的And I you其實就是And I will always love you的省略，因為will always love前面已提過，所以回答的人就不再重複了，而只說 And I you（我也會永遠愛你），因此它的文法是正確無誤的，只是這樣的說法比較老式。當然，你也可以用現在的說法Me too來回答。但從文法觀點來看，And I you比Me too合乎文法。

同樣地，在史詩電影或比較老式的電影中，你也可能會聽到這樣的對話："I will never forget you."，而另一人回答說 "Nor I you."。大家應該可以猜出Nor I you（我也絕不會忘記你。）就是Nor will I ever forget you的省略了吧！當然，你也可以用現在的說法Me neither或Nor me來回答。但從文法觀點來看，Nor I you比Me neither或Nor me合乎文法。

上述的文法觀點，就跟我們現在常說的一句話He is taller than me.（他比我高。）一樣。就文法而言，這句英文並不正確，正確的說法應該是 He is taller than I (am).（am 可以省略）；然而，後者已被歸類為老式的說法，因為現在這樣說的人越來越少。

006 Question

當有人問你What's your nationality時，你是回答I am Chinese. 還是I am a Chinese. 呢？

Answer

根據經驗及習慣用法，我會回答 "I am Chinese."。國內可能會有不少人認為應該使用 "I am a Chinese." 的說法，但實際的情況卻是以前者的說法佔絕大多數。不信的話，你可以隨便找個美國人，故意問他「你是哪一國人」，他會回答 "I am American."，而不會說 "I am an American."。

Can we not go there可能有兩個意思，一表厭惡、討厭，另一表渴望。是否可以説明 Can we not ...的用法呢？

Answer

沒錯！Can we not go there?有兩個截然不同的意思。

首先，它可以表達渴望的意思。當我們説Can we not (do something)?時，這是表示想要做某事，但我們認為那件事也許不可能辦到或不被允許。舉例來説，春嬌帶著志明來到一家旅行社，想要安排一個度假行程，共度夫妻甜蜜時光。兩人看完小冊子後春嬌説：

▶ Can we go abroad this year?（今年我們可以到國外度假嗎？）

春嬌當時認為到國外度假可能是OK的，所以她使用簡單的問句形式Can we go abroad this year?，沒有 "not"。然而，春嬌和志明也可能出現如下的對話：

志明可能説：

▶ We haven't got much money. Let's take a holiday in Taiwan this year.（我們的錢不多。今年在台灣度假就好。）

而春嬌可能回答：

▶ Well, we've been on holiday in Taiwan for the last five years. **Can we not** go abroad this year?（哦，過去五年我們都是在國內度假。今年怎麼又不行呢？／今年又不行哦？）

上句的意思是説，春嬌想要出國度假，但由於志明説錢不多，所以她認為這件事或許不可能或不被允許。是故，在此情況中，她使用Can we not (do something)? 這樣的問句。

當使用Can we not (do something)?來表達渴望之意時，也可以説成 "Can't we" — Can't we (do something)?事實上，Can't we (do something)?還比較常用。所以春嬌很可能是這樣説的：Can't we go abroad this year?

然而，Can we not (do something)?也可表示厭惡、討厭或不想做某事之意。舉例來

説，同樣是春嬌和志明在旅行社的對話：

志明説：

▶ I'd like to go to Iceland.（我想去冰島。）

春嬌回答説：

▶ Iceland sounds very cold. I don't like cold places. **Can we not** go there?（冰島聽起來很冷。我不喜歡寒冷的地方。我們可以不去那裡嗎？）

上句的意思是説，春嬌不想去冰島，因為她不喜歡寒冷的地方。但必須注意的是，當使用 Can we not (do something)?來表達不喜歡某事、不想做某事的意思時，一般並不使用縮寫的 "can't"。所以， Can we not (do something)? 不能縮寫成 Can't we (do something)? 就此意思而言，Can we not (do something)? 是一句非常口語的話，在美國比較常見，但英國人也已開始在使用這句話。

既然Can we not (do something)?有兩個截然不同的意思，那麼當別人使用這問句時，我們怎麼知道它是表達那個意思呢？事實上，若用寫的，它們看起來完全一樣。不過，它們通常用在口語中，是用重音的變化來表達不同的意思。當我們想要表達渴望的意思時， "can" 和主動詞要唸得比較重：CAN we not GO abroad this year?。然而，當我們想要表達厭惡或不想做某事的心意時，則把重音放在 "not" 上：Can we NOT go there?

順便一提的是，問題中所舉的例句 "Can we not go there?" 最近出現一個新的意思。如果我們説 "Can we not go there?" ，這可能意為「我不想談這件事」(= I don't want to talk about it; let's not talk about this.)。

008 Question

Didn't you used to eat breakfast?這個問句對嗎？

Answer

這是個正確的問句，意為「你過去不常吃早餐嗎？」或「你過去沒有吃早餐的習慣嗎？」不過，筆者猜想，這位讀者所要問的應該不是句子的意思，而是used to正確

的問句或甚至否定句的型態或寫法。

Used to是指過去習慣性和經常性的動作，但現在已經不做或不再發生，或過去存在的狀態或情況，但現在已不存在。根據*The New Fowler's Modern English Usage*一書及若干主流英英和英漢字典，used to的否定形式有didn't use to, didn't used to, used not to, usen't to, usedn't to和never used to等，而問句形式則有 Did/Didn't＋S＋use/used to, Used/Use(d)n't＋S＋to和 Used＋S＋not to等，其中藉助於助動詞did的形式僅用於極為非正式的上下文中，而未藉助於did的形式則略微正式一些，但Use(d)n't＋S＋to的形式大多用在口說英語和非正式信件中。值得一提的是，used to和use to的發音完全一樣。

現在我們以 He used to go to the cinema a lot.（他過去常去看電影。）這個敘述句為例來寫出它的各種否定和問句形式。

▶ He **didn't used to** go to the cinema a lot.
（他過去不常去看電影。）

= He **didn't use to** go to the cinema a lot.

= He **used not to** go to the cinema a lot.

▶ Did he **use/used to** go to the cinema a lot?
（他過去常去看電影嗎？）

= **Used** he **to** go to the cinema a lot?

▶ **Didn't** he **use/used to** go to the cinema a lot?
（他過去不常去看電影嗎？）

= **Used** he **not** to go to the cinema a lot?

= **Use(d)n't** he to go to the cinema a lot?

009 Question

Could I ask you a question?和 Could I just ask you a question?有何不同呢？

Answer

這兩句的意思都是「我可以問你一個問題嗎？」，但Could I ask you a question?只

是一般的問句，而Could I just ask you a question?卻是一種用來使請求更禮貌一些的問句。

這兩句僅有一字之差，那就是just。誠然，在口語的問句中，just經常被用來做為禮貌性的請求，以Could I just ask you a question?為例，它是表示，我想問你一個問題，但我並不想造成你的不便，而且這只會打擾你一下下的時間。在此，just 本身並無特殊的意義，它所含的意思跟「一下；一下下」差不多。茲再舉兩例如下供大家參考，相信這種含 just 的問句，會使請求獲致成功的機率大增，宜多加應用：

▶ Could I **just** borrow your pen for a second?
（我可以借一下你的筆嗎？）

▶ Can I **just** borrow some money from you?
（我可以跟你借點錢嗎？）

010 Question

I don't know what is the matter.和 I don't know what the matter is.那一句正確呢？

Answer

這兩句都對，但意思不同。首先來看I don't know what is the matter.，這句是由主要子句I don't know和附屬子句（名詞子句）what is the matter所構成，而名詞子句在此當know的受詞。在文法中，這個名詞子句又叫做間接問句，它是從直接問句What is the matter?（怎麼啦？）而來的，其中matter意為「問題；麻煩；困境」。

相信一定有不少人會質疑說，間接問句的詞序不是跟陳述句的詞序一樣嗎，為何還用直接問句的詞序呢？這正是本問題的重點所在！大家都知道，在含有疑問詞的直接問句中，其詞序為「疑問詞＋助動詞（若為be動詞，則主詞後面就沒有動詞）＋主詞＋動詞＋其他元素？」。當一個直接問句併入另一個句子（主要子句）時，該直接問句就變成間接問句，而後者的詞序為「疑問詞＋主詞＋（助動詞）＋動詞／be動詞＋其他元素」。例如：

▶ 1. Who is she?（她是誰？）-- 直接問句
I don't know **who she is**.（我不知道她是誰。）-- 間接問句

▶ 2. What do you want?（你想要什麼？）-- 直接問句
Please tell me **what you want**.（請告訴我，你想要什麼。）-- 間接問句

▶ 3. Who wants the document?（誰要這份文件？）-- 直接問句
Do you know **who wants the document**?（你知道誰要這份文件嗎？）-- 間接問句

在第 3 句中，直接問句Who wants the document? 的主詞是who，而在Do you know who wants the document?中，間接問句的主詞還是who，原本的主動詞位置並沒有改變；換言之，當疑問詞在直接問句中就是主詞時，在間接問句中的詞序維持不變。What is the matter?的情況就是這樣，what是這直接問句的主詞，所以變成間接問句後詞序不變。若疑問詞在直接問句中並非主詞，如第 1 句（主詞為he）和第 2 句（主詞為you），那麼在間接問句中，主詞與動詞的詞序必須恢復為陳述句的詞序。

現在來看 I don't know what the matter is.。為何這句也對呢? 因為這句中的 matter 意為「物質」(substance)，不是「問題；麻煩；困境」；它是直接問句 What is the matter? 的主詞，在間接問句中須調整詞序，位在 is 的前面。所以 I don't know what the matter is. 的意思是「我不知道這物質是什麼」。

011 Question

What happened?和What did happen?有何不同呢？

Answer

英文只有What happened?的說法或寫法，因為What did happen?的文法錯誤。請看下面的例句和解說：

▶ Benjamin Franklin invented the lightning rod.
（富蘭克林發明避雷針。）

上句若要改成問句，會有兩種情況。一是問主詞，另一是問受詞。若是問主詞，則句子變成：

▶ **Who** invented the lightning rod?
（誰發明避雷針？）

答案是Benjamin Franklin－當動詞invented的主詞。這種問句叫做「主詞問句」(subject questions)。

若是問受詞，則句子變成：

▶ **What** did Benjamin Franklin invent?
（富蘭克林發明了什麼？）

答案是the lightning rod－當動詞invented 的受詞。這種問句叫做「受詞問句」(object questions)。

所以，當問句是在問主詞時，我們係使用正確時態的動詞，無需助動詞，即 Who invented the lightning rod?；當問句是在問受詞時，我們要使用助動詞，而原來的主動詞則變成原形動詞，即What did Benjamin Franklin invent?。

現在來看問題中的問句：

What happened?
What did happen?

What這個疑問詞是在問happen這個動詞的主詞還是受詞呢？顯然地，這是主詞問句，是在問主詞。它的原句可能是：

Something happened to me.
Nothing happened to them.

根據上述，主詞問句係使用正確時態的動詞，無須藉助於助動詞do/does/did，所以What did happen?不合文法。

不過，若是yes/no問句，那就需要助動詞了。所以，問主詞的yes/no問句可以說成或寫成：

▶ Did anything happen?（發生了什麼事嗎？）
▶ Did it happen to you?（你發生了那件事嗎？）
▶ Has anything happened yet?（已經有什麼事發生了嗎？）

但不可能有 What did happen? 這樣的說法或寫法。

Excercise
綜 合 練 習

I. 圈圈看

1 Turn on the light, (please/couldn't you)?
（請開燈，好嗎？）

2 The dog is very cute, (is it/isn't it)?
（這隻狗很可愛，不是嗎？）

3 (What's his wife like/ How's his wife like)?
（他的太太是個怎麼樣的人？）
She's serious and shy. I've never seen her smile.
（她既嚴肅又害羞。我從未見到她笑過。）

4 (What/How) was your holiday like?
（你度假度得怎麼樣？）
Not wonderful. The hotel was awful.
（不是很好。旅館糟透了。）

5 I am (a Canadian/Canadian).
（我是加拿大人。）

6 I don't like fast food. (Can we not/Can't we) go to McDonald's?
（我不喜歡速食，可以不要去麥當勞嗎？）

II. 填空題

1 They had to take the early train, _____ they?
（他們必須搭早班火車，不是嗎？）

2 There used to be a banana tree in the garden, _____?
（這花園以前有棵香蕉樹，不是嗎？）

III. 改寫句子

❶ Didn't she use to go to that restaurant very often?
（她以前不常去那家餐廳嗎？）

= _____ she to go to that restaurant very often?

❷ Used you to eat ice cream a lot?
（他過去常吃冰淇淋嗎？）

= _____ you _____ eat ice cream a lot?

IV. 二選一

❶ ☐ What's the weather today?
☐ What's the weather like today?
（今天天氣如何？）

❷ ☐ What did happen?
☐ What happened?
（發生什麼事了？）

V. 合併句子

❶

A. Do you know?

B. Who knows the answer?

Do _____?

❷

A. Let me know.

B. Where is the box?

Let _____.

Answer

I. 圈圈看
1. please
2. isn't it
3. What's his wife like
4. What
5. Canadian
6. Can we not

II. 填空題
1. didn't
2. wasn't there

III. 改寫句子
1. Use(d)n't
2. Did; use/used to

IV. 二選一
1. 第二句正確
2. 第二句正確

V. 合併句子
1. Do you know who knows the answer?
2. Let me know where the box is.

Chapter 3 你的英文，用對了嗎？ | **句子篇**   **Unit 09 連接詞**

001 Question

在 There is no student but likes her.這句中，but是何種詞類，而整句的意思為何呢？

Answer

這句的意思是「沒有學生不喜歡她」，亦即「每個學生或所有學生都喜歡她」。句中的 but 為連接詞，與其前面的no或not構成「沒有……不……」的意思；由於這種句型中的 There be 都是用單數，所以其意思可更精確地説成「沒有一個……不……」。

問題中的句子也可改寫為 There is not a (not a = no) student that doesn't like her.。注意：在 there be 所引導的句子中，關係代名詞只能用 that。事實上，這個句子的原句應該是 Every student likes her.。再舉一例來説明之：

▶ There was not a person but had tears in his/her eyes.（沒有一個人不熱淚盈眶。）

= There was not a person that didn't have tears in his/her eyes.

= They all had tears in their eyes.（所有人都熱淚盈眶。）

002 Question

國內不少人使用的 Yxxxx字典有 The dollar has gone down against the yen, therefore Japanese goods are more expensive for Americans. 這樣一個例句。但這句對嗎？

Answer

這句犯了一個相當常見且非常嚴重的錯誤，也就是英文所謂的「逗點謬誤」(comma

fault or run-on error)，即兩個句子之間沒有連接詞而是用逗點來當連接詞。這種句子被稱為 run-on sentences。問題的癥結在於 therefore 是個副詞，卻被當作連接詞。所以問題中的句子應改為：

▶ The dollar has gone down against the yen, **and therefore** Japanese goods are more expensive for Americans.

= The dollar has gone down against the yen; **therefore,** Japanese goods are more expensive for Americans. －這句比較好。

（美元兌日元的匯率下跌了，因此日本商品對美國人來說比較貴了。）

上句係用分號來代替「, and」。除 and 外，分號亦可用來取代 but 和 or 等對等連接詞；分號後面的字須小寫。例如：

▶ The president did not approve the military operation; he suggested several options.（總統不同意這項軍事行動；他建議幾個選擇方案。）－在這句中，分號取代了「, but」。

在英文中，為了承接上一句的意思，我們往往在新的句子開頭使用however, therefore, consequently, nonetheless, nevertheless 或 as a result 等轉折詞 (transitional phrases)。這些轉折詞又叫做「連接副詞」(conjunctive adverbs, connectives)，亦即連接兩件對比、差異的事情或兩個對比、不同的觀念所用的副詞（並非連接詞）。

轉折詞有如上下兩句的橋樑，可使兩個句子之間的轉折比較平順。它們都位在下一句的開頭，其後通常有逗點，但前面絕不可有逗點，否則就會發生上述錯把連接副詞當連接詞的逗點謬誤情況，其中又以 however 最常發生這樣的錯誤。正如上述，我們亦可使用分號來使上下兩句更加無縫接軌。

例如：

▶ I am leaving now, **however**, I will be back on Saturday to attend your wedding ceremony.（我現在要離開了，但我禮拜六會回來參加你們的婚禮。）→（✗）錯誤。

I am leaving now. **However**, I will be back on Saturday to attend your wedding ceremony. →（○）正確。

I am leaving now; **however**, I will be back on Saturday to attend your wedding ceremony. →（○）正確。

▶ We talked until the early hours, and **consequently** I overslept. （我們聊到凌晨，結果我睡過頭了。） -- 不佳

We talked until the early hours. **Consequently**, I overslept. →（○）正確。

We talked until the early hours; **consequently**, I overslept. →（○）正確。

▶ John was ill, **as a result**, he could not come. （約翰病了，所以他不能來。）→（×）錯誤。

John was ill. **As a result**, he could not come. →（○）正確。

John was ill; **as a result**, he could not come. →（○）正確。

For example, of course 和 on the contrary 等片語也有轉折詞的功能。例如：

▶ Business is booming; **for example**, Peter has made one million dollars since April last year. （生意欣欣向榮；譬如說，彼得自去年四月以來已賺了一百萬美元。）→（○）正確。

▶ Everyone knows he has a mistress, **of course**, he will never admit it. （每個人都知道他有小三，當然了，他永遠都不會承認。）→（×）錯誤。

▶ I did not go to London, **on the contrary** I went to Paris. （我沒有去倫敦而是去了巴黎。）→（×）錯誤。

另外，so 除了一般常見的副詞和連接詞用法外，還有相當於therefore的連接副詞或轉折詞功能。

▶ Tom came down with a cold. **So**, he couldn't come to the party. （湯姆得了感冒。所以他不能來參加派對。）→（○）正確。

Tom came down with a cold; **so**, he couldn't come to the party. →（○）正確。

Excercise
綜 合 練 習

I. 填空題

1 There is _____ person _____ wants more money.
（沒有人不想要更多的錢。）

2 There is _____ customer _____ buys it.
（沒有一個顧客不買這的。）

II. 二選一

1 ☐ I did not go to London, on the contrary I went to Paris.
☐ I did not go to London, but I went to Paris.
（我沒有去倫敦而是去了巴黎。）

2 ☐ I love chocolate. Therefore, I've bought a lot of chocolate.
☐ I love chocolate, therefore, I've bought a lot of chocolate.
（我很喜歡巧克力，所以我買了很多。）

Answer

I. 填空題
1 no; but
2 no; but

II. 二選一
1 第二句正確
2 第一句正確

280

001 Question

The pen is 0.065 meter(s) in length.這句中的meter要用單數還是複數呢？

Answer

計量單位(units of measure)前面的數字，除非剛好是1，否則不管大於1還是小於1，單位都要用複數形式，所以問題中的meter要用複數形式，即meters。

另外，計量單位只有在與數字連用時才能縮寫，若其前沒有數字就不可以縮寫，如24 min, 55 mi, 200 m, 5 ft等，但inch（英吋）縮寫後須加句點，以避免與介系詞in混淆，如45 in.。再者，計量單位的縮寫，不管其前的數字是多少，都不能加 "s"，如The table is 4 m in width.（這張桌子的寬度是 4 公尺。）

最後必須注意的是，in length和at (some/great) length是意思截然不同的兩個片語，前者是指長度，後者意為「詳盡地；最後，終於」，如The matter will be discussed at greater length this evening.（今晚將更詳細地討論此事。）

002 Question

在That's a five hundred dollar (or dollars) dress.這句中，dollar要用單數還是複數呢？

Answer

當複數名詞修飾其他名詞時，它們通常會變成單數，所以That's a five hundred dollar/dollars dress.（那是一件500元的衣服。）中的dollar要用單數。事實上，在這句中，a five hundred dollar是由數字與量詞所構成的複合形容詞。這一規則適用於

大部分（並非全部）名詞，包括那些通常以複數型態出現的名詞。

例如：

- a race for horses
  = a horse race（賽馬）－ a race for horses 的寫法不多見
- a chair with arms
  = an arm chair（扶手椅－現在都拼成 armchair）
- a leg of a pair of trousers
  = a trouser leg（褲管）
- a sharpener for scissors
  = a scissor sharpener（磨剪刀用的磨刀石）
- a board for darts
  = a dart board（投擲飛鏢的圓靶－現在都拼成 dartboard）

但這規則也有例外：

- a depot for arms (i.e. weapons)
  = an arms depot（軍械庫）
- a race for arms
  = an arms race（武器競賽）－ a race for arms 的寫法比 an arms race 少見得多
- a committee on elections
  = an elections committee（選舉委員會）
- a tax on sales
  = a sales tax（營業稅）

值得一提的是，在數字與量詞所構成的複合形容詞中，過去每個字之間都會用連字號 (hyphen) 來連接，如 That's a five-hundred-dollar dress.，但現在連字號在英文中已變得有點像瀕臨絕種生物，許多人已完全不用連字號，尤其英文新聞更是越來越少用。這告訴我們，英語一直不斷地在改變。以下為一些未使用連字號的複合形容詞的例句：

- He's a **ten year old** boy.（他是個十歲男孩。）
- I recently ended a **four year** extramarital affair.（我最近結束了一段為期四年的婚外情。）
- I'm going on a **five day** business trip to Japan.（我即將到日本出差五天。）

003 Question

在a white and a black dog這片語中，dog是否要加s呢？有人認為應使用dogs，因為有兩隻狗，一隻白色，一隻黑色。再者，在ex-England and Barcelona coach此一類似名詞片語中，為何不使用coaches呢？若這個人在兩個不同時段擔任英格蘭隊和巴塞隆納隊的教練，那麼應該是兩項工作，這說法對嗎？

Answer

不對！第一個片語不能使用複數，因為它是a white (dog) and a black dog的省略。如果black的前面沒有a，即a white and black dog（一隻黑白相間的狗），那麼牠是一隻有兩種顏色的狗－只有一隻狗。至於ex-England and Barcelona coach，指的是同一個人，而這個人在兩個地方從事相同的工作，所以也不能用 coaches。現在就舉一個類似的例子來說明，如The winner and new president is Barack Obama.，當選者和新總統是同一個人，就是歐巴馬，所以動詞用單數。

004 Question

CSR是本公司用來指Customer Service Representative（客服代表）的縮寫，那麼 CSR的複數是CSR's還是CSRs呢？

Answer

現今的慣例是，這些縮寫字(abbreviations)的複數是直接在其後加s而不使用所有格符號，如My sister and I have identical IQs and we both have PhDs from Harvard.（我姊姊和我的智商完全一樣，而且我們兩人都擁有哈佛博士學位。）不過，這一慣例也有例外的情況，當縮寫字的最後一個字母是s時，該縮寫字須用's來構成複數，如We filed four NOS's in that folder.（我們將四個未列名項目歸檔在那個文件夾）--NOS為not otherwise specified的縮寫，意為「除非另有規定或指定」、「未另行規定或指定」，亦即不另外具體列出名稱的同一特定種類的商品或貨物。此外，26個英文字母和被當作名詞的字也須用's來構成複數，如He got four A's last term.（他上學期得到四個A。）；You'd better mind your p's and q's if you want to be invited again!（你如果想下次再被邀請，最好注意一下自己的言行！）；There are six and's in that paragraph.（那一段有六個and）－在此句中，and是個「被當作名詞的字」（原本是連接詞），這種被當作名詞的字也要變成斜體字，但其字尾的's則不用斜體。

如上述，縮寫字不使用所有格符號加s來構成複數，而是直接在其後加s。這一規則也適用於頭字語（acronyms－可發音的縮寫字），如LASER，IRA和URL等等。

再者，不可使用所有格符號加s來構成本身就是名詞的字（請注意本身就是名詞的字跟被當作名詞的字之間的不同）的複數，如 "ins and outs" of a mystery（神秘事物的內情），the "yeses and noes" of a vote（贊成票與反對票）。因此，在The shortstop made two spectacular outs in that inning.（游擊手在該局創造兩次漂亮的出局。）這句中，由於out本身就是名詞，意為「出局」，所以直接在其後加s來構成複數，而非使用所有格符號加s。然而，若某字是被當作名詞的字，那麼該字須變成斜體字，如I pointed out the usage of the word out in that sentence.（我指出out這個字在該句中的用法。）out 在這句中是介系詞或副詞；若為複數，則使用非斜體的所有格符號加s來使其變成複數，如In his essay on prepositions, Jose used an astonishing three dozen out's.（荷西在他關於介系詞的文章中使用了驚人的36個out。）不過，這一規則並非放諸四海皆準；在閱讀報紙時，吾人會發現，被當作名詞的字往往被寫成非斜體字且去掉所有格符號，如There are six "ands" in that paragraph.。

005 Question

Miss, Mr., Mrs., Ms.的複數為何呢？

Answer

Miss, Mr., Mrs., Ms.是商業書信中經常會用到的尊稱（courtesy titles）。Miss為「小姐」，用於未婚女子的姓或姓名之前，如Miss Chen is a popular teacher.（陳小姐是個廣受歡迎的老師。）Mr.為「先生」，是Mister的縮寫，用於男性的姓、姓名或職務之前，如Mr. Huang is a well-known scholar in ancient Chinese history.（黃先

生是個知名的中國古代史學者。）；Mr. President（總統先生）。Mrs.為「夫人，太太」，是Mistress的縮寫，用於已婚女性的夫姓或夫的姓名之前，如Mrs. Allen White lives in London.（懷特太太住在倫敦。）Ms.為「女士」，用於婚姻狀況不明或不願提及婚姻狀況之女性的姓或姓名之前，所以是未婚、已婚婦女均適用的稱呼，如 Ms. Smith is a student.（史密斯小姐是個學生。）

如上述，這幾個尊稱是單數，當書信要寄給或文章中同時提到兩個以上且尊稱相同的人時，它們必須使用複數。Miss, Mr., Mrs., Ms.的複數分別為Misses, Messrs., Mmes., Mses.，如Messrs. Ford and Brown are piano repairers.（福特和布朗先生都是鋼琴修理師。）；Dear Mmes. Lin and Wang（親愛的林太太和王太太）。顯然地，Mr.的複數之所以使用法文字，是因為如果直接在Mr.後面加s，那就變成了Mrs.，這是多麼嚴重的錯誤啊！

Mmes.是Mesdames的縮寫，而Mesdames除了是Mrs.的複數外，也是Madam和Madame的複數，換言之，Mesdames同時為Mrs., Madam和Madame（注意後面這兩個字的拼字）的複數，縮寫都是Mmes.。必須注意的是，madam（小寫）意為「（對婦女、尤其是女顧客的尊稱）夫人，太太，女士，小姐；老鴇」，複數為 madams，如Can I help you, madam?（夫人，我能為您效勞嗎？）；Are you being served, madams?（夫人，有人伺候妳們嗎？）。Madam（大寫）意為「（商業書信開頭的尊稱）女士；對女性官員的稱呼語，其後接她的職稱」，複數為Mesdames，如Dear Sir or Madam（親愛的先生或女士）；Madam President, may I ask a question?（女總統閣下，我可以提個問題嗎？）。至於Madame，這是法語中對已婚婦女的尊稱，意為「夫人，太太」，複數為Mesdames，如Madame Obama（歐巴馬夫人）。

值得一提的是，手機簡訊不使用 Miss, Mr., Mrs. 或 Ms. 等尊稱。反之，在簡訊中第一次提到某人時，係連名帶姓（first name＋last name）一起寫出來，而第二次提到時只寫出他或她的姓。

006 Question

「4 + 2 = 6」是Four plus two is six.還是Four and two are six.呢？

Answer

有關數學加法的主動詞一致問題，一直是許多人想知道答案的問題。截至目前，這兩種說法或寫法都可以。兩數相加所用的連詞plus（plus在此為介系詞）或and似乎會影響單複數的選擇。若為plus，數學人士一般都使用單數，如Sixteen plus sixteen is thirty-two.，若為and，則使用複數，如Sixteen and sixteen are thirty-two.。至於非數學人士，單複數都有人用，如Two and two make/makes four.。與乘法一樣，有些人是以加法中的第二個數字來作為單複數的判斷依據，如Nine and one is ten.，但One and nine are ten.。綜上所述，如果你要問人家「6加3是多少」時，你可以說What is/are six and three?或How much is/are six and three?（當然，句中的and可以換成plus。）

在乘法方面，也是單複數都有人用，尤其非數學人士更是兼容並蓄。但數學人士似乎都使用單數，罕見使用複數者。非數學人士也有不少人是以乘法中的第二個數字來作為單複數的判斷依據，如 Six times one is six.（6乘1等於6。）但 Six times three are eighteen.（6乘3是18。）

至於減法和除法，幾乎未曾與聞有使用複數者，亦即無論是數學人士或非數學人士一律使用單數，如 Eleven minus seven is four.（11減7是4。）；Three hundred and twenty divided by twenty is sixteen.（320除以20等於16。）

007 Question

在Approximately 15 minutes is (or are) allowed for questions and comments.這句中，主詞fifteen minutes是單數還是複數呢？

Answer

在 Approximately 15 minutes is (or are) allowed for questions and comments.（允許約15分鐘提問和發表意見。）這句中，fifteen minutes應被視為一個時間的總量，而以單數的實體來看待之；換言之，這裡要使用單數動詞 is，正如Fifteen minutes is not a very long time.（15分鐘不是一段很長的時間。）一樣。

當主詞為「一段時間」、「一筆金錢」、「一段距離」、「一個重量」時，若形式為複數，但意義上為單數時，須用單數動詞。然而，若這些複數名詞不是表示「單一的觀念」，則必須接複數動詞。例如：

▶ Ten miles **is** too long a distance for her to walk.
（走 10 英里對她來説太長了。）

▶ Five meters of cloth **have** been measured off.
（五公尺的布已經量好剪下來了。）

▶ Three hundred dollars **is** too much to pay for that book.
（花 300 元買那本書太貴了。）

▶ One hundred cents **make** a dollar.
（一百分就是一美元。）

▶ Twenty days **is** too long a time for me.
（20 天對我來説太久了。）

▶ Three years **have** passed since I graduated.
（我畢業迄今已三年了。）－複數時間名詞若與 pass 和 go by 等動詞連用，一般都用複數動詞。

▶ Thirty pounds **is** too heavy for me to lift.
（30 磅太重了，我提不起來。）

▶ Three hundred and one kilograms of heroin **have** been seized this year.
（今年已破獲 301 公斤的海洛因。）

He owns a farm, mansion, orchard, and estate.這句有四個名詞，但只有farm的前面有不定冠詞a，這樣對嗎？因為orchard和estate的前面須用an。

Answer

He owns a farm, mansion, orchard, and estate.（他有一座農場、一棟豪宅、一座果園和一座莊園。）這句不合英文語法，因為orchard和estate的前面須用an。所以，此一系列名詞的前面都要加上適當的冠詞，即He owns a farm, a mansion, an orchard, and an estate.。

不過，若句中一系列名詞都使用相同的冠詞，那麼就可以僅在第一個名詞的前面加上冠詞，其餘名詞前面的冠詞皆省略，以合乎簡潔的原則，如He owns a car, yacht, house, and company.（他有一部車、一艘遊艇、一棟房子和一家公司。）

茲將上述所牽涉的文法觀念詳述如下：在一系列名詞中，冠詞或介系詞可以只加在第一個名詞的前面，但前提是這個冠詞或介系詞須適用於每個名詞，而且不能有的名詞前面加冠詞或介系詞，有的前面不加，否則每個名詞的前面都要加上適當的冠詞或介系詞。

例如：

> ▶ In spring, summer, or in winter→（╳）錯誤。
> ▶ In spring, summer, or winter→（○）正確。
> ▶ In spring, in summer, or in winter→（○）正確。
> ▶ The French, the Italians, Spanish, and Portuguese→（╳）錯誤。
> ▶ The French, Italians, Spanish, and Portuguese→（○）正確。
> ▶ The French, the Italians, the Spanish, and the Portuguese→（○）正確。

總之，對於由一系列名詞或名詞片語所構成的句子，除了要使平行結構的元素在文法上對仗工整外，必要時還必須加上任何可使意思清楚，合乎文法規則或習慣用法的字，如冠詞、介系詞或動狀詞等。

009 Question

There's three books on the desk.這句對嗎？

Answer

若根據文法，這句當然不對，因為there is和there's的後面都要接單數可數名詞或不可數名詞，而there are後面接複數可數名詞。然而，在說話及非正式寫作中，像There's three books on the desk.（書桌上有三本書。）這種用there's來引導複數主詞的情況所在多有，如There's lots of cars in the parking lot.（停車場裡有許多車子。）這種用法在正式寫作或考試中會被視為錯誤，使用時不可不慎。

在書寫以there＋be動詞做開頭的句子之前，由於there在此為假主詞，真正主詞是there＋be動詞後面的名詞或名詞片語，所以我們必須先確定該主詞是實際上或概念上的單數或複數。在大部分情況中，這都沒什麼困難，如There is a book on the desk.（書桌上有一本書。）；There are three Mainland Chinese students in my class.（我的班上有三個陸生。）然而，當主詞是由兩個或更多個元素所構成時，情況會變得比較複雜。

例如：

▶ There were a table and some chairs in the room.（房間裡有一張桌子和幾張椅子。）－這句的主詞是由 a table 和 some chairs 這兩個元素所構成，所以主詞是複數顯而易見。

▶ There was a cypress table in the room and some wicker chairs which his father had produced several years before.（房間裡有一張檜木桌和幾張他父親幾年前製作的藤椅。）－這句看起來是由 a cypress table 和 some wicker chairs 這兩個元素所構成，但卻使用 there was，這是因為 a cypress table 靠近 there was，而 some wicker chairs... 意思非常清楚，因此把第二個元素排除在主詞之外，所以整句還是個可以接受的句子。

there is和there's的複數型為there are。有人可能會納悶，there's對應的複數型為何不是there're呢？這是因為there are通常不縮寫，儘管在非正式寫作中，there're 的寫法不時可見，但正式寫作並不接受這樣的寫法，這就是為什麼有些拼字檢查軟體會在there're底下劃紅線，但Word認為there're沒有錯。

I. 填空題

1 The closet is two _____ in length.
（這個櫥櫃長兩公尺。）

2 The elephant is 3 _____ in height.（縮寫）
（這頭大象高三公尺。）

3 I'm going on a _____ business trip to Japan.
（我即將到日本出差五天。）

4 She has an old and a new _____.
（她有一台舊的和一台新的電腦。）

II. 二選一

1 ☐ That's a nine hundred dollar toy.
　☐ That's a nine hundred dollars toy.
（那是個九百塊的玩具。）

2 ☐ There are three ands in this sentence.
　☐ There are three and in this sentence.
（這個句子有三個and。）

3 ☐ Ten minus seven are three.
　☐ Ten minus seven is three.
（十減七等於三。）

4 ☐ Approximately 30 minutes are allowed for lunch break.
　☐ Approximately 30 minutes is allowed for lunch break.
（允許約15分鐘午休。）

5 ☐ The French, the Italians and Japanese are proud of their culture.
　☐ The French, Italians and Japanese are proud of their culture.
（法國人，義大利人還有日本人都為他們的文化而感到自豪。）

6 ☐ There're a dictionary and three books on the desk.
☐ There's a dictionary and three books on the desk.
（桌上有一本字典還有三本書。）

Answer

Ⅰ. 填空題
1 meters
2 m
3 five day
4 computer

Ⅱ. 二選一
1 第一句正確
2 第一句正確
3 第二句正確
4 第二句正確
5 第二句正確
6 第二句正確

001 Question

He will make her a good husband.和He will make her a good wife.為何都對呢？它們有何不同呢？

Answer

這兩句的意思並不相同，其中所牽涉到的語法亦有不同。He will make her a good husband.（他將成為她的好丈夫。）是make接雙受詞的句型make + O(i) + O(d)，其中her為間接受詞，a good husband為直接受詞（注意：間接受詞和直接受詞指的是不同的人或物）；所以，這句相當於He will make a good husband for her.。此種用法並不難見到，如His ruthless behavior made him many enemies.（他的殘忍行徑使他樹敵眾多。）

至於在He will make her a good wife.（他將使她成為好太太。）這句中，a good wife 是受詞her的補語，換言之，her = a good wife（注意：當受詞補語為名詞時，它和受詞是指同一人或物。）同樣地，在He will make her a doctor.（他將使她成為醫生。）這句中，a doctor也是受詞補語。

002 Question

All children are not afraid of the dark.和No children are afraid of the dark.這兩句的意思為什麼不同呢？

Answer

按照句子字面的意思，All children are not afraid of the dark.應該與No children are afraid of the dark.同義，但其實不然，因為在英文中，"All/Both/Every ... not"的句型是在表達「部分否定」的意思，它們相當於"Not all/both/every ..."。所以問題中

"All..." 句的意思是「並非所有小孩都怕黑」（有些小孩不怕黑。）而 "No..." 句則是「完全否定」，意為「所有小孩都不怕黑」。

莎士比亞在「威尼斯商人」(The Merchant of Venice) 中所寫的 "All that glitters is not gold." 或相似的諺語 "All is not gold that glitters." （並非所有會發亮的東西都是金子，亦即所有會發亮的東西不全都是金子。）－但有些會發亮的東西確實是金子。這些都是在表達這種「部分否定」的名句。例如：

▶ **All** children of five **cannot** recite the alphabet.（有些 5 歲小孩不會背誦英文 26 個字母。）-- 部分否定

▶ **Not all** children of five can recite the alphabet. （並非所有 5 歲小孩都會背誦英文 26 個字母。）-- 部分否定

▶ **No** children of five **can** recite the alphabet. （所有 5 歲小孩都不會背誦英文 26 個字母。）-- 全部否定

▶ **Both (of)** his eyes were **not** severely burned. （他的雙眼有一眼沒有嚴重燒傷。）-- 部分否定，both of 以及 all of 和 half of 中的 of 可以省略。

▶ **Not both** his eyes were severely burned.（他的雙眼並非都嚴重燒傷。）-- 部分否定

▶ **Neither of** his eyes was severely burned. （他的雙眼都沒有嚴重燒傷。-- 全部否定

▶ **Everybody** in politics is **not** a good person. （有些政界人士不是好人。）-- 部分否定

▶ **Not everybody** in politics is a good person. （並非所有政界人士都是好人。）-- 部分否定

▶ **Nobody** in politics is a good person. （所有政界人士都不是好人。）-- 全部否定

事實上，除了 all, both 和 every 之外，always, altogether, completely, entirely, thoroughly, quite, wholly 以及 all the time 等副詞與 not 連用所構成的否定式亦是在表達部分否定的意思，其中 always 的否定式意為「並非總是；並非一直」，altogether, completely, entirely, thoroughly, quite 和 wholly 的否定式意為「不完全……；並非完全……」，而 all the time 的否定式意為「並非一直；未必老是」。例如：

▶ He is **not always** so bad. （他並非總是這麼壞。）

▶ I **don't** agree **completely**. （我並不完全同意。）

▶ What he did was **not** quite proper. （他所做的事並不十分妥當。）

▶ A foolish man **doesn't** make a mistake **all the time**. （愚蠢的人未必老是犯錯。）

若要對上述的all, both, every, always, altogether, completely, entirely, thoroughly, quite, wholly以及all the time等詞作完全否定，那就要分別使用與之相對應的完全否定詞，如no, none, neither, no one (nobody), never, not (never) ... at all等。

003 Question

(1) You are not John Cena.和(2) You are no John Cena.這兩句有何不同呢？

Answer

第一句的意思是説「你不是席納」(John Cena是美國著名的職業摔角手)，是席納以外的某個人。這句話可能是對某個自認是席納或非常像席納的人所説的。第二句的意思是説「你還不到當席納的資格」或「你不夠格當席納」，或許你也是個摔角手，但你的實力和技巧還沒有席納那麼好或還差席納一大截。

要注意的是，no在此種用法中常帶貶義，因此在使用上必須謹慎小心，如 "He is no teacher." 這句的意思是説「他還不到當老師的資格」或「他不夠格當老師」，或許他現在是個老師，但他的教學及其他行為表現都很糟糕，是個相當差勁或不適任的老師。

總而言之，no是當限定詞或形容詞用，可以放在單數名詞、複數名詞或不可數名詞的前面來限定或修飾名詞。但在一般用法上，no並不帶貶義，如：

I will watch no TV this week.
= I will not watch any TV this week.
（這個禮拜我都不看電視。）
(no = not ... any)

004 Question

(1) He is a man with over 20 years of experience in teaching English. (2) He is a man with over 20 years experience in teaching English.這兩句何者的文法正確呢？

Answer

根據*New York Public Library Writer's Guide to Style and Usage*，雖然無生命事物大多不能使用apostrophe- s ('s)的所有格型態，如「火車月台」不是寫成 the train station's platform而是寫成the platform of the train station，但在英文中，仍有為數不少的無生命事物被擬人化，可以使用apostrophe- s ('s)的所有格型態。例如：

❶ 國家、地名

表示國家、城市等地方的名詞可用's的所有格型態，如this country's industrialization（這個國家的工業化），the city's parks（這城市的公園），New Zealand tax system（紐西蘭的稅制）。

❷ 自然現象

表示自然現像的名詞也可用's的所有格型態，如the moon's surface（月球表面），the earth's atmosphere（地球的大氣層），the sun's rays（太陽的光線）。

❸ 時間、金錢、距離、度量

表示時間、金錢、距離、度量的名詞也可用's的所有格型態，如a year's time（一年的時間），3 years' salary（三年的薪資），dawn's early light（黎明的曙光），today's papers（今天的報紙），three weeks' journey（三週的旅行），five dollars' value（五美元的價值），ten pounds' weight（十磅的重量）。

是故，He is a man with over 20 years experience in teaching English.中的 "years" 後面應加上所有格符號，使其變成He is a man with over twenty years' experience in teaching English.（他有逾20年教英語的經驗。）不過，He is a man with over 20 years of experience in teaching English.也是正確的句子，而且是一種相當常用的時間所有格表示法。例如：

► After **three years of** mass treatment the infection rate had decreased to 6%. （經過三年的集體治療後，感染率降至了 6%。）

► At least 60 killed in **two weeks of** Mogadishu fighting. （在索馬利亞首都摩加迪休兩週的戰鬥中，至少有 60 人遭到殺害。）

► **Five days of** talks aimed at bringing China and the United States closer together on the issue of climate change did not yield substantial progress. （為期五天，旨在使中國和美國對氣候變遷問題的立場更趨一致的談判，未獲致重大進展。）

值得一提的是，experience意為「經驗」時為不可數名詞，如問題中的句子，但意為「經歷，閱歷」時為可數名詞，如I had a rather odd experience the other day. （前幾天我有過一次相當奇怪的經歷。）就前者而言，experience後面可接介系詞in或of，然後再接名詞或動名詞，若接動名詞，則in可以省略，如Have you had any experience of teaching English? / Have you had any experience (in) teaching English? （你有教英語的經驗嗎？）

005 Question

如何把想要表達的東西都寫在同一句，也就是說，如何延伸句子呢？

Answer

在英文中，許多功能都是藉由標點符號來達成，句子的延伸亦然。我們可以使用冒號 (colon) (:)、分號 (semicolon) (;)、破折號 (dash) (–) 和省略符號 (ellipsis) (...) 來延伸句子，把想要表達的東西都寫在同一句。此外，值得一提的是，冒號後面第一個字通常大寫，而分號後面第一個字則一定小寫。請看下面的敘述：

❶ 冒號

使用冒號係對句中前面提到的事物提供更多資訊或做進一步的解釋。

例如：

▶ There are three pets in the house now: A cat, a dog, and a hamster.
（現在屋內有三隻寵物：一隻貓、一隻狗和一隻倉鼠。）

▶ The management blamed the workers' sit-in for one thing: Paul's incitement.
（資方把工人靜坐示威歸咎於一件事：保羅的煽動。）

❷ 分號

使用分號可以起轉折(transition)作用而不必開始一個新的句子來敘述兩件相關的事物。分號的轉折作用比句點來得好。

例如：

▶ My professor did not approve of my App; he found it completely useless.
（我的教授不贊同我寫的 App；他認為那個應用程式毫無用處。）

▶ No one was killed in the explosion; the only damage was a house that was razed to the ground.
（無人在爆炸中喪命；唯一的損壞是一間房子被夷為平地。）

由於分號具有轉折作用，因此分號的後面往往接 however, therefore, consequently, of course, for example, as a result, on the contrary 等轉折詞，做為句子前半部和後半部的橋樑。

例如：

▶ I am leaving now; however, I will be back on Friday to come to your birthday party.
（我現在要離開了；不過，我禮拜五會回來參加你的生日派對。）

▶ I talked with my best friend until the early hours; consequently, I overslept.
（我跟我最要好的朋友聊到凌晨；結果我睡過頭了。）

▶ Angela is in your class; of course, you know her.
（安琪拉和你同班；你當然認識她。）

▶ John does not loathe wrestling; on the contrary, he quite likes it.
（約翰並不討厭摔角；相反地，他相當喜歡摔角。）

❸ 省略符號

使用省略符號可以起句子走文或說話停頓的作用，而且在引句中可以省略一些字。
例如：

▶ "I'm wondering if I ..." Jack said.
   （傑克說：「我想知道我是否 ……」。）

▶ A credit card stolen from a man in Taipei was used to pay for a
   Chinese meal 18 hours later ... in Los Angeles.
   （一張在台北竊自一名男子的信用卡，18 小時後在洛杉磯被用來支付一頓中式
   餐飲的賬單。）

▶ The ceremony honored ten brilliant athletes ... visiting the U.S.（這項儀
   式表揚了十位正在美國訪問的傑出運動員。）－原句可能是：The ceremony
   honored ten brilliant athletes from Taiwan who were visiting the U.S.（這項儀
   式表揚了十位正在美國訪問、來自台灣的傑出運動員。），其中省略了 "from
   Taiwan who were"，並代之以省略符號。

❹ 破折號

如果您想不起來上述任何一項規則，或者還沒完全弄懂冒號、分號和省略符號的用
法，那麼就使用破折號，因為破折號具有這三者的功能。例如：

▶ The management blamed the workers' sit-in for one thing – Paul's
   incitement. -- 破折號取代冒號

▶ No one was killed in the explosion – the only damage was a house
   that was razed to the ground. -- 破折號取代分號

▶ A credit card stolen from a man in Taipei was used to pay for a
   Chinese meal 18 hours later – in Los Angeles. -- 破折號取代省略符號

Excercise
綜合練習

I. 英翻中

1 I have made him a good daughter.

_____

2 She made him a mature man.

_____

3 A foolish man doesn't make a mistake all the time.

_____

4 You are no mother.

_____

II. 二選一

1 ☐ He is a man with over 10 years of experience in business.
　 ☐ He is a man with over 10 years experience in business.
（他有超過十年的商務經驗。）

2 ☐ John does not loathe wrestling; on the contrary, he quite likes it.
　 ☐ John does not loathe wrestling, on the contrary, he quite likes it.
（約翰並不討厭摔角；相反地，他相當喜歡摔角。）

Answer

I. 英翻中
1 我一直以來都是做他的乖女兒。
2 她使他成為成熟的男人。
3 愚蠢的人未必老是犯錯。
4 你不配為人母。

II. 二選一
1 第一句正確
2 第一句正確

Chapter 4

你的英文，用對了嗎？

—— 其他篇 ——

001 Question

英文名片上學位的順序如何排列呢 譬如說，我擁有J.D.和M.A？

Answer

一般而言，在英文名片上，學位是放在姓名的後面，而學位的排列順序是由左至右、由小至大，亦即由學士、碩士、博士依序排列。所以，您的姓名和學位可寫成：

George W. Bush, M.A., J.D.

註：M.A.為 Master of Arts（文學碩士）的縮寫，而J.D.為Juris Doctor (= Doctor of Jurisprudence)（法理學博士）的縮寫。

002 Question

在In Chapter 1 we will discuss how to use capitalization properly.這句中，Chapter 一定要大寫嗎？

Answer

如果chapter前面有修飾語（序數詞），則寫成the first/next chapter，亦即chapter小寫；但若chapter在前面，其後為數字（基數詞），那麼chapter與該數字都要大寫，如問題中的句子In Chapter One we will discuss how to use capitalization properly.（我們將在第一章討論如何正確使用大寫。）然而，這似乎與room的寫法相抵觸，如We'll meet in room 216.（room是小寫）。但在Please read Chapter Two (= the second chapter)中，Chapter大寫是公認的慣例。Lesson的大小寫情況亦同，如Lesson Twelve = the twelfth lesson（第12課）。

003 Question

postscript縮寫時，P和S是否一定要大寫呢？

Answer

根據*The Gregg Reference Manual* (by William A. Sabin. 9th Edition. McGraw-Hill)，信末簽名後的附言 "PS." 應全部大寫，P的後面不加句點（不過，大多數的英文字典在P的後面都會加上句點而寫成 "P.S." 或 "p.s."），而s的後面可加句點或冒號 (：)，然後空一格或兩格。

第二個附言，也就是信末附言之後的再附言，則寫成 "PPS."（但有些字典將它寫成 "p.p.s."），這是 "post postscriptum" 的縮寫。第三個附言寫成 "PPPS."。然而，除非是開玩笑，否則沒有人會寫三個以上的附言。

004 Question

有些專有名詞，尤其是公司名稱，不大寫，如eBay。若一個專有名詞平常不大寫，那麼當它們出現在句子的開頭時是否要大寫呢？eBay is an online company. 還是EBay is an online company.呢？

Answer

英文句子的第一個字一定要大寫，即使它們平常是小寫的，所以若以一家名稱平常不大寫的公司做句子的開頭，那麼它也要大寫，如 "EBay is an online company." (eBay 是一家線上公司)。要避免這種情況，唯一的方法就是把句子寫成這樣："The eBay corporation is ...."。

005 Question

Answer

根據*New York Public Library Writer's Guide to Style and Usage*，恆星、行星、衛星、星座以及其他占星名稱都要大寫，如Venus and Mars are the planets closest to Earth.（金星和火星是最接近地球的行星。）但sun, earth和moon則不大寫，除非它們跟上述的星體名稱一起使用，如（亦見上句）Jupiter is farther from the sun than Earth is.（木星比地球離太陽遠。）然而，如果earth的前面有定冠詞the，那麼它一定要小寫，如The moon came between the earth and the sun.（月球在地球與太陽之間。）

006 Question

報章雜誌名稱和文學作品名稱的大小寫是否有規則可循呢？譬如說，美國以前有個電視節目叫做This Is Your Life，為何它的每個字的第一個字母都大寫，而美國著名恐怖小説作家Stephen King的著作Riding the Bullet，則有的大寫有的小寫呢？

Answer

在書籍、報紙、雜誌、報告、文學與藝術作品、詩詞、戲劇、電影和電視節目的名稱中，第一個字和最後一個字的第一個字母都要大寫；此外，除了不定詞的 to、冠詞、對等連接詞（and, but等）以及4個字母或少於4個字母的介系詞外，所有字（名詞、副詞、代名詞、形容詞、附屬連接詞等）的第一個字母都要大寫。這些名稱通常以引號或斜體字來區隔。例如：

Riding the Bullet（《騎彈飛行》－美國恐怖小説、奇幻小説作家史蒂芬·金的作品）

Paul Revere and the World He Lived In （《李威爾及其生世》－美國女性小說家、兒童文學作家伊斯特‧福柏斯 (Esther Forbes) 的作品。）--最後一個字In的第一個字母要大寫

The Bridge on the River Kwai（《桂河大橋》－電影）
Midsummer Night's Dream（《仲夏夜之夢》－莎士比亞戲劇）
U.S. News and World Report（《美國新聞與世界報導》－美國雜誌）

007 Question

家庭成員的稱呼何時大寫、何時小寫呢？

Answer

在家庭或家族成員的稱呼中，如dad, mother, son和grandmother等等，若這些稱呼位在人名之前或代替人名（大多數人都不會直呼父母親、祖父母或其他長輩的名諱），那麼各該稱呼要大寫，如He sent an e-mail to Aunt White.（他寄了一封電子郵件給懷特阿姨。）；Did you hear that Dad now insists we study two hours every school night?（你有聽說爸爸現在堅持每個上學日的晚上，我們要讀兩小時的書嗎？）；You must study hard, Son.（兒子，你必須用功唸書。）

在其他情況，家庭或家族成員的稱呼要用小寫，如She sent an e-mail to her dad.（她寄了一封電子郵件給她爸爸。）；The student's mom met with the teacher.（那位學生的母親跟老師會面。）

再者，姓氏若要變成複數，千萬不可更改它們的拼字且不可加上所有格符號(')。對於以s, z, x, ch或sh作結尾的姓氏，只要在後面加上-es即可，如the Gonzalezes, the Jameses, the Edwardses；至於其他姓氏，包括大多數以y（即使y的前面為子音字母）作結尾的姓氏，則在後面加上-s，如the Clintons, the Kerrys（不是the Kerries）。當複數姓氏要變成所有格時，只要在最後一個字母s的後面加上所有格符號(')即可，如the Jameses' car, the Abernathys' home, the Clintons' holiday greeting（柯林頓夫婦的節日賀詞）－相較於Bill Clinton's holiday greeting（美國前總統柯林頓的節日賀詞。）

Question

阿拉伯人名（如 Bashar al-Assad）中的al為何沒有大寫呢？

Answer

Bashar al-Assad（巴沙爾・阿薩德）是敘利亞現任總統，為已故總統阿薩德（Hafez al-Assad）的次子。阿拉伯人的姓名頗為複雜，而人名中的al為定冠詞，一定小寫。許多阿拉伯人都在他們的姓名中使用al或它的變體。新聞界通常省略al，所以以Bashar al-Assad往往被寫成Bashar Assad。由於al是冠詞，因此在翻譯阿拉伯人名時切勿將它音譯進去。不過，無論是Bashar al-Assad或Bashar Assad，第二次提到時都寫成Assad。

阿拉伯國家的報章雜誌名稱和地名都會使用冠詞（往往還會加上連字號），如 al-Ahram（「金字塔報」－ 埃及第一大報）、al-Fajr（巴勒斯坦「黎明報」）、el-Alamein（阿拉曼－埃及北部的地中海濱海小鎮）和Dar el-Beida（達爾貝達－摩洛哥第一大城和海港。事實上，Dar el-Beida就是世界知名的卡薩布蘭加Casablanca。Dar el-Beida是阿拉伯文的名稱）。

許多阿拉伯人名中都會有Abd, Ibn, Bin或Abu等字，Abd意為「……的僕人」(servant of)，Ibn和Bin意為「……之子」(son of)，而Abu意為「……之父」(father of)，其中最知名的當非恐怖組織「蓋達」（al Qaeda － 但新聞報導經常將al寫成Al）已故首領賓拉登(Osama bin Laden)莫屬。這些字不能單獨存在，必須與其他字連用或結合在一起，如Abdullah（阿布杜拉－阿拉伯人常見的男性名，意為「真主阿拉的僕人(servant of Allah)」）、Abu Nidal（阿布尼達爾－1970和80年代世界知名的頭號恐怖份子，而 Abu Nidal 意為「鬥爭之父 (father of struggle)」）、Bin Laden 和 Ibn Saud。

Abd, Ibn, Bin或Abu在其所構成的人名中是不可分割的一部份，所以第二次提到時不可僅寫成Abu或Nidal，亦不可僅寫成Bin或Laden，而須寫成Abu Nidal及Bin Laden；因此，中文翻譯須將Abu和Bin音譯進去。當Ibn和Bin前面有其他名字時，它們通常小寫，如Osama bin Laden和Abdel Faisal ibn King Aziz al-Saud（沙烏地阿拉伯已故國王費瑟－King Faisal－的全名）。

009 Question

department這個字在指大學院校的學系時是否要大寫呢？

Answer

根據《衛斯理大學文體指南》(Wesleyan University Style Guide)，當系所和課程的名稱是以全名的形式出現時，該名稱應大寫。

例如：

▶ The English Department will have a meeting this afternoon.
（英語系下午要開會。）
→（○）正確。

The English department will have a meeting this afternoon.
→（✗）錯誤。

▶ The Math Department has a meeting every month.
（數學系每月開一次會。）
→（○）正確。

The math department has a meeting every month.
→（✗）錯誤。

雖然課程的全稱應大寫，如Economics, Biology 101，但如果學科跟系所的名稱分開的話，該學科名稱並不大寫，除非它是專有名詞（如語言、種族群體或地理實體等）。

例如：

▶ Samantha majored in biology and minored in **economics** and then she married the head of the **History Department**.
（沈曼莎主修生物，副修經濟，然後嫁給了歷史系主任。）

▶ Frank worked in the **Department of Behavioral Sciences** before he started to teach **physics**.
（法蘭克在教授物理學之前任教於行為科學系。）

▶ I'm taking a course in **bioengineering** this summer.
（今夏我將選修一門生物工程課程。）

010 **Question**

頭銜、稱號或職稱何時大寫、何時小寫、何時縮寫、何時不縮寫呢？

Answer

Dr., Mr., Ms., Mrs., Jr., Sr.無論位在全名或僅姓氏之前都必須使用這樣的縮寫形式。至於其他頭銜或稱號，若位在姓氏而非全名之前則不縮寫，如General MacArthur（麥克阿瑟將軍）；Professor Smith（史密斯教授）。不過，由於professor 也是正式頭銜，因此即使位在全名之前亦不縮寫且要大寫，如Professor Bill Smith（比爾‧史密斯教授），但Professor前面的修飾語則不大寫，如journalism Professor Bill Smith（新聞學教授比爾‧史密斯）。

若與全名連用，大多數頭銜或稱號都要縮寫，如Lt. Col. Neil Henderson（尼爾‧韓德森中校）；Sen. Edward Kennedy（愛德華‧甘迺迪參議員）。關於Honorable 及其縮寫 Hon.（尊貴的；尊敬的－常用在法官和一些政要的頭銜前）與Reverend 及其縮寫 Rev.（牧師－對基督教教士的尊稱），根據*The New York Public Library Writer's Guide to Style and Usage*，Honorable和Reverend若與全名連用則縮寫，如Hon. Robert White（尊敬的羅伯特‧懷特）；Rev. George Brown（喬治‧布朗牧師），但若其前有定冠詞the，則不縮寫，如the Honorable Robert White；the Reverend George Brown。

信封上常見、用於男性人名之後來代替Mr.的 Esq. (Esquire 的縮寫，意為「先生」)，不可再與Mr.連用。例如：

▶ The envelope is addressed to Peter Johnson, Esq. （信封上寫的是寄給彼得‧詹森先生 / 信封上寫的是彼得‧詹森先生收。）
▶ Peter Johnson, Esq. →（○）正確。
▶ Mr. Peter Johnson, Esq. →（✕）錯誤。

全名之前的職稱（job or position titles）通常大寫，如Attorney General Michael Wonder（司法部長麥可‧汪德）；Store Manager Brad Turner（店長布萊德‧特納）；Camera Operator George McCartney（攝影師喬治‧麥卡尼）；Water Quality Planner Paul Starkey（水質規劃師保羅‧史塔基）。當職稱單獨存在或以逗點跟人名分開時，它們須小寫且不縮寫，如Michael Wonder, the attorney general, spoke at the meeting.或The attorney general, Michael Wonder, spoke at the meeting.（司法部長麥可‧汪德在會議上發言。）；The attorney general spoke at the meeting.（司法部長在會議上發言。）。冗長的頭銜或職稱放在人名之後會比較通順，意思也會比較清楚。

如果組織、機構或公司內的某個頭銜或職稱僅一個人擁有，那麼若該頭銜或職稱為插入語句，亦即其前後都有逗點，則該頭銜或職稱的前面要加上定冠詞the，如The store manager, Brad Turner, addressed his staff.或Brad Turner, the store manager, addressed his staff.（店長布萊德‧特納對他的職員講話。）這種結構正好用來將冗長的頭銜或職稱與人名隔開，如Spencer Hope, the manager of the long-range service planning project, said ....（長期服務規劃專案經理史賓賽‧霍普說……。）

011 Question

First Lady（或 first lady）要不要大寫呢？

Answer

非正式頭銜、綽號（nickname－有人說這是暱稱）或描述性的稱號（epithet）通常要大寫。First Lady這個頭銜若用來指涉特定第一夫人時，通常大寫，但在一般的敘述中則不大寫。例如：

▶ The current **First Lady** of the United States is Melania Trump.（現今的美國第一夫人是梅蘭妮亞·川普。）

▶ Some countries have a title, formal or informal, that is or can be translated as first lady.（若干國家都有第一夫人或可被詮釋為第一夫人的正式或非正式頭銜。）

尤有甚者，總統及其配偶合稱為 First Couple（第一夫婦）；若他們有家庭，則被稱為First Family（第一家庭）。這兩個名詞通常也都要大寫。

綽號或暱稱及描述性的稱號通常要大寫。例如：

▶ Immortal Iron Fist Smith is a world-famous heavyweight boxer.（「不死鐵拳」史密斯乃舉世聞名的重量級拳擊手。）

- ▶ Sound of Nature Bananagaga has just released her single titled "I ain't a woman". (「天籟之音」香蕉卡卡甫推出名為「我不是女人」的新單曲。)
- ▶ In "Alfred the Great," "the Great" is an epithet. (「艾佛列大帝」中的「大帝」是個描述性的稱號。)
- ▶ Ivan the Terrible was the Grand Prince of Moscow from 1533 to 1547 and Tsar of All the Russians from 1547 until his death in 1584. (恐怖伊凡 1533 至 1547 年為莫斯科大公，1547 至 1584 年辭世為俄國沙皇。)

當綽號或暱稱與真實姓名連用以便進一步確認被指涉者的身份時，該綽號須加上引號（美國用雙引號，英國用單引號），而加上引號後的綽號則置於姓名之間，即插在first name (or given name)和last name之間；若綽號或暱稱不加引號，不無被誤以為是middle name (中間名)的可能。例如：

- ▶ Andy "Buffalo Bill" Cody will run for the city council. (「水牛比爾」安迪柯帝將競選市議員。)

Mexican drug lord Joaquin "El Chapo" (Shorty) Guzman, one of the most-wanted men in Mexico and the United States, may be spending some time in Honduras. (墨西哥和美國通緝最力的要犯之一的墨西哥販毒集團首腦赫昆「矮子」古茲曼，可能在宏都拉斯待一段時間。)

012 Question

e在10:30 a.m.或A.M.及11:00 p.m.或P.M.中，a.m.或A.M.及p.m.或P.M.何者正確呢？還是大小寫都可以呢？

Answer

從文法觀點來看，a.m.為拉丁文ante meridiem (= before noon，意為「上午」) 的縮寫，不是Ante Meridiem的縮寫，所以應該用小寫才對；同樣地，p.m.為拉丁文post meridiem (= after noon，意為「下午；午後」)的縮寫，不是Post Meridiem的縮寫，所以應該用小寫才對。它們均用於時間數字之後。然而，相信幾乎所有人都見過這兩種寫法，亦即大小寫都有人用。

a.m.亦可寫成am，而p.m.也可寫成pm。根據筆者參閱幾本著名的英文文體指南和手冊，美式英語都使用a.m.和p.m.，而英式英語則大多採用am和pm、甚至AM和PM的寫法。顯然地，無論大寫或小寫，都是可以接受的寫法或用法。

不過，有一項與a.m.或p.m.有關的用法經常發生redundant或wordy的情況，必須注意，無則嘉勉，有則改之。請看下面的例句：

▶ 1. The store will open at 8:30 a.m. this morning. （這家商店將在今天上午八點半開門營業。）

▶ 2. The library will close at 10:00 p.m. tonight. （這座圖書館將在今晚十時關門。）

上面這兩個句子都有贅字，不符言簡意賅的原則。在第1句，a.m. (= before noon) 與this morning同義，只能擇一使用，除非上午有兩個八點半；在第2句，p.m. (= after noon)與tonight或this evening的意思相當，也只能擇一使用，除非午後有兩個十點。所以，這兩句必須修改如下才符合簡潔的要求：

The store will open at 8:30 a.m.

The store will open at 8:30 a.m. today.

The store will open at 8:30 this morning.

The library will close at 10:00 p.m.

The library will close at 10:00 tonight.

The library will close at 10:00 this evening.

013 Question

在寫作中以全部大寫或粗體字來強調某段文字的作法適當嗎？

Answer

對於寫作中值得特別強調的某段文字(passage)，我們有一些方式可以為之，請看後面的說明。不過，問題所提的這幾種方式都應該或盡量避免。請注意：這些應該或盡量要避免的段落文字強調方式，只是針對文章的內容或本文而言，章節的標題則另當別論，亦即章節的標題是可以使用這些強調方式的。

首先來看以全部大寫字強調段落文字的作法，這絕對要避免，尤其是在正式寫作中。至於把字體加大的作法，也要避免。同樣地，粗體字亦被視為外行的作法。如果您經常閱讀英文書籍或其他出版品，那麼不妨多留意一下，看看內容是否有這些強調段落文字的方式，或許有，但非常非常罕見，可說是鳳毛麟角。專業寫作人士都知道，這會產生不良的後果。再者，驚嘆號亦應盡量少用。

不過，斜體字（或加底線－這兩者可以互換）可以吸引讀者注意某個字或某個短語，但即使如此，斜體字在使用上也要謹慎，當用則用，不可一而再、再而三地使用，否則將失去強調的效果。

最佳的段落文字強調方式是從造句方面著手，將最重要的字詞放在最顯著、最重要的位置。一個句子中最具強調作用的位置通常是句末，其次是句首。這似乎跟一般的認知有所出入，但英文寫作確實如此，所以我們應該將句中最重要的位置，即句子的開頭和結尾，保留給比較重要的東西如名詞和動詞。由於在寫作時經常會用到 however, additionally, moreover, therefore 等轉折詞，所以別把句子的開頭和結尾浪費給這些不重要的元素。

例如：

- ▶ However, the paper was finished on time.
  （然而，這份報告準時完成。）
  －不佳。句子最具強調作用的重要位置被浪費掉了。
- ▶ The paper was finished on time, however.
  －不佳。句子最具強調作用的重要位置被浪費掉了。
- ▶ The paper, however, was finished on time.
  －佳。句子最重要的位置放了名詞等重要元素，強調效果於焉產生。

總之，切記盡可能少用視覺感受的段落文字強調方式，如全部大寫、加大字體、粗體字、斜體字和驚嘆號，否則讀者很快就不會再去注意您要強調的東西了。

014 Question

president和vice president要不要大小呢？vice president要不要加連字號呢？

Answer

當 president 後面緊接一國總統的名字時要大寫，但其後若未緊接名字，只是指總統，則不大寫。例如：

▶ U.S. **President** Donald Trump cannot run for his third term.
（美國總統川普不能競選第三任。）
→（○）正確。

▶ The politician has decided not to run for **President** next year.
（那位政治人物已決定明年不出馬角逐總統寶座。）
－這裡的 president 是個普通名詞，不可大寫，所以有誤。

▶ Thousands of people demonstrated against **President** Donald Trump yesterday.
（數以千計的民眾昨天示威抗議川普總統。）
→（○）正確。

▶ Lee Myung-bak, the former South Korean **President**, appeared on Wednesday for questioning by prosecutors.
（南韓前總統李明博週三出庭應訊。）
－這裡的 president 並非官銜而是一個意思為「總統」的普通名詞，所以不大寫，所以有誤。

對於公司和組織的president（董事長、總裁）以及大學的president（校長），當它是後面緊接人名的頭銜時，有些刊物（包括許多美國刊物）會將它大寫。但其他刊物（包括許多英國刊物）對於公司、組織和大學等的president則都不大寫。顯然地，這沒有規則可尋。一般而言，比較安全的做法是，除非它是後面緊接人名的一國總統，否則president都不大寫。

至於presidential，那更沒有理由大寫，除非它位在句子開頭的第一個字或是某個專有名詞的一部份，如美國的Presidential Award for Excellence in Mathematics and Science Teaching（數學和科學卓越教學總統獎）。

就vice president而言，當它後面緊接一國副總統的名字時一定大寫，如U.S. Vice President Mike Pence（美國副總統彭斯）。當vice president是指公司和組織的副董事長、副總裁、大學的副校長或其他機構的類似頭銜時，平面刊物鮮少大寫，但在各該公司、組織和大學的正式文件中通常大寫。

當vice president是正式職稱的一部份時，也要大寫，如Vice President of Marketing（企業行銷副總裁）、Vice President of Investor Relations（投資人關係副總裁）。若vice president後面未緊接名字且不是正式職稱的一部份，那麼都不大寫，如 They escorted the vice president to a safe and secret location.（他們護送副總統到一處安全且秘密的地點。）

在美國以外的國家，vice president在所有應用中都會加上連字號，即 vice-president。美國的出版品通常不加連字號，但vice-presidential都會加上連字號，因為它是個片語形容詞。順便一提的是，我們找不到vice-presidential要大寫的理由。

然而，上述有關vice president的說明都不是既定的規則，因為不同的寫作者和刊物有不同的偏好。譬如說，在加拿大、英國和澳洲的刊物，很容易找到正式職稱不大寫而vice president不加連字號的實例，有時甚至會看到vice president後面緊接名字卻沒有大寫的情況。

Excercise 綜合練習

改成正確的大小寫：

1 Romeo And Juliet
《羅密歐與朱麗葉》

_____

2 Neptune is farther from the sun than earth is.
（海王星比地球更遠離太陽。）

_____

3 Dennis is a computer science major, but he also loves his courses in Chinese and east Asian studies.
（丹尼斯主修電腦學，但他也喜歡中文和東亞研究課程。）

_____

4 Melania Trump is the first lady of the USA.
（梅蘭妮亞‧川普是美國第一夫人。）

_____

5 There are a few people in the USA who usually criticize their President.
（美國有一些人經常批評他們的總統。）

_____

6 The first chapter of this book is very important.
（這本書的第一章非常重要。）

_____

7 Would you please pass me the salt, father?
（爸，請你把鹽遞給我好嗎？）

_____

8 My Mom usually tells me not to go out with any indecent girl.
（我媽媽經常叫我別跟不三不四的女孩交往。）

_____

Answer

1. Romeo and Juliet
2. Neptune is farther from the sun than Earth is.
3. Dennis is a computer science major, but he also loves his courses in Chinese and East Asian studies.
4. Melania Trump is the First Lady of the USA.
5. There are a few people in the USA who usually criticize their president.
6. The first chapter of this book is very important.
7. Would you please pass me the salt, Father?
8. My mom usually tells me not to go out with any indecent girl.

001 Question

C 有兩種發音，一是發[k]，如 call, cup，另一發[s]，如 city, cent。這是否有規則可循呢？

Answer

c的發音確實是有規則的。如果c後面接的字母是e、i 或y，那麼它發[s]的音，如cell, cent, center, city, decision, receive, license, distance, recently, pronounce, cycle, juicy, cylinder；若是接e、i和y以外的其他字母，則發[k]的音，如call, correct, cup, cross, class, rescue, fact, public, panic, ache。這一規則幾乎沒有例外－至少到目前為止還沒看到例外的情況。

無獨有偶地，g的發音也遵循這一規則。如果g後面接的字母是e、i 或y，那麼它發[dʒ]的音，如 general, giant, gymnastic, large, energy, intelligible, changing；若是接e、i和y以外的其他字母，則發[g]的音，如golf, pig, great, gum, fragrant, grasp, glut, progress。這一規則僅有少數例外的情況，如gear, get, gelding, give, girl, gift, tiger, geisha－這些例外都是原本要發[j]的音，現在變成發[g]的音。另外，兩個g連在一起(gg-)是發[g]的音，如trigger, outrigger。

有趣的是，有些英文字當中同時含有兩個c，其中一個發[s]，另一個發[k]；或者同時含有兩個g，其中一個發[dʒ]，另一個發[g]，如success, circulate clearance, bicycle, vacancy, garage, gauge, geography, gigantic, gorgeous。

002 Question

英文中有不少字雖然拼字中有d或t，但在讀音時卻不發音，如
pos(t)card, pos(t)pone，請問要如何知道這樣的d或t在說話時
是不發音呢？或者這只是一種經驗的累積呢？

Answer

事實上，這是有規則可循的。當單字中或相鄰兩個字中的 "d" 或 "t" 出現在兩個子
音之間時，它們通常不發音。這在英文中叫做「省音」(elision)。

例如：

- ▶ san(d)wich
- ▶ oin(t)ment
- ▶ I'm going nex(t) week.
- ▶ I borrowed one thousand dollars from my girlfriend las(t) week.
- ▶ That was the wors(t) job I ever had!
- ▶ Jus(t) one person came to the party!
- ▶ I can'(t) swim.

另外，值得一提的是，當一個字的最後一個字母是子音，而下一個字的第一個字母
也是相同的子音或同組的子音時，它們只發一個音（不是發兩個音）－所謂同組
的子音是指發音方式相同的有聲音和無聲音，如[d]和[t]、[b]和[p]、[g]和[k]、[v]和
[f]、[z]和[s]等。這在英文中叫做「子音的重複」或「複音」（germination或sound
twinning）。

例如：

hot dog－t不發音，只發d的音。
I'm a bit tired.－只發一個t的音（第一個t不發音）。
We have a lot to do.
Tell me what to say.
She's slept for three hours.－第一個s（發[z]的音）不發音，只發第二個s的音。
I've finished.－v不發音，只發f的音。
I look forward to seeing you soon.－d不發音，只發t的音。

除上述外，英文還有所謂的「連音」和「變音」。它們都是英美人士在講話時真正的發音，所以如果能夠掌握「省音」、「連音」和「變音」等的發音，對於英文聽力的大幅提升會有莫大的幫助 — 這意謂您將可以在多項英檢考試的聽力測驗項目中拿到高分。

003 Question

電子郵件位址中的@要怎麼唸呢？

Answer

@是個大家再熟悉也不過的符號了，因為它是電子信箱或電子郵件位址(email address) 中用來分隔用戶名稱(username)和提供電子信箱的主機的字元，如 cybertranslator@gmail.com，其中cybertranslator是用戶名稱，而gmail.com為主機名稱。

@在國內叫做「小老鼠」，因其形狀而得名。但如果有一天你必須告訴英美人士你的電子信箱，那麼不要說你跟他們講「小老鼠」他們聽不懂，即使跟他們說little or small mouse，他們也肯定會一頭霧水。相信許多人已知道@的英文要唸成 "at"，但這只是其中一種說法而已。@亦可唸成 "arroba"、"commercial at"、"at sign" 或 "at symbol"。以cybertranslator@gmail.com為例，如果你要告訴老外這個電子信箱，那麼一般都是這樣說cybertranslator at gmail dot com，但如果要將它拼出來，那麼通常這樣說 c－y－b－e－r－t－r－a－n－s－l－a－t－o－r－arroba (or commercial at, at sign, at symbol)－g－m－a－i－l－dot－c－o－m。

茲將一些常用的標點符號和特殊符號的英文臚列如下供大家參考：

- ▶ , 唸成 comma
- ▶ ` 唸成 apostrophe
- ▶ " " 唸成 speech marks, inverted commas 或 quotation marks
- ▶ & 唸成 ampersand
- ▶ + 唸成 plus sign
- ▶ - 唸成 minus sign
- ▶ → 唸成 arrow

▶ © 唸成 copyright sign
▶ ? 唸成 question mark
▶ #（符號－井字號）唸成（美國）pound sign, number sign；（加拿大）number sign；（英國等）hash, hash symbol 或 hash sign。（有此符號的手機或電話按鍵－井字鍵）（美國）pound key；（加拿大）number sign key；（英國等）hash key。
▶ *（符號－米字號）唸成 asterisk, star symbol。（有此符號的手機或電話按鍵－米字鍵）star key。
▶ （）唸成 brackets
▶ （ 唸成 open brackets
▶ ）唸成 close brackets 或 closed brackets
▶ _ 唸成 underscore
▶ : 唸成 colon
▶ ; 唸成 semicolon
▶ / 唸成 forward slash
▶ \ 唸成 backslash

001 Question

(1) 如果冒號前面是個縮寫字，那麼該縮寫字還要不要使用句點（例如：RE.:或 ID.:）呢？ (2) 在John shook his head, no.和Mary nodded yes.這兩句中，no和yes是否要加引號呢？

Answer

關於問題(1)，我們不可把縮寫字後面的句點省略掉，除非該縮寫字是句子的最後一個字，此時該縮寫字的句點剛好做為句子結束的句點，如My grandfather always gets up at 5 a.m.（我祖父總是在清晨 5 點起床。）－ "m" 後面的句點也是句子結束的句點，亦即兩者共用一個句點。但是，如果縮寫字的句點後面須用到其他標點符號，如逗點，那麼縮寫字的句點和這個逗點都要存在，如The students were up by 5 a.m., and they gathered on the campus by five-thirty.（這些學生清晨5點不到就起床，5點半之前就在校園集合完畢。）一樣的道理亦適用於冒號(:)，如The following steps must be accomplished before 11:30 a.m.: First, ... second, ...（下列步驟須在11點30分之前完成：第一……，第二……。）不過，對於問題中所提到的 "RE" 和 "ID"，大多數的寫作者都不用表示縮寫的句點，如The following forms can be used as a proper ID: A driver's license, a passport, a birth certificate, ...（下列證件都可用作身份證明：駕照、護照、出生證明書等。）

關於問題(2)，根據筆者查閱有關英文文體（style）的專書，無論搖頭表示 "no"（「不」或「不同意」）或點頭表示 "yes"（「是」或「同意」），它們都不使用引號，而且不需要逗點，如I am shaking my head no.（我搖點表示不同意。）

順便一提的是，冒號(:)後面第一個字母要大寫，而分號(;)後面第一個字母小寫（專有名詞除外）。

002 Question

在書寫一系列項目時，如I like to eat apples, kiwis, bananas and oranges.，and前面是否要加逗點呢？

Answer

在書寫一連串（三個或三個以上）的項目時，筆者向來都會在最後一個項目前面的and前面加上逗點，但你也可以不加，這要視個人的習慣而定。在該處加上逗點，一定都是對的（但在新聞寫作中除外，新聞寫作都是把這個逗點省略掉）。為何加上這個逗點一定是對的呢？因為在某些情況中，倘若不使用這個逗點（尤其是此一系列項目很複雜或冗長時），最後兩個項目可能會結合成另一個與這兩個項目完全不同的事物，如macaroni and cheese（macaroni是「通心麵」，cheese 是「乾酪，起司」，而macaroni and cheese或macaroni cheese卻是「起司醬通心麵」，與macaroni或cheese已經是不同的食物了）。因此，筆者建議，最好使用逗點來分開一系列項目中的所有項目以避免這問題。

然而，如果一系列項目中只有兩項，那麼and前面不可有逗點。

例如：

▶ Mom bought grapes and bananas. （媽媽買了葡萄和香蕉。）→（○）正確。

Mom bought grapes, and bananas. →（✕）錯誤。

值得注意的是，我們有時也會見到沒有and的情況，如I like to eat apples, kiwis, bananas, oranges.，這時句子所表達的意思已不盡相同；它是在表達「等等」、「諸如此類」（et cetera, and so on, and the like）的意思。換言之，它的意思是說，除了apples, kiwis, bananas, oranges之外，我還喜歡吃其他水果。

註："Macaroni and cheese" 意為「起司醬通心麵」(a dish made from macaroni and cheese sauce)，為美國用語，在美國部分地區往往被縮寫為mac 'n' cheese，在英國則稱為macaroni cheese，但同樣的東西在加拿大卻叫做 "Kraft Dinner"。

003 Question

在 In 1998 then President Clinton issued a memorandum ....這句中，then的後面要不要加連字號(hyphen)呢？

Answer

許多人不喜歡then的這種用法，但它自16世紀末期以來就一直存在，且被廣泛使用。在此用法中，then是形容詞，意為「當時的」。然而，當它的後面加上連字號，尤其是當它與另一個修飾語（形容詞）連用而又加上連字號時，then就變成了副詞，如 "then-executive producer"（當時的監製－執行製片）、"then-White House Chief of Staff"（當時的白宮幕僚長），那麼整個片語看起來就顯得笨拙，不好處理，有時甚至會造成意思上的誤解，所以then的後面不要加連字號。

004 Question

如果句子的最後一個字是有句點的縮寫字，那麼要怎樣標示標點符號來表示句子的結束呢？下面哪一句才正確(1)The meeting ended at 10:05 p.m.(2)The meeting ended at 10:05 p.m..

Answer

縮寫字後面的句點就足以結束句子，亦即縮寫字的句點兼具句子結束的句點，所以句(1)是正確的寫法。但如果這是個問句，那麼除了縮寫字的句點外，我們還要加上問號，如 Did the meeting end at 10:05 p.m.?（會議在下午10時5分結束嗎？）

005 Question

My question is should this have a question mark是一句以問句做結尾的陳述句,請問這種句子的正確寫法和標點符號為何呢?

Answer

上句要寫成 My question is, should this have a question mark? (我的問題是,這句要加問號嗎?),亦即在問句前面用一個逗點將問句隔開,並在問句句末加一問號。不過,在這句中, "should" 也可以大寫,如 My question is, Should this have a question mark?。如果問句前面是個完整的句子,那麼要使用冒號 (:)。

例如:

▶ The question is, Who will foot the bill for the reprinting?
（問題是,誰要付重印的費用呢?）
= This is the question: Who will foot the bill for the reprinting?

006 Question

年份的所有格也是在年份的後面加's嗎?還是只加s就可以了?
2009s results were excellent.和2009's results were excellent.
何者正確呢?還是都可以呢?

Answer

年份的所有格是在年份的後面加's,不能只加s,因為兩者的意思截然不同。所以,2009's results were excellent.（2009年的決算結果非常好。）是唯一正確的句子。不過,筆者建議使用「of 片語」,亦即寫成The results for/of 2009 were excellent.,因為有人可能會誤以為 "2009's results" 是某種複數型態（當然它不是,但有人就是會搞混。）

如果僅在年份的後面加上s,如1980s,其意思就變成「1980年代」,是指從1980年到1989年的10年期間;同樣地,2000s意為「2000年代」,是指從2000年到

2009年的10年期間。由此可知，年份後面加's的意思和加s的意思有天壤之別，兩者千萬不可搞混。

007 Question

頭銜的後面是否要加逗點呢？例如，Elizabeth II, Britain's Queen(,) pleaded for world peace in her first visit in five decades to the U.N. headquarters.。

Answer

一般而言，當頭銜位在姓名的後面時，它是屬於插入語句，亦即自句中移除也不會改變句子主要意思的語句，因此，頭銜前後都要加逗點。由此可知，Elizabeth II, Britain's Queen, pleaded for world peace in her first visit in five decades to the U.N. headquarters. （英國女王伊莉莎白二世在其50年來首次訪問聯合國總部時呼籲世界和平。）才是正確的句子。

然而，當頭銜位在姓名的前面時，它是屬於必要的語句，所以不能加逗點，如 Britain's Queen Elizabeth II pleaded for world peace in her first visit in five decades to the U.N. headquarters.。不過，若頭銜前面用定冠詞來表示特指時(The Queen)，姓名就變成插入語句，前後要用逗點來隔開，如 The Queen, Elizabeth II, pleaded for world peace in her first visit in five decades to the U.N. headquarters.。

008 Question

在He is an internationally(-)known scholar.這句中，internationally和known之間要不要加連字號呢？

Answer

以-ly做字尾的副詞在與其他修飾語（尤其是過去分詞）構成複合形容詞時不加連字號(hyphen)。所以，問題中的句子應寫成He is an internationally known scholar.（他

是一位國際知名的學者。）亦即internationally及其所修飾的known之間沒有連字號。這類複合形容詞相當常見，俯拾即是，如a widely used device（廣泛使用的裝置），scantily clad girls（穿著清涼的女子），publicly held securities（公開發行的證券）等等。

不過，若字尾非-ly的副詞與過去分詞構成複合形容詞，則要加連字號，如an ill-equipped laboratory（設備簡陋的實驗室），an ill-favored man（其貌不揚的男子），ill-gotten gains（不義之財），a well-chosen name（精挑細選的名字），a well-behaved child（行為端正的小孩），well-dressed ladies（穿著體面的女士）等等。

009 Question

條列項目中應使用分號還是逗點呢？再者，分號或逗點是位在and的前面還是後面呢？

Answer

下列為問題中所舉的例句，為了避免問題過長，因此將其移到此處：

Your duties as teacher are as follows:
(1) Take attendance;
(2) give lectures, exams, and speeches;
(3) assign homework; and
(4) dismiss the class.

或

Your duties as teacher are as follows: One, take attendance; two, give lectures, exams, and speeches; three, assign homework, and; dismiss the class.
（身為老師，你的職責如下：(1)點名；(2)授課、考試和演講；(3)指派家庭作業以及(4)下課。）

英文的條列項目可以直列或橫列，如上面的例句。條列項目中最後一項的前面須用連接詞and，分號或逗點一定位在and的前面，而且不能在and的後面再加上分號或

逗點。所以，在問題的例句中，直列句的寫法是正確的，而橫列句的寫法不對，因為and的前面須用分號，而後面不該有分號。

在此必須強調的是，一般的條列項目只要使用逗點就可以了，如The company's current focus should be on revenue, clients, profit-sharing, and communication.（這家公司當前的重心應放在營收、客戶、分紅和溝通上。）條列項目須使用分號的唯一理由是，所臚列的項目中已經有逗點，如問題中的例句。此外，值得一提的是，冒號(:)後面第一個字要大寫，而分號(;)後面第一個字是小寫。

事實上，問題中有編號的直列句亦可橫列，如Your duties as teacher are as follows: (1) Take attendance; (2) give lectures, exams, and speeches; (3) assign homework; and (4) dismiss the class.。不過，許多人習慣不使用編號，而將句子寫成Your duties as teacher are to take attendance; to give lectures, exams, and speeches; to assign homework; and to dismiss the class.。

010 Question

在The software development plan is described in this chapter (for related information, see the references cited in section 2.3.3).這句中，句末標點符號（句點）是位在括弧內還是括弧外呢？

Answer

如果括弧內的語句是位在一個句子當中，那麼不管這個嵌入句中的括弧所在的位置為何，括弧內皆不可使用句末標點符號之一的句點，即使括弧內的語句是個完整的句子亦然。因此這個例句是個正確的句子：

▶ The software development plan is described in this chapter (for related information, see the references cited in section 2.3.3).（軟體開發計畫將在本章做説明（至於相關的資訊，請參見 2.3.3 節所引用的參考文獻））。

句點可以放在括弧內的唯一情況是，括弧內的語句是個完整且獨立的句子，亦即這個句子不是位在另一句子當中，如：

▶ He thought he could live to be 100. (Actually he died at 78.) He was a good guy. （他認為他可以活到 100 歲。（事實上，他 78 歲就過世了。）他是個好人。）

由於上句括弧內的語句是個完整且獨立的句子，所以句子的開頭Actually要大寫。

然而，儘管嵌入句中的括弧內不可使用句點，但卻可使用另外兩個句末標點符號，即問號和驚嘆號；此外，在嵌入句中的括弧內，句子的開頭不大寫，如：

▶ He's the mayor (but how many people does he know who are out of work?) of that big city. （他是那個大城市的市長（但他知道現在多少人失業嗎？））

011 Question

Ms.既然不是縮寫字，為何它的後面有句點呢？

Answer

"Ms." 意為「女士」，用於婚姻狀況不明或不願提及婚姻狀況之女性的姓或姓名之前，所以是未婚、已婚婦女均適用的稱呼。Ms跟Miss一樣都不是縮寫字，所以其後不應加句點，但Ms的後面往往加句點，猜想這可能是為了跟Mr.和Mrs.保持一致。

不過，要注意的是，Ms, Mr和Mrs後面加句點是美國的用法，英國的用法是都不加句點。這是英美用法上的差異。

012 Question

Inc.和Ltd.的前面需不需要逗點呢？

Answer

對於公司或企業的名稱（以及其他大多數專有名詞），它們每個字的第一個字母都要大寫，除非某公司有自己喜歡的其他字母的大寫，如eBay，但若這個公司名稱是位在句子的開頭，它也要大寫。

切勿將公司名稱的所有字母都大寫，如Subway（不是SUBWAY），除非那些字母是個別發音，如IBM。有些公司會在企業標誌(logo)及其促銷宣傳品中使用驚嘆號、星號或加號，但在書寫這些企業名稱時不可使用這些符號，如Yahoo（不是Yahoo!）。

若公司法定名稱中有company, corporation, incorporated和limited等字，則它們通常分別縮寫為Co., Corp., Inc., Ltd.，如Boeing Co.（波音公司）、Chevron Corp.（雪佛龍公司）、Apple Inc.（蘋果公司）。但在商業書信中，這些字並不縮寫；換言之，在商業書信中，若這些字是公司或企業名稱的一部份，那麼它們要完整拼出，如Boeing Company。若第二次提到時，company, companies或corporation是單獨出現，那麼這些字須完整拼出且小寫，如The company showed a big loss in the fourth quarter.（該公司第四季出現重大虧損。）不過，當上下文不需要正式及完整的公司名稱時，這些字經常被整個省略掉。

至於Inc.或Ltd.的前面是否需要逗點，根據*New York Public Library Writer's Guide to Style and Usage*一書，它們的前面無需逗點，然而，在實務上，許多公司名稱的Inc.或Ltd.前面都有逗點，尤其是緊接在Co.之後，如Nissan Motor Co., Ltd.（日產汽車）、Merrill Lynch & Co., Inc.（美林證券），但Time Warner Inc.（時代華納）、ASUSTeK Computer Inc.（華碩電腦）、Pangang Group Company Ltd.（中國攀枝花鋼鐵集團公司）則沒有逗點。

在一本英文書中，引句都使用單引號，而其他標點符號幾乎都位在引號外，如「...'going to God'.」。這裡的第一個問題是，書中為何都使用單引號呢？這又不是引句中的引句。第二個問題是，句點不在引號內對嗎？

Answer

筆者幾乎可以確定問題中所提到的書是採用英國標點符號寫法。英國人在處理引號及引號旁的其他標點符號的方式與美國人截然不同。

在引號方面，英國人使用單引號而美國人使用雙引號。至於引號旁的其他標點符號，英國人的處理方式是根據邏輯而非慣例。在美式用法中，逗號和句號（又稱逗點和句點）是位在引號內，分號和冒號位在引號外，而問號和驚嘆號只有是引言的一部份時才位在引號內。在英式用法中，逗號和句號除非是引言的一部份才位在引號內，否則位於引號外，而其他標點符號則都位在引號外。

例如：

- ▶ Mike said that he was "very angry."
  = Mike said that he was 'very angry'.
  （麥克說他「非常生氣」。）
- ▶ The teacher said, "Call it a day."
  （老師說，「今天到此為止。」）
- ▶ What is "neologism"?
  = What is 'neologism'?
  （「neologism」是什麼意思？）

所以，問題中所述的片語在美國將會這樣寫："going to God."（句點在引號內）。Go to God = go to heaven（往生，逝世）。

Excercise
綜合練習

I. 請加入標點符號

1 Cinderella you have to do the following things before 12 a m First mop the floor Second do the laundry Third do the dishes

2 I have three friends John David and Lily

3 I am going to buy a beautifully decorated house

4 The mother but how much does she know about her son is regretting

5 He asked me How to plan for a vacation（請使用雙引號）

II. 二選一

1 ☐ The question is, Who will do the housework?
☐ The question is: Who will do the housework?
（問題是，誰要做家事呢？）

2 ☐ Jazz music was very popular in 1920's.
☐ Jazz music was very popular in 1920s.
（爵士樂在1920年代非常盛行。）

3 ☐ The attitude of Trump, the President of the USA, is the crucial factor.
☐ The attitude of Trump the President of the USA is the crucial factor.
（美國總統川普的態度是關鍵因素。）

Answer

I. 請加入標點符號

① Cinderella, you have to do the following things before 12a.m.: First mop the floor. Second do the laundry. Third do the dishes.

② I have three friends: John, David, and Lily.

③ I am going to buy a beautifully decorated house.

④ The mother (but how much does she know about her son?) is regretting.

⑤ He asked me, "How to plan for a vacation?"

II. 二選一

① 第一句正確

② 第二句正確

③ 第一句正確

NOTE

語研力 *E020*

你的英文用對了嗎？〔基礎篇〕

英文翻譯專家教你搞定易混淆文法！

作　　者	俞亨通
顧　　問	曾文旭
總 編 輯	黃若璇
編輯統籌	陳逸祺
編輯總監	耿文國
行銷企劃	陳蕙芳
執行編輯	賴怡頻
封面設計	海大獅
封面圖片來源	圖庫網站 Shutterstock
內文排版	王桂芳
文字校對	賴怡頻
法律顧問	北辰著作權事務所

初　　版	2018年04月
出　　版	凱信企業集團-凱信企業管理顧問有限公司
電　　話	（02）2752-5618
傳　　真	（02）2752-5619
地　　址	106 台北市大安區忠孝東路四段250號11樓之1
印　　製	世和印製企業有限公司

定　　價	新台幣349元 / 港幣116元
產品內容	1書

總 經 銷	商流文化事業有限公司
地　　址	235 新北市中和區中正路752號8樓
電　　話	（02）2228-8841
傳　　真	（02）2228-6939

港澳地區總經銷	和平圖書有限公司
地　　址	香港柴灣嘉業街12號百樂門大廈17樓
電　　話	（852）2804-6687
傳　　真	（852）2804-6409

國家圖書館出版品預行編目資料

你的英文用對了嗎？〔基礎篇〕--英文翻
譯專家教你搞定易混淆文法 / 俞亨通著.
--初版. – 台北市：凱信企管顧問,
2018.04
　面；公分

ISBN 978-986-95443-5-1（平裝）

1. 英語　2. 語法

805.16　　　　　　　　　107000786

凱信企管

用對的方法充實自己，
讓人生變得更美好！

凱信企管

用對的方法充實自己，
讓人生變得更美好！